In His Office

Mia Faye

Mia Faye

ISBN: 9798614960414

For my readers

TABLE OF CONTENTS

1

Robert

"Where is she?"

I stand over the office receptionist, and I am aware that I am towering over her. She is short and seated, a tiny little ball of nervous energy. She looks up at me like she would a skyscraper. I smile inwardly. A fearsome reputation is built on such moments. The kind of reputation I am exceedingly proud to have.

"Sir?" the receptionist mumbles, almost inaudibly.

"My assistant. Where is she?"

I wave in the general direction of her desk, but I don't look away from the receptionist. The color is rising steadily in her cheeks. She is also sinking slowly into her chair, lower and lower, and part of me is tempted to stand there just long enough to see if she'll eventually slide completely off it.

"I don't know, sir," she says. "I think I saw her head out a few minutes ago, but I don't know where to."

I continue to stare at her, my eyebrows furrowed, letting my displeasure wash over her. It wasn't really her job to keep an eye on my assistant I remind myself after some time. Leave the poor woman alone.

"Very well," I tell her. "When she does show up, please tell her to come to my office right away."

The receptionist nods, the relief on her face is evident. I think I hear her sigh as I turn and walk away from her desk. Eyes follow me as I make my way back to my office. As they always do. Conversations trail off, smiles are wiped from faces, and there is a false, unnatural silence at every station I pass. Good. Still terrified of me.

Back at my desk, I pull out the Mandel files and begin to rifle through them. This is going to be a tricky case. Possibly the trickiest one with which I have ever had to deal. But then again, all my cases have been tricky. Back in the day, when I was just starting out before I had an unbeaten record to worry about, all I wanted was to win every single case, dominate every battle in the courtroom. And as the wins started to stack up, the pressure grew exponentially. Now, every time I get a new case, the worry is there, in the back of my mind. What if this is the one I can't crack?

Usually, I shrug it off fairly easily. No case is unwinnable I like to tell myself. But this isn't like the other cases. This time, I'm going up against the might of the greatest manufacturing company in the country. The pressure is the highest it's ever been. I cannot afford to slip up on this one, which is why I don't understand why that damn assistant chose today, of all days, to vanish from the office. She should be here. We should be discussing the strategy I had her draw up, talking about the details of the case. Instead, I'm twiddling my thumbs as I wait for her. No. I won't have it.

The more I wait, the more agitated I get. After checking the clock for the hundredth time, I get fed up and slam the folder shut. I push my chair back and stand up. I pace the length of my office for a minute, then turn to the door, intending to go back to the receptionist and grill her some more. But I don't have to. I look up to see my assistant half-walking, half-running toward the office. Her shoes make tiny little clopping sounds that echo down the hall as she approaches. Her arms are laden with several bags, which she deposits at her desk outside before rushing into my office.

Her expression is several variations of terrified. No doubt she has heard that I was looking for her, and she knows how bad it is that she wasn't there. It is literally her job. And one of a long list of absolutely inflexible rules I drummed into her head when I hired her. No matter what, be there when I need you.

"I'm so sorry, Mr. Hardy," she says, wringing her hands anxiously. She stares at me with pleading eyes, imploring, willing me to let it slide, just this once. As if that is possible.

"Do you remember what I told you during your interview?" I ask her, my voice way calmer than I actually feel.

"Uh, yes, sir." She sounds unsure.

"What did I say about your ass?"

"That you own it, sir."

"And?"

"That I should be here if and when you need me. Before you think you're going to." Ah, good. She remembered the exact wording.

"So. Where were you?" I ask her.

"I ... uh ... I'm ... I had some personal business ..."

"During working hours?"

"I'm really sorry, sir—"

"You already said that."

She looks like she is about to cry. Her eyes are wide, and she is blinking a bit too fast. Her lips are trembling too. She mouths wordlessly, clearly at a loss on what to say.

"Clearly, you have more important things to attend to," I say. "I would hate to get between you and whatever it is that was so urgent you needed to leave the office in the middle of the day. Without telling me. Perhaps I should free up your schedule, so you won't have to run back and forth like this."

"No! Please, Mr. Hardy ... I'm so— uh, I apologize. It was a mistake; it won't happen again—"

"How long have you been here, Miss Woods?"

"Two weeks, sir."

"Shame. You lasted longer than most."

The current record is four weeks and five days.

She registers the use of the past tense, and I can see the dilemma on her face, wondering whether there is still something she can say to salvage the situation or whether it is a lost cause.

"Did you write this?" I reach over to my desk and pick up a thin sheaf of documents, then wave them at her.

"What is that?" she asks, forgetting for a minute to look scared and going for confused instead.

"I have no idea what it is," I say. "At first, I thought it was the brief I asked you to write this morning, the summary on all the cases we've handled involving embezzlement. But when I went through it, I realized it cannot possibly be that. No, this, if it is anything other than a plagiarized, grammatically abhorrent jumble of words, must be your final plea to me to put you out of your misery. And alas. I think I must."

"I don't ... I didn't ..."

"You're fired, Miss Woods."

This is usually when they start to cry. Or beg. Or get angry and launch into insults. If I'm lucky, they would have been working on a 'fuck you' speech, and this is about the time they usually decide to let loose with the expletives. What else is there to lose?

To her credit, Miss Woods— and I can't seem to remember her first name— doesn't do any of that. She purses her lips and stares blankly at me for several minutes. Then her whole body just deflates, and she shrinks in resignation. No fight in her. No attempt to bargain or threaten.

And that is how I know I made the right decision. I need someone with a tougher exterior and the ability to fight for what they want. Miss Woods has her good qualities; she is very good with clients, and she has mastered my schedule almost to a tee. But she will never stand up to me or anyone. She has never gone above and beyond for the job, preferring to stick to the strictest margins of her job description. She isn't a fighter. Frankly, I'm surprised she's worked for me this long.

"I, uh … thank you for the opportunity, Mr. Hardy," she manages to say. Her voice is shaky and low. I can bet she's putting on a brave face, trying to hold onto her dignity, but that she's going to break down as soon as she's out of my sight. I feel a brief urge to say something kind to her, to try and soften the blow in any way I can. But the urge is gone in a second. It would be unprofessional. Robert Hardy does not have time for hand-holding.

"Please clean out your desk by tomorrow morning," I tell her. "Susan down in HR will sort out your final check. Oh, and I'm going to need my keys, please."

Once, I forgot to take my keys back, and a former PA snuck back into my office and shredded all my documents, then left me a big pile of actual shit on the carpet. I'm not making that mistake again.

Miss Woods looks absolutely morose as she drops the keys on my desk. I watch her quietly as she goes back to her desk. I hear the dull sounds of her dropping things into a box, packing her belongings. Her process is slow, methodical, almost like she's hoping I will change my mind in the process. Like I'll see her packing away her stapler, be overcome with guilt and nostalgia for all the documents she stapled for me, and then call her back and let her off with a warning. Well, she is sadly mistaken. I am many things, but I am not nostalgic.

And now I need to find another Personal Assistant. Again. I am beginning to lose count.

The phone rings, sudden and shrill, and I reach for it absently.

"Bobby fucking Hardy!"

I know that voice. I would recognize it anywhere, and it makes my skin crawl.

Even on the phone, Daniel Goldman sounds like a complete asshole. He is smug and assured, and he speaks with a slow, almost Southern drawl that is dripping with unearned confidence. In all the years I have known him, he has never once been to the South. It's just something he decided he would start doing, probably because he thought it would give him character. It did not.

"What do you want, Goldman?" I ask, trying to keep the irritation out of my voice. I can hear the smile in his voice, and I don't like it. It's never good news when Daniel Goldman is happy about something, and it's especially bad news if he's calling me about it.

"Oh, you still don't know?" he says, still chortling. Gloating. Dangling the bait in front of me.

"I don't have time for this. Don't know what?"

"Hmm. Now I almost wish I didn't call, just so I can see the look on your face when you show up for the deposition and see me sitting across from your client. But then I couldn't live with myself if you found out some other way …"

"Why would you …" Then it dawns on me, the thought sudden and unwelcome, and the realization is like having an icy bucket of water upended over my head. "Mendel hired you? You're prosecuting the case?"

"Ding ding ding! They want to win, so yeah. I advised them to go with someone who would guarantee them a win, and they did just that."

"And since when is that person you?" I say, my lip curling.

"Funny, they asked me the exact same thing. And you know what I told them? Simple. There's only one man who has gone up against you and won."

"You didn't win, Goldman. The client settled. Out of court."

"I had you beat, and you know it."

"You keep telling yourself that if it helps you sleep at night."

"That's okay, Bob. I don't need that little win by technicality. I'll let you have it because I know how much your silly unbeaten record means to you. But I'm coming for you this time, buddy. And I can tell you for free before we even go to court; we will not be offering or accepting a settlement at any point in the case."

"Well, it's good to know you're still deluded, Goldman. Now if you'll excuse me, I have actual work to do." I slam the phone down a little harder than I had intended.

Things have just gotten trickier than they ever were.

Daniel Goldman. Shit.

The man who I identified on good days as my arch-nemesis, and on worse days as my mortal enemy. The biggest asshole I knew and, as much as I hate to admit it, one of the best trial attorneys in the country. I have not been preparing to go up against him. Whatever strategy I was considering was automatically going out of the window.

Battling Daniel requires a different approach. The legal side of things is important, and the man is a brilliant lawyer. But that isn't where the battle is going to be won. With Daniel, the key is to keep his attention off the actual case, in whichever way possible. Over the years, we have faced off a few times, and that simple strategy worked almost every time. I have to distract him. But how?

This is exactly the kind of thing one needs an assistant for. If only the bastard had called before I dismissed my latest assistant. But no. This is the wrong case for Miss Woods. She wouldn't survive a second against the pressure Daniel is capable of exerting. I need a fresh face, someone new enough that Daniel won't see them coming, and yet competent enough to handle the rigor of working a case.

I usually rely on temp agencies to send me applicants for the position of my Personal Assistant. I have become something of a legend there, thanks to the fact that I keep sending their applicants home. The lady who handles my requests once joked that the day she provides me with someone who lasts through the month, she will retire because no career achievement would top that.

Today, though, I won't be using the agency. I'm not up for the scrutiny and having to explain to some snotty lady over the phone, 'What happened to the last one?' knowing she is rolling her eyes and marking another x on my page. Besides, I have grown tired of the same young women they send me. It's almost like they think I have a type.

I need something different. Someone who doesn't just do the job because of the paycheck. Someone who actually cares about representing the client and doing whatever it takes to help them. I need someone who can keep up with me, someone who can double as an assistant and a second chair. And I need someone who can dive into the trenches and get their hands dirty because this case is going to demand it.

If they happen to be good-looking and young, then that will be a delightful bonus. A necessary one, considering. People never change, and Daniel Goldman is a sucker for a young, pretty face if I ever saw one.

2

Amelia

I stare at the page without really seeing it. Words jump out at me, some making sense, others just a collection of meaningless letters. I read and reread the same sentence over and over again, understanding it less each time. Eventually, I give up. I snap the book shut and look up at the wall in front of me.

Exam in two weeks.

Even that unfortunate reminder isn't enough to get me in the mood to study. I have a permanent lump in my throat now, every time I think about the exam. But instead of that fear and panic driving me to my books, it does the exact opposite. I just can't seem to concentrate. I have no idea why. It's a vicious cycle; I'm too stressed to study, and not studying makes me stressed.

Ness doesn't seem to have the same problem. She is sprawled out on the bed on her stomach, her legs dancing in the air this way and that as she taps away at her phone. I envy her freedom, her carefree attitude. Every second that I am not studying, I'm panicking or actively freaking out. But not Ness. You wouldn't have known we both have to sit for the same exam.

Ness and I have been roommates since the very first day of college. We met on the quad. Cliché, but we bumped into each other and clicked right away, and we were too scared to risk living with anyone else. She is also my best friend, even though we couldn't be more different.

While I am anxious and obsessive, Ness is perky and outgoing, an endless source of energy. She wants to do it all; go to every party, kiss every guy, dance to every song. Most of the time, this contrast is drastic, like it is with our approaches to studying. There is more to life than school she likes to say. Ness doesn't believe in killing herself in the name of grades, which is the polar opposite of my own philosophy of panicking constantly about getting good enough grades and passing the bar exam so I can achieve my goals. Not that she doesn't try; Ness is one of the more naturally brilliant people I know. She can see or hear something only once, and it sticks in her head. It's another thing about her I am insanely jealous of.

So, naturally, she seems to have forgotten that we have an exam in a few weeks. A very essential exam. I don't think I've seen her crack open a book once.

"Hey, you know the Smith twins?" she asks suddenly, looking up from her phone for the first time in a long while. The implication is not lost on me. Everyone knows the Smiths, yes, but do you?

"Yeah, everyone knows the Smith twins on campus," I say.

"They're throwing this end of year party at Delta Hall, and from what people are saying online, it's going to be epic."

I shrug. "What's your point, Ness?"

"My point? Jesus, Amy. Why are you like this? My point is that we should go!"

"Oh. No, thanks. I have to study …"

"You've been studying all day! And all week! At the very least you need a break. Come on. You can't slouch over that chair every waking hour of your life."

"You know I hate parties, Ness." I'm trying to change the topic. The only way to successfully say no to Ness is to throw so many excuses at her she can't deflect them all.

"This isn't just any party. It's probably the last one before we graduate."

"I'll celebrate graduating when I pass these fucking exams."

"Oh my God, woman. Stop. That's exactly why you should come to this party. You've been so worried about the exam you're not even yourself. Look what it's doing to you. I bet you didn't even notice you have chips in your hair."

I reach up into the unruly mess that's my hair, and sure enough, my hand comes away with crumbled potato chip dust.

"I'm not listening to your bullshit today," Ness continues. "You're coming with me to the party."

"I probably won't know anyone there," I say, my voice small.

"That can only be a good thing. Means you can make some mistakes, and no one will remember it. Plus, I'll be with you all night, so you don't need to worry about that."

"You mean until you get dragged off by some guy and disappear for the rest of the night?"

"I won't do that, I promise. Although I won't lie, I've been looking to get into that Smith sandwich …"

"Ew, Ness! That's disgusting!"

"Such a prude. Come on, then. Let's get you dressed. I don't even want to think about what monstrosities are in your closet."

The party is exactly as loud and in your face as I expected. The blare of music hits us even before we get into the hall, and it's amplified to the nth degree when we step inside. There are more people here than I think I have ever seen in any one place on campus, and that includes lecture theaters. It seems everyone has shown up. The press of bodies is like a wall pushing in on all sides. I regret coming right away.

Ness grabs my hand, as if sensing my hesitation, and leads me into the heart of the party. She stops every few feet, saying hi to random strangers, stopping to converse briefly with others. Clearly, she is extremely popular, but that's not news.

I'm dressed in a regretfully short skirt and a floral shirt that's hidden away behind a warm sweater. Ness had fought valiantly against the sweater, insisting that it covered up my best feature, which to her is my chest. But I had already compromised on the length of the skirt, so she wasn't going to win that one. My hair is tied up in a loose bun at the top of my head, from where single strands keep sneaking out and falling around my face. Overall, though, I think I look pretty good for someone who didn't want to be here in the first place.

Ness leads the way to the alcohol almost on autopilot. She pours us both a drink and hands me a glass, lifting hers in the air for a toast. "Here's to us making some mistakes, and hopefully a lot of memories."

We clink glasses, and I take a tentative sip of my drink. The whiskey fires straight into my brain, and I close my eyes and cough violently for a few seconds. Ness laughs and claps me on the back. I think I hear her mutter 'virgin' under her breath. Once my eyes stop streaming, she pushes the glass back to my lips. I manage to swallow this time; the taste took me by surprise the first time.

"Are you trying to get me drunk?" I ask Ness. I can't help noticing how keen she is to help me empty my glass.

"Just enough that you stop worrying and have some fun," she says.

I don't say it, but I doubt that's going to happen. The few times Ness has managed to get me liquored up in the past, it led to me passing out and waking up the next day with no recollection of what happened. I'm not good with alcohol. I never have been.

I see the two guys approaching, and I know right away that they're the Smiths. They're immaculately dressed and very cool-looking with their identical velvet suits and their steel-toed boots polished to a high sheen. The Smiths are kind of legendary around campus. Their father is none other than the university's Dean of Students, and their name precedes them. They're wild and unhinged and showy. I think the first time I met them was at another one of their parties.

The guys themselves are good-looking in the classic, 90's movie star sense. They're identical twins, but they have over time distinguished themselves through their clothes and personality. Frank likes his bowties, and he is by far the brasher of the two. His brother Miles is quieter, more reserved, but you can see in his eyes he has a mean streak about him.

They say hi to Ness with exaggerated kisses on both cheeks. I take a step back, not wanting to get dragged into the conversation, wishing I could blend into the nearest wall and stay there until it's time to leave.

I hear them talk about the party and how it was the perfect opportunity for people to squeeze in the things they never got a chance to do all year. And there is something a bit too mischievous in the way Ness grins at that remark. Holy shit, she was serious about the sandwich.

That conversation does not seem to be dying down any time soon, so I take several more steps back, turn, and head off looking for a bathroom.

The crowd seems to have gotten thicker if that is even possible. I bump into countless shoulders, step on what seems like hundreds of toes. I mumble my apologies, but they get snatched up by the music and the collective hum of shouted conversation. Eventually, I locate a bathroom on the floor I'm on, and I duck in with relief. I stay in there for as long as I can. Only when I start to fear that Ness is looking for me do I get out of the stall I was sitting in, wash my hands, and reluctantly rejoin the party.

In that short time, the mood seems to have changed. The music is slower, more soulful, not as loud as it was. The people I pass are all versions of high or slightly drunk. I figure it is the point in any party when the drugs have finally kicked in for everybody.

Ness isn't where I left her. I look around to confirm I'm in the right place. As I am about to leave and go looking for her, I notice the slicked-back hair of Miles Smith. His brother is nowhere to be seen. Neither is Ness. I approach him and tap him gently on the shoulder.

He turns and lets his gaze travel over me. His expression is strange; I feel like he's undressing *and* judging me all at once.

"Where did Ness go?" I ask him. I have to shout so he can hear me. And stand on toes so I can speak directly into his ear.

He shakes his head, then hands me a glass I recognize as mine. "She went off with Frankie," he says. "If you know what I mean."

"I thought she wanted you both?" I ask him, the words spilling out of my mouth before I can stop myself. *Filter, Amelia. Filter.*

But Miles only grins. "She did, but I wasn't into it. I like my women more …" His eyes travel over my body once more. I feel the x-ray of his stare all the way through my sweater and top. I am almost tempted to tap his chin and say, 'My eyes are up here champ.'

"… unconventional," he finishes, and he grins again like he has just said the funniest thing.

My heart has begun to patter. I take an unconscious gulp of the alcohol to calm my nerves, and then another. It is so typical of Ness to promise not to leave me alone, then do it at the first opportunity, knowing how uncomfortable I get around people I don't know. And how much I hate parties. I make a mental note to give her a piece of my mind tomorrow. I should really be studying right now. Maybe I still can.

I pull out my phone to look at the time. The digits swim maddeningly in front of me, and for a second, I'm convinced the floor is spinning. I look up and around, wondering what just happened. How strong was that drink? I try to take a step back into something solid I can hold on to like a wall. My foot comes up, but there doesn't seem to be anywhere to put it back down. It hangs, for an eternity, in the air, and then I'm falling. I don't know how or why, but the next thing I know, my balance is completely shot. I can't remember which side is up, down, left or right. The whole room gives an almighty lurch, and the floor rushes up to meet me.

Strong hands grab me before I get to the ground. I think. I can feel fingers burning the exposed skin on my arm, as the stranger steadies me and holds me up. I can't be that drunk already. It happened too fast. I know I'm a lightweight, but it still feels strange how fast I got here. Unless …

But my mind is a puddle of half-formed thoughts. I can barely string a thought together. I feel suddenly weak and uncoordinated.

"Steady there," a voice says from somewhere above me. I try to focus on my savior, but my vision is blurry. "You should lie down. Let me help you …"

And then I'm being carried away. I think I feel my feet kicking against someone's hard torso. I lift my arm to touch his face, inches from my reach. I feel a slight brush of stubble. Lower, my fingers slide against something soft and rich. Velvet. Miles is the one carrying me. I remember his eyes, how they cut into me. I remember the assessment, the observation, the way they lingered ever so slightly over the swell of my chest. And I remember how uncomfortable he made me feel.

Something is wrong. Something bad is happening. I can feel it.

I try to speak, but the words come out in a string of unintelligible noises. I try to lift my hands again, to hit him, maybe, or push him away. But each of my fingers suddenly weighs a ton.

Scream, Amelia. Try and scream.

He can't hurt you. He is in the middle of a crowd. Everyone can see him carrying you away. But he is Miles Smith. No one will bat an eyelid. To them, this might just look like him carrying a drunk girl away to get some air.

I'm on my own.

Despair floods through my body. I close my eyes and focus on the singular effort it will require for me to scream. My brain seems lethargic, my mouth even more so. When I finally open my mouth, all that comes from it is a meek little whimper.

"Help."

I doubt anyone hears it. I barely hear it myself.

I hear Miles push open a door, and then he walks into a large room, still carrying me. My world is still swimming. I am floating, suspended in the air, then a plush mattress hits my back, and I lay still.

3
Robert

This was a terrible idea.

I am horribly, laughably out of place. I am at least twice as old as the youngest person here, and it shows.

The music is too loud. There are too many people. It's too hot. None of which are good signs for me, but they may be promising for why I'm here. Narrowed eyes follow me as I walk through the house. Suspicious. Confused. Amused. Ever so slightly hostile. I feel old and unwelcome. But I'm not about to back down from this just because I'm a little uncomfortable. Still, not exactly the best idea. Or maybe the execution is the problem. Maybe I should have given this a little more time, let the idea sit before diving straight in. It just seemed like the perfect opportunity cropped up out of the blue.

How long had it been since someone called to tell me about a college party? Too long. A lifetime ago. But that's exactly what happened. I reached out to an old college buddy of mine who still worked at the university and mentioned my situation without going into too much detail. It was an odd request to make I realized as I scrambled for words over the phone. It was good that he knew me personally.

The best place to find some bright young college minds? Probably an educational setting of some sort. A lecture or a symposium or talk. But I wasn't just looking for some nerdy legal mind. Hints were dropped. Throats were cleared. My friend ooohed in comprehension and finally informed me of the party. The last one there was going to be for a lot of the students, most of whom were graduating in a few weeks. It was the perfect setting.

The practicality of it was another matter entirely.

I pace around the house, my eyes scanning the faces around me. It's your typical college party fare. Tall skinny stoners, drifting around the house. Young single girls clearly out in search of a good time. Hawk-eyed predators scoping the scene. Nothing stands out; no one hits my eye enough to warrant a second look. I need a drink, a stiff one. But it's never a good idea to risk the drinks at a party. A college party at that. I let my eyes wander over to the drinks table. Maybe I can manage a beer?

That's when I see her.

She is standing at the table but leaning away from it like she's trying to slide away without being noticed. She is clearly uncomfortable; her body language is screaming that she doesn't want to be there. She keeps throwing furtive glances at a short, shapely brunette who is flanked by two men and clearly unconcerned about her friend's discomfort.

But all these observations come second to the most glaring one, the one that hits me like a ton of bricks: she is absolutely stunning.

Whether deliberately or not, she has managed to put together a look that says she couldn't be bothered, but if she had tried, she would have looked incredible. I think she looks incredible anyway. Her hair is just the right amount of loose/in place. It is tied back in a bun, leaving her heart-shaped face open. Hair that is a striking dark red, framing a pale, almost sun-deprived face. Her eyes are large and quick. Her nose is long and narrow. Her lips are full and inviting, painted a lush shade of plum red that almost matches her hair. Her body is half-hidden behind the drinks table, but from what I can see, she is tall and leggy. Her posture is rigid, reserved, almost too cautious. It's like she's afraid of spreading out like she wants to remain in her shell and not be bothered by anyone. I feel for her. Clearly, she doesn't want to be here.

"Hi!" Someone glides into my field of vision, completely out of the blue. Blonde. Blue eyes. Wide, inviting smile.

I have a second to register her, and then she has thrown herself at me, wrapping me in a bold hug. I am too stunned to react, so I stand there stiffly as she pats me on the back. It's a familiar hug, one that says she knows me, if a little too intimately. Yet I'm sure I've never met the girl in my life. I would remember. I never forget a face.

She is beaming when she pulls back.

"I'm sorry, who are you?" I ask her, brushing her hand from my shoulder where it is resting. She looks taken aback, offended even. I try to think about where I could have seen her, but nothing clicks.

"You're Robert Hardy, right?" she asks. "*The* Robert Hardy."

"Yes ... but how do you ...?"

"I'm sorry. It was presumptuous of me to come up on you like that. I assumed you'd remember me. I'm so sorry."

I open my mouth and shut it, still confused.

"My name is Veronica Sharpe. My class worked with you on a mentorship program for young law students last year. I'm a student here."

The memory finally falls into place. Yes, I did do a mentorship initiative for the school a while back in collaboration with the university, working with the college student body president. But that had been a young man, hadn't it?

"I think I know why you don't remember me. I wasn't exactly at the forefront. But I was an assistant student body president, and we interacted on a daily basis for several weeks."

"I'm so sorry," I tell her, and I mean it. I have no recollection of her at all.

"That's okay. You're a busy man, Mr. Hardy. I would expect nothing less."

"Well, it's nice to know I left an impact with someone, even if I don't remember it."

"Oh, you definitely left an impact. I've been following your cases for a long time, Mr. Hardy. I'm your biggest fan. And if I may be so bold as to say, I think your defense in the State vs Colin case was a stroke of genius."

This is strange. I don't think I've ever encountered a fan before. But it is also deeply flattering. I am almost reminded of myself in college, eager and desperate to prove myself, to follow in the steps of the lawyers I idolized.

"That's very kind of you to say, uh, Veronica."

"It's such a weird coincidence to see you here!" She looks around as if expecting our surroundings to vanish and be replaced by a courtroom. "Can I ask why you're here?" She gasps. "Oh my God, are you recruiting?"

The excitement in her voice is palpable. Her eyes are now two large orbs of brilliant blue.

"No," I say quickly. I mean, I am, but I don't want to give it away.

16

"Because I would love to work with you, sir, in whatever capacity," Veronica goes on. Her gaze is steady. She is staring at me, unflinching, and I have to admire her forwardness, how aggressive she seems to be. These are all great qualities of an assistant.

And why not her? She is certainly attractive. A girl that bold and that hot would definitely be a force to reckon with. Goldman wouldn't know what hit him. She seems eager, and she has done her research on me. That could actually be a plus for her. If she is already aware of how I work, then there would be no need for the initial training and hand-holding as she tried to figure out what was what.

So, why not?

I look back over at the drinks table. The gorgeous redhead is gone, as is her friend. One of the guys has remained behind, though. Waiting for her? Had he made a move while I was talking to Veronica? I start to look away, but a surreptitious movement of his hand catches my eye, and I turn back to him.

He does it with the practiced nonchalance of someone who has gotten away with it many times before. It's so quick, too, a casual flick of his wrist over the glass. If I blinked, I would have missed it.

"Mr. Hardy?" Veronica is positively bouncing up and down on the balls of her feet in front of me. My eyes refocus on her.

"Right. Sorry." What were we talking about? Ah, yes. She wants to work for me. "Listen, Veronica. You're a very impressive young woman. Of that, I'm sure, even though I've only been talking to you for five minutes. You seem brilliant, and you have the perfect attitude for the murky world that is the legal system. Never lose that. It will serve you well. Have you finished law school?"

"Technically, I am. We're graduating in a couple of weeks."

"Well, like I said. Impressive. How about this. Give me your information, and I'll keep you in mind in case anything ever comes up." It's the least I can do. It's the only thing I can do.

Veronica beams and she pulls out a strip of paper from her handbag and scribbles her information on it. I nod at her as I pocket it, and she departs with a cheery wave and a 'Nice to meet you!'

My eyes fly back to the drinks table. Right on cue, too. Gorgeous redhead is back, and she is conversing with the asshole who just spiked her drink. I take a few steps to my left so I can get a better look at him.

He looks vaguely familiar, even beyond the clear wealth and affluence that mark him out as a spoiled brat. I definitely know his type: rich, arrogant, powerful. Which is probably why he thinks he can get away with anything. Well, he's about to discover he cannot.

I watch with dread as she teeters, already feeling the influence of whatever he put in her drink. The man reaches over and scoops her up just before she crashes to the ground. Very chivalrous, asshole. I swing into action, making my way through the crowd I had assumed was thinning, but which is still very much a factor. I keep my eyes on them, on his purple coat, his broad shoulders taut as he carries her through the room and around a corner.

I am now elbowing people, toes crunching under me, startled cries of pain following me as I pass. I barge through what must be the entire student population until, at last, I round the corner, just in time to see that purple tailcoat disappear into a room at the end of the hallway.

I break into a brisk jog. I get to the room and fling the door open. The asshole is in the process of fumbling with his pants. The girl is sprawled out on the bed, writhing in blissful unawareness of just how much danger she is in.

"What the fuck?" the guy says, and he has the guts to look offended.

I walk forward slowly, or so it seems in my head. I am only vaguely aware of raising my hand, and then swinging. I hear a dull thump, and then the man recoils. His yell is loud and surprised. He staggers back and then falls, his arms flailing as he tries and fails to find something to steady himself.

"What the fuck?" he screams again. His hand goes up to his face and comes away, slick with blood. I look down at my own hand, coiled into a fist.

"I know what you were trying to do," I say through gritted teeth. "That's a criminal offense, one you could go to jail for. Drugging her and trying to rape her. Two criminal offenses."

"I don't know what you're talking about," the guy says, still clutching his nose. "I didn't rape anybody."

"But you drugged her. I saw you."

He doesn't seem to have an answer to that. I walk over to him with my fist raised again, and he recoils in fright. Wow. An asshole and a pussy.

"Give me your wallet," I tell him.

His hands are shaking. His whole body is. I take a photo of his driving license and student ID. Something about the name Smith rings a bell slightly, but I don't linger on it.

"Here's what you're going to do, Miles Smith. You're going to report yourself to campus police first thing tomorrow. And then you're going to go to the Dean and explain to him what you almost did. And then you're going to serve whatever punishment the school decides. Do you understand me?"

He nods.

"I have your information. I will make a follow up in a few days, and if I find out you haven't done as I asked, we're going to have a problem. Now get the fuck out of here."

He doesn't need a second telling.

I go over to the bed and lean in, looking at the girl. Her eyes are closed, almost like she's sleeping. She looks beautiful, at peace. I shake her gently awake.

Her voice is weak, her words incoherent. I look around the room, and luckily, there are some bottles of water over by the bedside table. I take one and shuffle her body into a roughly upright position. I tip the bottle into her mouth and force her to drink some of the water. It takes some time, but she eventually stirs, and her eyes slide open a fraction.

"Hey," I say to her. "I need your address, so I can get you home."

She doesn't seem to hear me. After some time, her eyes slide back shut, and she drifts off.

Stumped, I reach for her handbag and delve inside. It takes some rummaging, but I finally find a card with her address. Relieved, I put everything back into her bag and get up off the bed.

She is a bit heavier than she looks, but I manage to lift her without much trouble. I heave her over my shoulder and slowly make my way out of the room. It is much harder to navigate the crowded party, but I manage. Something about the sight of a man with a woman slung over his shoulder helps to part the seas.

I think about walking, as her hall of residence isn't too far away, but in her state, it would be hell getting across the campus. It's been a while too. I don't think I know my way around all too well anymore. So, I get her in my car and drive her to her building. Pulling her over my shoulder again, I carry her down the long hallway of identical rooms until I find 46A. I fumble with her keys but manage to get the door open and push inside. I fumble around for a light switch and flick it on.

I am standing in a very girly room with bright posters all over the walls and identical pink bedspreads over two single beds. I lay her gently on one of the beds. It's a bit of a struggle, keeping my eyes off her pale, creamy thighs, but I do. I shake her shoes off and try and tuck her into bed. My face is close to hers. I can hear her soft breathing, feel it on my face.

Amelia. Her card says her name is Amelia Brooks.

Beautiful name.

Beautiful girl.

She stirs again. This time, when she opens her eyes, I can tell she's lucid. They travel over me, green pools, half-lidded. I realize how strange it must be for her, waking up to a stranger like this. Must be scary and confusing. I straighten up, intending to turn and leave.

Her hands shoot up suddenly. She is stronger than I thought. Or maybe it's the surprise of it all. But she pulls me down on her, and her lips crush onto mine.

4

Amelia

The first thing I become aware of is that I am back in my room. Somehow. And on my bed. The events of the night play in my mind like a bad dream. I am not even sure they were not a dream. I cannot make sense of them.

I was there with Ness and the Smiths … I went to the bathroom and stayed in the stall for almost twenty minutes … and then I came back and started chatting with one of the Smiths … and then nothing. There is a gap in my memory; my mind tells me there is. I can't recall what happened after that. I have a vague recollection of being carried, and someone pushing water past my lips … and I think I may have been in a car … and then nothing.

Wait. I do remember something. Someone. Once or twice, when I flicked my eyes open, I found myself face to face with the most beautiful man I have ever seen. Jawline cut from granite. Light stubble. Dark, dangerous eyes. And he was looming over me, his hands patting my cheeks, my forehead. I didn't imagine that part, did I?

I drift off, my head full of images of the man. In my waking dreams he was towering over me, protective and caring. He watched over me, he touched me ever so softly. He lowered his head and planted a chaste kiss on my forehead and said something that sounded like goodnight.

My eyes fly open, and there he is. My dream. The knight who saved me. He isn't a dream. He is flesh and blood and strong jawline and dark eyes. He is sexier than I can believe, hotter than I've been imagining. And he's right there, in front of me, his lips parted slightly, begging me to dive in.

And I do.

I don't know what has come over me, but my inhibition is screaming at me from a very thick window in the back of my mind. *Not today, bitch.*

I reach up and grab him. He is trying to leave for some reason. I'm not about to let him. I give him a gentle tug, and he falls onto me. His weight is delicious, and I spread my legs as he writhes on top of me.

I find his lips with ease.

They are hot and moist and slightly parted. I reach up and seize them with mine, and his initial shock is all the window I need to grab his neck and pitch him forward even further. I kiss him hard, a sudden fire of desire tearing through me, making me bolder, making me need him. I feel his face with my hands, tracing the hard, masculine features, trying to draw his profile with just my fingers. And then he gives in and kisses me back, and the roar in my head is loud enough to drown out all other sounds.

He kisses me with passion and wild abandon. I thought I was kissing him hard, but he now shows me I was but teasing him. He shifts his weight on top of me, and I feel a hard pressure on my belly that sends shock waves through my core.

His hands are on my neck, on my cheeks, tussling in my hair. I am in a cloud of scent and taste and sound, his heavy woodsy cologne swirling around me, his lips, tasting of gum and something fruity, and the sound of moaning that can't be coming from me, surely?

The kiss is simultaneously hot and soft and urgent and demanding. He suckles, nibbles at my lips like they are life-affirming. I probe gently with my tongue, and when he meets it with his, my whole body trembles and my eyes roll back in my head. Nothing else in the world exists; there is only this man and his wonderful lips, cutting me to pieces, our bodies dancing a slow conga.

Every nerve in my body is on fire. I want more of him. I need to feel him. I am torn between wanting to savor this sensation, this moment, and giving in to the growing roar in my head that's demanding more.

My hands move between us, trembling, tentative, determined. I feel the heat pouring out of him in waves as my fingers brush against his shirt and pry the buttons open. Finally, I run my palms across his chest; it is granite, sculpted from the same unforgiving material as his jawline. He feels amazingly solid, and just below, my fingers locate a row of impossible abs.

I feel rather than hear him curse into my mouth. In retaliation, his hands unentangle themselves from the depths of my hair. His fingers are quick and nimble as they travel down my body, igniting sensations I am sure will cause me to explode as they go. He alternates between slow exploratory flicks and heavy patting with hot palms. My body is aching with lust. And then he is at my thighs, working his way upwards, my body bucking uncontrollably. I will die from this pleasure. I won't survive this onslaught of sensations.

He stops, suddenly, maddeningly.

"What? Why did you stop?" The voice is not my own. It is thick and laden with lust. My eyes are open now, and I can see through the mist into his eyes, dark and sharp and definitely aroused. So why did he pull back?

He is crushing me. His hard maleness is still pushing into my thigh. I don't want him to ever move. I want us to remain like this for the rest of time. Or we could take our clothes off and then get into that position again.

"I'm sorry," he says.

"What? Why?"

"I lost control for a minute there."

He lifts himself from me and gets off the bed. His absence is like a cold gust of wind hitting me in the face.

"How are you feeling?" he asks. What is that—concern?

Horny. Like I want to sit on your face and ride you till kingdom come? Horny! Did I mention horny?

"I'm fine," I manage to say.

"That was quite the ordeal you went through back there," he says.

"I don't actually remember what happened."

"Oh, some douchebag drugged you and tried to take advantage of you back at the party. Thank God I stopped him before he could do anything."

Smith? Miles Smith had tried to take advantage of me?

"My hero," I say. *Fuck me. Please?*

I don't know who I have turned into and where she is from. This is nothing like me. I'm Amelia Brooks, sensible, polite law student who didn't seize men and kiss them at random. To think that there was a version of me brave enough to do that is mind-boggling.

"I'm just glad you're okay. You really shouldn't accept drinks from strangers at parties like that."

"He isn't a stranger. I mean, he is. But I know him. Everyone does. He's the Dean's son."

I see a light flit across his face like that information means something to him. Now that I am thinking straight, I realize I have no idea who this man is and how he got into my room. I feel comfortable around him, enough to be making out with him in my own bed, despite the fact that he is a complete stranger. Why is that?

"I think I'd better be going," he says. He stands up from my bed. Tall, but not reedy. His arms are muscular; they strain the fabric of his shirt, and I don't need reminding just how ripped he really is beneath that shirt.

I feel myself blush and look away.

He walks around the room, taking in everything from our silly posters to the books still open on my study table.

"Won't you at least tell me your name?" I ask him, watching him with fascination.

He ignores me and continues his tour of my room. He stops at the desk and flips through some of the books. "So you want to be a lawyer?" he asks without turning to look at me.

"I'm going to be one," I say. "As soon as I ace these pesky little exams coming up."

"The bar exam? That little thing? I'm sure you'll do great. And when you do pass it? Where do you want to work?"

This conversation has definitely gone off the rails.

Sir? Can we have more of you doing things to my body?

"I'm not sure, to be honest. I think an internship first, maybe? I want to learn under someone established because hands-on experience is the most important thing in this field."

He nods as if he knows exactly what I'm talking about. Wait. Maybe he does!

"Are you a lecturer here?" I ask him. He looks older, so it's a possibility. But also, not old enough, if that makes sense? He speaks like a lawyer. Or, at the very least, someone well versed with the field. And he is here, at the university. What am I missing?

Whatever his secrets are, he seems determined not to divulge them. When he finishes his tour of the tiny space I call my room, having inspected everything, including the visibly aroused woman on my bed, he rubs his hands together in a theatrical show of winding up and getting ready to leave.

"Have a good night, Miss Brooks," he says. "It was fun meeting you."

"Wait. How do you know my name? As a matter of fact, how did any of this happen? How did you get me back here?"

He merely smiles.

I watch him as he walks out, and I have to resist the temptation to get up and watch him walk away. Instead, I slump back in bed and will my pounding heart to be still. Without a doubt, this has been the wildest night of my life.

The only thing worse than the stress and pressure of preparing to sit for the biggest exam of my life is the stress and pressure of worrying about work and internship. Okay, so it's not worse, because nothing trumps the big bad wolf that is the bar exam. But still, it has become a constant source of anxiety for me.

I have started sending letters out. I have applied everywhere I ever wanted to work, and a lot of places I don't. I am growing desperate now. Either I'm doing something wrong, or nothing is going to work out the way I planned. Finish law school. Ace the bar exam. Get a fancy job at a top firm in the city. Crush it at the job. Make junior partner in three years. From there, the rest just falls into place. Maybe marriage. Three kids. Gorgeous house and life.

But it all falls apart if the first milestone isn't complete.

I am just about to give up when I get the phone call. Ness and I sit across from each other in the room, trying to decide from a pile of things who gets to keep what when we leave. It isn't going so well.

"Hello? Is this Miss. Amelia Brooks?"

"Yes."

"My name is Susan Rance. I'm Head of Human Resource at Galweather & Meyer."

"The law firm?" Ness asks, clearly eavesdropping.

I shoo her away and get back to the call. "Okay …"

"I am pleased to announce that you've made it through our first round of applications for an entry position at our firm, Miss Brooks. Congratulations."

I don't actually remember applying to Galweather & Meyer. But then again, I applied to so many places, so who knows. "Thank you!" I say.

"As such, I would like to invite you for a personal interview to be conducted this coming Friday at our offices on 5th and Madison. I'm calling to confirm your availability."

"Uh, yes. Of course. I will be available."

"Excellent. We look forward to seeing you."

It's fantastic news. I didn't realize how much I had been hoping for something like this to happen, a confirmation that I was on the right path.

I spend the rest of the week researching G&M and going over their cases. I'm thrilled to learn that it is one of the most powerful young firms in the city. The more I read about them, the more I'm shocked that I actually managed to get an interview there. Everything about the firm suggests it is impossible to get to. But I am determined to put my best foot forward. There must be a reason I was considered in the first place.

I don't even get nervous until I'm standing right at the large glass door into the building, and I can see my own reflection staring at me with wide eyes. I have chosen a cream blouse with tiny patterns, and sleek, stylish pants for this interview. Why not play with what you've got?

I am surprised to see that I am the only one here. I check my watch to confirm that I'm not too early. I sit down primly in the reception area, and minutes later, a sallow-faced older woman signals to me that I should follow her.

She leads me down a long hallway with offices on either side. We walk in silence. I go over my preparation in my head, making mental notes to be brief and concise.

Presently, the lady stops at an office marked 'ROBERT HARDY' and gives the door a gentle tap.

A deep voice calls out that we should come in. The lady

swings the door open, but instead of going in first, like I expect her to, she steps aside so I can walk through.

"Good luck," she says. "You'll need it."

How incredibly rude, I think, as I walk into the office. I barely have time to register how large and well-furnished it is before I see him. He is seated on his desk, looking at me as I walk into his office.

It's him. Even if he hadn't been in every one of my dreams since that night, I would recognize that jawline anywhere. It is my dark knight.

5
Robert

I would never admit this to anyone, but I love the interview process. It is one of the few guilty pleasures I have, which is why I always insist on doing it myself whenever possible. Not only is it the best way to figure out if someone can handle the unique pressures of working under me, but it also gives me a rare opportunity to go all the way with my 'insanity.' Anything to test the applicant's mettle and nerve. It's when I truly get to shine, pushing the narratives of my perceptions. It has not been a good interview if the applicant is not crying at the end of it. Or a very good one.

I have been looking forward to Amelia's interview. A bit too much if I'm honest. And I can already tell it's going to be a good one.

She has made quite the effort today. Unlike the last time I saw her, she is definitely dressed to impress. She is in a lovely, cream blouse with tiny patterns on it, and sleek, stylish pants that draw attention to her long, shapely legs, rounded off by a pair of simple black heels. Her hair isn't held up today; it falls in neat little ringlets around her face and down to her shoulders, a thick mane of dark red curls. She looks lovely.

She looks … shocked.

Her eyes are like two large marbles when she walks into my office. She actually stops in her tracks, frozen in place. I watch as she tries to make sense of it. I can almost hear her mind whirring, turning.

"Miss Brooks," I say, stepping forward and offering her my hand. "Please, have a seat."

She moves almost in slow motion. Her hand comes up slowly, slides into mine, and shakes once. Her grip is firm, and her fingers feel warm. I am transported for a moment back to her room, with her working those fingers all over my torso. I shake myself out of the unwelcome reverie. I step aside to indicate the chair, and she glides to it gracefully.

Her scent hits me as she passes me. It's distinctly feminine, with notes of something flowery and a rich vanilla essence that lingers in the air long after she has passed. She sits down and crosses her legs, then blinks up at me expectantly. I wonder if she's going to bring up the fact that we have met before. I have my response ready. Or my non-response. We met where? And did what? No, miss. You must have me confused with someone else.

"Can I get you anything?" I ask her as I sit across from her. We are both on the same side of the desk. No barrier. The proximity is supposed to do half the job of intimidating her.

"No," she says. "Thank you."

I reach for a file on my desk and flip it open. The file is full of blank sheets of paper. Usually, this file would contain the applicant's information, resume, and application. But Amelia never applied to Galweather & Meyer. The file is a visual prop.

"So, Miss Brooks. Let's hear the pitch. Why should I hire you?"

She takes a big breath, no doubt to steady any frayed nerves. When she launches into her speech, it comes out rigid and concise, like she spent hours in front of a mirror perfecting it.

"I just graduated in the top 5th percentile in my law class at DePaul University. I'm very passionate about the law, and I hope I can apply what I learn here to augment my career and journey. I have done one internship while on summer break at a small law firm back home in Marietta. I acknowledge that I'm not experienced, but what I lack in that regard, I believe I make up for in hard work and desire. You should hire me because I will kill for you."

Not bad. And delivered in under two minutes. Still, not exactly mind-blowing. "What do you know about me, Miss Brooks?" I ask.

Her hesitation is brief, a mere flicker across her face. But it is enough to tell me what I need to know; she has read up on me.

"Uh, you're a peerless defense attorney," she says. "You've handled a range of cases, but your specialty is criminal law, and you have yet to lose a case."

I wave a hand, and she falls silent. "That's all very well. But what do you know about me, Miss Brooks? Not my Wikipedia entry."

Her mouth falls open slightly, and her eyes widen. She has to have heard something about me. Anything. I take a lot of pride in my reputation.

"I don't know what you mean, sir," she says. Either she knows but is too afraid to say it to my face, or she didn't bother to go beneath the surface with her research. If she did any research. Both scenarios are disappointing.

I change track. "Do you have any trial experience?"

"Not from any actual case, no."

"What did you do at the law firm you interned for?"

"It was mostly office work. Preparing court documents, reviewing, and correcting motions …"

"Fetching coffee?"

She blushes. "Yes."

"So, to summarize, you have no actual experience, you've only worked at one firm, and all you did there was grunt work?"

She shifts uncomfortably in her seat, and for once, she looks rattled. "I did what was required of me, sir," she rallies. "As I will do for you. And as for experience, I believe my lack of it will be to my benefit and yours as I am hungry to learn and to grow."

I'm silent for a while, thinking.

"I hope you are aware, Miss Brooks, of the scope of your responsibilities as my Personal Assistant? Because I'm going to require so much more from you than simply getting my coffee."

"Yes, sir. Of course."

"While it's refreshing that you are as yet unaware of my reputation, I find that it would also be instructive for you to learn all you can about me. Much of what you're going to hear is exaggerated or wildly inaccurate, but you will do well to remember it anyway. I like to consider myself fair, Miss Brooks. I am not a perfectionist, but I do expect you to perform to the best of your ability, and should you fall short of my expectations, you will be out the door. The minute you start working for me, I own your ass. You will make yourself available when I need you; the minute I need you, Miss Brooks. Not five minutes after or as soon as it is convenient for you. The second I ask for you, I expect you to be there, pen and notebook in hand. Do you understand?"

"Yes, sir."

"My Assistant should be a reflection of myself. I don't make mistakes, so I don't expect you to make mistakes. Please remember, your job is to help me do my job as effectively as possible. I don't need to tell you what will happen if I feel, at any point, that you are not doing so. Understood?"

She nods. Her eyebrows are pulling together, though, and she looks like she wants to ask me something.

"What is it, Miss Brooks?"

"I'm sorry, sir. But it sounds like … am I hired?"

"Frankly, I have seen better applicants. Your shortcomings aside, however, I find myself in dire need of an assistant, and you will simply have to get up to speed on the fly. But yes, Miss Brooks. The job is yours."

Her reaction is muted. Barely a smile. But her whole body relaxes, and the relief on her face is evident.

"Now, I cannot stress this enough: I need you to learn what is required of you. Your job description is whatever I say it is, and I say it stretches from office tasks to helping me on actual cases. The one thing I cannot abide is ill-preparedness. So, take an hour or two to get acquainted with the office and your environment. Then report back to me for your first assignments."

She nods curtly, then stands up to leave. She brushes imaginary lint off her pants.

"One last thing, Miss Brooks."

She turns to me, eyes expectant.

"While you're here, I think it might be best to keep your personal life out of the office as much as possible. I will not abide gossip or wanton affairs with the lowly office staff. I hardly need to say it, but I expect you to be a consummate professional."

There is nothing professional about the look I find myself giving her as she walks out. Her pants are tight, and her legs are oh so long. My eyes fall to her bottom as she sways out of my office, and they remain there, stubbornly following the delicious swinging motion until she has disappeared out of sight. I don't remember seeing *that* ass at the party.

I'm still staring at the spot from where her figure just disappeared when a fresh pair of legs struts into sight. I recognize

Susan from HR immediately. Considering how often she has to deal with me and my rotating door of assistants, I see her more often than anyone else in the office. Always, she shows up with an exasperated expression, like she knew it was just a matter of time before she had to sit down with me again to discuss a new assistant. Today, though, she doesn't look resigned or embattled. She looks flustered. It's a new look for her. In all the time I have worked with Susan, I have never seen anything fluster her.

"Susan," I say as she walks in. "If you're here about the new hire ..."

"Oh, you hired someone already?" she asks, genuinely surprised.

"Yeah, just now. You probably walked past each other in the hallway."

"I look forward to meeting her, however briefly."

Damn, Susan. Not pulling any punches today, are we?

"But that's not why I'm here."

"Oh. Is everything okay?"

"I ... uh ... she's back, Mr. Hardy."

"What do you mean? Who's back?"

But I can see it written all over her face. And from the way she looks around like she's afraid she'll catch someone with their ear pressed against the glass.

The realization settles, heavy and uncomfortable, in the pit of my belly. I get up and walk quickly to Susan. She is still standing suspended in the doorway. I pull her into the office and close the door, then grab her by the hand and march her to the window. The city hums and speeds just outside us.

"Why is she here?" I ask, and I am vaguely aware of my fingers digging into her arm where I'm gripping her.

"You're hurting me," she says, almost casually. It's my favorite thing about her; she may be the one person in the office who is not flat-out terrified of me. "And I don't know why she's here. She wouldn't say. She just showed up and demanded to see you."

Her arm slides out of my grip, but rather than step back, she stands there looking coolly up at me. "I can send her away," she says after a beat. "Or have security see her out ..."

"No, that will only cause a scene." Which is exactly what she wants. "I guess there's only one way to find out what she wants. Send her in."

Susan nods. She turns and leaves the office quietly.

A minute later, I hear the gentle tapping of heels on the floors and the low, inaudible whisper of conversation. Then someone is tapping at my door, and I turn around to see Susan retreating fast, and the tall, willowy figure of the woman formerly known simply as 'Number 10' leaning into my office.

She hasn't changed a bit. Still gorgeous. Long blonde hair falling past her shoulders. Flawless heart-shaped face. Body swathed in an elaborate, over the top and completely out of place blue dress. She trots in, hand extended delicately in my direction. I walk stiffly to her, meet her halfway and take the offered hand in a reluctant handshake. Her skin feels cool to the touch, a coldness that extends all the way to her eyes.

"Was that the new one?" she asks, smiling that knowing smile of hers.

"I don't know what you're talking about," I say mechanically.

"I saw her, the cute little redhead wandering around, looking at the names on doors. I must say, Robert, you're losing your touch. That bumbling child won't last a day."

I flinch at her use of my first name. So personal. So aggressive. Cocky, too, like she knows she's untouchable. "As I said, I don't know what you're talking about."

She only smiles, an indulgent flash of gleaming white teeth. "Right. Of course. Well, aren't you going to invite me to sit down?"

"What do you want?" I snap at her. "I don't have time for your games."

Her eyes never leave mine as she steps around me, swiveling her body completely so I remain in her line of vision. She locates the chair with her foot and drops into it, then crosses her legs and nods at the chair across from her. I'll be damned if I'm pushed around in my own office. I cross my arms and remain standing. She smiles again.

"This takes me back," she says after some time. She looks around the office, and there is a wistful fondness in her eyes. "So much time wasted in here … I actually spent more time here than in my own house. Or anywhere else, really. Good times."

I bite back the retort that springs to my lips.

She must realize I'm not going to indulge her because she clears her throat, and her demeanor is suddenly business-like. "I want more money," she finally says.

"What?"

"You heard me. More money. Or our deal is off."

"I don't think you understand how this works," I say. "We already have a deal in place. One that prevents exactly this sort of thing from happening. You can't just show up whenever you want and make more demands."

"And yet here I am."

This was a bad idea. It had always been a bad idea. Clearly, it had been foolish to expect this woman to disappear and stay gone. "I can't help you," I tell her. "You know I can't."

"Oh, don't give me that crap, Robert. You paid me off once, so you can definitely do it again. I'm not even asking for much. I just need a little something to sort my affairs out."

I shake my head, unconvinced. I'm not about to fall for some sob story. Keep your focus on the facts. And the fact here is that this woman is trying to exploit me. "Like I said. I can't help you."

Her eyes assess me quietly, deliberating, and I see the exact moment she realizes she's not winning this one. Her whole body tenses, and her expression changes in a heartbeat. "I'm not asking, Robert." She is now terse, her voice ringing with authority. "I am ready, as I was last time, to go public with my story. We both know that won't look good for you. Particularly now, when you have this big case coming up."

Of course, she knows about the case. For all her faults, the woman was always meticulous and thoroughly informed. It was what had made her a good assistant.

"I don't respond well to threats," I say. I step back and indicate the door with a sweep of my hand. "And I think you should leave."

"Are you sure about that, Robert?"

It's a challenge, a final salvo where she goes for broke in the hope of landing a significant blow. I know that tactic all too well; it's an old Robert Hardy specialty.

I gesture once more toward the door. I hope I'm projecting a cool and unbothered exterior, but the gears are turning in my mind. Yet another thing to worry about, as if my plate isn't already full.

She seems to get the message. She smiles sweetly as she gets up and walks past me. She gives her hair a theatrical toss, then leaves me with a cryptic, "You'll be hearing from me."

6
Amelia

It doesn't dawn on me just what I've gotten myself into until I'm sitting in front of a short, weary-looking woman, with a stack of endless books and files tottering dangerously on her desk. She pauses for a minute and then reaches behind her, somewhere in the depths of the paper mountain that makes up her work area and pulls out yet another file. But this one is unlike the others. This one is, in fact, a binder, with a thick, glossy cover and the appearance of age and wear.

"So," the lady says, and I remember she told me her name is Susan. I make a mental note to start keeping track of faces and names. She flashes a brief smile at me. "These are all the cases you need to get yourself acquainted with. I know it's a lot, but you need to internalize all this to help him prep for the big case he has coming up." She points to a second batch, smaller, but still substantial. "These are all the cases Mr. Hardy has tried in the past year. Useful reading, so you can familiarize yourself with his strategies, tactics, and how he goes about his work."

She lifts a thick looking folder and places it in front of me. "This is everything you need to know about Galweather & Meyer. You'll find a standard contract, the company HR manual, which I must insist you go over with a fine-tooth comb, and a few other documents detailing your job description and everything else you'll need in terms of paperwork."

Already my head is swimming, but Susan does not appear to be even close to finished.

"But this …" she pushes the thick, worn binder in front of me. "This is the most important one of all. It's essentially a Robert Hardy dossier. I'm not joking. This is everything Robert Hardy. There's a list of all the people who have worked as his Personal Assistants. You'll find notes on his preferences, some of the things he'll ask you to do, and crucially, a list of fireable offenses."

I can tell from the way she speaks that this is a speech she has given many times. Judging by the size of the dossier, there is a lot to learn about Robert Hardy.

"Listen …" Susan sighs, and at that moment, I notice how

very old she looks, how tired. I can't even begin to think about what
her job must entail. "It's not an easy job, being Robert Hardy's
assistant. In fact, I'll go so far as to say it's an impossible job. All you
can do is your best, really. So just buckle up, go over these files, and
stay on your toes. You'll be fine."

I'm not convinced or reassured. The terror has been building
slowly inside me since I walked into the building, and it has since
blossomed into full-blown panic. I feel overwhelmed and confused,
and unsure where to even begin.

"Amelia?" Susan speaks softly. The terror must be showing
on my face. "Are you okay?"

It all comes spilling out in a rush. I don't know this woman
well enough to feel this comfortable with her, but I need to vent; I
need to speak to someone about all this, or I'm going to lose my shit.
I tell her about the interview, how badly it went, and how the fact
that I still got the job means I'm already working from a
disadvantage. I admit that I'm terrified of Mr. Hardy, confess that I
had no idea what I was walking into and that I doubt I'll be able to
handle whatever it is my job entails. Maybe not the best thing to say
to your new employer, but I'm past caring at this point.

I stop just short of telling her about the night in my room
because I can't even wrap my head around that one myself. Was it
him? Of course, it was. I'm not crazy. But why does he not
remember it? What does that mean?

"And he keeps talking about his reputation! And I don't
know that much about him, but apparently, he is this big-time lawyer
with a streak of wins, but he's had all these assistants, and I don't
know what to make of that …"

Susan listens quietly. There is something comforting about
her presence; she is at once maternal and friendly, and there is a
knowing glint in her eyes. I am almost certain she has had to deal
with similar breakdowns before. I do not realize I'm crying until she
pushes a box of tissues in my face. I pluck one out and dab my face,
frustrated at my weakness and lack of professionalism. *Not the best first
impression, Amelia.*

"I'll be honest with you, Amelia. You seem like a nice girl.
This is a difficult job. It's probably a good thing that you haven't
heard that much about Robert Hardy because I doubt you'd still want

to work with him. He is a brilliant lawyer, of course. Exceptional. But that means he's a bit of a character behind the curtain. He won't win any awards for his management style. He's relentless, cold, disassociated, and some have even called him mean. The reputation he spoke of is one of fear. Everyone who has interacted with the man comes away with the same feeling of fear. It's much worse when you work for him.

"I'm not telling you this to scare you. I think you should know the kind of man you're working for. Yes, Robert is all these things and more, but there's much more to him than the coarse, occasionally brash exterior everyone sees. He cares about his cases, sometimes to an obsessive degree. It's why he wins so often. It's what makes him a great lawyer. If you can understand that, then I think you'll understand why he's the way he is."

"How many assistants has he had?" I ask her. That dossier looks mighty thick.

"You would be Number 16."

"Oh. That's not too bad."

"That's in the last two months."

"Oh."

"This month has been a bit tricky. Whenever he gets a big case, he gets a bit more … impatient. But don't worry about that. Just do as I told you, and you'll be fine, okay?"

I nod. I feel better, having unburdened myself like that. The weight is still there; I still get a pang of terror every time I think about Mr. Hardy and his steely eyes. But it's not as overwhelming. The sense of impossibility is gone. I appreciate that it's not going to be easy, but at least it doesn't seem as daunting. All I have to do is go through the binder, as Susan said.

I get to the door before I remember another question that has been playing on my mind. I turn back, shifting to settle the pile of files in my hands.

"What's the longest an assistant has lasted with him?" I ask Susan.

Her response is disconcertingly automatic. "34 days, 6 hours, and 10 minutes."

My eyebrows go up. So, someone is keeping count. More

importantly, though, someone somewhere was able to survive for that long. The thought fills me with a sense of purpose. What if I treated this as a challenge? What's one month? Whatever he throws at me, I bet I can suck it up for a month. If I can hold out for that long— longer, even— then I will have proved something to myself and Mr. Hardy. Already he thinks I lack experience. Well, I'm going to show him just how diligent I can be.

I think about the night in my room once more as I'm walking back to my desk. It's still so fresh in my mind. Every touch, every kiss, still lingers on my skin and in my memory. How could he not remember any of it? Or maybe that's just my naivety shining through. Just because the incident was a big deal for me doesn't mean it was for him, too. He probably forgot about it as soon as he walked out. Just another college girl who couldn't hold her liquor.

I remember asking him who he was and how he cleverly avoided answering; because it didn't make sense why he was there at the party. And then weeks later I interview for him? There is too much going on there for it to be a coincidence.

I've gotten so lost in my thoughts I'm not really watching where I'm going. She comes out of nowhere, a blur of motion, a flash of blue fabric, and blonde hair. I walk right into her, and the files fly from my hands. They land with a dull thunk on the floor, and a hundred pieces of paper, once meticulously arranged, are now cascading around us like falling snow.

"Damn it!" I hear myself curse.

The woman I have collided with materializes slowly in front of me, like a picture getting clearer as the lens is adjusted. I don't have enough time to take her in. I notice only that she is perhaps the most beautiful woman I have ever seen, with lustrous long blonde hair, come hither eyes, and a lovely little dress that would not look out of place at an awards show.

Then that beautiful face contorts, and she blinks rapidly as the expletives flow from her mouth. "What the fuck! Are you blind?"

There is a phone in her hand, still lit. I doubt I'm the only one at fault here, missy. But I am too preoccupied with the scattered papers to worry about her at that moment. I get down on my haunches and scan the pattern of the chaos. The papers have spread out in all directions. It seems only the three or four top folders were affected, but that is still hundreds of individual files, and judging by how far and wide they have scattered, it would be virtually impossible for me to figure out what came from where.

"Excuse me!" the blonde woman snaps, calling my attention back to her.

"I'm sorry, miss," I say quickly. "I wasn't watching where I was going."

"Damn right, you weren't. I almost dropped my phone." And she somehow manages not to look ridiculous while saying it.

"I'm sorry," I say again. "But I really need to sort these out."

The courteous thing would be for her to get down and help me gather my things. But this woman clearly has no need for courtesy. I'm sure she has … other things going for her. She clicks her tongue in disgust and steps around me. Her shoes are golden stilettos with tiny little crystals inlaid along the heel. The front of her shoe makes contact with the batch of files still remaining and pushes the top one just enough so that the glossy 'Robert Hardy' binder is exposed.

The foot, already stepping away, hangs for a minute in midair, and then it is returned slowly to where it was.

"Oh, you're the new assistant!" the woman says. "I thought you looked familiar."

There is something like glee in her voice. I don't recall seeing her before.

"I'm sorry," I say, straightening up so that I'm looking into her face. "Do I know you?"

She shakes her head, her features twisting again. "Oh, sweetie. If you don't know who I am, you might not last very long at this job." The look she gives me is full of quiet scorn.

It takes a second, but it finally dawns on me. "You're one of his old assistants," I say.

"I'm his best assistant. I worked here the longest, and I would still be here if I wanted to. I'm basically the template."

So this is the 'someone.' I would never have put her face to the mysterious assistant who went where none had gone before. I expected simple, hardworking, maybe even a little nerdy. Not this tall, snarky, model-type. Is this what I was supposed to turn into? Is this what it took to survive Robert Hardy? Except she hadn't really survived either, had she?

"Couldn't have been much of a template," I blurt out.

"You wouldn't know anything about that, would you?" she scoffs at me. "Everything about you is wrong. If I were you, I wouldn't get comfortable. You won't last a day with Robert."

In another world, I would be pulling this woman aside and asking her for survival tips. But she gives off such negative energy I find myself instantly disliking her. "I guess we'll see about that," I tell her.

We stare at each other for a long time. Hostility seems to ooze from her pores. I match the intensity of her stare, refusing to be cowed. If this is a staring contest, I'm determined to win. But it's so much more than that, and we both know it. She is trying to flex authority she no longer has. She is trying to show me she's better than me, that I will never be as good as she is. And I refuse to indulge her. Eventually, she blinks. She smiles, but there is no warmth there. Then she takes one step back, and I realize we were actually inches from each other's faces. She steps around me and walks away with a final withering glare.

I get back down and gather up the scattered pages, trying to disturb them as little as possible. I am tempted to go back to Susan and ask for her help sorting through them, but I have already endured a moment of weakness in front of her, and I don't think she'd take kindly to another.

I stack the files and folders back together and lift them up, then resume walking toward the desk outside Robert's office. My desk. As I approach, I sneak a glance into the office to see where he is. I see him standing against the window, looking out into the street. He looks so silent and docile it's hard to imagine he is the same person I've been hearing so many negative things about.

It takes me less than ten minutes to arrange my desk. I didn't expect the job to start right away, so I have nothing personal to put on it. I rifle through the drawers, but there's nothing in them but lint. I pull the binder closer and flip it open.

Now that I'm working for him, I might as well get to know the devil himself.

7
Amelia

Robert's voice is loud. It doesn't seem that way when you're in front of him, and he's practically muttering with that quiet baritone of his. But when you're say, a few feet away, at the desk just outside his door, and he is agitated for some reason, then you realize just how loud he can really get. It carries, vibrates through every bone in my body, and I have jumped out of my skin each of the last six times he has shouted for me today.

The first thing I learn about him is that he is incredibly impatient. He wants things done his way, and he wants them done right when he says them, which means that when he first called my name and I didn't materialize like a genie in front of him, a small vein appeared at the base of his neck and did not go away for the rest of the day.

Another invaluable lesson I have picked up is that Robert Hardy does not like to be corrected. I made that mistake earlier today when he called me 'Amanda' and I stupidly mumbled, "It's actually Amelia." It was also when I learned that he had a stare that could curdle milk. So when he shouts for 'Amanda' for the seventh time, I leap up off my chair and speed into his office, where I stand in front of him, notebook and pen in hand, trying to keep my breathing steady. I am mostly unsuccessful.

"I need the McKinley interview," Robert says, and he stretches his hand out.

"I'll get that for you right away, sir," I say.

My heart is hammering in my chest when I get back to my desk. I am not aware of any McKinley interview. I throw open the folder containing the case files and peruse through the documents with trembling fingers. The panic is rising like a bubble in my throat. Any second now, he is going to yell out my name and remind me of the value of his time.

Who the hell is McKinley anyway? I am scrambling now, flipping through pieces of paper, the words jumping out at me and blurring into each other. McKinley … McKinley.

And then I remember where I heard the name. Heard. Because the interview is one of the recordings Robert emailed to me when updating me on the case. The momentary relief from figuring out what he needs vanishes in a puff of smoke. The McKinley interview is an audio recording.

I traipse back to Robert's office with shaky legs. "Sir? Did you mean the audio interview …?"

"There is only one interview, Miss Brooks," he says. Ah, so he remembers my name after all.

"Right," I say. "It's just that … the interview …"

"Do you mean to tell me, Miss Brooks, that you have yet to transcribe the audio files I sent over to you?"

I want to protest that he did not tell me to transcribe the files, but I can already hear that conversation play out in my head. Why did I think he was sending me the files in the first place? I was to anticipate his needs, not stand there looking at him. The obvious defense would be that I couldn't possibly have had time to transcribe the files. In between shuffling back and forth around the offices tracking down all the documents he needed and simultaneously being present for when he shouted for me, my plate was already so full as to be spilling over.

But that would be an excuse, and excuses do not sit well with him.

"I'll get right on it, sir," I say, hoping he'll let it slide. I don't wait for his response but turn and practically run out of the office.

Once at my desk, I soon realize the job is much harder than I could have imagined. The interview is over an hour long, and one of the speakers, probably McKinley from the sound of it, has a thick Southern accent that I simply can't decipher. I let my head drop onto my desk, defeated.

Not for the first time, I consider simply giving up.

It has only been four days, and already I am thoroughly overwhelmed. The workload is immense. The pressure is constant. Robert Hardy is indeed the slave driver I feared he was, and he is unrelenting. From the minute I walk in, I am inundated by lists of increasingly difficult tasks, all of which I'm apparently supposed to work on simultaneously.

The case appears to be one involving a big telecommunications company called Mendel Technologies. The former CEO, Mr. Gregory Mandel, is being sued by his partner and the company for fraud and embezzlement. And Robert Hardy has the unenviable job of proving that the lawsuit is, in fact, part of a larger plan to get Mr. Mandel's shares in the company. It's an extremely complicated case, with an endless list of documents and files, and a rotating door of people to speak with. I have a near-constant headache just from trying to keep the facts of the case straight.

And then there is the other stack of documents I'm supposed to have read and internalized, as per Susan's instructions. And the binder. It's enough to make anyone lose their mind. Which is exactly what is happening. I can feel myself unraveling. Four days in. I keep telling myself that the first few days are always the hardest, that I'll figure it out ... things will get easier. But in moments like this, that doesn't seem likely.

The Amelia who swore not to quit, to soldier on regardless of what happened, is somewhere in the recesses of my mind, biting her lip. Her logic does not seem so sound anymore. What exactly am I holding out for? Galweather & Meyer is a great firm, but it isn't the biggest in the city. I'm almost certain I can get a job someplace where I don't feel like my will to live is being dragged out of me. So why am I so determined to make it work?

Initially, even though it took me some time to admit it, the fascination with Robert was a big part of the appeal. The man was an enigma. He was everything Susan said he was, dialed up tenfold. In one word, he was intense. I had been watching him, telling myself I was learning him so I could understand what he needed me to do. But I was also studying him, waiting for those tiny human moments to shine through, when he would turn back into the man I met that night at the party. The man who saved me; my dark knight.

"Amelia?"

It is his use of my first name that causes me to jolt upright. Not his sudden presence, although I didn't hear him approach. Not the fact that it looks like I was taking a nap on my desk instead of working. No, it's the tiny detail of him using my actual name. It sounds intimate like he just whispered it directly into my ear.

I start to apologize, but I notice his expression for the first time, and the words die in my throat. The scowl I have grown used to seeing on his face isn't there. He looks sympathetic. When he reaches out and places a hand on my shoulder, I forget to flinch, struck by the unexpected softness of the gesture.

"I'm sorry," he says, and it is so low only I can hear, so soft I wonder if I've misheard him. "I know it must be overwhelming, all this."

His hand is still on my shoulder, and it's proving to be quite the distraction. The heat from his palm seems to burn through the fabric of my blouse. The jolt travels through my body, all the way down. I press my knees together and force myself to focus on his face. Nope. Bad idea. His eyes are almost beetle black ... he has shaved since last time, I notice, and it makes his jawline look even stronger.

Voice. Focus on his voice.

"... how about that?"

"Hmm? I'm sorry?"

"Coffee," Robert says. "Why don't you get us some coffees, and we can go over these files together?"

"Yes. Coffee."

Stop the presses. Robert Hardy isn't completely heartless.

I get up, and his hand slides off my shoulder. He lets it hang in midair for a moment as if he didn't realize he was still holding me. Then he stuffs it awkwardly in his pocket, nods curtly, and retreats to his office.

He likes his coffee black, with two sugars, and no cream. I memorized his order on the first day. I balance the cups gingerly as I walk back to the office. I can feel curious eyes on me all the way. Everywhere I go, it's always the same. And I know exactly what they're thinking. I can almost feel the bated breath, the surprise that I've lasted so long, the anxiety on when I would inevitably drop. I know they whisper behind my back. I know, because the conversation always dies down whenever I walk past.

I put my coffee down and walk with the other one over to his side of the desk. He is immersed in something on his computer, and he mumbles his thanks without looking up. I have to skip over a constellation of wires to put his coffee down on the desk. The cup wobbles slightly as I lean over to him.

Then it happens.

A little coffee sloshes over the brim of the cup. I don't expect it to be so hot, but it is. Scalding hot. Before I know what I'm doing, excruciating pain shoots through my fingers, and I let go of the cup. It falls, almost in slow motion, and my spur-of-the-moment thought is that it's going to spill into his lap, and I can't let that happen. I make a swipe with my burnt hand with some half-formed idea that I have better reflexes than I actually do.

All I do is redirect the mess.

The coffee sloshes over Robert's shirt, and the cup topples over to his lap and, when he shoots back in his chair with a startled yelp, clatters onto the floor.

"Oh my God, I'm so sorry!"

I have no idea what to do. I reach for the nearest item of clothing I can find, a thick woolen scarf on one of the other chairs, and dab at the growing stain on his shirt. I am aware that it's pointless, that the white shirt has already been ruined, and I'm basically making things worse. But I can't seem to stop myself. In between apologizing repeatedly and fussing over his shirt, it's a hectic few minutes.

Robert eventually stands up and unbuttons the shirt with quick, deft flicks of his wrists. He throws it off to reveal a predictably chiseled body. No undershirt or T-shirt. As if I'm not confused enough as it is.

I can't help it; I know I'm staring, but I can't tear my eyes away from his body. I'm physically unable to. He has the sculpted physique of someone who works out every waking moment of his life. I follow the single trail of hair from his chest, down past washboard abs and down into the V in front of his pants.

"Miss Brooks? I'm sure it's not your intention to stand there gawping like that for the rest of the day?"

"Uh … no, sir. Of course not." And just like that, I'm back to being Miss Brooks. Hey, at least it's better than Amanda.

"I need something to wear."

"Right."

For the second time today, I dash out of the office without the faintest idea what I'm going to do. I wander in the direction of HR, thinking vaguely of Susan. There has to be something she can do. Maybe someone has a spare shirt? Which is ridiculous and impractical, but I quicken my pace.

Someone says hi to me in the hallways, and I grunt back at them. At him.

I freeze. What if ...?

"Hey!"

I hate that I can't remember his name. He has said hi to me every day since I started. He's one of the junior lawyers, I think. And I'm about to bet my job that those genial little hellos mean he has a little crush on me.

He turns back with a puzzled smile.

"I need your shirt," I tell him.

I cover the distance between us in a few short steps. He is roughly the same build as Robert, but with slightly narrower shoulders. I would know. I just got an eyeful of those shoulders. And abs.

"What?" His eyebrows are knitted together.

"Shirt. I need it. Please, I'll explain later."

It occurs to me how strange a request it must seem to him. I'm expecting him to say no and walk away. *It's a stupid idea, Amelia. Maybe go back to the HR thing.*

His eyes search mine, and I'm sure he sees the desperation in them. "Okay ..." He sounds uncertain. But he reaches up and starts to unbutton the shirt.

"Thank you so much. You're a lifesaver."

At least *he* had the foresight to wear a T-shirt inside.

"Uh, sure. Am I getting this back, or ...?"

"Yes?" *Probably not.* "I'll make it up to you, I promise!" I say, and then I take off running back to Robert's office. Without even getting his name. Damn it; I'm turning into a monster.

Robert is examining his shirt when I burst back into the office. His ruined shirt. His eyes flick up to me then to the shirt I'm carrying.

"Whose shirt is that?" he asks suspiciously.

"Doesn't matter," I say. "Put this on while I rush yours over to a laundromat."

I throw it over at him, afraid to approach in case I spill something else on him. Like myself. He catches the shirt in one hand and lifts it up to inspect it.

"This won't fit me," he says.

"Oh, it will."

His eyes flick to me once more, and I feel my cheeks heat up. I have no doubt he heard the subtext of what I just said. 'I've been checking you out, so I know it will fit.'

It turns out the shirt does fit him, even though it's a bit snug around the arms.

I grab the soiled shirt and turn to leave.

"I'm sorry again, Mr. Hardy." I haven't gone through the full list, but I'm sure 'pour coffee on your boss' is one of the fireable offenses.

"Just get it fixed," he says curtly.

And for once, his voice isn't loud or demanding. It's quiet and disappointed, and it announces the return of the cold, heartless man I've been working for.

8
Robert

Amelia Brooks is a problem.

I should have fired her by now. If she were anyone else, I would have fired her by now. But then I shouldn't have hired her in the first place if I'm being honest.

She is inexperienced, and from the onset, she had that fish-out-of-water look about her. Not a big deal. As she said herself during her interview, experience in itself isn't necessarily a strength, and her lack of it didn't constitute weakness or inability.

Her performance of the job is okay, considering the amount of work I have so far thrown at her. More than usual. I needed to test her mettle, see how she handled the kind of relentless workload that was inevitable in this business. And to her credit, she did as well as can be expected. But it was always with a drop of her head. Any time she encountered something challenging, her shoulders slumped, and I knew she was thinking about quitting.

So, I upped the dosage. I assigned her more and more work, dialing up the pressure, curious to see what it was that would make her finally crack. And finally, she did. Never mind that it was in the face of a virtually impossible task. Finally, her head went down, and I knew she would not be picking it back up again. Not without my intervention.

That hand on the shoulder should have been a dismissal. Hell, I fired my last assistant for something significantly smaller. I should have walked up to that desk and told her to get her things and go. It irked me to no end that I couldn't do it.

The easy excuse would be that I did not hire her because of her ability to do office work. In that regard, she did not pass muster. No, I need her for something bigger. She has a crucial part to play in the upcoming trial, one that doesn't involve filing motions and transcribing interviews. I have the right weapon; I just have to wait until I can actually deploy it.

But there is more to my reluctance to let Amelia go, and I know it.

The woman is a problem.

I didn't expect her to be such a distraction.

She is a walking disaster, a total klutz on heels. Which for some reason, I find adorable. She has a childlike innocence and approach to most of what she does. It's both endearing and frustrating. Like how every time she does something she thinks is wrong, her eyes go wide— and they're pretty big, to begin with, and her lip trembles as she looks up at me for mercy. It's probably unconscious. It takes a lot not to burst into laughter every time she does it.

Or how she is always out of breath when I call her into my office, and she tries to hide the fact by pressing her lips together and actually trying to breathe slower.

I have found myself noticing the strangest things about her. Things that I have no business seeing, much less looking out for. Her shoes, for example, are always different. She must have a rich collection of them because I haven't seen her wear the same pair to work yet. She uses them to imbue her outfits with a little personality, and it only took me two days to figure out how to read them. Generally, the simpler the shoes, the more confident she feels on the day. She has only worn heels, and they may have had something to do with the coffee she just spilled all over me.

She has a small tattoo on her leg, one which I have not gotten close enough to examine, but which looks a lot like a bird.

She chews her pen when she gets nervous. And considering how often that is, her current pen now looks like a dog's chew toy.

I am always aware of her it seems. I have become accustomed to her scent, her walk, her presence. Once or twice, I walk past her desk just to watch her fidget. I don't know what it says about me that I love watching her fuss about, especially when she knows I'm watching her.

Either way, Amelia has become such a distraction I'm finding it hard to concentrate. I don't know how I managed to bury the memory of our little tryst so successfully for the first few days. Now, it's like a broken record in my mind. The way she grabbed me and took charge. The way she felt crushed under me. The gentle pressure of her lips. How her tongue probed, pried my lips apart. It's all I think about.

I hear the sound of heels on tile, and it snaps me out of my reverie. Not a second too soon, either, because I would have moved on to undressing her in my head. And then lifting her onto my desk and clearing its contents with an impatient swipe of my hand.

She is back. So soon, which means she must have run all the way there and back. Even if she had gone to the closest laundromat a few blocks away, there's no way she would have gotten the shirt washed in that short time. This time, she doesn't even try to hide how tired she is. She leans against the door and heaves, her chest rising and falling as she catches her breath. I wait patiently, feeling the smile tug at my lips and fighting the urge.

Eventually, her breathing slows, and she says, "I dropped it off. The guy told me to come back in an hour, so …"

"You could have stayed and waited for it," I say.

"Oh. I just thought it would be better if I were here, in case you need anything."

"How thoughtful of you, Miss Brooks. Alright. We can use that hour to go over the case files."

Normally, going over case documents is a tedious, boring affair. But Amelia brings the same application and exuberance to poring over documents as she does everything else. She takes it all in, scribbling down notes every other minute and asking questions to help her understand the specifics. It reminds me that she is still a student in some ways, eager to learn and hungry for the hands-on experience. It's in those moments that I begin to see just how smart she is.

"So, let me get this straight," she says after I'm done breaking down the case for her. "Gregory Mandel started this company with his best friend, Thomas Wagner. They worked on it together, grew it into one of the biggest tech companies in the world, then Gregory decides to step aside from management, leaving Thomas in charge but retaining a controlling stake in the company. Then a few months later, Thomas is suing him for fraud and embezzlement?"

"That's about it, yes. It looks like a pretty straightforward case, but Gregory has a completely different story. Says Thomas has been trying to push him out for years, and it seems the only way he can now do so is by proving to the board of governors that Gregory risked the financial future of the company with fraudulent financial practices."

"Which is all bullshit, right?"

"Well, there's a mountain of paperwork going back several years, as you may have noticed. Even if it's bullshit, which I believe it is, yes, it would seem Thomas has been planning this for a very long time now. The paperwork shows hundreds of thousands of dollars were being stashed away into several offshore accounts over the course of around three years, and those accounts are in Gregory's name."

"But you believe Gregory?" Amelia asks.

"I do. I wouldn't take the case if I didn't. It's a very risky case for me, but that also means it's an opportunity to make a big splash. If I land this one …"

"Okay. So, all we have to do is discredit Thomas Wagner and prove that Gregory had no reason to defraud his own company."

"That's right. I'm still working on a strategy, but I think a good place to start would be digging into those financial statements and figuring out where the paper trail started. That's why we need McKinley. He's the financial advisor for Mandel Tech."

Amelia nods. "I'll go work on those."

"You're sure you can handle it?" I ask. "He has a bit of an accent, McKinley."

Amelia laughs. It transforms her face completely. The tension seems to drain from her body, and for the first time since she started working here, she looks like the woman I met at the party.

"You noticed that too? I thought that was just my city ears."

"Oh, no. The man definitely has an accent. If we can wade through it, though, I bet there's something there that won't show up on the financial statements."

"Okay." She closes her notebook and stands up. "I think I'll go for your shirt first, and then I'll sit down and figure out the audio file."

"No, I'll handle the shirt. I can pick it up on my way home." I stand up too, and now we are facing each other. This is the closest we've been since that time she was shoving her tongue down my throat. "Where did you get this shirt, really?"

She blushes and looks away.

"Because I could swear, I saw it on one of the second-year associates earlier."

"You said you needed something to wear!" Amelia says, throwing up her hands. "So I got you something to wear."

I smile. "I'm not faulting your resourcefulness, Amelia. I just hope the young man isn't walking around the office naked. Susan doesn't take kindly to office nudity."

"Oh, no. He had the good sense to put on a T-shirt inside his shirt ..."

She trails off, but her meaning is clear. "Unlike some people."

So, she *was* looking at me when I had my shirt off. I thought I noticed her eyes flick over my torso.

We both fall silent, but something has passed between us. The air between us is suddenly crackling with energy, with possibility. I look into her eyes, and they are so green, so beautiful, I forget where we are for a moment.

I raise my hand and lift it to her face. She is frozen in place. I brush once across her cheek, and my fingers pick up a stray lock of hair and tuck it behind her ear.

I feel her body tense. She licks her lips with a slow, deliberate flick of her tongue, and that ends any notion I had of holding back.

Our eyes still locked we communicate wordlessly. I'm not sure who steps forward first, or whose hands go around the other first. But the next moment, we are locked in an embrace, and our lips meet.

Her lips are soft and slick. They dance along mine, against them, pushing and nibbling and sucking all in tandem. Kissing her is like falling into a bottomless pool; my head is swimming with the pleasure of it, and my mind is wiped clean of all thought. I am lost in her embrace, and I am blissfully unaware of anything outside those magical lips.

She kisses me with the same hunger she did the last time. It's strange, this woman seems timid and slightly held back in every other aspect of her life. But when we kiss, she comes alive, and she is suddenly wild and unrestrained and passionate. I push past her lips with my tongue, and she meets it with her own as the kiss deepens. I hear her moan. Or it may have been me.

I let my hands roam the small of her back, down to the sweet curve of her hip and the swell of her ass. It feels full in my hands, and I give it a gentle squeeze. This woman is sexy; I cannot deny it any longer. I want to do things to her. I want to …

I reach around her and feel around for the desk. I lift her and lay her on it, and the action forces her legs apart and her skirt to ride up past her thighs. My hands reach down and fall on silky thighs. I caress them slowly, using the tips of my fingers so the touch is feather-light. Amelia moans deep in my mouth. Her breathing grows more ragged as I work my way inside her thighs with painfully slow motions. Circling, rubbing, brushing. I can't get over how soft her skin is.

My fingers keep exploring, widening their reach until they brush against the heat and moistness of her womanhood.

Her body is rocking against me now. She breaks the kiss as her head falls back, and I lay a trail of kisses from the nape of her neck down to her collarbone and chest.

My fingers feel around the soft, damp cloth and work them aside slowly. I'm not ready for just how wet she is. I use one finger to trace the outline of her lips, once, then again, lingering over the clitoris each time. When I withdraw my hand, she moans in my ear and pushes herself back into my palm. I start the motion up again. Drawing random patterns along her lips, circling, and then gently rubbing her clitoris. I tease and cajole, flick and rub, and finally, I slide one finger into her.

Her whole body jerks and she is moaning in ecstasy now. Her waist gyrates to meet the thrusts of my fingers. Her hands go around my neck, and her grip is so tight I can feel her nails digging into my back.

I add a second finger, and my rhythm is faster now. In and out, rub, circle, dip. I can feel her falling apart. Her mouth is somewhere in my hair, the heat of her breath like a pleasant tingle on my ear and neck.

And then she unravels completely. Her body lurches, then clenches, then it bucks wildly. She grips me harder than ever as the orgasm rocks her over and over again. My eyes slide open, and I am just in time to see the look of pure bliss on her face before her body stops trembling, and she is finally still.

Before I can say anything, before I can even react, she shimmies off the desk, pushing me gently away. I step back and watch silently as she adjusts her skirt, which had been pushed up well over her waist. Then she steps around the desk and rushes out of the office without another word.

At that moment, all I can think of is that I've never been so turned on in my life.

9

Amelia

The laptop lies open at my feet, the image on it frozen. The screen is blurry, but I can just make out a pair of pale thighs and long shapely legs. The wind whistles in from the window above my bed, swirling gently over me, caressing me. I'm sprawled out on the bed, naked except for a pair of silk panties. I've been trying and failing to keep my hands out of them. I've also been trying to watch my favorite show, but it seems to have way more sex scenes than I remember. Not to mention my internet is incredibly poor today, and it freezes at the most inopportune moments. Like the moment just before Kitty Delacour gets seduced by the rich, handsome billionaire.

Of course, none of it is as frustrating as the fact that I cannot stop thinking about Robert Hardy. And the things he did to me. The things I let him do to me.

Every time the image pops up in my mind, I try and convince myself I imagined it because there's no way I just had an orgasm on my boss's desk.

The laptop screen unfreezes, and the pair of thighs slide out from view to be replaced moments later with the strong, beautiful face of Lord Mackenzie, the show's main protagonist. His eyes are cast downward. He has not missed that generous reveal of Kitty's body. His gaze, when it returns to Kitty's face, is full of lust and purpose. He steps forward and seizes her, then grabs her bottom firmly and wraps her leg around the back of his thigh ...

And I am instantly transported back to that desk, and my own legs dangling uselessly behind Robert as his fingers explored the insides of my thighs and beyond ...

Now Mackenzie is whispering something in Kitty's ear, and it is salacious enough that she blushes and smiles sweetly up at him. Then he pulls her closer and crushes his lips against hers.

I can feel the dampness in my panties, and the heat, like a sweet pulsing ache, forcing my thighs apart. The screen freezes once more, but I am too far gone now to care. My mind has taken over, feeding me the scene from Robert's office on a loop.

I slide my hand down the front of my panties, and I'm truly surprised by how slick my fingers get. What has the man done to me?

I can't remember the last time I was so horny. It's like he flicked a switch inside me, and now all I do is get aroused even at the slightest things.

My eyes flutter shut, and even when I hear the screen of my laptop unfreeze and the scene continues to play out, I don't open my eyes. A different scene is playing out in my head.

I think of Robert, and the intensity of his stare, the way his eyes blaze and burn. I remember his hands on me as he kissed me, the gentle exploring of his fingers as they slid further and further down. I start to twitch and shudder as desire flames out from the point of my touch and radiates into every nerve, every cell in my body. My fingers rub down along my puffy lips, gently coaxing them apart, and the dampness builds until I can hear a soft squishing sound with every movement I make. It's sheer bliss, the pleasure mounting steadily as I rub faster and faster.

I continue to tease at my lips, and then my finger brushes against my clit, and I gasp. The touch sends shivers running through my body. My other hand reaches up, gliding over my skin until it finds a heavy breast and a hard, pert nipple. I cup and squeeze the breast, pinch the nipple, tease, and fondle until a hot pulse starts in my belly.

My fingers are almost a blur as I continue to play with myself. The pleasure builds, growing more urgent until I feel I cannot rub fast enough. I need more ... I need him. I flick at my clit again, and I lose control of my body for a few seconds. I am vaguely aware of my back arching and my toes curling. I think I'm moaning. Harsh, ragged breaths are spilling from my mouth. My chest is heaving. I cannot stop. I don't want to stop. I delve my fingers deeper so that they are buried well beyond my swollen lips. I alternate the pressure, the speed of my shallow thrusts, the angles ... I pause after each change to savor just how good each variation feels. My fingers feel slick, so slick I'm struggling to find purchase. But I keep going, feeling the ecstasy growing, the moment of release nearing with every second.

The sensation I keep thinking of is heat. I am in heat. My body is flushed. A sheen of sweat has dampened my sheets. My body is buzzing, my pussy screaming with need. My legs are wide apart, and I am definitely on fire. I return my fingers to my clit. It's unbelievably sensitive, and a few lazy circles with my fingers make me fall apart completely.

And then I'm coming.

I arch and twist once more, but this time the sweet agony of release is more than I can bear. My whole body is trembling, jerking. My toes grip the sheets beneath them tightly. My body clenches and pulses for what seems like an eternity. I kick out involuntarily, and my foot connects with something hard, which I realize seconds later is my laptop, and that the dull thunk is the sound of it falling to the floor. But I'm too far gone to care. It takes me a long time to finally lie still.

My breathing comes in gasps and pants. I try to open my eyes, but they feel heavy and uncooperative.

When I can finally string a thought together, I realize this might be the first time I've masturbated to completion. Amelia Brooks does not masturbate. Or think about her boss as she does. This is all uncharted territory for me, being sexual at all, let alone playing with myself like that. That orgasm may be one of the most powerful I've ever experienced. But I also know, deep down, that it was nowhere near as intense as the one I experienced in Robert's office. And for a long time, I just lie there, thinking about that strange little fact and what it means.

My one meeting with Robert after 'the incident' is stiff and awkward. I walk into him as I'm rushing into the office ten minutes late and afraid for my life. I'm looking down at my watch one second, and the next, I'm crushed against the hard torso of my boss. He jumps back so fast I'm initially afraid I've hurt him somehow. But that's impossible, I think, confused. If anything, I should be the one checking for injuries; I've just walked into the human equivalent of a brick wall.

And then I see his expression, and it dawns on me. He is studiously avoiding my eyes. He has tucked his hands defensively into his pockets, and his body language screams that he wants to be anywhere but here.

I mumble my apologies, but he's already waving me silent.

"Do you have the financial records?" he asks, and it can't be clearer he's desperate to keep the interaction as professional as possible. I'm not sure what I expected, but I'm momentarily thrown.

It's not like we were going to start grabbing each other and making out every time we pass each other in the hallway. Still …

"Miss Brooks?"

"Huh? The records. Right. I have them on my desk. I'll just get them to you …" I make an attempt to side-step him, but he holds out a hand, blocking my path.

"Don't bother. I have a meeting downtown, so I'll be out of the office for most of the morning. Have the records scanned and send them to my email."

"Will do, sir."

The hand drops, after hovering for a long, agonizing moment over my chest.

"And you're late," Robert says as he walks away. I can't tell from his voice whether he's simply pointing it out or if it's an actual warning. I have for some time now suspected that Robert has been taking it easy on me. I've flouted at least three of the things on the list of fireable offenses, but I haven't as yet attracted the fiery temper I was warned about. Any time I do something wrong, he shakes his head, and I hold my breath, expecting the dismissal, dreading it. But he hasn't so far.

For some time, I allowed myself to think that maybe he had taken a liking to me, which was why he was being soft on me. It was a fanciful thought, given weight by the recent 'encounter' in his office. But I realize now, as I stare at his gruff, retreating figure, that maybe I'm simply on my second strike, and the next mistake I make will likely be my last.

I snap out of my trance and break into a run. Robert wants what he wants when he wants it. He probably expected those records in his email the minute he finished speaking. And here I am, daydreaming instead of working.

I dump my bag on my desk, grab the file containing the financial records, and rush back out. The printer is located in the financial hub of the building. It serves as the water cooler for Galweather & Meyer. It's where people meet and gossip or catch up. The working areas are cordoned off by low, separate walls, and 'interpersonal frolicking' during working hours is frowned upon by HR so people steal away to the printer to chat, or trade gossip. It's the perfect place to do it; they can't exactly flag you for making conversation while you wait for documents to print or scan.

Of course, none of this applies to me. So far, I'm still attracting only the sympathetic stares, the hushed whispers, the stolen looks. I can't say I've made many friends. Or any friends, really. But I refuse to blame myself. Working for Robert is taxing. There's simply no time for fraternizing.

Today, I have the fortune of finding Susan there. She looks agitated. Her arms are crossed, and her eyebrows are knitted together as she stands over the printer. She gives the printer a hearty thump with her hand, and the machine growls in protest.

"This damn thing is completely useless these days," she says, then looks up and sees me. "Oh, hey, Amy."

"Hey, Susan. What are you trying to do?"

"I've been trying to print a document for the last ten minutes. You think you can work some of that millennial magic?"

I pull out the paper tray and peer inside.

"Can't be the paper," Susan says. "I just put in a new stack."

I pick the papers out, restack them, and push them back in. Then I reach behind the printer, yank the power cord out, and plug it back in. The printer whirrs and growls as it comes back to life. After a few moments, and more clunking and whooshing, it starts to print the documents.

"Look at that," Susan says, shaking her head. "The old unplug and plug-in routine."

"Always works," I say, grinning.

"Thanks, Amy. How are you doing, by the way? Robert driving you crazy?"

Ha! More than you can imagine, Susan.

"I'm doing okay, I think. I mean, I'm still here, so that's something, right?"

"Of course, dear. You've surprised a lot of people here. And disappointed almost everyone."

"What? Why?"

Susan looks up at me, and she smiles in that genial, good-natured way that endeared me to her in the first place. "You know about the betting pool, surely?"

"The what?"

"There's a betting pool on how long you'll last. There usually is, with Robert's assistants, but you seem to have stumped even the experts."

"How long did they expect me to last?" I sweep a look around the office, feeling hurt that people who knew nothing about me would be making bets on me.

"Honestly? And this is a compliment to you, Amy—no one thought you'd survive the first day. And when you did, you sent them scrambling. It's been a while since they lost money the way they have."

"What about you?" I ask her. "How long did you think I'd last?"

Susan smiles. "As Head of HR, I cannot even acknowledge the existence of such a thing as a betting pool." She picks up her printed documents and puts a hand on my shoulder. "But I have you down for setting a new record." She winks as she walks away.

It's a tiny gesture of faith, but it softens the blow a little. At least someone here believes in me.

There is a large, well-dressed man sitting on my desk when I get back to Robert's office. *On* my desk. He is bouncing his leg absently, watching with an unreadable expression as I approach. I have all but memorized Robert's schedule, and I'm sure he has no appointments today. He looks even bigger up close. I get to him, and a strong musky scent hits me right in the face. He has a round, friendly face, but his eyes are anything but friendly; they are gray and cold, and when he smiles and shoves a pudgy hand in my direction, the smile does not extend to his eyes.

"Daniel Goldman," he says as I shake his hand.

He is impeccably dressed. His suit is sleek and rich. He wears a crisp white shirt, with a slightly askew bowtie resting just below his chins. An aura of power and authority seems to ooze from him, in addition to whatever cologne he lathered himself with. He must be a lawyer, I figure. Something about how assured he seems, how comfortable he has made himself at *my* desk, reminds me of Robert.

"How can I help you, Mr. Goldman?" I ask, injecting as much sweetness into my voice as I can.

Daniel Goldman leaps down off the desk and steps up to me. He is taller than I had assumed, but he still has to look up at me. His eyes wander almost casually over me, and I immediately feel like I'm being x-rayed. His gaze feels inappropriate, dirty. He looks me over, from head to toe. I almost expect him to walk around to my backside and continue his inspection. Somehow, I have a feeling he will if I face away from him.

"Sir?" I prompt him, and his eyes flick back to me.

He smiles a slow, assured smile. "I see Mr. Hardy isn't in," he finally says, waving casually at Robert's office. His voice has a Southern twang to it.

"No, Mr. Hardy has stepped out briefly."

"Has he really? I thought he would have his head buried in paperwork this close to the case … But I suppose that's what you're here for? You must be the intern."

"I'm Mr. Hardy's assistant," I say, a bit more sharply than I had intended.

And then it hits me from where I know his name. Daniel Goldman is the lawyer representing Mendel Tech. This is the man Robert is going up against in the big case.

"Feisty," Goldman says, grinning. "I like that in a woman." His eyes go right back to undressing me, and I have to stop myself from physically recoiling.

"Like I said, Mr. Goldman. Mr. Hardy isn't in. Perhaps you could come another time? Or is there a message you would like passed on to him?"

Goldman pauses, apparently lost in thought, then he turns and steps away from me. He bends over a brown bag I had not seen on the desk and unzips it, digging into it with stubby fingers and emerging moments later with a stack of files.

"I would have liked to hand these to Mr. Hardy in person, so I can look him in the face when I tell him he's fucked." He pushes the stack into my hands, stepping back in front of me so that his cologne is almost overwhelming. "But I guess you'll have to do. Yes, I would like a message passed on to dear old Bobby."

Somehow, I can't imagine Robert entertaining anyone calling him 'Bobby.'

"Tell him ..." Goldman's hand reaches up before I can react and taps me slightly on the chin like a parent would a mischievous child. It's incredibly patronizing. "Tell him when I'm done with him, he won't be able to call himself a man, let alone a lawyer."

"I will inform Mr. Hardy that you dropped these off." I step around him and walk quickly into Robert's office, grateful for the lungful of fresh air. I am hoping Goldman is done with his little show and is leaving. But when I drop the files onto Robert's desk and turn around, he is right there, behind me. He moves too fast, too quietly for me to hear. I gasp and take hurried steps backward, but there's nowhere to escape to. The backs of my thighs hit the desk, and I'm trapped.

Goldman sees my discomfort, and it brings a smile to his face. "You're a pretty little thing, aren't you?" he says.

I swallow, unsure how to react or what to say.

"Robert does tend to go for the pretty ones ..." he goes on. He has gone right back to undressing me with his eyes. "You, though ... you're a bit on the young side. What are you? Twenty?"

I remain silent. I must look terrified because Goldman backs away. He puts up his hands, almost in an apologetic gesture.

"I'm not going to hurt you, gorgeous. You can calm down."

I'm disappointed in myself for showing weakness, for letting this man get to me. I want to scoff at him, tell him I am calm enough, thank you very much. But more than anything, I just want this interaction to end.

"You're new, aren't you?" Goldman says. He nods to himself, seemingly taking my silence as confirmation. "Yeah. I can tell. What's your name?"

I think about it for a long time. Why should I tell him my name? Why is he asking? But eventually, I realize there's no point trying to keep it from him. He is on the other side of Robert's case. As much as I hate the thought, we're going to be seeing a lot of each other in the coming weeks.

"Amelia Brooks," I say in a flat voice.

"Amelia. Lovely. Well, Amelia, you probably don't know who I am, but I can assure you, there isn't a person alive who knows Robert Hardy better than me and let me tell you, that man is a deviant. He eats girls like you for breakfast and spits them right out. I'm sure you've heard about his former assistants? The stories are a bit of an open secret in the legal community."

"I don't see what any of that has to do with me, Mr. Goldman," I tell him.

"You're a beautiful woman, Amelia. Young, smart. I just don't want to see you end up like the women who pass through this office, because trust me, it's not something you can come back from."

I have no reason to trust this man, let alone believe him. But there is an uncomfortable ring of truth to what he's saying, and it ties into everything I've heard about Robert so far.

"My advice?" Goldman presses on, sensing my doubt. "Run. There's plenty of other places you can work. As a matter of fact, here …" He reaches into his pocket and draws out a stack of cards, one of which he hands me. "That's my card. My private cell is on there. You can come see me, and I'll find something better for you to do."

I hate that I take the card. It's almost an involuntary motion; when someone hands you something, you take it. I hate that I think about it, even just for a second.

And I hate that when I look up from the glossy card, the slouched figure of Robert is standing in the room, an expression of disgust written all over his face.

10

Robert

I make it all the way to the interstate before I realize I've left my laptop in the office. The very same laptop with all the documents I need for the meeting I'm going to. And the one I need to use to review the case files I've just asked Amelia to send to me.

I can't go without it. There's simply no getting around that fact. I think about calling her and having her bring it to me at the venue, but I immediately dismiss the idea. Things between us have gotten increasingly awkward, and I don't want to spend any more energy trying to keep our interactions civil.

Because it takes a huge amount of energy. I have to discipline my eyes and keep my mind blank, otherwise, it wanders, and inevitably lands on such distracting things as the dipping swoop of her neckline. And then my tongue gets heavy, and I forget what it was we were talking about, and I am no longer Robert Hardy, breaker of men.

No, I need to stay away from that woman. Twice I've taken her magnetic appeal for granted, and twice I've found myself entangled in her arms. And her legs. Not anymore. I'm worried I may have already chipped away at the authority I had over her. Like it or not, our relationship isn't strictly that of a boss and his employee anymore. God knows what it is now, and all because I couldn't keep my hands to myself.

It's the reason I have decided to take a step back from her. Henceforth, the only interactions we'll have will be in passing. Me asking her to do something and her doing it. No more huddled sessions in quiet rooms. And certainly, no unnecessary phone calls, which will only mean I have to endure her presence throughout the meeting and probably for the rest of the day.

I have no choice but to turn around and go back for the laptop. I curse silently as I drive back to the office. I glance at my watch and hope I won't be late.

The scent hits me while I'm still in the hallway, and I know right away that Daniel Goldman is here. It's another of his defining traits; his insistence on dousing himself too liberally with whatever dark, musky cologne he uses.

I quicken my pace, wondering what he's doing here. We're not due to meet for discovery exchanges for another week, but then again, Daniel has never been one to play by the rules. Knowing him, he probably sprang this surprise visit to get a sense of where we were on the case, maybe even dig some dirt. Reconnaissance, I would respect it if I didn't despise the man, which means, though, that he has by now met Amelia and is no doubt trying to put those lecherous paws of his on her.

Indeed, when I walk into the office, the scene that greets me is exactly the one I pictured. Amelia backed defensively into my desk. Daniel bearing down on her, his short, thick frame rather imposing. Amelia's eyes go wide when she sees me. For a few seconds, I register her surprise, and then relief floods her face.

"Robert!" she says, stepping away from the desk and away from Daniel. She sounds genuinely thrilled to see me. I'm sure it's because Daniel was being Daniel, but her reaction is so earnest and endearing I can't help smiling. Then there's the fact that she used my first name. Not Mr. Hardy. Not 'sir.' I'm not sure what to make of that.

"Amelia? What's going on here?"

Daniel finally turns to look at me. His smile is calculating, and as always, it doesn't reach his eyes.

"This gentleman ... uh ... Mr. Goldman is here to see you."

"Bobby!" Daniel bounds over to me, arm extended. Anyone watching would think he is an old friend I haven't seen in a while.

I keep my arms at my side and look at Amelia instead. "I imagine you informed Mr. Goldman that I'm not available?"

"I did ..."

"And that even if I was, I don't just take walk-ins? Does Mr. Goldman have an appointment?"

"Not that I'm aware of, no."

"Then why did you not dismiss him?"

Amelia bites her lip, and her whole body seems to deflate.

"Oh, leave the poor girl alone," Daniel pipes up. I don't know what's more annoying, his presence here, or the fact that him taking her side makes me look like the asshole. Which is absurd, considering I'm in a room with the king of assholes.

He leans into me and whispers: "You keep treating them like that, soon no one will want to work for you. Much less someone this beautiful."

"What do you want, Daniel?" I ask him.

"Oh, my business here is concluded. I just wanted to drop off all the documents on the case. You know, as agreed."

"We agreed on a discovery meeting next week," I say through gritted teeth.

"Yeah, but I figured why wait, you know?" He looks cocky and flippant, and I don't like that at all. "My team and I are ready, so I just assumed you were as well. But that does not appear to be the case. You're losing your touch, old friend."

I motion for Amelia to leave the office, and she peels away quietly. I wait until the door closes behind her, then I turn to Daniel.

"You have no case," I tell him.

"Are you sure about that?" he scoffs. "Really? Is that why you're still scrambling around? Do you even have a strategy yet, or are you just going to wing it, as usual?"

"Is that why you're here, Daniel? Trying to snoop around and see what I'm planning?"

"If you think I need to snoop around to beat you ..."

"I think you need a miracle to beat me."

We stand there staring at each other, mutual dislike radiating almost tangibly between us. That was the first salvo. Two cowboys sizing each other up, hands hovering over the guns at the hips. Daniel likes his mind games. This is only the first of an endless back and forth that we will engage in until the case is done.

"I guess we'll see," he says after some time.

"I guess we will," I reply in the same tone.

I step around him and pick up the stack of papers that I assume are the files he has brought over. I don't need to go past the first file to see what he has done.

"These are all redacted," I say.

Daniel grins triumphantly. "My client insisted that these documents contain crucial intellectual property that simply cannot be handed out willy nilly. I have taken the liberty of redacting sections we feel contain company secrets."

"And let me guess," I say as I flip through another file. "That means all the sections?"

Daniel shrugs. "What can I say. It's a large company." He claps his hands together to indicate he is done with the conversation. "Have fun with those. I should probably be on my way."

"This is both unprofessional and illegal, Daniel," I tell him. "We both know I need full access to all your documents."

"Eh. Let's leave it to a judge. What do you say?"

Ah. So that's his plan. Take me round in circles just to get the documents. Bury me in pre-trial motions which are essentially irrelevant to the case, to distract me and exhaust me before the real business of the trial even gets underway. Smart. But he assumes I don't know his playbook.

"You know what, Daniel. I don't think that will be necessary. We'll try and make do with these." I pat the files and flash him a smile.

His eyes narrow in suspicion, but he shrugs as if he couldn't care less. "Great."

"Fantastic."

He grins and walks out. I see him stop at Amelia's desk, and then his voice carries over to me, loud and brash. "Do give me a call, sweetheart. Let's do dinner some time, and I'll tell you all about Robert Hardy."

Amelia trots into my office shortly after Daniel leaves. She looks nervous but determined. And breathtaking, in a peach suit that hugs her body perfectly. But I'm not going to actively notice that. Shit, did I already do that? Focus, Robert. Professional, just like you said.

"How can I help you, Miss Brooks?" I ask.

"I'm sorry about Mr. Goldman. I tried to get him to leave, but he was … persistent."

Too true. When he wanted something, Daniel was almost obsessive.

"It's fine, Miss Brooks. I know dealing with him can be difficult."

I continue looking for the laptop. I turn files and binders

upside down, recheck the drawers, and even flip over the couch cushions. Nothing.

Amelia watches me passively. I can feel her gaze following me across the office.

"Was there something else?" I ask her.

"Well, yes," she says. I make a motion with my hand to indicate that she should go on. "While you were with Mr. Goldman in here, I sort of flicked through his briefcase bag. I didn't have much time, but I saw their financial records, and the documents I looked through are definitely different from the ones they sent over."

"What?" I'm reluctantly impressed that she would even go looking in the first place. But if what she's saying is true, it could be a huge break in the case.

"I'm almost certain the records are different."

"Almost certain? We can't afford to make a mistake on this, Miss Brooks." I hear the urgency in my voice.

"I'm certain," Amelia says.

I sink into the couch, lost in thought. If Mendel has somehow doctored even one set of financial records, then this case could be over even before it begins. It would make sense because they would need to show that their former CEO Gregory was somehow funneling money through the backdoor of the company. And if that isn't true, as I know it's not, then it's not unthinkable that they would resort to such tactics. I can feel my excitement mounting. This could be the quickest win of my career. But …

"I need those records," I say, looking back up at Amelia.

"Sir?"

I leap to my feet and walk up to her. "I need you to go to that dinner with him."

Her eyes go wide, and color seeps into her cheeks.

"I know he made a pass at you. That's just what Daniel does. We can use that to our advantage. He gave you his number, right?"

She blushes again.

"This is important, Amelia. There's no need to be coy."

She nods.

"Good. Call him. Tell him you've thought about it and

decided to hear what he has to say. Or something … I don't know. Set up the date for tonight, so we know he'll still have the bag with him. You'll have to do something to distract him, get him out of the room, then grab those documents and photograph them for me. Do you understand?"

"I don't think I can do that," Amelia says, shaking her head.

"What? Why?"

"Well, it's Mr. Goldman. He's …"

"Sleazy? Handsy?"

"Inappropriate. He made several comments about my appearance, and I don't think it's a good idea to be alone with that man."

"You won't be alone. You'll be at a public restaurant."

Amelia shrugs. I'm beginning to lose my patience.

"I'm really not comfortable with this, Mr. Hardy," she says. "And I don't think I can do what you're asking. What if he doesn't leave his bag? What if he catches me?"

Just like that, I'm irritated.

"Frankly, Miss Brooks, this is not a request. I'm asking you as your boss, to go and get me those documents. Or don't bother coming in tomorrow. I've looked the other way on all your little mistakes so far, but I think your honeymoon period is over. This is the job. Either you can do it, or you can't. And if you can't, then you have no business working for me."

She looks absolutely stunned like I slapped her across the face. This is it, I think. This is the moment she quits. But all she does is nod slowly as if she's still processing what I just said. Then she straightens up and purses her lips.

"Of course. I'll set up the dinner right away."

"Good. I'll expect those documents as soon as you have them."

She nods again, but her whole demeanor has changed. Stiff upper lip. Determined expression. The faintest hint of disdain in her expression.

She starts to leave then pauses, looking at something under my desk. She walks back to the desk and gets on her knees. I look away pointedly as she bends down under the desk, fishing for something. Somehow, even while looking away, I can see the shape of her ass, the swell and curve, so feminine. She straightens up, and she is holding my laptop. She puts it on my desk and turns to leave.

"Looks like someone pushed it under the desk," she says. I'm almost sure I see the corners of her mouth twitch in the ghost of a smile.

11
Amelia

What does one wear to a dinner date they have been coerced to go to by their asshole of a boss? A date with a vile, odious man?

It feels wrong to even think about dressing up, and I wonder whether the suit I wore to work is right. One thing is certain; I'm not going to give Goldman any opportunity to make me even more uncomfortable than I already feel. That means covering up from head to toe. Bland, boring white blouse. Dinner jacket buttoned all the way. Hair tied up in a severe, hopefully, unapproachable bun.

I still can't believe Robert is making me do this. I blame myself, to some extent; I was the one who brought the information to him in the first place, and, by extension, I'm the one who went snooping through Goldman's bag. I don't know what I was expecting, but it wasn't more time around Daniel Goldman. Especially not on a covert operation, one which is apparently going to determine whether or not I stay employed.

For the hundredth time, I wonder why I didn't just tell Robert to take his job and shove it. The impulse is always there. Every time he snaps at me or asks me to do something near-impossible, I get so close to quitting, and every time, something holds me back. I'm particularly frustrated by his dogged determination not to acknowledge what happened between us. And yet I can't seem to shake the desire to impress him, to prove that I can handle whatever he throws at me.

Goldman was delighted to hear from me. I could hear the laughter in his voice when I called him minutes after he left the building. Which Amelia, he had asked? The lovely vixen with the ass to die for? Cringe. Apparently, he had a standing reservation at The Sarova Hotel, one of the best hotels in the city. And he would be delighted if I joined him for dinner that evening.

I find him waiting for me at reception. The Sarova is opulent; pristine marble floors, high, vaulted ceilings, and smooth jazz playing in the background. The foyer alone is absurdly large, and I feel out of place. Goldman is waiting in one of the lounge chairs, a handsome golden settee that matches the atmosphere perfectly. He is dressed in a dark grey tux with a maroon bowtie. When he sees me, he beams his creepy smile, and I can't help thinking he must have not been sure I would show up.

"Lovely Amelia!"

He steps forward with the clear intention of wrapping me in a hug. I sidestep his large arms, grabbing one hand and shaking it quickly, then letting it fall.

"Playing hard to get, I see." He laughs. "Good, good. I like a challenge. Shall we?" He holds out his arm, and I take it reluctantly. We walk into the hotel in silence. I notice he has not brought his bag with him, and my heart sinks. Already, the plan has gone to shit.

A cute little blonde woman ushers us into the restaurant. Goldman's hand drops to my lower back as he hovers behind me, and I quicken my pace to escape his touch. As expected, he has reserved what appears to be the best table; it's set apart from the rest of the restaurant, close to a window with a stellar view of the gardens outside, and the city in the distance.

"So," Goldman says once we're seated. "I didn't think you'd call me. Or show up tonight."

I shrug. "You were right. Robert is an asshole. I can't run away from that fact." I don't even need to fake the emotion on that.

"He said something to you after I left, didn't he?"

I remain silent, hoping he'll take it as confirmation, and he does.

"I don't know how he does it, to be honest," Goldman goes on. "How he keeps getting young women like you to work for him."

"Isn't it obvious?" I say. "He is a top lawyer in the city. Few people will turn down the opportunity to work with him. The experience, the hands-on knowledge … it's a dream for someone just coming out of school."

"Oh, you're fresh out of school, are you?"

"Yeah, I graduated a few weeks ago."

"I see. And what did you want to get into?"

"I haven't really thought about it, to be honest, but I've always loved criminal law."

Goldman looks impressed. "Really? I wouldn't have pegged

you as a criminal law type."

"Why? What does that type entail?"

"Let's just say you need to be a lot more duplicitous and ruthless to be a good criminal lawyer. Like your boss, for example. Completely heartless, and therefore a great lawyer."

"And you don't think I have these qualities?" I ask, feigning hurt.

"Oh, not at all. I know for a fact you have at least one of those qualities."

"And which one would that be?"

Goldman grins. "Let's just say I don't think you agreed to go to dinner with me because of my charming personality."

So he's not a complete idiot. For the first time, I wonder if he may be onto me. I had not considered that maybe Robert and I are playing right into his arms. Maybe he tricked me into coming here; he knew I would see the files and seek him out to get a second look. And then he conveniently forgot his bag. Is it possible we underestimated him?

The blonde waitress shows up with our drinks, and after some debate, we order. I'm not surprised to learn Goldman likes his steak bloody. I wouldn't be surprised if halfway through dinner he reveals that he's actually a vampire.

"How long have you known Robert?" I ask him as we wait for the food.

"Hmm. Almost ten years, I think. He won't admit it, but Robert and I are old friends. We started around the same time, with different firms, but we hung around the same circles. We knew a lot of the same people, so I guess it was only a matter of time before we officially met."

"You two don't seem to like each other very much," I comment.

Goldman laughs. "I don't know about liking each other. We have a competitive professional relationship. But I suppose I can understand why Robert doesn't like me. I'm the only person who's ever beaten him in court."

"I thought he has never lost a case."

"Oh, he wants everyone to think that. When he came up

against me a couple of years back, I had him on the ropes. He was scrambling to save face. It would have been a loss for the ages, but my client had a change of heart and decided to settle the case."

"So technically, you didn't beat him?"

"Oh, I did, and he knows it. But he doesn't like to talk about that. No, Robert wants everyone to buy the narrative of his invincibility. And most people do, but I know him too well. He has a glaring weakness."

He sounds so confident, so assured, I almost believe him. Robert did say this is the biggest case of his career. And by the way he's preparing, it does seem like a big deal. But I don't believe for a second that he's scared of this man.

"What did you mean, back in the office, about his assistants?" I ask.

"You mean the stories?"

"Yeah."

"Honestly, I wouldn't know where to begin. The one that springs to mind right away is the one about some young woman who slaved for him for so long, and he worked the poor woman to insanity. Literally. She had a mental breakdown, and Robert paid her off so the story wouldn't be made public. But lawyers talk."

"That can't be true," I say, horrified. I've pored over the Robert Hardy Binder, and there is nothing in there about anyone having a mental breakdown.

"As I said, it was kept hush-hush. Robert wouldn't want a story like that coming out. It would ruin his reputation. Frankly, I don't know anyone who wouldn't immediately believe it when they heard it. But you must know what it's like, surely? How long have you worked for him?"

I want to argue, tell him that despite his gruff exterior, Robert wasn't half the monster everyone makes him out to be. But I'm suddenly picturing him during one of his fits of rage, and it's not so hard to imagine the person on the receiving end of his fury cracking. I've been there too many times myself, and I'm almost sure Robert has been taking it easy on me.

I'm spared having to answer by the arrival of our food. It serves as a welcome distraction; Goldman turns right away to his steak, and he attacks it with verve.

I hate that he has instilled some doubt in me. Or, more accurately, fanned the embers that were already there. I keep trying to reassure myself that Robert would never go so far as to scar someone mentally, but it's a bit difficult to convince myself having just decided a few hours ago that the man is a total asshole, a regular Jekyll and Hyde. He swings wildly, unpredictably, from charming and almost human, to unpleasant, rude, and cold. From kissing me with surreal tenderness to threatening to fire me. Maybe I really don't know the man.

"I hope I haven't upset you," Goldman says in between forkfuls of steak. My own food lies untouched in front of me.

"No, no. I just didn't think ..."

"That he was that bad? I told you, very few people know the man that well. As I said, the best course of action for you would be to get away from him as soon as possible, before it's too late. I'm still willing to get you a job at my firm if you're interested. I assure you; we don't have slave drivers over there."

"I don't know ..."

"Consider it a favor. From a friend. And sometime in the future, I'm sure we can find a way for you to repay me."

His eyes travel over my body. I reach a hand up unconsciously, checking to see if I buttoned all the way up. I did, yet somehow his gaze makes me feel naked. And disgusted. I'm surprised it took so long, but there he is; the inappropriate man I knew I was going to be having dinner with.

"Excuse me," I say. "I have to use the bathroom."

This whole thing has been a massive failure from the get-go. I don't actually know why I'm still here. Will Robert believe me if I just tell him Goldman didn't have the bag with the documents with him? Somehow, I doubt he'll even give me the chance to talk. 'Get me the files, or don't bother coming in tomorrow.' Not much wiggle room there.

I walk back in the direction of the bathroom, or at least I think I do. I emerge into the foyer, and I realize I've somehow walked in a complete circle back to where we started. I step up to the reception desk, intending to ask the lady where the bathroom is.

And then I notice the bags, tucked neatly away in the low shelves around the receptionist.

"Excuse me, miss?" I say, excitement suddenly coursing through my veins. "The gentleman I came in with, Mr. Goldman? Did he leave his bag here?"

The lady frowns and looks around. "Mr. Goldman ... Ah, yes. I believe he did."

Lightbulb.

"I need to check something in there, please," I tell her.

"In the bag?"

"Yes."

"I don't know if I can do that, ma'am."

"No, it's okay. I'm with him. I just need to look at some documents real quick. Please."

I think she hears the desperation in my voice. Or sees how bright my eyes are. Either way, she pauses for a long moment, considering. And then she reaches behind her and pulls out the bag, swings it over the reception desk. She gives me a quick wink and then disappears behind her computer.

I dig into the bag and pull out a bundle of documents. It doesn't take long to find the ones I'm looking for. The financial records. I pull out my phone and open the camera, already feeling relieved. It looks like I'll be keeping my job, at least for today.

Without warning, my phone starts to blink, and I realize, with a growing sense of dread, that my battery is dying. "Shit," I mutter to myself. I have just enough charge to finish taking photos of the documents. Then the red LED light blinks a few more times, and the phone dies.

My mind is whirling as I rush back to the table. Robert specifically said he wants those documents as soon as I have them. And while I'm sure even he won't be anal enough to expect them during dinner, I don't feel like testing his patience. I need to figure out a way to get the photos to him as soon as possible. I don't think I can wait until I've charged my phone. No, I need to physically get them to him. Or is it that I want to?

"Is everything okay?" Goldman asks as I slide back into my chair. His plate has been cleared; he already finished eating and is now swirling a glass of wine.

"Yeah!" I say. "I just had a bit of a feminine emergency." I give him a significant look, so he knows exactly what I'm referring to. I expect him to flinch, but he doesn't so much as bat an eye.

"You barely touched your food," he says. "Shall I order you something else?"

"No, no," I say, quickly. And then it occurs to me I have the perfect excuse for leaving. "Actually, I have to go. My boss just called me; there's some work he needs my help with."

"Now?" Goldman stares at me in disbelief.

"You know what he's like," I say without missing a beat. "He wants what he wants when he wants it. Thank you for the dinner, Mr. Goldman, but I have to run."

"Please, call me Daniel. We will pick this up at a later date, no? I feel we've barely had a chance to get to know each other."

Oh, I know you well enough, you creep.

"I would like that, yes."

I get up, and Goldman does as well. He makes a big show of walking around to me and pulling out the chair for me, and I dodge his hands with practiced ease. I thank him repeatedly, and as I leave, I wave away his offers to have his driver take me back to the office.

"I'll be fine, really," I assure him. "Thank you, though!"

Then I'm out the door, and the fresh air in my face is a momentary relief before I remember I have to figure out where Robert lives and somehow get there. The thought terrifies and excites me in equal measure.

12
Robert

I consider myself an excellent cook, but this chicken parmesan recipe is making a fool of me. I've followed it to a tee, yet it looks nothing like the pictures on the website. I bet it tastes nothing like the target dish, too. My breading is soggy, soaked through with cheese, and the chicken is flavorless. I'm not sure where I went wrong, but what I have now is far from the thing I set out to make in the first place.

I take a tentative bite and scrunch up my face. This one is going in the trash; there's no helping it. I'll try again tomorrow. Right now, the growling in my belly means I have to figure out something else to eat for dinner. It sucks, considering how much time I spent on that damn chicken. I consider going out, but I decide against it. Tonight, I want a quiet night in, just me and my case files. I have the beginnings of a strategy, and I want to tighten it. Hopefully, Amelia will send the financial records in the course of the night, and I can go over them with a fine-tooth comb.

Which only leaves the option of ordering in. Again. The fast-food joint a couple of blocks away has probably got my order on file by now.

At least I tried my best. I pick up my phone, trying to remember the number of the restaurant.

The sound of the doorbell takes me completely by surprise. I'm not expecting anybody—not at this time of night, anyway. I almost never get any visitors, something of which I'm actually quite proud.

I pad over to the door and peer into the keyhole.

Amelia Brooks is standing in my doorway, jiggling anxiously on the balls of her feet. She looks like she's just come from a difficult job interview; she's dressed in an even more prim suit than the one she had on at work today, which is odd because she's supposed to be on the 'date' with Daniel.

I swing the door open, curious. "Miss Brooks?"

She opens her mouth, but whatever she means to say freezes on her lips. Her eyes drop to my torso, and I realize I am dressed only in sweatpants and an apron. I close the door quickly and shake my head. Damn it, why am I always shirtless in front of the woman? I throw a T-shirt on and go back to the door. Amelia hasn't moved. She looks like she just saw a ghost.

"Sorry about that," I say. "I wasn't expecting anyone."

She shakes her head. "No, of course. I'm sorry to bother you so late, but you said to get you the financial records as soon as I got them."

I didn't exactly mean the second you got them, you mad woman.

She goes on, speaking quickly like it's important that she explains why she's at my doorstep at 10 p.m. "My phone died while I was at dinner, and I didn't know when I would be able to send you the photos. And since you said you want them as soon as possible …"

"It's fine, Miss Brooks. Really. Come on in."

I step aside, and she walks into my apartment. She smells wonderful. I notice, for the first time since I met her, that she has a small tattoo on the back of her neck, which is a pleasant surprise. I wouldn't have taken her for the kind of person who would get a tattoo at all.

She takes in the apartment with hungry eyes. I follow her gaze, watching her as she walks around slowly, turning this way and that. It feels strange, like I'm awaiting her approval, eager, desperate.

"So you got the files," I say, jogging her out of her bubble.

Her eyes snap to me. "Oh, yes. I did."

She pulls out her phone and waves it in front of me. "But my phone is still dead, so I'm going to need to juice it up a bit."

I take it from her and excuse myself. My charger is in my bedroom. I walk in and plug it in. I pause for a moment, considering how messy the room is. But it's not like she's going to be coming in here, so I shrug and walk back to the living room. Except that Amelia is no longer in the living room.

"Amelia?"

"Here, sorry!" she calls from the kitchen.

I find her in the kitchen, peering innocently into the mess

that is my chicken parmesan.

"It smells wonderful," she says defensively.

"I hope you didn't try to eat that," I say, grabbing her by the hand and pulling her away from the stove. It's the first time I've touched her since ... Her skin is so soft.

"What? Why? It looks so good!"

Her words come out slightly slurred, and it occurs to me she must have been drinking. The Amelia I know would not be so forward. This version of her is closest to the woman I met on campus a lifetime ago. Bold. Playful. Adorable as fuck.

"It only looks that way, trust me. It's disgusting."

"Really?"

"Yeah. It turns out there's much more to recipes than following the instructions."

"That's a shame. I'm starving."

"Didn't you just have dinner?" I stop before adding 'with Daniel.' I don't want to think about Daniel just now.

"I didn't touch my food. As soon as I got the photos, I fled as fast as I could."

I feel myself smiling. "I would have loved to see that. Come on; I was just about to order take-out."

I pull her back into the living room, and she sits down on the couch as I call the restaurant. I ask her if pizza is okay, and she nods. I place the order, then go back and sit on the couch next to Amelia. Close enough that I can smell her perfume. And see the stunning green of her eyes.

It's so strange how we interact. There are moments like now when for whatever reason guards are dropped, and everything is pleasant and friendly, and I feel so at ease with her presence. And then there are the other moments when things are not so warm. I never know what I'm going to get. Or how I'm going to react to her.

"How did you know where I live?" I ask her.

"It's in the binder," she says, then she blushes like she just revealed something she wasn't supposed to.

"Why did you come here, Amelia?" I ask. I'm looking into her eyes, and she meets my gaze with unwavering intensity. I feel the familiar tug of static, the electric buzzing between us.

"To bring you the files you asked for," she says in a whisper.

"You could have sent them to me as soon as you got home and charged your phone."

"You say that now, but a few hours ago, you were threatening to fire me if I didn't zap them to you the second I got them. Never mind that what you asked me to do was almost impossible."

"And yet you pulled it off," I say.

"I got lucky."

"Don't sell yourself short, Amelia. You're more resourceful than you give yourself credit."

"It helps that I thought my job was on the line."

"You haven't answered me," I say quietly.

For the first time, her gaze drops to the ground. "I wanted to see you," she says, her voice so low I'm not sure I've actually heard right. When she looks up, the fire is back in her eyes. "I shouldn't because you've been horrible to me, and I don't understand why you treat me the way you do. But I wanted to see you. Goldman said all these horrible things about you, and I know half of them are true, but for some reason, I don't care. I didn't even think about waiting. Or trying to get my phone charged. I jumped at the opportunity to come here the second it came up."

She exhales a long, drawn-out sigh. It took a lot of guts for her to say that I'm sure.

"I'm sorry," I tell her. And I mean it. "You're right. I've been horrible to you. The truth is, I don't know how to act around you. I haven't known how from the moment I met you. You ... affect me, more deeply than I want to admit, so I lash out, and I push you away until I can't anymore. But no one should have to deal with that, and I'm sorry."

Amelia is silent for a long time. She looks so delicate, so beautiful. Why am I playing games with this woman? It's clear I'm crazy about her.

"I have a confession to make," she says.

"Yeah?"

"I've never ... I ..."

She's blushing now. Her cheeks are completely flushed. I reach over and tip her chin up so she's looking into my eyes once more.

"You can tell me," I prompt her. "You've never what?"

"No one has ever made me … orgasm the way you did, back on your office desk."

I grin, completely wrong-footed. I didn't expect her to go there. I remember how she fled afterward, and it suddenly makes sense. I also remember how turned on I was at that moment. I can feel the front of my sweatpants start to get taut.

For the second time tonight, the doorbell rings, the sound cutting into our little cocoon with shrill urgency. I get up awkwardly, shifting my growing boner and waddling to the door. I don't even look at the delivery guy. I grab the box and push a small wad of cash at him. I'm sure I've over-tipped him. I couldn't care less just now.

I settle back onto the couch, snuggling closer to Amelia than I was before. She doesn't seem to mind.

"You're not too hungry, are you?" I ask her, my hand going to her cheek and stroking her silky skin.

"Why?" she asks. "Did you have something in mind?"

"Oh, I've just been made aware of some puzzling stats, and I was hoping we could test them out, so we can be sure it wasn't a fluke last time out."

I stroke her chin, and she leans into me and closes her eyes.

"I need you to promise me something first," she says suddenly, pulling back and putting a hand on my chest.

"Sure," I say, impatient.

"No more Jekyll and Hyde. No more mixed signals."

"Fair enough," I say. "Now, shut up and kiss me."

13
Amelia

Robert Hardy is a phenomenal kisser. I may be biased, but I know it for a fact.

The first time we kissed, it felt like a stolen moment, a fleeting gush of need and desire forcing our lips together. It had been sweet, but it felt restrained, and when we broke apart, I was left bereft, wanting more.

The last time, it was more urgent, simultaneous, unanimous. It was magical, passionate … every motion of his lips sent a bolt of pleasure straight to my vagina. With just his kisses, Robert turned me into a wild woman whose body was reacting and doing things I had never imagined it capable of.

This kiss feels different, and yet all too familiar. His lips are soft, too soft. He asks *me* to kiss him, but when I close my eyes and lean into him, it is his mouth that brushes mine, and it is his hand that goes behind my neck and pulls me in.

It's almost chaste at first. Like he's teasing me. I'm impressed and angered by the restraint he seems to have because I suddenly want to jump him and rip his clothes away. Not him—everything he does is slow, meticulous. I feel warm and fuzzy and a bit stunned. This is really happening. With *him*. The kiss lingers. He nibbles so gently at my lips with his, taking turns, alternating between lower and upper lip. Slowly. It's driving me mad.

He moves closer, and his hands are suddenly around me. Up and down my back. He grabs my butt, and the way he squeezes is both possessive and delicious. He lifts me with no apparent effort, and I feel myself settle onto his chest. Then he stands, his hands securing me by the butt as he starts to move. His kisses have slowed even further to intermittent pecks, but he does not stop. As he carries me, he does not stop kissing me, and I keep expecting him to walk into furniture, and for us to go tumbling to the floor.

I don't want to close my eyes. I love the feeling of being in his hands; it feels safe. And I love the tiny little kisses, how I don't know when the next one will come, so I keep my eyes shut and wait.

I know we're in his room. The aura has changed, as well as the lighting. I slide my eyes open a fraction, and I am momentarily aware of being in a very large, spacious room with atmospheric lighting.

Robert carries me over onto a large, cushy-looking bed, and I think again, *It's happening.*

He lays me down slowly, then drops down on top of me. His lips are on me again in seconds. He seems a bit more urgent now. His tongue brushes and probes, and I meet it with mine. But just before I can deepen the kiss, he is gone.

I moan in protest, my eyes flying open. He is grinning; he knows what he's doing to me.

His fingers are quick and practiced as he unbuttons my blouse, spreading it to expose my skin. My bra comes off and is tossed impatiently away. I lift my butt so he can pull my pants off. I feel incredibly self-conscious as he peels away my panties, and I thank heaven I put on the sexy silk lingerie Ness got me. Just like that, I'm naked, and I refuse to allow myself to think about it because if I'm worried, I'll lose my nerve.

Robert leans back down and plants a wet kiss on my neck, nibbling lightly on the skin, and then he sets off downward, leaving a trail of moist kisses all the way from my neck to my navel. My breath hitches as he goes lower. Already my body is shaking from anticipation and excitement. I close my eyes and let the warmth spread outward from the points where his lips touch me, radiating out to the very tips of my fingers. He is slow and torturous. His progress barely registers; having closed my eyes, I'm only peripherally aware of him, and it seems he has been at my collarbone for an eternity.

Finally, his exploring mouth finds my breasts; it wraps around one nipple and sucks softly. My fingers dig into the bedding. I'm gritting my teeth to stop the moans threatening to spill out of me. I don't know why, but I'm afraid I'll unravel in front of him, and I won't know what to do like the last time. His tongue lashes out, flicking against my hardened nub. He flicks and sucks, and it feels so good I can't hold back the moans any longer.

My body is betraying me. I have no control over it anymore. My legs are twitching. My back arches and twists of its own accord.

And my fingers are clenching and unclenching Robert's sheets. I want to touch him, but I can't seem to figure out how to. Not with the waves of pleasure I'm currently enduring.

I feel Robert's fingers close around my other breast, and he starts cupping, tweaking, and rubbing it in time with the motions of his tongue. It's a vicious assault on my senses; I'm overwhelmed in seconds. I don't know if it's the anticipation of it all, but I feel the tension in my body mount until I'm taut as a spring. Then, with a scream that sounds nothing like me, I release.

I feel myself jerk wildly. Somewhere in the back of my mind, I marvel at the fact that Robert just made me come without even touching me there. I don't fight it; I let the motion take over me, the orgasm wracking through me, setting my toes curling and my teeth chattering.

I don't know how long I thrash about like that, but when I regain my senses, Robert is still hovering over me. Except he's gone lower, much lower.

I'm still sensitive from the orgasm, and I worry for a second about him touching me. But he seems to know this. He works his way around my vagina, circling it but not quite going there just yet. He kisses and licks my thighs. He caresses me like that for some time, until my breathing has slowed down, and the sense of need is growing once more.

I let my eyes flutter open, and I see him watching me as he caresses me with his hands. He is studying me, reading my reactions to what he's doing. It's strangely erotic, the sight of him between my legs like that.

I gasp as his finger brushes past my swollen lips. I must be sopping wet and getting wetter. He makes small, circular motions around the lips, and its torture. I'm panting again, heaving, twisting. I want him inside me. I push my hips upwards towards his face, an invitation, a plea.

I haven't seen him, I realize. Unlike me, he is still dressed, even though I'm fairly certain he has nothing on under those sweatpants.

"I want to see you," I mumble. My voice is thick and almost inaudible, but Robert hears me. He nods, but he doesn't pull away. Next thing I know, his tongue is on me. He licks along my lips, and when his tongue touches my clitoris, all thought is wiped from my mind.

"Fuck!" I say. I feel like I'm spiraling, completely out of control. "Please, Robert."

I feel the rustle of fabric, and then the delicious weight of him, the presence, the scent, moves away. I try, but I can't seem to open my eyes. I hear a drawer open, and the sound of things being shuffled.

He returns, and I feel his skin on me. He is naked this time, finally. I lift my hand and run it along his chest. He feels solid, wonderfully warm—hot even. I open my eyes a fraction, and he is inches from my face. He smiles at me, and it strikes me just how beautiful this man is. I feel a pang of joy that he's here with me. That he wants to do this with me.

"Ready?" he asks me in a soft voice.

I nod. *I've been ready ever since I walked into your apartment.*

He slides one hand under my thigh and lifts my leg slightly. Just enough so he can position himself right at my vagina. He slides into me with a sure stroke. I'm so wet I actually feel embarrassed.

Robert is huge. Bigger by far than anything I had expected. I've been stealing glances at him, looking at the outline in his pants, trying to guess what *he* looked like. Even my best estimates were wildly off.

He isn't all the way inside me, but I feel stuffed. I spread my legs and throw them around him, lifting my hips to accommodate him. He slips in a bit deeper. I can feel his eyes on me. I'm holding my breath, and I realize I'm a bit tense.

Relax, Amy. This is happening.

I let out the breath in a whoosh, and I feel my muscles relax. He pushes all the way in, and I hold him there, my lips pulsing around his girth as I adjust to his size.

I risk looking into his eyes; they are bright coals, burning into me with an intensity I definitely can't match. I lift my hands to his head and pull him down, bury my head in his neck. He starts to move then, as gentle and unhurried as he has been all night. He pulls almost all the way out, and then he slides back in, sheathing himself completely until his thighs brush mine. It's so deep, so intense, my eyes roll into the back of my head.

He lifts his head to look at me again. I'm so emotional I can feel the tears welling up in my eyes. I blink them away and try to meet Robert's gaze.

"You floor me, Amelia Brooks," he says, so earnestly I have no doubt he means it.

I want to tell him just what he does to me because it's so much more, so much deeper. But I don't know where to begin. Or how to put it into words.

Robert doesn't seem to be waiting for a response. He picks up his pace now, moving faster, grinding against me with renewed urgency and vigor. He shifts, lifting his torso and pulling my legs all the way up and resting them on his shoulders. His thrusts are almost mechanical now. It's all I can do to hold on to the headboard as he rides me.

Already, I can feel this warm sensation, beginning in the pit of my stomach and growing, pulsing, pushing out. It's like a growing heat in my vagina that's building and shooting out to my extremities. My cheeks feel flushed, my heart is pounding, and I'm sure I have drenched the sheets with my sweat. Robert is groaning, and I'm moaning, and between us, the sound of his thighs slapping into me fill the room.

Still, he pounds into me, all ideas of gentleness apparently abandoned. He is fucking me, I realize. Proper fucking, like I've never experienced in my life. But then I've never experienced any of this with anyone.

Suddenly, without warning, my mind goes blank, and I feel the release wash over and through me. Every part of me is tingling. If I'm shaking, then Robert is shaking right with me. I cannot be still. My body feels liquid; a warm sensation of pleasure is flooding every cell in me. My vagina lips are pulsing too, clenching and unclenching against the unrelenting thrusting of Robert's thick hard dick. This climax lasts much longer than the last. It just keeps going. I grab Robert, and I cry out, and I jerk uncontrollably, and then I'm lying still, and it starts up again, and my back twists up off the bed, and my legs are spread so far apart, and Robert is still pounding me into a pulp, and I'm sure this is how I die.

Then he groans loudly, and his whole body goes rigid. He

pushes into me once more, hard, and then he falls forward as he climaxes, and we are both shaking and thrashing about the bed, and our limbs are intertwined and coiled around each other. It's the single most intense orgasm I've ever had.

I drift away almost immediately. I don't even roll away or detangle from Robert. My eyes flutter shut, and I fall away, lost in a cloud of happy, sated thoughts and stunned disbelief.

It's the hunger that wakes me up. I jerk awake, and I look around wildly, suspicious of just how comfortable I am. The room is dark, even with the filtering of sunlight from outside. I'm sprawled out indolently on the bed. Alone. I don't remember covering up, or Robert leaving, but the sheets smell of him, so he must have slept with me. I take a quick peek under the covers to confirm that I'm definitely naked, and that last night wasn't a dream. It's a silly thought, I know. I'm in his bed. Of course, last night wasn't a dream. Not to mention the sweet ache in my vagina.

I'm grinning as I slide out of bed. I look around, trying to remember where my clothes were thrown. They are nowhere to be seen. I can't walk around naked, although I'm tempted for a fleeting moment to do just that if only to see how Robert would react. I walk over to the huge closet in one corner of the room and pull out the top drawer.

His clothes are meticulously arranged, as expected.

I grab the first T-shirt I come across and put it on. Robert's scent wraps around me. I smile and walk out of the bedroom.

I find him in the living room, his head bent over a collection of documents and files. I spot my phone on the table as well, and I gather he has been going over the case files, including the photos I took last night.

I sneak up to him, intending to startle him, see his reaction. But as I approach, he turns his head slightly to the side and smiles.

"You're adorable," he says.

"How did you hear that?" I protest. "I was being sneaky!"

"Not sneaky enough."

I wrap my hands around him from the back. "Morning," I say

into his hair.

"Good morning. Did you sleep well?"

"I don't think I've ever slept so well in my life," I tell him truthfully. "You knocked me right out."

He laughs, the sound reverberating through him, a rich, delightful timbre. "I'm sorry?"

"You had better be, mister. Trying to get out of feeding me by putting me to sleep like that."

"Oh, yeah. You still haven't eaten. Sorry." He starts to get up, pulling my hands away from around him.

I shake my head and hold him tighter, not wanting to let go. "No! Let me hold you a bit longer." It occurs to me I've never felt this free with him, never been this forward. It's like we've crossed a silent boundary, and I can now be myself around him.

He laughs again, and then, without warning, he gives me a not-so-gentle tug, and I fall over the back of the couch onto him. He shifts me around so I'm on his lap, and then he holds me by the chin and kisses me. It's a quick kiss, but it goes straight to my vagina. I still don't understand how this man can turn me on so easily.

"Stop," I say, pushing him away playfully. "I know what happens when you start that. I'll die of starvation. And dehydration." I blush, remembering the orgasms. "And exhaustion."

Robert grins. "Fair enough. Let me make you some breakfast."

"Oh, you don't need to," I say quickly. "I'll just eat this." I untangle myself from him, reach over for the box of pizza from last night, still unopened. I pull out a slice and take a big bite.

"You won't even heat it up a bit first?"

I shake my head. "You know what they say about cold pizza."

"I don't think I do."

My mouth is full, so I simply hold up a thumbs-up sign as I chew.

Robert laughs. "You're so adorable it's unbearable," he says. He looks different, happy, at ease.

"So?" I ask him when I finally stop chewing. "Where are we with the case?" I sweep my hand around the table, where the documents are littered.

Robert runs a hand through his hair, sighing deeply. "I have a strategy, and I think I know what Goldman is planning to do. I've gone over the financial records—the actual ones which you got. Good work on that, by the way. Mendel was trying to hide that the financial transactions to the offshore accounts, which were initially in Gregory's name actually went to a joint account. And guess who co-owns that account?"

"His partner, Thomas …?"

"Wagner. Right. So, either they were both in it, and they were both secretly stealing from the company, or Thomas wasn't so careful when he was planting the decoy paper trail. It may even be that he's the one who has been stealing from the company and he's trying to pin it on Gregory."

"Sounds messed up."

"It is, yeah. And these two are supposed to be best friends."

"What do you think Goldman's strategy is going to be?"

"From everything I've gone over, these financial documents have to be his smoking gun. I think he's pinning his whole argument on them. With the records you obtained, we can challenge the authenticity of the records, question them completely so the judge throws them out. If we can do that, we may get the case dismissed before it even begins."

I nod slowly, mulling it over. It makes sense, although it seems a bit simplistic. From what I gathered of Daniel Goldman, he is a bit more complicated than he seems. "What if he has another trick up his sleeve?" I ask.

"I know Daniel," he says. "He usually has one big gun up his sleeve, and this is it. Everything else he tries will be to test me out, and when that fails, he's going to pull his big gun out. Except he doesn't know we've already checked it and replaced the bullets with blanks. All thanks to you, Amy."

"Just following instructions, boss," I say. "Speaking of which, I should probably get going. I need to get home and get ready for work. My boss is a real slave driver."

Robert grins. "Is that so?"

"Yeah. Total asshole."

"Well, I'm sure even he will be softened by your effortless

charm."

"I don't know …" I pause as if deep in thought. "He's a pretty tough nut to crack. Nothing impresses him."

Robert shimmies closer and gathers me into his lap once more. "Well, you'll tell him you're running a bit late because you were working late last night. And this morning."

"This morning?"

He reaches for the hem of the T-shirt, and his hand slides easily up my body, finding and grabbing a breast. My nipple stiffens immediately.

"Maybe I can be a little late," I whisper.

14
Robert

The week leading up to the first preliminary hearing passes by in a flash of activity, almost none of which is related to the case.

I will be the first to admit that I'm distracted. More than I've ever been in my professional career. I'm finding it hard to focus on the case with the gorgeous woman seated outside my office.

I'm quietly confident about the case. In the moments when I've not been lost in Amy's body, I've been going over the case files as thoroughly as I can. The facts are clear enough. If Daniel uses the angle of attack I expect him to, I have no reason to worry.

The problem is that I'm not even worried to begin with. I feel, for the first time in my career, like the case is really not all that important. I still have the desire to win. But in those unguarded moments when I've been honest with myself, I realized that desire does not consume me as wholly as it once did. The case will take care of itself.

I'm consumed by a different desire, one that burns like an eternal flame. And one that I can't seem to put out.

Amy and I have been sneaking around the office like a couple of horny teenagers. It's entirely her fault. A few days after we made love, she showed up to the office with a flimsy, see-through blouse, under which she had decided to forego a bra. I didn't even have to squint to see the dark circles of her areolas pushing against the fabric.

That may have been the longest morning of my life. And she knew exactly what she was doing. She made a point of coming into my office every few minutes, to 'hand over some files.' And boy, did she hand them over. Always, there was a playful smile on her face. Always, her eyes flicked downward, and I knew she knew I was turned on.

By midday, I couldn't take it anymore. I pulled her into a bathroom, locked the door, and took her in one of the stalls.

From there, it was a freefall. Lunch breaks. Coffee breaks. Random times. Her dressing grew bolder but more subtle. Several times I caught some male worker following her as she passed, and the look on their face was probably identical to mine.

It's remarkable what a little confidence has done for Amy. She seems different, and I know it's simply because she's more comfortable with herself and with me. She has bloomed. She is more intelligent than I gave her credit for and better suited to the job than I expected. If anything, she's more prepared for the case than I am.

Yesterday, I walked up to her desk with my hands behind my back. She looked up at me and beamed, that special smile she seemed to trot out just for me. It made me think of all the times in the past when she had seen me and her face fell immediately. It was a welcome change.

"Yes, sir?" she said softly, her eyes twinkling. A few days previously, she had whispered to me that every time she called me 'sir' what she was really saying was 'sexy.'

"I came to give you this," I said, sliding a tiny velvet box across her desk.

Her eyes popped.

"Where is the horse-drawn carriage? The mariachi band? Where are the flowers? What kind of proposal is this?"

"Just open the box, you lunatic," I said, grinning.

She pulled the pin out of the box and stared at it for a long time, her face blank.

"It's a pin celebrating you breaking the record," I explained. "See? The little #1 engraved on it?"

"But I haven't broken the record," she protested. "I've only been here 25 days. Not that I'm keeping count or anything."

"Call it an early gift, then," I told her. "Because I know you'll be here much longer."

I leaned in and stole a quick kiss.

Today, I have brought a bottle of champagne. I haven't presented it to her yet, because it's a celebratory gift. We will pop it when we win the case.

She looks nervous, and that in turn makes me nervous. The big day is finally here. For the first time in a long time, the only thing on my mind is the case. I have finally snapped into battle mode.

Today, Amy has ditched her naughty attire for a simple black suit. She looks stunning in it if a little too professional. We sit down for one final brainstorming session in my office, and then we head out to court.

She is unusually silent on the ride there. I have gotten so used to her quirky, offbeat humor; it feels strange for her to be so silent. I catch her eye a few times and give her a couple of smiles and winks to put her at ease, but I must not be convincing, because the worried expression remains pasted on her face.

Gregory is already in court. Always the businessman, he showed up an hour early to scope out the 'enemy,' and he promptly updates me as we walk in.

"Mendel didn't send the barrage of lawyers I thought they would," Gregory says. "It actually looks nothing like the spectacle I expected them to make it. No press, no crowd of people screaming for my blood. I hate to say it, but it looks relatively low-stakes. Either Goldman is overconfident, or there's something we don't know."

"One moment," I say, placing a hand on him so he stops walking. "Go on," I add to Amy, and she walks on into the courtroom.

"Let's try and be a little more positive, Gregory, okay? The woman is already half-scared to death. No need to make her even more nervous."

"Who, Amy?"

"Obviously."

"Amy is a trooper. She'll be fine."

"I know she is, but it's her first case. Let's keep the talk of impending doom to a minimum, okay?"

"Okay, okay. But you're sure you know what Goldman is thinking? I don't know him as well as you do, obviously, but something doesn't seem right."

"I've got this, Greg, don't worry."

Gregory lifts his hands up in resignation. "Oh, and he brought some woman with him as his second chair, I think."

"What?"

"Yeah. She's already in there. I didn't catch her name ... Gibbons, or something."

It's like Gregory just slapped me across the face.

"What?" I say again, even more thickly than before.

"She's in there, you can just take a look," Gregory says, puzzled.

I nod, but my heart is suddenly racing. It couldn't be. He couldn't have. I lift legs made of lead and propel them forward into the courtroom. Emptier than I thought. Only a handful of people. Maybe Gregory is right. Maybe something *is* up. My eyes travel the length of the courtroom, all the way to the front. Amy is looking over at me, but my eyes are drawn to the woman seated across from her on the other side of the divide.

Tall. Skinny. Straw-colored hair. Large oval glasses. It's her. Damn it, it's her.

I make my way to the front slowly, trying to think. This is Goldman's doing. This has his fingerprints all over it. And if it is, then I have grossly underestimated the man. All along I thought I was the one with the upper hand, getting Amy to go to him, hoping his penchant for pretty young girls would work to my advantage, while he had this card up his sleeve the whole time.

The man himself appears out of nowhere, which is shocking for someone his size.

"Bobby!" he booms, stepping between me and the two rows separating *her* from me. "You came! I thought you would wake up, realize you're doomed, and simply not show."

I'm so confused that I don't know what to say to him. I look over his shoulder at the woman, hoping against hope that I'm hallucinating, and it's not actually her.

"Oh," Goldman pipes up, noticing where my attention is. "How rude of me. Come, let me make the introductions." He throws his hand around my shoulder like an indulgent tour guide. "Although I daresay we don't need introductions in this case, eh?" He laughs his annoying laugh, and for a brief moment, I seriously consider just punching him in his stupid face, if for no other reason than to shut him up.

But then we are there, and he gives me a slight push towards *her*.

"This is Laurie Gibbons. I'm sure you two have met."

Laurie gives me her hand, and I reach out and shake it stiffly.

"We have," I say, forcing myself to smile.

"Oh, come on, Bobby. There's no need to be so modest. It's an open secret you two used to date, isn't it? Way back, too, before you became a hotshot lawyer."

I know exactly what Goldman is doing. He isn't exactly subtle about it, either. Throwing her in my face like this. Forcing me to confront the reality of my past and the fact that I would now have to deal with her for the duration of the case. I would have applauded the ingenuity if I wasn't so furious.

"A long time ago," Laurie says, smiling sweetly. "Too long ago to even warrant mentioning, right, Robert?"

Her eyes are like darts as she stares at me.

"Right," I say.

"It's good to see you again," she says, and for a second, I almost believe it.

"You too. Are you …?"

"Daniel's second on the case, yes. He literally begged me to help him out with this one. Apparently, I have experience that will be invaluable to him."

By experience, I know Goldman meant 'knowledge about me.' And for all her sweet smiles and innocuous small-talk, Laurie knows that, too.

"Where did he drag you from?" I ask.

"Oh, I actually have my own practice in the city now. I moved here about six months ago."

"Oh."

"She's being modest," Goldman chips in. "It's more than just a practice. The Law Monthly called it the fastest-growing law firm in the city. In a year's time, she'll be competing against the big boys in the area. You know, might even overtake Galweather & Meyer."

I shrug. For the second time today, I have no comeback for Goldman, and that bothers me. Already, his plan is working. I'm shaken. I'm discombobulated.

"Hello?"

Amy pops her head around Goldman's massive frame, and

we all turn to look at her. She must have been wondering what the meeting was all about.

"Ah, the lovely Miss Brooks!" Goldman pulls her into a very uncalled for hug. When he lets her go, she throws me a look of disgust, and it almost makes me smile. Almost.

"Sorry, doll, we didn't mean to leave you out of the ménage. We were just saying hi, getting to know each other. Of course, these two old lovebirds were catching up."

He makes a casual gesture, pointing first at Laurie and then at me, but his eyes, like mine, are fixed on Amy. And I have to give it to him; he has played this whole thing perfectly. Even if he doesn't know about Amy and me, he is using that information to drive a wedge between us. And judging by the way his greedy eyes were devouring Amy, he knew. Or suspected.

Already, the fucker was two for 0 on me.

To her credit, Amy's expression doesn't change. She barely flinches. There is only a flutter of eyelids as the information registers, and her eyes flick to me ever so slightly. But then she smiles, and she holds her hand out to Laurie.

"Hi, I'm Amelia Brooks," she says to her.

Laurie shakes her hand and smiles at her. "Nice to meet you, Amy. Can I call you Amy?"

"Of course."

Goldman watches intently, a slight frown on his face. No doubt he expected this to blow up into a scene of some sort. Well, he doesn't know Amy as well as I do. She may be smiling now, but I have no doubt there will be a reckoning when we're alone.

"We should get back to our own side of the divide," I say. "The hearing should be starting any time soon."

"Right, right," Goldman says. "Good luck, buddy." He claps me on the back with a heavy paw and throws a lewd wink at Amy.

Amy and I step away and move quietly to our own table. I sit down and immediately reach for my bag, pulling out documents, taking my time, avoiding the gaze I know she's throwing me.

"Look," I begin, but I don't get a chance to finish my doomed attempt at an explanation. A baritone-voiced man steps out from behind the judge's chamber door and announces that court is in session. I manage to steal a glance at Amy as we stand, and her expression is less than friendly.

"Everything okay?" Gregory asks me as we sit down.

I nod, but everything is definitely *not* okay. And as soon as the hearing begins, everything starts to fall apart in spectacular fashion.

Daniel and Laurie are content to present the financial records as the primary evidence against Gregory. The documents they present are wildly different from the ones Goldman brought to my office, and from the ones Amy 'stole' from him. I look through the records, realizing, too late, of course, that Goldman has played me. He pulled a triple bluff on me, bringing me false documents knowing I'd immediately suspect there were others, and then letting Amy get those 'others,' except those were fake too.

I have been outplayed, and the realization hits me like a ton of bricks. And at the worst time. I have no rebuttal for the evidence. I can only stare wordlessly at it, wondering how I let this happen.

Amy nudges me under the table when I don't speak for almost two minutes, and I scribble 'NOT THE REAL RECORDS' on a piece of paper and slide it across to her.

That was my entire defense, rebutting the financial records. With that taken away, I have nothing. I look over at Goldman, and his grin is sickening.

"Your Honor, we have a witness who can speak to Mr. Mendel's fraudulent transactions," he declares after the dust has settled over the financial records.

That is pretty much the final blow. The noose is tightening. Thomas Wagner takes the stand, and his testimony is about as incriminating as it can get. They had a partnership, yes, but he soon realized the discrepancies in the financial records, and he confronted Gregory about them. Gregory denied any involvement, but soon afterward resigned his position. After an internal audit, the company discovered the money stacked away in offshore accounts and decided to pursue legal recourse against their former CEO.

Gregory squirms in his chair, throwing murderous looks at me every other minute. He mumbles, "Lies," under his breath from time to time, throwing up his hands all through Wagner's testimony. Amy does a good job cross-examining the witness, but even while she manages to call into question Wagner's duties in the company and implying his jealousy towards his more gifted partner, the damage has been done, and we both know it.

When the gavel comes down, it does so with the verdict that the case will go forward. The judge finds that there is more than sufficient evidence for there to be a full trial, and just like that, he hands me my first loss in a very long time.

I go through the motions, calming Gregory down, assuring him it was only a small loss. We'll simply fight them in court, I tell him. I'll be better prepared next time. This one was on me, and I apologize.

"I told you not to underestimate him!" he barks at me. "I fucking told you!"

He storms out of the courtroom, and I am left with a quieter-than-usual Amy and a grinning Daniel Goldman. I don't feel like dealing with his gloating. I doubt I'll be able to. So I shake my head and head out of the courtroom. I don't slow down until I'm out. And then when I get to the car, I realize with a sinking feeling that I came with Amy and I have to wait for her.

As if I've not been humiliated enough.

15
Amelia

The thing that strikes me most about the loss isn't the fact itself, though it's pretty remarkable that the great Robert Hardy has lost something as simple as a preliminary hearing. From what I've heard and read about him, that's essentially unprecedented.

No, the thing that I can't wrap my head around is how it happened. And what the tall, beautiful woman had to do with it.

I've never given much thought to Robert's romantic past. He has never given me any reason to think about it. But I know he has a type, and if ever there was a walking advertisement for that type, it would be the woman I found sitting across from me when I walked into court. Tall and beautiful are an understatement; she's stunning in all the ways models are supposed to be. Perfect posture. Perfect hair, perfect face. She reminds me of the woman I met on my first day working for Robert, the one who claimed she was his best ever assistant. But this woman is different. She is class and intellect personified. She oozes the easy grace and effortless charm of someone who has lived their life navigating social circles.

But Robert's reaction to her was by far the most heartbreaking thing. He looked like he had seen a ghost. If I could put the loss down to one thing, it would be that woman's presence, plain and simple because Robert was focused and confident before he walked into the courtroom. Once he saw the woman, his whole demeanor changed, and I saw for the first time what he looked like when he got flustered.

And then I learned that they used to date. In the flurry of emotions that were competing for attention, I recognized Goldman's manipulative hand in all that was happening. I saw it, clear as day. So why didn't Robert? Or did he see it and shrug it off? He had clearly underestimated Goldman every step of the way. Was this him dismissing what was clearly an attempt to distract him, throw him off his game? Because that's exactly what happened. I know Robert, when he calms down, will want to point to Goldman's real subterfuge coming in the form of the financial reports. But the Robert I know would have countered that inconvenience, even if he didn't see it coming. If he was in his right mind. If he hadn't just seen his former lover and her perfect breasts.

And there it is. That's what really bothers me.

There have been no words exchanged between Robert and me. What we have has been unspoken for the most part. There was that huge shift in our dynamic when I went to his place, and after that, we sort of crossed over the boss/employee threshold. But we never talked about what we had stepped into. It was whirlwind in the classical sense. It was giddy and passionate and in the moment, knowing I wanted him and he wanted me just as bad, if not more. It meant so much for me because it felt like he was helping me discover myself in ways that went beyond the physical. I was a new version of myself, a better me. I was on a journey, and he was leading me on it. We never sat down to talk about what it meant in the greater scheme of things. Somehow, I doubted Robert was the kind of guy who would want to sit down and discuss labels.

Yet I'm still angry at him for letting that woman affect him like that. It bothers me to no end. No one has ever put Robert off his game like that. Who exactly is Laurie Gibbons?

The question plays through my mind throughout the hearing. I am vaguely aware that it is going badly for us. I can see Gregory growing more restless, and Robert retreating further and further into his shell. And all I can think of is the woman, and how she smiled at Robert, and how her hand lingered in his when she shook his hand.

The realization that I'm jealous dawns on me slowly, festering like a wound until I can't deny it any longer.

When the hearing finally ends, and everyone has cleared out, I walk slowly over to the prosecution desk, where Laurie is bent over a document, alone. Goldman is thankfully nowhere to be seen.

"Hi," I say, sounding more timid than I would like.

Laurie looks up and smiles. Radiant. Gorgeous. Irritating. "Hey, Amy," she says. She sounds almost kind.

You just lost against her, Amy. This woman is not your friend.

"You guys did a great job in there," I hear myself say. I wonder what I'm doing, why I even approached her in the first place.

"Sweet of you to say, Amy. I appreciate that it can't have been easy for you."

I nod, and just like that, I've said all I can. My lips are suddenly dry. I'm staring stupidly at this woman and wishing I never walked up to her in the first place.

"You want to talk about Robert, don't you?" Laurie asks me, smiling slightly. Of course. She's perceptive too.

I don't respond, but I don't need to. Laurie is already stuffing her papers back into the folders and the folders into a handsome black bag. She gathers her things and steps beside me.

"Let's take a walk, shall we? I know this cute little coffee shop a block away."

I fall into step beside her. She is even taller than I thought, thanks in part to the heels she's wearing. We walk silently out of the courtroom. I wonder what she's thinking, how she sees me. It must be strange for her, this random girl walking up to her and then clamming up after only one sentence. If she finds it weird, she doesn't let it show.

She beams at me, and at the world, and at almost all the people we meet between the courtroom and the coffee shop. Clearly, she is a hit around these parts. Not surprising in the least.

"So how long have you been sleeping with him?" she asks as soon as we sit down.

I had been staring at her cleavage; my eyes zip back up to her face. I'm sure I've misheard. "What?" I sputter. Is the woman psychic?

Laurie smiles. "You're a beautiful girl, Amy. I know Robert. I'm sorry, I didn't mean to be presumptuous."

"You weren't," I say after some time. "Robert and I ..." What? Have been screwing each other's brains out at every opportunity but haven't sat down to discuss it? "It's complicated," I say. "But yes, we're sort of involved. Is it that obvious?"

"Oh, no. Nothing like that. I mean, I did see the way he looked at you, but I may have been imagining things—"

"I saw the way he was looking at you too," I jump in before I can stop myself.

Again, Laurie smiles. She flags a waiter over and asks for two coffees.

"As I was saying, I did see the way he looked at you, but

Daniel strongly hinted that there was something going on between you two, so it wasn't that big a leap."

I remain silent, waiting for her to address my accusation.

"What is it you want to know, Amy? It seems you have a lot you want to say."

"You and him ..."

"Are a thing of the past. Ancient history. You have nothing to worry about if that's what this is."

Bullshit.

"Why did Goldman hire you?" I ask her. My tone has gotten abrasive, forceful.

"Because I'm a damn good lawyer?"

This time I say it out loud: "Bullshit."

Laurie laughs softly. "How about you tell me why you think he hired me?"

"Because he knew you and Robert have history, and he wanted to use you to distract him, throw him off his game."

"Not bad, Amy. It's certainly part of it; I won't deny it. Robert and Daniel have an old rivalry that dates back years, and whenever they've faced each other, it tends to be about everything but the case. I took the case because I want my client to win, and the only way to do that is to keep the case on track. Left to their own devices, those two would probably find a way to drag this out for an eternity without actually trying the case."

"So, what, you're the arbitrator? Between them?"

"If you like, sure. But I have a more important question for you, Amy. Do you know what you are?"

"What do you mean?"

"You've worked out my role in this whole mess. But do you know yours? Do you know why Robert hired you?"

I fall silent. Mostly because I have thought about that very question myself several times. And never been able to give myself a satisfactory response.

"We're not so different, you know," Laurie goes on. "But unlike you, I know when I'm being used. I turn it to my advantage any chance I get."

"What do you mean? How am I being used?"

The waiter materializes with our coffees. Laurie takes hers and starts dropping sugar cubes into it. I count four before my eyes snap back to her face.

"Like I told you, Amy, a case between Robert Hardy and Daniel Goldman is an exercise in mind games and manipulation. A chess match, if you will. They know each other so well, and yet they don't really know themselves well enough to guard against their obvious weaknesses."

"I still don't understand ..."

"You're the bait, Amy. The Trojan Horse. You're the distraction. Remember how you so astutely worked out that Daniel hired me as a way to throw Robert off his game? Well, why are you not as astute when you're involved yourself?"

In a way, it makes sense. The way Robert had pimped me off to Goldman just to get some case files. How little he seemed to care about me in the beginning. His own admission that I was a cog in a long line of his assistants. He had even told me during my interview that I did not have the qualifications for the job. So, he had hired me for something else, then.

The only problem with that argument was ...

"I know what you're thinking," Laurie says. Apparently, she can read minds. "But he slept with you, right? He was intimate with you on more than one occasion? You probably think you're in a relationship, right? And even though you know deep down that he is not the kind of guy who gets into a relationship just like that, you're telling yourself that he really cares about you."

It sounds uncomfortably close to the truth of what I'm feeling. And I know it's why I approached her. I had my doubts about Robert. I wanted to speak to someone who really knew him.

"What happened between the two of you?" I ask her.

"Are you sure you want to know?"

"Tell me," I say resolutely.

Laurie takes a long sip of coffee before launching into her story. Mine remains untouched, growing colder by the minute.

"Robert and I met at a small law firm we both worked for in the city. I was a junior partner, on the fast-track to becoming a senior and then name partner, and Robert was an intern, just fresh out of school. He was brilliant. I remember noticing him right away, among the hundreds of applicants, and as fate would have it, I was assigned to him as his mentor. He was a fantastic lawyer. In a few short months, he had already impressed the big names at the firm, and there was already talk of making him the highest-paid first-year associate in the history of the firm. I was behind him the whole time, watching him grow, proud of his progress. There had always been an undercurrent of attraction between us. I fought it because I knew it was inappropriate. I was much older than him, and the firm had strict rules against interpersonal relationships. But in many ways, we were inevitable. We made love one night in my office, and after that, we started carrying on this secret affair."

I swallow hard, remembering my own 'incident' with Robert in his office. And the bathroom. And the elevator. And the stairway. And in his car.

I drag my attention back to Laurie with some difficulty.

"It was thrilling," she goes on. "The sneaking around made it all the hotter, and after some time, we started to get sloppy, careless, taking more risks. I don't know how it happened, but word started going around that I was sleeping with a junior associate, which was a very big deal at the time. We were both called in and asked to explain what was happening. I figured it shouldn't be a big deal, and I confessed to the relationship. But Robert didn't. He told them I had coerced him into having sex with me, that I had taken advantage of him, and he couldn't say no because I was his direct superior. It was quite the scandal.

My career took a massive hit, naturally. I was scapegoated, and any notion I had of promotion went out of the window. After some time, I figured the only option I had was to move away and start over in a new city."

"And Robert?" I ask breathless.

"Nothing happened to Robert. I suspect he would have kept up his trajectory to success anyway, but the sympathy certainly helped him, and the firm doing all it could to bury the scandal so it wouldn't incriminate them. He ascended the ladder fairly quickly after that. Junior partner in a year, senior in another year. Eventually, he left to join a bigger firm, but by then, he had already acquired a reputation as the fiercest lawyer in town, and everybody soon forgot that little story about the junior partner who took advantage of him that one time."

"That's awful," I say, and I'm truly horrified. Like the time Goldman was slinging dirt on Robert, I want to dismiss the story as malicious lies, but somewhere in there is a kernel of truth, and I know it. It doesn't sound like him, but it also sounds exactly like him.

"So, you see, Amy, Robert Hardy doesn't care about anyone but himself. He will use you to advance his own cause. He will do whatever it takes to get ahead, even if it means feigning an entire relationship to make it happen. That's just what he does. Don't kid yourself that he cares about you. He's using you, just like he has used countless girls before you."

16
Robert

I have had what may be the shittiest day I can remember. But I realize as soon as I get to my office, it's about to get much worse.

Emma is waiting for me. Or, as I called her the whole time she worked for me, Number 10. Clearly, today is my day of reckoning. This is the second ghost I'm meeting today. But this one is much less friendly.

I drop my bag onto the floor, grateful that I didn't come back with Amy. She's already seen enough of my demons. I don't need her witnessing this. I can feel a headache starting to pulse at my temple.

I walk into the office, keeping my eyes on Emma. She is seated at my desk, her eyes following me keenly as I approach her. She looks less glamorous than she did the last time she was in my office. Somehow, the sheen is not as glossy; she is still beautiful, her dress is typically over the top, but she has lost some of her glow.

"Robert," she says coldly as I lower myself into a chair.

"Emma."

"Oh, you remember my name now?"

"What do you want? I've had the shittiest day, and I really can't deal with you right now."

"Oh, you couldn't get the case thrown out, could you?"

I'm still impressed by just how much information the woman still has about me. Maybe she has someone here who tips her off?

"Shocking," she says. "The great Robert Hardy. Felled at last."

"What do you want?" I snap, louder than I wanted. My patience is gone, and the headache is now a full migraine. I take a deep breath and force myself to calm down. "If you're going to ask me for money again, you can save your breath. The answer is still no."

"Oh, no. We're way past that now." She draws a sheet of paper from her bag and pushes it across the desk toward me.

It takes all the restraint I have not to grab it, crumple it into a ball, and chuck it at her. Taking another deep breath, I pick it up and begin to read it. My frown grows deeper as I continue to read it. And deeper. When I finish, I can barely see through the red mist that has settled over my eyes.

"What the fuck, Emma?"

"I told you," she says, and she has the nerve to look unbothered. "You should have given me the money when I asked for it."

"No one will publish this," I say, but I know that's not true. This is as explosive an expose as the papers have probably seen in a while. Never mind that a big chunk of it is fabricated, and the other part a complete misrepresentation of the truth.

It's official. This *is* the shittiest day ever.

"Are you sure about that? I already have three reporters waiting for this story. I'm not even the one who wrote it. I spoke with a freelance journalist and dictated my story to him. This is his write-up. All I have to do is give him the go-ahead, and he splashes this on tomorrow's front page."

I get up from the chair and start to pace the office. I need to think. My mind feels clogged. I'm under duress, a result of losing the case and now this. I need to get away. I need ... Amy. I want to vent to her. I want her to make silly jokes and laugh at mine. I want to bury my head in her bosom and forget any of this ever happened. But Amy is not here. And if she was, I doubt she'd want to do anything with me.

"Okay," I say finally. I'm cornered, and I know it. "What do you want?"

Emma smiles, a sick twisting of her lips that contorts her features so she's no longer as stunning. "I want twice what you gave me last time," she says without missing a beat.

"I don't think ..."

"And I want a monthly stipend."

"That's completely unreasonable," I say. "And impossible. I don't have that kind of money right now."

"Somehow, I find that hard to believe."

"I really don't. I'm going to need some time."

"So, you can figure out how to worm your way out of this?

No way, Robert. I leave here with my money, or this is tomorrow's front page."

"I could just rip this into pieces, you know."

"Don't insult my intelligence, Robert. Or yours. That's a copy. One of many."

"Well, I definitely can't budge on the stipend. I may be able to get the money together, but I need at least two days."

"This really isn't a negotiation, you know."

"It's the best I can do!" I yell, losing my temper once more. My head is pounding now, a slow, agonizing throbbing at my temples. I need this day to be over. I need this woman gone. I need to fall asleep and never wake.

"Okay," Emma says after a moment. "One day, but that's it. If I don't see the money in my account by this time tomorrow, I won't even call. Front page, Robert. And I don't think you want that, especially now that you've lost a huge case."

"I haven't lost the case, just the first hearing." For some reason, it's important to clarify. At least for myself.

"Keep telling yourself that."

Emma gets up and walks around the desk to where I'm standing. She leans over and plants a kiss on my cheek, whispering: "Pleasure doing business with you, Robert. As always."

When I hear the shuffle of feet approaching my office, I think it's Emma coming back, and I simply refuse to deal with her.

I look up, the nastiest expletives I can think of dancing on my tongue, but they die right there. It's not Emma darkening my door but Amy, and I don't think I've ever been so happy to see anyone in my life. I almost go up to her and hug her. I get up from my chair, but then I see the expression on her face. I know Amelia Brooks well enough to realize I'm in trouble.

"Amy! I'm sorry I didn't wait for you," I begin. "I needed to get away. I don't think I would have been able to deal with Daniel just then. I don't know if I can at all."

Amy shrugs, and she steps into the office. "I took a cab; it's fine."

Okay. So she wasn't mad about that.

"If this is about Laurie, I don't know what Daniel told you, but I'm sure he exaggerated. We were together, yes. But that was a long time ago. A lifetime ago, actually."

"Really?" she asks, her face twisted into a disbelieving mask. She is at my desk now, looking down at me, the full extent of her anger washing down at me like a high tide.

"Yes. Daniel only hired her to distract me, I'm sure. I'm not proud of it, but he outmaneuvered me this time."

But Amy has stopped listening to me. Her eyes fall on the piece of paper Emma left, the one that is still on my desk, the very last thing I wanted Amy to see. I make a desperate swipe for it, but she is faster. She snatches it off the desk and steps away, her eyes already darting across the paper.

It's hopeless, I realize. Even if I can somehow get it out of her hands, she has probably already read enough to guess what it is. And there's no way I'm getting it out of her hands when she's in that mood. So I sit quietly, knowing her wrath is coming, trying to remember her as she was; shy, gentle Amelia Brooks. Funny, warm, adorable, awkward, clumsy Amy. Because I know all that is about to change.

Right on cue, she turns to me, and the look on her face is truly heartbreaking. "Is this true?" she asks.

"It's a misrepresentation of the facts, Amy, at best."

"Don't lawyer-talk me! Is this true."

"I'm not. If you'll just let me explain …"

"Yes or no, Robert. Did you work this woman until she had a mental breakdown?"

I shake my head. One of my professors used to say that yes and no answers are the worst things a lawyer can be faced with. "I can't give you a yes or no answer, Amy, because it's way more complicated than that. Yes, she did have a mental breakdown. But no, I did not work her hard enough to trigger it."

"So, you're saying you didn't play a part in it?"

"Again, Amy …"

"Yes or no?"

I sit back in my chair, and for the first time, a stubborn edge creeps into my voice. The old defense mechanism. Never let them dictate the attack.

"I think you already think I did," I say. "You've made up your mind about that letter, and about me, and you're looking for validation so you can decide how you feel about me. Well, I'm not going to give you the satisfaction, Amy. I can tell you the details of that story if you want, but only if you want to hear the truth and not just confirm your biases."

She falls silent. I can almost see the gears turning in her head.

"What happened between you and Laurie?"

"What?" I ask, wrong-footed by the sudden side-step.

"You heard me."

"I told you, that was a long time ago."

"What was a long time ago?"

I know it's the wrong time, but I'm struck by just how pressed and cornered I feel, and the nagging realization that Amy would make an excellent lawyer, the way she is grilling me.

"I don't know what you heard, Amy, but I wish you'd give me the benefit of the doubt, at the very least."

"I'm trying to, but you don't seem to be able to give me a straight answer, Robert."

I have no idea what to say to that.

"Okay. Here's a simple one. Why did you hire me?"

It is at that moment I realize she must have spoken with Laurie. When I left her alone in the courtroom, Laurie must have pulled her aside and fed her the usual story she liked to peddle around. If that's the case, then I'm fighting a losing battle here. Amy knows the answers to these questions; she's simply giving me a chance to dig myself even further into my own grave.

"Let me put it this way. In terms you can understand. Did you hire me specifically so you could dangle me in front of your nemesis like some sort of bait?"

I want to joke that I plead the fifth, but I doubt she will take it in the tone I want her to. She seems to take my hesitation as an unspoken agreement, and her face sets. She reaches into her pocket and pulls out something, throws it onto my desk.

"I guess I won't be needing this," she says. "Look at that. The record is still intact. I quit."

She turns and walks away, and for the life of me, I can't think of a single way to stop her from leaving.

17

Amy

"You look different."

Ness holds me out at arm's length, much like a concerned parent would, and inspects me with narrowed eyes. I'm so happy to see her, I melt into her arms, hugging her tightly.

"Seriously," she says again. "Something has changed … your whole vibe is different."

I shrug, smiling sweetly. "Maybe it's that whole 'not seeing my best friend for months' thing. Messes up one's vibe, from what I hear."

"You're being dramatic. It's only been a few weeks."

I gasp, a bit too theatrically, and clutch my heart in horror. "A few weeks? Do you have any idea how much has happened in my life since the last time I saw you?"

She has a point, though. It has not been that long, but it seems like it. With all that went down with Robert and the case, I've been living in the fast lane, and it was only when I stepped away from it all that I realized how drab my life was otherwise. How simple.

"How was I supposed to know you would go and get cool after law school?" Ness says. True to character, Ness decided to travel after school, see the world. She only got back from her latest jaunt a few days ago.

"What are you talking about? I didn't get any cooler than I already was."

"Look at you being cute. As if the streets are not alive with gossip about what you did. *Who* you did."

"What streets? What gossip?"

"Come on, let's sit down. People are starting to stare."

She shimmies into the booth and drags me in with her. We sit on the same side, just like we always have in restaurants. It's a shot of nostalgia.

"Lawyers talk, you know," Ness says. She leans towards me and stares at me like she's reading my mind.

"When did you find time to seek out gossip?" I ask, attempting to deflect the direction the conversation was heading in. "You just got in."

"Like I said, lawyers talk. They're gossips, the whole bunch of them. I kept in touch with some of our old law school friends. And from what I hear, you have been one busy little bee, Amelia Brooks."

"I'm sure you've been misinformed."

"Well, then, it's a good thing we got together, isn't it? You can straighten the story out. It won't make up for the fact that you didn't tell me any of this while it was happening, but still …"

"Really, Ness? I wasn't about to burden you with my trivial nonsense while you were climbing the Kilimanjaro or exploring the Louvre."

"Oh my God, Amy, you should definitely come with me next time. The world is so much more beautiful than this." She waves a hand around, her lip curled in distaste at the drab streets around us.

I imagine, after all she has seen, coming back home must be a big letdown. "What was it like?" I ask her. "Where did you go? Come on, tell me everything."

"Uh, uh, Amy. We're talking about you here. What is this I hear about you and infamous prick Robert Hardy?"

"You know him?" I blurt out.

"Of course I know him. Everyone in town knows him, and not for the right reasons. Every douchebag lawyer wants to be him; every shallow, vapid woman wants to sleep with him. He has quite the reputation. When you told me you'd gotten a job at Galweather & Meyer, I had no idea you meant working for him. I would have told you to turn it down."

"Really?"

"Absolutely."

"Well, it was more complicated than just turning the job down."

"What are you talking about?"

I take a deep breath and let it out in a long sigh.

"Remember the Smith party you dragged me to that final week of school?"

"Yeah?"

"And you remember how you left me alone with one of the Smiths?"

"Miles. He wasn't up for the threesome."

"Ew, Ness."

"Hey, you're the prude here, not me."

"Right. Anyway, Miles slipped something in my drink, and he tried to take advantage of me."

Ness's eyes pop, and her mouth drops open. "What!"

"Yeah. And he would have too if some handsome stranger hadn't stopped him and taken me home."

"Why didn't you tell me any of this?" Ness asks.

"Honestly? I was embarrassed. And I knew you were friends with the Smiths ..."

"Really, Amy? That's how little you think our friendship means to me?"

"It's not that, no. I just didn't want to make a big deal out of it. Nothing happened, and Robert made sure Miles was punished by the school ..."

"Wait. Robert? As in Robert Hardy? He was the stranger?"

"Yes. I was getting to that, but yeah. He was at the party for reasons that were not clear at the time, and he saw Miles slip something in my drink, followed him as he led me away, and stopped him before he could do anything. Then he drove me to the dorm and ..." I feel the color seep into my cheeks. I try to look away, but Ness is too sharp to miss it.

"Holy shit, you slept with him!" Her voice is louder than I would like, and it carries through the restaurant. I think I hear it echo back at us, but I may be imagining things.

She grabs me by both cheeks and turns me to face her. Her eyes are burning in the unique way they do when she's involved in salacious gossip. "Who are you, and what have you done to my sweet, innocent best friend?"

"Calm down; I didn't sleep with him." I want to add 'that night,' but I'm afraid Ness will shriek in excitement and draw even more attention to us.

"But you did something. I can see it in your eyes."

"We made out. Well, I kissed him."

"Holy shit, woman. That's why you decided to work for him?"

"As I said, it's complicated. I got a call a few days later from G&M asking me in for an interview, even though I didn't remember applying. Then when I got there, I see Robert sitting behind that desk, ready to conduct the interview, and he acts like he has never met me before."

"He didn't remember sticking his tongue down your throat? I told you he's an asshole."

"That's not even half of it, though. He did go on acting like nothing happened between us, but then he was also treating me like a sorority pledge or something. Working there was hell, Ness. I can't even tell you."

"And then you slept with him."

"Damn it, woman, will you let me tell the story or not?"

"Well, get to the good stuff already!"

I shake my head. It's very typical of Ness. But I've been stalling, and she knows it. I tell her about Robert and me, keeping the story as concise and PG 13 as I can. She prods and pushes, asking for details at every stage. When I tell her about the office sex, she stops speaking for a full minute, and her shock is only topped by me telling her about the apartment sex.

"Shit." That's all she seems to be able to say once I'm done. She shakes her head in disbelief. "I had sex on an island, with a native who could not speak a word of English, and somehow I had the more boring month of the two of us."

I don't know what to say to that. I want to shrug it off, tell her it was nothing to write home about, but I'd be lying, and if there's one thing Ness is infuriatingly good at, it's calling me out on my bullshit.

"I knew something was different about you," she says, bringing her eyes back to my face. "You've been ravished. You have that glow about you." Her gaze is unrelenting, cutting me into ribbons. "But there's also a world of pain in your eyes." Her tone is suddenly somber, serious. "You love him, don't you? And he broke your heart."

She drags the rest of the story out of me, with some deductive work aided by her knowing me so damn well and pointed questions that remind me just how good a lawyer she is going to be. I thought I would be angry talking about Robert and what he had done to me. I thought I would be disaffected, aloof. But I am far from disaffected. Reliving the truth, that Robert had set out to use me from the get-go, reopens the wound, and the emotions that bubble to the surface are betrayal and shame.

"The thing that hurts the most is that I knew who he was. I knew exactly what I was dealing with. But I kept going back. I kept talking myself into giving him chances, turning a blind eye to his shadier qualities. It's my own fault, really."

"Don't be absurd, Amy. None of this was your fault. I won't let you take credit for some guy's stupidity. Actually, you know what? We're not going to talk about Robert Hardy anymore. If he couldn't see how incredible you are, then that's his loss. Forget about him."

Ness reaches over and wipes away a tear I didn't realize I had shed.

"Not to ruin the mood, but we should order something. The waiter over there has been giving me the stink-eye the whole time we've been sitting here."

Castor & Sons is a small, decidedly intimate firm. It feels as I'm sure Mr. Castor intended, like a small family. Everyone is upbeat and friendly. The atmosphere is one of cheeriness, and the office setting is open and inviting. As soon as you walk in, you feel comfortable and welcome. It's a far cry from the cold, often clinical feel of Galweather & Meyer.

I'm ushered in by Mr. Castor himself, which is in itself very telling. No overdressed young intern waving me into an empty room with the promise of a coffee. No stuffy, cocky young man leering at me as I wait in the reception. I am met at the door by the man himself and offered a warm handshake.

"You must be Miss Brooks."

"Mr. Castor?"

Castor is a tall, middle-aged man with a spectacular handlebar mustache. His hair is greying in spots, but it adds to the overall sense of calm authority on his face. His eyes are heavily wrinkled around the corners, and when he smiles, his thick eyebrows come together almost comically. "Call me Ed, I insist."

"It's very nice to meet you, Ed."

"Come, Ms. Brooks. Let me show you around our little shop."

The little shop is not so little. The building is modest, compared to G&M, but then everything is modest compared to that behemoth. A large open floorplan with several desks, each customized to suit its owner, opens up into what Ed calls the 'business end.' This is comprised of a few offices with completely transparent walls and open doors lining each side of the room. It doesn't look like any law firm I've ever been to. Hell, it doesn't look like any office I've ever been to.

Ed takes me around the office making booming introductions to his staff. I'm thrown by this. It's not exactly standard procedure for a manager to be introducing an applicant to the staff *before* their interview. What if I don't get the job?

"And this," he says finally, standing and waving for me to walk into the largest of the transparent offices. "This is my office."

I walk in and sit down on the chair he indicates. He mutters something about getting me a coffee, then pirouettes and rushes back out of the office.

I pull out my documents and place them on the table. I am determined not to have a repeat of my last job interview. This time I'm going to be professional, assured, confident. I spent the whole night preparing, looking up this firm, reading up on some of their cases, and brushing up my CV. I am confident I'll do well.

Ed returns with a cup in his hands and sets it on the desk in front of me. "Sugar?" he asks, producing tiny white sachets from his pocket. I nod, and he empties one into my cup and stirs.

It feels weird that I'm being served by the boss. Unsettling, somehow, but I put that down to the long period of torture under You-Know-Who. Imagining him getting me coffee is almost farcical.

"Thank you," I say, and Ed smiles. He sits right across from me, not on the other side of the table. He leans back and watches me quietly, until, after some time, I start to wonder if perhaps he is waiting for me to say something.

"Drink your coffee," he prompts, and I bring the cup up to my lips.

"Right then," he says after I take a sip. "Where to begin? As you can see, we're not exactly a big firm. But we're a very good one, and we take a lot of pride in our work. We are a family here, and we run our business based on that core concept. If you join us, Ms. Brooks, you will be joining a team that works diligently to solve cases and help our clients, pooling all our resources, chiefly the human resource, to make a difference. I know we cannot compete with some of the other, larger firms in the city, certainly not in terms of pay. But I'm confident enough to tell you that you won't find a better working environment anywhere else. I guarantee it."

"I'm sorry, sir," I say, confused. "I thought I was here for an interview?"

Because it sounds very much like he is the one being interviewed.

"And you are, yes," Ed says. "I already looked through the papers you sent over. And even if those were not convincing enough, I have had the pleasure of speaking to someone who worked closely with you, and I must say, they couldn't recommend you highly enough."

My stomach sinks. He has spoken to my former boss.

"Frankly, Ms. Brooks, we'd be lucky to have you. Which is why *I'm* the one pitching Castor & Sons to you. I'm confident you would be an asset to us."

"May I ask who you spoke with, sir?"

"Please. Ed."

"Sorry. Ed."

He leans forward and frowns. His brows knit as he thinks, and I wonder why he hesitated.

"I spoke with a charming lady by the name of Susan, I believe. She had only wonderful things to say about you."

The relief on my face must be visible because Ed notices and smiles. "Ah, did you think I was referring to Mr. Hardy?"

There's no point denying it. "I did, yes."

"And you're worried Mr. Hardy would not say the same

about you? I imagine because of the disastrous way his case turned out?"

At that moment, I see the lawyer in Ed. He is clearly intelligent, well-informed. But he leads with charm and polite banter, and that is a deadly way to disarm your opponent. He is the complete opposite of You-Know-Who.

"I'm well aware of Mr. Hardy and his methods. As I am with Daniel Goldman and his. I think it's unfortunate that you found yourself in the middle of those two matadors, because the result of that collision is always going to be mutual distraction, and in the worst-case scenario, a shocking amount of collateral damage. I have nothing but respect for anyone who worked for Robert Hardy for as long as you did, Ms. Brooks. It shows, if nothing else, grit and resourcefulness. So you don't need to worry about what Mr. Hardy thinks of you. Having met you, however briefly, I am inclined to believe the glowing recommendation our mutual friend Susan provided."

Whether it is his intention or not, his words have a profound calming effect on me. I feel relieved, comfortable, at home. It would be nice to work at a place like this for a change, where I'm met by positivity like this. And where I don't have to question whether or not I'm wanted.

"Thank you, Ed," I say, and I can't help smiling myself.

"Good," Ed beams. "Now, I've already given you the tour, you've met the team. All that's left is for you to say yes, Ms. Brooks."

There is a pause, during which the tiniest flicker of doubt crosses my mind. Why? It's a perfect place to work, and it represents the opposite of everything I hated about G&M. So why am I hesitating?

"Tell you what," Ed chips in, sensing my hesitation. "You can take the rest of the week to think about it. No rush. And then we can sit down Monday and discuss your contract. That's how confident I am that you'll be joining us."

"Okay," I say. "That would be wonderful, thank you."

"Excellent."

I start to rise, but Ed holds out a hand, and I fall back into the chair.

"Please, Ms. Brooks. Finish your coffee. No one is kicking you out."

18
Robert

I think the briefcase is a stroke of genius.

It strikes just the right balance between theatrical and businesslike. It's comically large, for one, and it reminds me of mob movies, where cash is always trading hands in the form of an inconspicuous black briefcase.

Emma sees it and scoffs. "Was that really necessary?" she asks, plopping down onto the seat across from me. We are in an open park area, where a food truck has set up for the day, and the owner has set out a few small tables and chairs for his customers. Having the meeting outside was another inspired idea, I think. Less chance of Emma's shenanigans. She is crazy, but not crazy enough to try anything stupid in public.

"This old thing?" I ask, smiling. "How else am I supposed to hand over a hundred thousand dollars?"

"How about like a normal person? Check, money transfer. This isn't 1980."

"Well, maybe I'm just old-fashioned like that. I believe any transaction, especially one where such money is involved, should be done face to face."

"You didn't share this sentiment with the last payment." She is getting irritable. Good.

"Do you want the money or not, Emma?"

She makes a clicking sound with her tongue and reaches over the table for the briefcase. I yank it away and put it on the ground beside me.

"Not so fast, sweetheart," I say.

Emma's eyes narrow in suspicion. "What is this, Robert?"

"Like I said, old-fashioned. I have the money. Now you just have to assure me your reporter won't publish that story. If you can convince me that he won't, you can have it."

"He won't. You have my word."

I laugh, a short, disbelieving snort. "You seriously expect me to leave here on the strength of your word? Come on, Emma. This moved beyond verbal excuses when you started making threats."

"Well, what do you want me to do? I'm telling you he won't run the story. He already killed it."

I sit back in the chair and stare at her, my mouth a thin line. "Prove it."

Emma stares at me for a long moment. She really is a beautiful woman. Even while she looks a bit shabby, she is still stunning to look at. It's a shame she doesn't have the character to go along with it. Eventually, she grabs her phone and dials a number. She pushes the hair out of the way and puts the phone to her ear.

"No," I say. "Put it on speaker."

She frowns at me, but she lowers the phone, puts it on speaker, and lays it on the table.

After a few rings, a voice on the other end cuts in, sleepy and slightly irritated. "Hey, baby. Is everything okay?"

Baby? Of course.

"Yes, yes," Emma says quickly. "You're on speaker. I'm here with Robert Hardy. He wants our assurance that you won't publish the story I had you write."

"Oh. I was never going to run that story. Not without sitting down with him and getting his side of things. I'm a journalist, you know, not a tabloid reporter."

Emma glares at me as if to say "See?"

"To be clear," I say, leaning forward so I can speak directly into the phone. "If I see any version, any permutation of this story anywhere, I will sue you and everyone you work with. If I hear of any of this again, I will sue you and your accomplice here for extortion. Do you understand?"

"That sounds like a threat, Mr. Hardy."

"You're damn right it's a threat." I reach over and end the call. "Baby?" I say to Emma. "You're sleeping with him?"

"I don't believe that's any of your business," Emma says, her voice heavy with scorn. Defiant. Defensive. I've hit a nerve.

"Let me guess," I plow on, thrilled that I have the advantage for the first time since the woman showed up at my office. "You promised him you would share the loot? 50-50? Maybe a little more for you since this was your idea? But you're not really going to give him anything, are you? You just used him, and now that his role is done, you'll dump him and ride off into the sunset, until you blow all your money and need to weasel your way into some more."

"Not everyone makes a living using people, Robert," she says, but she looks rattled. "As I said, it's no longer any of your business who I sleep with."

"And what is that supposed to mean?"

Emma grins and leans forward. "Oh, come on, Robert. I saw the way you used to look at me. The comments you used to make about me, the way I dressed. The long nights you'd make me stay in the office in the pretext of working. I know you wanted me. Maybe you still do?"

I feel something brush against my leg, and the next thing I know, Emma's foot is on my crotch. "You're deluded," I say, reaching down and pushing her leg away. "As always."

"You can pretend all you want, Robert. But I know you. I know that tough exterior you like to put up is a front. I know you only abuse your assistants like that because deep down, you're angry you can't have them. And even when you do get them, you know they'll run as soon as they see the real you."

She slumps back in her seat, satisfied that she has landed a blow.

"I do not abuse my assistants," I tell her. I hate that she has regained the upper hand. Now I'm the one backpedaling.

"No?"

"No. I push them to be the best versions of themselves. I work them hard, yes, but that's because I'm a perfectionist, not out of some sadistic desire to punish them for anything. If they can't handle the pressure and the demands of the job, that's not my fault."

"*If* they can't? Is that a sly dig at me, Robert? Because I'll have you know, you'll never get another assistant like me. I gave everything for that job. I was young and naïve, and I thought I was doing it to impress you, so I killed myself for a stupid job I didn't even want. If *I* couldn't handle it, and no one has been able to since, what do you think that says about you?"

"I think it says more about you than it does me. You said it yourself. You couldn't handle it. Whether it happened a week after you started working for me or a month later, you having that breakdown was inevitable."

"What a callous thing to say, Robert. Even for you. So now I'm responsible for my own mental breakdown?"

"Do you even remember what happened to cause your breakdown? Or are you too caught up in your little narrative to care about the truth?"

"You know what I think? I think you're wasting my time. I don't think you have my money, and you're trying to weasel your way out of paying. Enough talk. Pay up, or I redial my journalist lover."

"You mean the guy who just admitted he doesn't have a story?"

"I see you've decided not to take me seriously again. That was your last chance, Robert."

She gets up and gathers her things in a huff, clearly intending to storm off.

It's now or never, Robert.

"Sit down, Emma. I have your money."

I reach into my coat pocket and pull out the contract. I slide it across the table and indicate with a nod for her to sit back down.

Her eyebrows crease, and her frown deepens, but she does sit down. She grabs the contract and begins to read it.

"That's a legally binding document stating that this is the last payment I'm making to you and that once this is done, you have no grounds to come after me again."

"This was not the agreement."

"I'm changing the agreement. Surely, you don't expect me to keep doing this with you, do you? I shouldn't have paid you off the first time. That was my mistake. But if you don't sign that document, then nothing is stopping you from holding me at ransom every other month for the rest of my life. This is it, Emma. Either you take this money and walk away, or I give you nothing, and you do your worst."

I lift the briefcase and put it back on the table to emphasize my point. Emma's eyes dart from me to the briefcase. I can almost see the cogs turning in her mind as she tries to work out how to dodge this little complication. But she has no more moves, and she knows it.

"Pen," she says, and I hand her one from my pocket.

She scribbles the document angrily and slides it back to me. As I look it over, she grabs the briefcase and starts to fiddle over the lock.

"You disappoint me, Emma," I say, shaking my head.

"What?"

"You were supposed to be the best of them. The great Number 10. The one all the others aspired to but never quite emulated."

"What are you talking about ..."

She clicks the briefcase open, and the sight of her confused expression is genuinely cathartic. She grabs the recording device, the only thing in the suitcase, and holds it up to me.

"So you were recording our conversation," she says, shrugging. "It doesn't matter. I didn't say anything incriminating."

"I didn't think you would, to be honest. I just needed something to put in the briefcase. I was going for a subtle mafia/mob boss thing, but it didn't quite come together. No, Emma. *This* is the document that spells out your defeat."

I wave the contract she just signed in her face.

"How many times have I told you, Emma? Always read the document before signing it. That is literally the first lesson I taught you. Or tried to, anyway."

She looks panicked now. Her eyes are wide, and her mouth is hanging open.

"This is a statement admitting to attempted blackmail, duly signed and dated, thank you very much. Now, I may not be the lawyer I once was, but I'm pretty sure this would convince a judge in the event I chose to sue. What do you think?"

I'm grinning now. I can't help myself. I can smell my victory, and it is a heady, intoxicating scent. My favorite part of any legal tussle has always been this exact moment. When the opponent realizes they have been beaten. When they feel the jaws of the trap closing in around them. When their soul crumbles, and the little flicker of hope is extinguished in their eyes. It's a beautiful moment. It's the reason I became a lawyer.

Emma thinks for a long time. I sit quietly and watch her,

knowing there isn't anything she can do to retake the initiative. This little war is over, and we both know it.

"Okay," she eventually says. "Okay."

Still grinning, I reach back into my coat and pull out another slip of paper. Emma watches me silently. She doesn't even reach for the paper when I slide it over to her.

"This is a check for five thousand dollars. It's all I can afford to give you right now. I wish it didn't have to go down this way, Emma, I really do. I wish you had just come to me and told me you needed money. I would have found a way to help you out. But. I'm not the monster you think I am. I'm not giving you this money because you threatened me, or because I'm trying to shut you up. I'm giving it to you because once upon a time we were friends, even if you don't remember it, even if it was colored by a frosty boss-assistant dynamic. I know you're in trouble. So here. I hope this helps you, even if only in a small way. But please. Enough with the blackmail attempts. Frankly, it's beneath you."

19
Robert

The new assistant reminds me of Amy.

She looks nothing like her; she is perky and bubbly, with a restless energy that spills over to her work. Amy was more nervous and twitchier and constantly looking over her shoulder. Veronica is more confident, but then I already knew that when I hired her.

For the first time since I started looking for assistants, I decided to forego the whole temp process and even the traditional method of advertising. It has proven largely ineffective, if the endless string of failed or departed assistants is anything to go by. I remembered Veronica completely by chance. I was going over my contacts, trying to figure out who I could call to recommend a good assistant for me when I saw the name Veronica Sharpe and a phone number scribbled on a piece of paper, tucked away in the depths of my wallet.

I remembered her right away. The girl who had come up to me at the same party where I met Amy. The eager blonde who had virtually begged me for a job. The timing couldn't have been any more perfect.

As expected, Veronica is an excellent worker. She is brilliant at the legal side of things; she has a near-photographic memory, and she has already proven herself useful at pointing out precedents in cases she's assigned. Her work ethic is flawless. She is always the first person in and the last out, even when I work late. She has perfected the art of anticipating my needs; it has become something of an inside joke that when I ask her to do something, she has already done it. Like the time I asked her to get me a coffee and she pointed to the steaming cup on my desk. I haven't had any cause to even raise my voice at her.

It seems I may have finally solved my assistant crisis, because, by all indications, Veronica is going to go all the way.

And yet.

My only problem with her is how much she reminds me of Amy.

She doesn't even do it consciously. It would be more accurate to say I am reminded of Amy by things Veronica does. Her personality is so radically different from Amy's that I find myself comparing the two of them all the time. Like when I ask Veronica for information on a case, and she goes into a detailed breakdown of all the aspects of that case. Yet all I can think about is how flustered Amy would have been by that very same question, and how her cheeks would have flamed as she tried to answer, how she would have wanted to be sure she had done her research before providing me with an answer.

Or how Veronica's wardrobe consists entirely of different shades of black and blue suits, and she dresses with prim professionalism that is both impressive and a bit off-putting. Amy had a very loose sense of what could pass as work attire. Often, she threw the rule book completely out the window and went for something she would be comfortable in, or something she knew would draw my attention and keep it for the rest of the day.

I have been unable to stop thinking about her since she left. It has only been a few weeks, but I could swear it's been months. There is a certain drabness to everything now that she's gone. I'm no longer excited about work, even though I need to come up with a new strategy for the Mendel case. For some time, the situation with Emma kept me busy and focused all my obsessive energy. But once I was done with that, I was forced to confront the fact that there wasn't much else I liked about my life.

Susan let it slip today that Amy is fielding offers from several law firms in the city, and I'm not sure how to feel about it. On the one hand, I feel proud of her for standing up for herself and getting out of a situation that ultimately wasn't what she wanted. But on the other hand, I know that it wasn't really the job she walked away from; it was me.

I want to talk to her so desperately it's almost an ache. I need to make things right with her. I need to apologize to her; admit I was wrong, and maybe things would get back to how they were. Except I'm not sure I want them to go back to how they were. I want more. I want the Amelia who would sit on my couch and open up to me, the woman who would eat cold pizza in my T-shirt and watch me work. I want the version of her she didn't show to anyone but me.

But the harsh reality is that I'm not going to get any version of Amy back, and that is almost unbearable.

Almost.

I have fallen back into old patterns.

For the past two days, I have been coming to an exclusive club I used to frequent back when I was a young, hotshot lawyer. I didn't do anything the first time I went. Yesterday, I ordered a drink, then another, and then I asked the waiter to leave the bottle.

Today, though, something has happened. I have been approached.

I wouldn't have noticed her if she didn't come up to me. She probably only comes up to me because she realizes I am blind to my surroundings, and that I wouldn't have seen whatever signals she was throwing at me.

She is older, wealthy, and attractive. Not the overstated beauty of some of the other women who frequent the club. Hers is more subtle, the well-kept beauty of a woman who has been around the block a few times and learned to take care of herself. Her hair is short, falling softly around a handsome oval face. Her eyes are gray, and she has a tiny button nose and lush, moist lips. Her dress is silk; it hugs her body all the way down to a visible swell in the hips. Curvy. Feminine without being overly sexual.

"Are you done checking me out?" she asks. There is no trace of shame in her voice.

"For now," I say.

"And? Do you like what you see?"

"I don't hate it."

"Hard to impress, I see. Well, I'll take it as a challenge." She slides onto the high chair next to me. She does it in one fluid, graceful motion. Her dress parts as she sits down, revealing thick, soft-looking thighs. "I would introduce myself, but I have this nagging feeling you don't really want to know my name."

"What makes you say that?" I ask her.

"Let's just say I know how to read people. Besides, by my count, you had two drinks, and now the bottle. I doubt you'll be able to remember my name even if I told you."

"Been watching me, have you?"

"You're a hard man not to notice. I must admit, I'm a little disappointed that I didn't strike you as much as you did me. But then again, I don't blame you. I know that look you have on your face. Drinking to forget. Never works, but it's always fun to try, right?"

I don't respond, gulping down my drink and pouring out another.

"Here's my proposal," she goes on. Confident. Undeterred. "You're clearly going through something, and I understand that. I don't want anything complicated. I don't think you do either. But that doesn't mean we can't have some fun with each other. I've reserved a suite upstairs. Room 12. I'm going to go up in a few minutes. I'll leave the door unlocked. I hope you join me."

She leans over and plants a kiss on my cheek. She smells wonderful. Then, with another generous flash of her thighs, she gets down off the chair and floats away.

I take my time finishing my drink, even though I'm no longer enjoying it. It occurs to me that this kind of proposal would have thrilled me a few months ago. I wouldn't even have thought about it. So why am I hesitating now? The woman has been clear; she does not want anything complicated, which used to be my favorite kind of relationship. She is definitely attractive, and her decisive, go-getter attitude is definitely a big plus. What's there to think about? I can't make a convincing argument for holding out and I know it. Amy is out of the picture, no matter how much I wish she weren't. If anything, a tryst with someone different might finally get her off my mind. Because nothing else has worked so far.

I get up, still thinking. Maybe I'll figure it out when I get to the door. Maybe that will be the moment of clarity.

I feel the room spin as I walk out, and I realize I'm actually drunk. Just. I amble along to the elevator, and it's only once I'm inside that I realize I have no idea what floor I'm going to. Room 12. That could be anywhere. I decide to take my chances on the first floor. Luckily, I find the room easily enough; it's the farthest one from the lobby.

I pause at the door, my fist raised.

There is no whoosh of clarity, no sudden epiphany. If anything, my mind is completely blank. But I cannot turn back now. One way or the other, this is happening. I tap gently on the door, then try the handle. It swings open as promised, and I walk in slowly.

She is perched on the edge of a couch, looking towards me with a huge smile. So she wasn't sure I would come, despite her confidence. She has shed her dress in favor of a sheer cream nightgown. Sheer enough that I can make out the contours and outline of her.

She gets up and walks toward me, her hips swaying seductively as she does. "I'm so glad you decided to come," she says, putting her hands around my neck and pulling my head down towards her.

"I haven't actually decided," I say.

She shakes her head and kisses me on the mouth, a soft, inquiring peck of her lips. "Yes, you have," she whispers. "You're here, aren't you?"

"Maybe I just wanted to see the rest of you," I say.

She smiles and lets her hands slip from around my neck. Her eyes never leaving mine, she reaches for the shoulder straps of her gown and lifts them, and lets them fall one at a time. The gown slinks to the floor, and she is naked.

Even with the room spinning, I have no difficulty focusing on her. She is extremely curvy, even more than I initially thought. Her body is full of soft swells and dips, curves, and contours. This is a woman, a full-bodied woman who knows she's sexy and owns her figure. Her breasts glisten in the low light of the room, two large globes begging to be touched. Her hips curve outward and backward, into what I'm sure is a voluptuous behind.

I feast on her with my eyes, appreciating how sexy she really is.

"How about now?" she asks after a while. "Do you like what you see?"

"Oh, I like it very much."

Reassured, she takes a step towards me and starts to undress me. Her fingers are nimble and quick. In a few moments, my shirt is crumpled in a heap on the floor, and she is helping me out of my pants. She pushes me back against the door and kisses me hard. She tastes of wine. She feels soft all over. I let my hands explore; on her shoulders, down her back, down to her ass where I cup and squeeze.

She moans into my mouth and deepens the kiss. Her tongue

darts out, and I send mine out to meet it. They lock and clash in the space between our mouths, and now she's writhing and grinding against my midriff.

"What's wrong?" she asks after some time, speaking mostly into my mouth.

"What?" I mumble, and then I realize what she's talking about. My dick is still soft. "Oh. I've been drinking. Takes a while to get going."

She nods, but there is an unreadable expression on her face. She steps away, takes my hand, and leads me across the room. It is large and luxurious, with plush furniture and thick, soft rugs, and large abstract paintings lining the walls. She leads me into the bedroom, a smaller room off to the right of the suite.

Her hands are slightly sweaty as she pushes me onto the bed, and I wonder if she may be more nervous than she's letting on. She climbs onto the bed after me and mounts me. She reaches for my eyes and draws them shut with her fingers. The weight on me shifts, and then I feel damp lips peck at my forehead, then start to work their way down.

She trails soft, feathery kisses all over my face, lingering for a delicious moment on my lips, nibbling, and suckling on them. Then she pulls away again, and now she is at my chest, then at my navel. She has clearly done this before. She is using the anticipation of her touch as a tool, bringing me right to the edge of longing, not knowing when she's going to kiss me next, where her lips will be. Which is why it takes me completely by surprise when I feel those inquiring lips close around my still soft dick.

She starts to suck, letting her tongue travel along the full length of my shaft, teasing the slit at the top of my head, then wrapping her mouth all the way around and taking me all the way to the hilt.

My dick twitches and starts to grow hard, but not nearly hard enough for my liking. I'm starting to worry now. This has never happened to me. I've never had to worry about my ability to perform, no matter how drunk I've gotten in the past. Something is wrong.

I let my eyes slide open so I can get a good look at her. Maybe the sight of her head bobbing up and down will stoke the fire. Or the visual of her ass, curved sweetly in the air, a small pale mountain disappearing off the edge of the bed.

Think of her breasts, Robert. Think about how perfect and rounded they are. Think about what you can do to those tits.

She is picking up the pace now, sucking faster and faster. Her hands are fondling my balls, in time with the motion of her neck and mouth. I should be loving this. I should be halfway to orgasm by now. Why am I not?

She straightens up without warning, and her lips make a smacking sound as she lifts her head from my groin. I don't need to look down to see that her best efforts have done nothing to improve the situation. Defeated, she shifts and drops onto the bed beside me. "Well, that's unflattering," she says after some time.

I'm too embarrassed to look at her, so I keep my gaze fixed on the ceiling. "I'm so sorry," I hear myself say. "You're gorgeous, really. Sexy. I know it's a cliché, but this has never happened to me before." When I finally gather enough courage to steal a glance at her, I'm surprised to see her smiling.

"What's her name?" she asks me.

"What?"

"What's her name?" she asks again. "The woman you're in love with."

"What has that got to do with anything?" I ask.

"Most of the time, nothing," she says. "But this happens sometimes. I've seen it before, I should say. There's no shame in it at all. I think it's beautiful."

"I'm pretty sure I have no idea what you're talking about."

She laughs, then lifts herself and swings one leg over me, mounting me once more. She leans forward, and I wrap my hands around her waist.

"It's a remarkable thing, the human body," she says, looking deep into my eyes. It feels rather intimate and uncomfortable, but I'm pinned under her weight, and part of me is still hoping my treacherous dick will spring to life at any moment. "We can lie to ourselves all the time, but our bodies always reveal the truths we're not willing to admit to ourselves. Let's try this again. What's her name?"

Something about how close we are makes it incredibly

difficult to lie to her. "Amelia," I tell her. "Amy."

She smiles, then leans forward and kisses me again on the lips. "Shame. She's a lucky girl, Amy." She pushes herself off me and gets up off the bed. "I'll go get us some drinks, and you can tell me all about her."

20
Amelia

I wake up with a start, jerking upright in bed and looking wildly around in the dark, not sure what woke me up but convinced that something did. In the time it takes my eyes to adjust to the darkness, my breathing slows down, and I repeat to myself that there is no one else in my bedroom.

But something did wake me up, a dream. The details are foggy, and the memory of the dream, so vivid mere seconds ago, is now fading faster than I can make sense of it. I was in an arena, I think, an open arena with low stands all around me, and sand digging into the soles of my feet. A bullfighting arena, I remember.

And two bulls were charging at me. That's what woke me up. The sickening crunch of their horns clashing. The sound, and the feeling, and the knowledge that I was about to be impaled by two bulls charging at each other. I was right in the middle, too, paralyzed with fear, unsure which way to duck or what to do.

I go into the kitchen to get myself a glass of water. It does not take me long to figure out why I was dreaming of bulls and matadors. Just before bed, I had been thinking about my interview with Ed Castor. My week was up. Tomorrow, I have to give him my final answer, whether I will be working for him or not. Or as I'm sure he'll insist, *with* him.

I've been going back and forth about that dilemma all week. But that's not what I had been thinking about just before drifting off. It was something Ed had said during the interview, in reference to Robert and Daniel going up against each other. "The result of that clash is always going to be mutual destruction."

It makes sense that when I did fall asleep, my dreams were full of bulls and tall men with distinct jawlines. I didn't know why my mind lingered over that statement, but as I stand in the moonlight in my own kitchen, the full realization lands on me like a lead weight.

Mutual destruction.

Excited, I dash into the living room. It takes some finding, as I have not made any effort to clean my house in a long time, but I eventually locate the thick folder and stacks of papers representing the remnants of my career at Galweather & Meyer. My ill-fated, woefully short-lived career.

I flip through the papers, eager to test my theory, but I realize pretty quickly that the financial records are the smoking gun I need, and the last time I saw those I was on Robert Hardy's couch. But I'm on to something. I can feel it. If I'm right, I may just have figured out how to salvage the Mendel case. If only I can figure out a way to get a copy of those documents without having to see or speak to Robert …

I pick up the phone and dial Susan. I realize a second too late that it's 3 o'clock at night, and that I really shouldn't be calling anyone.

"Hello?" Susan sounds groggy. I'm surprised she picked up the phone at all.

"Hey, Susan. I'm sorry to call so late. I didn't realize the time."

"Amy?" she asks.

"Yeah. Hi."

"You owe me five hundred bucks."

"What?" I ask. "Why?"

"The betting pool!" I can almost picture her indignant face. "I was the only one who still had an active bet on you when you quit and cost me five hundred dollars and the eternal respect of my colleagues."

"I thought you were not supposed to acknowledge the betting pool, let alone take part in it."

"Completely beside the point, Amy. You couldn't wait one more week to quit?"

"How do you know I wasn't fired?"

"Because I know Robert Hardy. And I know you."

"Well, I'm sorry, Susan. I wasn't thinking about betting pools or anything of the sort. I had to get out of there, that's all."

"I get it, relax. I'm only teasing. So, why are you calling me in the middle of the night? What's going on?"

"Right. I need your help with something. By the way, thanks for putting in a good word for me with Ed Castor and whoever else you called."

"It was the least I could do. You were a good assistant, Amy."

"Thanks, Susan. You may be the only person who ever believed in me."

"So, how can I help you, then?"

"Is Robert still prepping for the Mendel case?"

"Yeah, he is. Although ..." Her voice trails off.

"What?"

"He has a new assistant," Susan says in a small voice.

Oh. Already? Why am I not surprised? Hopefully, this one will have better luck than I did. I speak quickly, to stop myself from thinking about the fact that I was ultimately just as disposable to Robert Hardy as all the women who came before, and probably the ones who will come after.

"Good for him. Anyway, if he's still on the case, then that means his case files are in his office. I need you to do a little sneaking around for me, Susan. There's a couple of files I need to look over."

I have spent all day thinking about what I'm going to say when I finally see him. The reason I'm having such difficulty surely has to do with the fact that I don't know how to feel toward him. I promised Ness I would put him out of my mind, and I did, for the most part. Off my lips and out of my mind. But my subconscious dredged him up easily enough. After all, he has done, here I am, still fighting to win his case.

And now, here I am, at his doorstep, again, nervous and anxious and more excited than I should be.

I knock, ring the doorbell, and stand there for almost twenty minutes before I accept that he isn't in. And that this was poor planning on my part. I was his assistant. I should know his schedule like the back of my hand. I should have confirmed if he was home first. All that mental preparation and I'm not even going to see him today.

I feel ... disappointed.

I stuff the documents back in my bag and turn away from his

door. So much for confronting my demons.

The clouds have darkened in the sky outside, and I can feel the first few drops of rain starting to fall. Another thing I did not plan for. I stop at the entrance to Robert's apartment complex, thinking. I could wait for him right there and not risk being rained on. It might be more practical than risking the rain when I'm still going to have to make this trip again, possibly tomorrow. After calling Susan and getting his schedule for the day, of course. I don't think I can handle another fruitless trip. I'll lose my nerve completely if I have to keep—

"Amy?"

He comes out of nowhere. Much like he did in my life. He is just there, suddenly materializing from thin air and filling my line of vision, along with the rest of my senses.

He is carrying flowers, which is nearly as unnerving as the accompanying rugged look he is sporting. He has grown out a small, neat beard that somehow makes him look even more attractive. His hair isn't slicked back and combed through like I'm used to. Whether it is because of the drizzle or a conscious decision, he looks like he just rolled out of bed and ran a hand through it. Accidentally unkempt on purpose. He looks divine. My heart aches at the sight of him, and my mouth dries up. Why am I here again?

"This is such a pleasant coincidence," he says. "I'm just coming from your place."

"What?"

"Yeah. Your neighbor told me I just missed you. I'm guessing we just missed each other."

"Wait. How do you know where I live?"

He shrugs, and I remember him asking me exactly the same question the last time I showed up here. He must be thinking about that too because he says, "Maybe I have a binder on you."

"It would be a very thin binder," I say.

"You would be surprised."

My eyes dart to the flowers. "Are those …?"

"For you, yes," Robert says, and he offers them to me. White roses. How very charming. "We should head upstairs. Before it starts raining in earnest."

He starts to take my hand but changes his mind halfway through it. His hand hangs in the air for an awkward second, and then he tucks it into his pocket and shoulders past me into the building. He is silent throughout the elevator ride, and as he opens the door and stands aside to let me in. Once inside, he walks to his bedroom, leaving me in the living room. He returns a few minutes later having changed into a gray T-shirt and sweatpants. Which I must now keep my eyes away from.

"Can I get you anything?" he asks as he sits down on the couch. I shake my head. He pats the spot on the couch next to him. I sit down reluctantly, a fair distance away from him. I do not trust myself around him at all.

"I think I'll go first," he says. "I owe you an apology. Several apologies, in fact. I wasn't honest with you from the beginning about why I hired you. I admit I had an ulterior motive when I came to your school and met you. I was recruiting with my case against Daniel in mind, and I was hoping to find a beautiful young girl I could use as bait to distract him. It was wrong, I don't deny it, and I'm truly sorry.

"The truth is, Amy, I got a lot more than I bargained for when I followed you into that room. And when you came to interview for a job here, I knew there was so much more to you than the silly role I hoped you'd play. I'm sorry I reduced you to that when you're such a wonderful, complicated person with way more to offer than I ever let you show.

"But most importantly, I'm sorry I wasn't open and honest with you about myself, my past, and everything else that's been going on in my life. The fact is, Amy, I was using our professional relationship as a shield, because I was afraid of caring about you, wanting to be more than just your boss. I hope you can forgive me, Amy. I need you to forgive me, because I can't do this case, or any other case, without you. I can't seem to do anything right without you."

There is such uncharacteristic vulnerability in his voice and demeanor I almost can't believe it's all coming from him.

"I guess this is probably not the best time to tell you I took a job with another firm," I say. "So I'm not sure I'll be able to help you with any cases going forward."

"Old man Castor's firm? Yeah, Susan mentioned it. Congratulations, Amy. They're lucky to have you."

"I hear you got a new assistant anyway, so you won't need me."

"Haven't you been listening? I *do* need you. Not as my assistant. As Amy, the woman I fell in love with."

He tries to reach out and take my hand, but I move it away. I still need answers. "What happened with the woman I found in your office the day I left? The one who claims you caused her mental breakdown?"

"Emily was helping me with a sensitive case involving rape and domestic abuse. I think it got to her, dealing with all that violence and unpleasantness. Coupled with the pressure I was piling on her to deliver, it was almost inevitable that she would crack. I'm not saying I was innocent in all this; I did ride her pretty hard. But she exaggerated the story and changed a lot of facts to paint me in a negative light. I was in the middle of a landmark case, and I didn't want the negative press, so I paid her some money so she would keep it quiet. That was my mistake. She was trying to extort me when you found her in my office. I only just managed to get her off my ass."

"So Robert Hardy is not the asshole everyone thinks he is?"

"Oh, I'm definitely an asshole," he says. He reaches for my hand again, and this time I let him. "But I'm trying to do better. I'm trying to be a better man for you." He brings my hand up to his lips and kisses the back of it.

I believe him because the Robert Hardy I know would never be this openly affectionate. His touch sends the usual tremors through my body. Unable to help myself, I lean forward and seize his lips in a kiss. I have missed him so much. But my body has missed him more. Within seconds, I am pressed up against him, like a jigsaw piece, and he is kissing me like he hasn't seen me in months.

"Wait," he says suddenly, breaking the kiss. "Why did you come here?"

"Oh. I figured out how to win the Mendel case. Or at least how to get Gregory's partner to back off. I realized why the financial records were so murky. The money being stashed in offshore accounts is in both their names. So if we go after Thomas for the same crime he's accusing Gregory of, I think it should be enough to make him reconsider."

Robert pulls me even closer and kisses me again. "I don't think I've ever been more attracted to someone in my life."

"Clearly," I say, rubbing my groin against his straining erection. "Now, what was that you were saying about being head over heels in love with me?"

But in the next moment, his hands have found the hem of my top, and his fingers on my nipples wipe every coherent thought from my mind.

21

Amelia

We are seated at a corner table in an unusually quiet restaurant in the middle of town. Robert is right next to me, so close I can feel the heat spilling from him, can almost taste his scent. I'm practically pressed up against the wall, and with Robert boxing me in, it's almost overwhelming. Almost. Because we're so close, it's all too easy for him to slide his hand slowly under the table and run it along my thigh. Because we're at the corner table of an almost deserted restaurant, there is no one watching. So I don't have to pretend to repress the shudder that goes through my body, or the way my cheeks immediately get flushed.

I snap my knees together, trapping Robert's wandering fingers in the space between my thighs. If my plan was to stop the heat from his hand flushing through my body, then it is a bad idea.

"Stop it," I admonish him in a whisper. He looks over at me with a smug smile.

"Are you sure?"

His eyes are glowing with mischief. And intent.

"Not here," I say, but I make no move to brush off his hands, and after a brief pause, he resumes the stroking motion. I throw panicked glances at the door, and then around the restaurant. No one has taken any notice of us. Our coffees are steaming quietly on the table, getting colder by the minute. Beneath the table, Robert's fingers breach the side of my panties, my last line of defense.

"I can't help it," Robert says, his lips right against my temple. "You know what this dress does to me."

I suppose I'm partly responsible. Besides the fact that we have both been finding it difficult to keep our hands off each other, I have not made things any easier for him with the dress I'm wearing. I knew we were coming for an important meeting, but I just couldn't help putting on the gorgeous sundress Ness brought me back from France. It sways and sashays in the wind, and it fills out my figure in ways I did not think possible. And, of course, it rides all the way up to my thighs when I sit down.

I try again: "You shouldn't start something you can't finish."

Somehow, my legs seem to have been spread even further apart. Even without the heated dampness of Robert's fingers, I know I'm soaking wet.

"That sounds like a challenge, Robert says. "Which I gladly accept."

He looks around the restaurant, his eyes eventually going into the corner where I know the bathroom is.

"Meet me in the men's washroom in five minutes."

He is off before I can protest. Do I even want to protest?

It amazes me that he can still get me this excited, even after all that has happened between us. I allow myself a moment of indulgence, but I know I'm kidding myself. When have I ever been able to say no to Robert Hardy?

I wait a little more than five minutes, just in case anyone is watching. I get up anxiously, nervously, feeling like someone somewhere definitely knows what I'm about to do. That they saw Robert head into the bathroom and will be proved right when I walk in after him.

But that worry is put to bed almost immediately. I hear a gentle tinkling sound, and the doors to the restaurant open. Daniel Goldman shoulders his way in with the usual exuberance and arrogance. His eyes sweep the entirety of the dining area, and ultimately fall to me, half-sitting, half-standing. Laurie Gibbons walks in behind him. She smiles and waves when she sees me, and they both turn and walk over to me.

"Hey, Amy," she says cheerfully, ignoring my hand and going in for a hug.

"The lovely Amelia Brooks," Goldman says. It may just be me, but his voice sounds creepier than I remember. How have I never noticed how short he is?

"Daniel." I give him a curt nod.

"I hope we haven't kept you waiting too long?" he booms. Knowing him, he did hope the exact opposite of that. I'm willing to bet it's a strategy of his, keeping us waiting, letting us get agitated and, therefore frustrated, which would, in turn, make it harder for us to focus on the business at hand.

He glances down at the pair of steaming coffee cups on the

table. "Where's dear old Robert?"

"Oh," I glance desperately in the direction of the bathroom. "I think he went to take a phone call. You guys take a seat. I'll see if I can locate him."

It's a flimsy excuse, and I know it. But I can't think of any other way to get Robert back here. I can't have him waiting indefinitely in some bathroom.

I sidestep Daniel and make a beeline for the bathroom. I look around quickly, then duck into the men's room.

My first thought is that it is a large room; way larger than the ladies, and certainly cleaner than I had anticipated. The fruity scent of citrus hits my nostrils.

"Took you long enough."

Robert emerges from nowhere. The next thing I know, large, strong hands are lifting me off my feet, and I am pinned against a wall. My protests spill into his mouth as his lips crush into mine. He kisses me hard, and I can already feel the pressure from his erection somewhere in my waist. I am momentarily dazed, lost in the rush and urgency, the desperate need his kissing evokes. It reminds me of that first night in my room, and how badly I wanted this man, how much I still do.

His hands are roaming everywhere on my body. His palms are like hot irons, finding several inches of exposed skin and caressing, fondling, squeezing. Somehow, my dress has ridden up way past my waist, and I can feel the cold press of the wall on the backs of my thighs. Robert's fingers are deft and eager. All too suddenly, they are brushing the mound in front of my panties, and the shock of it is enough to jolt some sense into me.

I break the kiss with an audible smacking sound. Robert's eyes are unfocused, but his brows are furrowed in confusion.

"Goldman is here," I say quickly. "And Laurie. They're waiting. I told them you were on a call."

"Damn that inconsistent asshole! If he was going to be late, why couldn't he be proper late?"

He swoops down and plants another one on me. It is a promise, I know. A little something to remind me where his mind will be during the meeting. I think I feel him throb against my pubic bone.

"Damn it," he curses again. It seems to take him a lot of effort to step away from me, but he does. His eyes go over me from head to toe, and the expression on his face is so tortured it gives me an ego boost.

"To be continued, I guess," he says. He straightens his shirt, tucks it back in, and then runs a hand through his hair. Then he turns to leave.

"You are the sexiest thing I have ever seen in my life, Amelia Brooks."

I'm smiling stupidly long after he is gone. My heart is fluttering, soaring. I feel giddy, like a child, and I know it shows. I step in front of a mirror, and indeed, my face is flushed. My cheeks are rosy, my eyes have a far-away look, and my hair is disheveled. I look like I was just rolling around in bed with someone, which I suppose I kinda was.

I straighten my dress and do my best to re-order my hair. I take several deep breaths, splash some water on my face, and hope the color in my cheeks isn't too telling. Then I sigh and walk back out of the restroom. It's a minor miracle no one came in while Robert was feeling me up.

There is an annoyingly covert look on Laurie's face when I rejoin them at the table. A little too knowing. Her lips curl up in a smile that she immediately suppresses. Her eyes dart from Robert to me and back again. But she doesn't say anything. Goldman hasn't noticed the exchange, and possibly even our return; his head is buried in a menu. He emerges minutes later, waves over the waiter, and places his order, which includes "Your largest plate of fries".

"So, Bobby," he announces once the waiter leaves. "As I was just telling Miss Brooks here, I apologize if we kept you waiting too long? I had a quick walk-in I couldn't reschedule in time."

"Oh, it's not a problem," Robert says. "Amelia and I found ways to pass the time."

He says it with a straight face as if I'm not seated next to him, growing redder by the minute.

"Good! Good!" Goldman beams, somehow innocuous. "Shall we get this thing on the road, then? Some of us have actual clients to represent, you know."

"I have twice as many clients as you do, Daniel."

"I highly doubt that."

"Boys! Boys!" Laurie cuts in, putting up a hand. "Let's not make this another dick-measuring contest, okay? You're both pretty. Robert? If you could tell us why you summoned us here?"

"Well." Robert sits back and crosses his hands. "To keep it simple, we wish to urge you to drop your case against our client."

Goldman actually snorts. "I guess this will be a short meeting. Shame. I was looking forward to those fries."

"I think you'll find we have a strong case," Laurie says. Unlike Goldman, her eyes are narrowed, suspicious. "Unless there's been a development?"

"Look," Robert says. "You have me on the financial document. I can admit it. As far as a defense goes, it's pretty useless for me. But here's the thing. We've done some digging, and we found out those documents are actually a double-edged sword. You can't bring them up without risking exposing your own client."

Goldman shrugs, unconcerned. "My client isn't on trial. Yours is."

"What do you mean?" Laurie asks. "Expose him how?"

Robert looks from her to Goldman, and a small smile flashes across his face. "It might be a good idea to be honest with your second chair, Daniel. You know ... because she's on your side?"

"What is he talking about?" Laurie turns to Goldman, who continues to look unbothered.

"He's fishing. He has nothing. This is a cheap ploy to get me to offer up new information."

Robert reaches into his pocket and pulls out a document, which he slides across the table to Laurie.

"That's the initial agreement between Gregory and Thomas. Back when they were starting Mendel. If you'll read it, you'll notice the agreement that all accounts are to be held jointly. I don't need to tell you what this means, of course."

"Give me that," Goldman snaps, snatching the document from Laurie's hands. He reads quickly, his expression guarded, but I can see the vein on his temple begin to throb.

"This doesn't mean anything," he says when he's done. "Like

I said, my client isn't on trial."

"You're very slow today, Daniel." Robert is smiling again. Sensing blood in the water. "Your case hinges on these offshore accounts your client claims my client opened and was using to defraud the company. I've just presented you with a document that I will use to show your client was part owner of these accounts. He knew about them, maybe even used them himself. Double-edged sword, you see? If my client goes down, yours does too. I got the idea from Amy here."

Goldman shakes his head. "You're bluffing. This is blackmail. You wouldn't dare."

"Are you sure about that, 'old friend'?"

They stare at each other across the table, and for once, I understand everything I've heard about them and their strange rivalry. There is a wordless war going on between them. I glance over at Laurie, who has gone back to poring over the document. She looks up at me and shakes her head as if to say "Men, right?"

"Let me get this straight," she says, probably eager to break the silence before Robert and Goldman come to blows. "You're threatening to sue Thomas for the exact same thing he's suing Gregory for?"

"That's right."

"Come on, Robert. Your client won't go for that. It will just be a waste of his time and money because we both know your theory is bullshit."

"My theory ... well, our theory ..." He glances sideways at me and the corner of his lip twitches. "Our theory is no crazier than yours. We both know this whole case is a sham to push Gregory out of his own company. "

"Our answer is no," Goldman says. "You can go ahead with your case, and I'll finish wiping the floor with you on mine."

Laurie speaks over him, addressing Robert. "What are you proposing?"

Robert leans back and turns to me. "Amy?"

"Right." I clear my throat. "I think there's a way for both Gregory and Thomas to get what they want. Gregory wants to still have a say in his company, which I think is fair. I mean, it's his baby.

Even if he doesn't get final say over the day to day, it's important to him to still be part of the family. And Thomas ... well, Thomas is being a bully. He wants Gregory out completely, and for that to happen, Gregory has to give up his controlling shares. So. The solution is simple. We get Gregory to sell some of his shares to the other board members. He can work out the details on who gets what, but essentially, he keeps enough without being the majority shareholder. It's the only compromise I see working out. Because this could all have been solved by these two just sitting down and talking it out."

Laurie and Goldman are silent for a long time. The food arrives, but Goldman appears to have lost his appetite.

"You're sure you can get your client to agree to this?"

"Of course."

"I know what you're doing, you know."

"What?"

"This is you sensing defeat and running away like you did last time. So that you can keep going around saying you're undefeated."

"Honestly, Daniel? I couldn't care less about that now. I have bigger fish to fry. We can put this down as a win for you if you want. I just think we both have better things to do with our time and resources than handle petty disputes."

He reaches for a handful of fries and eats them slowly, one at a time.

"I'm not promising anything, but if you get me a document detailing this proposal, I'll show it to Thomas."

"Look at that," Robert says. "Compromise. Who would have thought it possible." He grabs the document from the table and tucks it back into his pocket. "Pleasure doing business with you, Daniel. As always. Come on, Amy."

I reach for my bag and get up to leave with him. As I do, Laurie reaches over and puts her hand on me.

"Show me to the ladies, Amy?"

It's a strange request. I'm fairly certain she doesn't need my help locating the ladies' bathroom, particularly when its signage is so clear. But I recognize that she's trying to get me away from the men. And what better place to do it than the most universal female safehouse?

"Sure."

I lead the way to the bathroom, wondering whether this is going to be anything like our last meeting. She doesn't have any more dirt on Robert, does she? Because I really can't handle any more skeletons.

"I see you two have gotten even chummier since our last meeting," she says as soon as the door closes behind us.

It sounds like an accusation. Like she's asking me why I'm still with Robert after what she told me about him.

"I guess you could say that, yes," I say.

"He was always a charming bastard, Robert. Which is fine. But you, Amy. I thought you were smarter than that."

"Smarter than you, you mean?"

"Frankly, yes. I mean, after what I told you … Did you ask him about what happened with me? What he did to me?"

"I know the kind of person Robert was," I say. I resent that she's making me explain myself to her, that she's bringing up these issues I've only just wrapped my head around. "I can't hold his past against him. I've done things I'm not proud of in the past, too, and I hope someone won't use them as the basis on which they judge me for the rest of my life."

"This is not just something he did, Amy. This is who he is."

"No," I say stubbornly. "It's who he was. He's different. Or at least he's trying to be. That's enough for me."

I can see the exact moment when her disappointment turns to resignation.

"I hope you're right," she says. She touches up her hair briefly in the mirror, then turns and opens the door. "Good work on the case, by the way. I know that agreement was your idea."

"Thanks."

I'm silent all the way home. Despite my best efforts not to let Laurie's intervention bother me, it has darkened my mood. Robert picks it up right away. He tries to make a few jokes, prod some life back into me, but I can't give him the smile he's looking for.

"What's wrong, Amy?" he asks after a while.

I realize I don't know what to tell him. Nothing is wrong? I've just gotten a cryptic warning from your former lover, who wasn't entirely wrong about you the last time? He's already owned up to what happened with her. It wasn't flattering, he said, and he wasn't proud of who he was back then. What is the point of bringing it up again?

"I never asked you," I say, trying to deflect. "What happened to make you and Daniel hate each other so much?"

"Oh. It's silly, really. He stole my assistant during our first case. Long story. But come on, Amy. I know this is not what you want to talk about. What's really going on? What did Laurie say to you?"

"Just promise me one thing, Robert."

"Of course."

"Promise me you're not using me like you did her."

Robert pulls the car over and stops, turns to me. He grabs my face and stares deep into my eyes.

"I would never do that to you, Amelia Brooks. I love you too much."

It's the first time I've ever heard the words from him. They hang in the air, heavy like a cloud, and I feel a smile creep up on me.

"There she is!" Robert says happily. "You've turned me into an old sap. I mean it, though. I've never had this with anyone else. I would never do anything to jeopardize what we have."

"I love you too."

Part II

22

A few years later
Robert

I once heard a story of a wise Buddhist Zen master who was admired by everyone for how happy and balanced he was. One day his students went to see him to discover his secret.

"Master," one of them asked, "what are you doing to be happy and content? I would also like to be as happy as you."

The old man replied with a mild smile: "If I lie down, then I lie down. When I get up, I get up. When I go, I go and when I eat, I eat."

The students looked at each other in confusion and shook their heads in disbelief. One of them gathered all his courage and said: "Please, don't mock us. We do the same things. We sleep, eat and go. But we are not happy. So what's your secret?"

The same answer came: "If I lie down, then I lie down. When I get up, I get up. When I go, I go and when I eat, I eat."

This time even some of the students rolled their eyes, it was clear that they did not believe the master. After a while he smiled: "Sure, you are doing these things, too.. But while you're lying, you're already thinking of getting up. As you get up, you think about where you're going, and as you go, you wonder what you're going to eat. So your thoughts are always somewhere else and not where you are. Real life takes place at the intersection between past and future. Allow yourself to be immersed in this immeasurable moment and you have the chance to be really happy and satisfied."

I have always derided such esoteric wisdom. Ultimately, these are nothing more than perseverance slogans for unfortunate failures who didn't have the guts to really make something out of their lives. For me, life is about success. Setting goals and then achieving them. What if you do that? Then you need new goals. This is the only way to be really happy. At least I always thought so. Well, you're always smarter afterwards.

Today I would probably make some decisions differently. Everything could have been so nice with Amy. The right woman, the right job, the right life. But afterwards you are known to be always smarter. If only I...

"Are you ready?"

Gwen puts her hand on mine, and I realize it's shaking. She grips and squeezes, reassuring me silently. Her gaze holds me, and I know she's trying to get me to focus just on her, to ignore the swell of noise from the crowd outside. It's not easy, as they are literally on the other side of the curtain. It's a small crowd, but you couldn't tell that from how loud it is.

"I thought you said it's just a few reporters," I tell Gwen.

"It is," she says. "You've got this under control, Robert, don't worry. You've done it a thousand times."

"In court, not in front of ... people."

"Exactly. It's much harder to do it in front of a skeptical jury and a gallery of biased people. This is easy."

"You're right," I say, nodding. We've been planning this for months now. I've been picturing this very moment, the first step in the plan for my future. Somehow, it never seems quite the same as you picture it in your head. Suddenly it's all too real.

Gwen stands on the tips of her toes and kisses me lightly on the lips. "Just read the cards. I know you'll be great."

She gives me a gentle shove before I can say anything else, and I find myself on the other side of the curtain. My appearance is greeted by a flurry of camera clicks and an uptick in mutterings and whispers. A hundred different questions are shot at me as I approach the lectern. Somehow, the nerves are gone by the time I get there, and I stand overlooking the small gathering.

I glance down at the cards Gwen squeezed into my hands. I look back to the side of the mini podium, where she is standing. She gives me a quick wink and a thumbs up.

I clear my throat, and the crowd gradually grows silent.

"I'm a proud member of this community," I begin. Lead with a joke, Gwen had said. And we had gone back and forth with it, before ultimately agreeing that it wouldn't be believable. I have no problem admitting that. I come off as many things, but funny has never been one of them.

"I was born in Glendale, and I grew up here. Some of you may know of my work here as a lawyer. I have seen first-hand the challenges this community has gone through, the struggles we've had with our justice system, the journey we still have to take as members of this community. If we're being completely honest, we're nowhere near where we need to be, and that buck starts with us."

It's a compelling speech. I've gone over it a hundred times with Gwen stopping me every other sentence to remind me to emote differently or emphasize a certain phrase more. The key, she had said, was to go for honesty. Not philosophical or political rhetoric because people have an innate ability to tell when someone is being dishonest, and it puts them off when they feel the speaker doesn't believe the message they're selling.

"I believe it's time for change. Our legal system is rife for reform, and this reform may be a long time coming if we don't act now. For this reason, and many more I hope to share with you in the coming weeks, I wish to declare my candidacy for Glendale County District Attorney."

The applause is hesitant at first, and then it picks up amid a breakout of excited muttering. I let out a low sigh of relief. In several of my nightmares, my announcement is met with stunned silence. And not the good kind.

The rest of my speech flows out with practiced ease. It's like I've gotten over the hump, the difficult part is done with. The rest is 'politicking' and that is easy. Make no promises. No negative statements about the incumbent District Attorney. Lay out a clear strategy for what you're going to do. And, most importantly, be brief.

"I look forward to working with you to restore Glendale to its former glory. Thank you."

The applause is much warmer as I walk off the podium. The questions come at me, more aggressively. People are jostling to get to me, shoving microphones, phones, tape recorders in my face.

"What made you decide to run, Mr. Hardy?"

"What do you think about the current administration?"

"Have you spoken with the DA?"

"How many challengers do you think there will be?"

"Do you think your current win streak will extend to the

DA's office if you win?"

"What are your chances of winning against the incumbent DA?"

I nod and smile, waving politely as I make my way back to the rear. Gwen is beaming when I rejoin her. She throws her arms around me and hugs me tightly.

"See?" she says. "I told you it was easy. You were a natural up there."

"I don't know about that. I felt stiff and severe."

"No. Serious and honest. Trust me, people are tired of the same brand of politicians they see every other year. You're a breath of fresh air."

"Well, it's only because I have the best campaign manager. I couldn't have done this without you, Gwen."

She shakes her head, and light brown curls bob around her face. "We'll celebrate when we win. Come on, let's get back to HQ."

HQ means my office. Months ago, when I first arrived at the decision to run for political office, I had imagined I would have a large office with an open floor plan, and several eager interns running around with clipboards and blinking earpieces. It didn't exactly work out like that. I still do most of the planning and strategizing in my office, or occasionally at my house. Gwen agrees that we will eventually have to think of something more official, but for now, the office works just fine. I can still get my work done, and when I need to switch to campaign mode, I'm saved the hassle of running around town.

I replay the speech over in my head. It feels surreal, but the stone is in motion now. All those months of planning have led up to this. I'm officially a politician.

"Hey," Gwen says, and my eyes snap back to her, and to the present. The car is pulling up outside the office. "Are you okay?"

"Yeah. Still a bit stunned, I guess."

"You should be proud, Robert. The announcement went well. See this?" She holds up her phone, showing me 30 missed calls.

"These are reporters, looking to get quotes, statements, book interviews. We've had it easy up to this point. Now the real work begins. Now you're a public figure."

"We're not taking interviews already, are we?" I ask her.

"We'll pick and choose those that will present the best image of you. Don't worry about that. That's for me to figure out. I want you to focus on internalizing your message. Strategies, plans, all that."

"Will do, boss."

"One more thing, Robert."

"What?"

"Simms has requested a meeting."

"The District Attorney?"

"Yeah."

"When?"

"He reached out this morning, just before your announcement. I'm actually surprised it took him so long to hear about it. He must have assumed he was going to run unopposed again."

"Huh. Okay. He wants me to go to him, or ...?"

"I'm not sure yet. But I'm working on it. Just giving you a heads up."

"Smart," I say as the car rolls to a stop. "He wants to size me up, see what he's up against."

"I'm not worried about him. Whatever happens, it will be a good visual. He'll look rattled."

"Great."

I knew she was serious about me being a public figure, but I had not expected it to happen so fast. As I walk into the building, I notice people staring, pointing, whispering urgently to each other. It will never cease to amaze me how fast news travels in this town.

Veronica meets me at the door. She looks flustered, which is very much out of character. She is usually the picture of prim, professional, and competent.

"Everything okay, Veronica?" I ask her.

She falls into step beside me. "Something came for you, by courier."

"Okay?"

"It's in your office. But before you go in, the partners want to see you in their office. They want you to go in right away."

I sigh and hand my coat and briefcase over to Gwen. "Wait for me in my office."

Anthony Galweather and Phillip Meyer are the name partners at the firm. They have been at the helm since I first joined the firm. In recent months there has been talk of them leaving and promoting one of the senior partners to a management position, but I know them too well, and I'm sure Anthony and Phillip have no plans of leaving any time soon. The firm is their whole life; they wouldn't know what to do in 'the real world.'

Their office is on the first floor. It's actually two offices which were redesigned into one large one. Anthony likes saying that it's so they can both keep an eye on the other; that way they're always on the same page, and no one can plan anything without the knowledge of the other. In truth, it has created the belief among their employees that they function as a single unit, which has its benefits.

The office is just as lavish and over the top as you would expect. Two large mahogany desks pushed up against walls on opposite sides of the room. A pool table in one corner, a rich cabinet lined with drinks, half of which I've never seen, a full sitting area with two three-seater couches, a coffee table, and a love seat. It looks like a small apartment.

"Robert!" Phil booms when I enter. He gets up and bounds over to me, seizing my hand in a firm handshake. "Good God, man, I thought you were joking about running. You're actually going for it, you mad bastard!"

"If you thought he wasn't serious, then you don't know Robert Hardy," Anthony says, coming up and clapping me on the back. "We had better keep him in our good books, Phil. Or we'll wake up one day, and he'll be President."

"Oh, I wouldn't go so far," I say modestly. "I think DA might just about be the highest office I can handle."

Phil grins. "Modesty. The mark of a true leader."

"Yeah. Just what Alexander used to conquer the world," Anthony says, and they both laugh.

"Come on, Robert. Sit."

He ushers me into the couch, and he sits in the one across from me. Phil goes over to the cabinet, from where I can hear the clinking of glass. He comes back balancing three glasses, two of which he hands to Anthony and me.

"Isn't it a bit early ..." I start to protest.

"Drink," he insists. I bring the glass up to my lips, take a sip. The whiskey is so fine it practically evaporates in my mouth.

"Holy shit," I say.

"It's good, right? 40 years old. Vietnamese."

"I want to be you when I grow up," I say.

"Ah, if only. You chose the politician's path instead. Anyway, Robert. We need your help with something."

"Sure," I say. It's not every day you get asked for a favor by the partners.

"We know you're not going to be able to work your cases while also focusing on the campaign. Even if you could, it won't be for long. Now, you've been our best lawyer since we hired you, so we'll let you decide when you want to step away officially. We'll even let you decide what happens with your active cases. But there's one last case we were hoping you could help us out with."

"What is it?"

"It's a bit personal, so I'm going to need your word that you'll be discreet."

"Of course. Lawyer to lawyer confidentiality."

I know it's serious because neither of them registers the joke. They exchange one final look, and then Phil sits back in his chair.

Gwen and Veronica are both standing over my desk when I get back to my own office, and I quickly surmise that something is not right.

"You need to see this, Robert," Gwen says without even lifting her head. I walk over to the desk, and she steps aside so I can see what she's looking at. My laptop, playing a grainy, unclear video. It takes me a minute to figure out what I'm looking at. Who I'm looking at.

The couple in the video are thrashing about on a large, four-poster bed, clearly making love. And I know, even before the dread starts to flood my system, that this is bad. The man shifts. The woman twists and turns, and his face is suddenly visible to the camera. My face.

I have no recollection of any of it. The woman, the hotel, the video. I reach over and slam the laptop shut, then whirl around to face Gwen.

"What the hell is this?" I ask her.

"I was hoping you would tell me," Gwen says. Somehow, her voice is steady. Somehow, she has kept her cool.

"It came for you," Veronica says from somewhere behind me. I turn around and look at her; I had completely forgotten she was in the room. "Courier. The package had no address, no name or anything. The guy just said he had a delivery for Robert Hardy."

"We need to get you a security detail," Gwen says. Always on the job.

Veronica holds up the package, and I take it from her with shaky fingers. It is a small brown envelope, unmarked, unremarkable.

"The only thing inside it was this thumb drive," she says.

"Maybe you should have waited for me to open it," I say angrily.

"With all due respect, Robert," Gwen says, "that's the last thing I would have done. Do you know when this was taken? Who the woman is?"

I shake my head. "I think it's from a year ago. Maybe a year and a half." The period I think of as 'the great depression.' "I was going through some things. But I don't remember filming this. Heck, I don't even remember the woman. I must have been drunk or drugged because I would never have let her film it."

Gwen shakes her head, and for the first time today, the chipper optimism is gone from her face. "I know someone in IT. I'll put them on this, see if they can find out anything for us."

She turns to leave. I grab her hand, and she lifts her eyes up to me.

"What does this mean, Gwen?"

"Blackmail, Robert. This means someone is trying to blackmail you."

23
Amelia

Ness stands at the entrance to the house and frowns, her hands coming to rest at her sides.

"I don't like it," she says, twisting her face into a disapproving grimace.

"I didn't think you would, for some reason," I say, pushing past her and into the house.

"Okay, fine. So maybe the house isn't bad. I just don't understand why you have to move out at all. Don't you like living with me?"

Here we go. The patented Ness technique. Step 1: The guilt trip.

Ness and I have been living together ever since she came back from her 'world tour' two years ago, and it has been just as fun as it was when we lived together in college.

"Come on, Ness. You're doing it again."

"Doing what, trying to understand why I'm being rejected?"

"Oh my God, why are you so dramatic? No one is rejecting you."

"Feels like it. You're moving out, completely unnecessarily, I might add."

"It's anything but unnecessarily. For the hundredth time, Ness, I want to be closer to the school."

"It was only a forty-minute drive."

"And now it's a ten-minute drive."

She pouts, but before she can argue some more, a pair of hairy arms snake their way around her torso, up to her breasts. She squeals in alarm, then falls back into Jeremy's torso. "Jeremy! You naughty boy!"

Jeremy grins sheepishly. "How did you know it was me?"

"Uh, because I know you're obsessed with my breasts, and you went right for them?"

Jeremy flips her around and crushes her body against his. He brings his head to hers, touching her forehead with his. "It's your own fault for having the most perfect breasts in the world."

Even from a distance, I can see Ness blushing. And just like that, they're gone, disappeared into their own little world where it's just the two of them. This has been happening so much in the last few weeks I don't even flinch anymore. Or get embarrassed. Ness has been wildly flagrant with her sexuality for as long as I've known her, and now she has found someone who is just as sexual as she is who can't keep his hands off her.

We met Jeremy at a bar a month ago. He was out with a group of his friends, and apparently one of them dared him to go pick Ness up. Jeremy didn't return to them. I tried valiantly, but by the end of the evening, I had failed to extract Ness from his arms, and I've been failing to do so every day for the last month.

"You smell amazing," Jeremy whispers, his face inches from Ness's. "I want to strip you down with my teeth and lick every inch of you."

"Ooh," Ness says. "And then what?"

"And then I'll blindfold you," Jeremy goes on, "and use my tongue to bring you to orgasm over and over again until you pass out."

I clear my throat as loudly as I can. I have learned that it's usually best to cut them off before they get a good rhythm going. Their verbal foreplay usually turns into actual sex at the drop of a hat. I learned it the hard way. Ness and Jeremy have a truly remarkable ability to tune the world out when they're together.

Jeremy snaps his head around, his eyebrows going up as if he is only just noticing me. "Sorry, Amy," he says. "I'll get started with the boxes."

He gives Ness one final slap on the ass before turning and walking back out of the house.

Ness skips over to me, shaking her head. "I swear to God, that man can turn me on just by showing up."

"I know. I'm the one who has to watch you two teenagers fooling around. Everywhere."

She grips my hand suddenly, her eyes going wide. "I just got the craziest idea."

"Whatever it is, no."

"You don't even know what it is!"

"No. But I know you."

"Hear me out. Jeremy has a roommate I think you would like. No, no, listen, Amy. He is actually really cute. A bit nerdy, but I think you two would get along."

"Really?" I ask her, trying not to sound skeptical. "Why do you think that?"

"Look, Amy. You're my best friend, so I'm just going to give you some tough love. You need to get back on the horse. I don't know what happened between you and …"

"Don't you dare say his name," I snap.

"Okay. Okay. I don't know what happened between you and X, but it's been over a year. Even by your standards, this slump is going on a bit long, don't you think?"

Another Ness trademark: brutal honesty to the point of being mean.

"Who says I'm in a slump?"

"Then come out with Jeremy and me tonight. We'll invite his roommate. You don't have to do anything, Amy. Just give it a chance."

Jeremy comes in with a large box balancing loosely in his hands. Behind him, the moving guys are carrying in my old couch, which I had seriously considered giving away. In the end, sentimentality won over reason. Glad for the excuse to escape Ness, I walk over to them and direct them on where to set the couch down, and then I follow them out and continue directing traffic. It is a bit dispiriting that the entirety of my possessions barely fit one small truck, but it's also a huge relief because moving is so much easier.

The hardest part of it all was boxing my things up because that brought on random fits of nostalgia, most of them unwelcome. As a precaution, I threw out all my documents from as far back as I could. College and after, even the files from my brief stint at Castor & Sons. I didn't want to risk stumbling across something that would send me back down the spiral of depression. It had happened before, and I wasn't going to let it happen again.

A lot of my clothes went into the 'give away' box. I've

outgrown most of them, and those that I haven't are completely inappropriate for a college lecturer. I ended up keeping very little, which is how we're able to move most of my things into the new apartment in such a short time.

I spend the rest of the morning avoiding Ness. I keep myself busy, ordering the handymen around, arranging the furniture, trying to recreate the lived-in feel of our old place, and mostly failing.

The truth is that I've been thinking of moving out for some time now. I love Ness, but I'm finding more and more that I like my own company best. On a typical day, Ness is a hurricane, a bundle of relentless energy. This dynamic, how our personalities were so different, somehow worked when we were in college. She would always take charge and push me, drag me to things just like she's trying to steer my social life now. I love her for it, but sometimes she can be a bit much. None of which I can say to her face, so I hide behind the excuse that I want to be closer to the university. Not exactly untrue.

Once or twice, I notice both she and Jeremy have vanished, and I have no doubt they have found a room and are doing inappropriate things to each other.

By the time evening rolls around, I'm basically done moving. The house has a stark, cold feel to it, but it's now my home, and I'm proud of it.

Ness finds a bottle of wine somewhere, then drags us into the living room, where we huddle on the carpet, and she pours out glasses for each of us.

"Here's to my best friend, finally grown up and setting off on her own," she says, lifting her glass high.

I blush as they toast me, and we drink.

"You know, Amy, this place isn't half bad," Jeremy says. "Your bathrooms have excellent acoustics."

I make a gagging sound. "Gross, Ness!" They look at each other and laugh.

"So, Amy," she asks. "We're going to go home and change. You're coming, right? We're thinking of checking out that new club downtown." She gives me a suggestive wink.

"I'm really tired, Ness," I tell her. "I just want to grade papers and then get some rest."

"It's the weekend, Amy. You can't seriously tell me you'd rather work than go out with us. Come on."

I would. I actually would. God, I've turned into an old woman.

"I'm invoking the sacred code of best-friendship. You owe me this, especially since you've moved out and abandoned me."

Oh, good. We're still on the guilt trip.

I know Ness well enough to realize she is not going to drop this. Not when she's being backed up by Jeremy and his puppy eyes.

"Fine," I sigh, defeated. "I'll come out for a couple of hours. But only for a couple of hours. And you don't get to guilt me about moving out ever again."

"Deal!" Ness grabs the bottle and the glasses and dances into the kitchen.

"Come on, babe." She grabs Jeremy, and they make for the door. "We'll come to pick you up at exactly eight. Wear something sexy. Like that flowery dress I got you from Jamaica. Yes. Wear that."

I can't bring myself to tell her the dress she's referring to didn't survive the purge. So I just smile and nod.

I glance at my watch. It's just after 6 p.m. I have less than two hours to get ready and I know it's going to be hellish. I can't remember the last time I got dolled up for anything. My school outfits are basically variations of the same blouse/pants combination with the occasional jacket thrown in, or a scarf.

I take a quick shower, and I'm instantly impressed by the pressure of my new shower head. It feels therapeutic, the scalding heat, the knowledge that I'm alone in my own space. But the real struggle is picking out an outfit. Nothing in the heaps of clothes I own seems appropriate. It makes me realize just how little effort I've been making. I wouldn't go so far as to call it a slump, but it has been a while before I cared enough to make myself look like a sexually viable woman.

With the clock ticking down, I settle on a simple black cocktail dress, the one I wore to the dinner celebrating my appointment to the university. It's just short and sexy enough to draw the eye.

I go back and forth on whether to put on any make-up at all, before deciding to dab a little rouge on my cheeks and a quick shade of eyeliner. Nothing too fancy. I'm not out to impress anyone, after all.

Ness and Jeremy show up at exactly eight. Ness is in a body-hugging gold dress with an open back and a plunging neckline. Jeremy has worn a blue shirt that brings out the blue in his eyes. I look nervously behind them, but Ness assures me that Ethan said he would meet us at the club.

"Not bad, Amy," she says, inspecting my outfit. "Not bad at all."

Ethan is exactly what I imagined he was going to be. He is tall and skinny, with long sinewy arms that he never seems to know what to do with, so he twiddles his thumbs or sticks them in and out of his jeans. He has long, unruly brown hair that keeps falling into his face. He is definitely cute, in that awkward teenage-boy way. And he is definitely shy.

He goes in for a hug when Ness introduces me, then changes his mind halfway through it and reaches for my hand instead. He keeps avoiding my eyes, but when we are finally seated, he leans over and whispers that he thinks I'm gorgeous. It's subtle yet charming in a way.

"Let's go get drinks," I say to him. His eyes go wide like he doesn't believe what he just heard. I want to get him away from the others so I can speak with him. No point leading the poor boy on. I get the drink orders from Ness and Jeremy, then grab Ethan's hand, and we start ducking and weaving through the crowd, heading for the bar. Once I've ordered the drinks, I turn to Ethan and lean in so he can hear me above the gentle thrum of the music.

"Listen, Ethan. I'll be completely honest with you. I'm not really looking for anything serious right now. Ness dragged me here. I don't know if you know her, but she can be very persistent. Anyway, you seem like a great guy. I just don't want to give you the wrong idea."

Ethan shakes his head. "No, I completely understand. Jeremy dragged me out as well. I think he's trying so hard to set me up so I can get out of the house a bit more. Probably so that they can ruin perfectly good furniture."

"Oh my God, they're handsy in front of you too? I thought that was just me!"

"Me too! I mean, those two are disgusting. No shame at all. Can you believe the other night we were watching a movie, and then they just started doing it, right there on the couch, without warning or anything?"

"I can definitely believe that," I say. "And that's nothing. I once had to pretend not to hear them doing it in the back of the car I was driving. On a six-hour road trip."

Ethan laughs. "Fair enough. Yours is worse. At least I had the option of leaving."

I smile, suddenly feeling less resistant to the idea of a night out. I extend a hand, and Ethan takes it hesitantly.

"Friends?"

He nods. "Friends."

We share more horror stories on our way back to our table, and I'm so glad to have someone to talk to about Ness's madness. I'm actually laughing out loud for what feels like the first time in forever.

"Oh-oh!" Ness exclaims as we take our seats. "Are you seeing this, Jeremy? We have sparks!"

I blush slightly, and I turn around to see Ethan blushing as well.

"We have actually found out that we do have something in common," I say to Ness. "Who would have thought?"

She squints her eyes in suspicion, and I continue to smile innocently.

"You know what," she says after some time. "I don't even care about your implications and innuendos. I'm just glad you're taking my advice for a change."

"You were right," I concede. "Maybe this might actually be fun."

"It's good to have you back, Amy. Really." And she sounds like she means it.

Then the music changes and her face lights up. Without another word, she grabs Jeremy and they disappear onto the dancefloor.

"Ten bucks says they're making out in five minutes," Ethan says, leaning into me.

"Five? Ridiculous. You're on."

24
Robert

If I had to describe Jeremiah Simms in one word, it would be shrewd. I've only ever seen him on television, but even then, he always gives off a certain vibe, like he knows something you don't. He is a large man, over six and a half feet tall, and wide; he must have played a sport or something because he has the girth of a football linebacker or a bouncer. His face is genial enough, with greying hair trimmed neatly and bushy black eyebrows also with hints of grey. But his smile, on the rare instances when he offers it up, does not reach his eyes. And that is the thing that stands out most about him; his eyes. They are cold and grey, the eyes of a man who will not hesitate to crush anyone in his path, the shifty eyes of someone who is always thinking of the best way to turn any situation to his advantage.

I can tell he is going out of his way to show me the weight of his authority, to impose his personality on me. It's quite aggressive, but it's not something I haven't encountered before. I have come up against many prosecutors with this very brand of alpha aggression, and I know how to deal with it.

He insists on the meeting taking place in his office, the first of many power moves. The significance is not lost on me. He wants to show me the throne I had the balls to challenge him for, and which he will ensure I never sit on.

His handshake is firm, almost painful. When he ushers me in, he does not ask me to sit, but he drops into a chair himself and looks up at me with his chin resting on steepled fingers. I look around and settle on the chair right across from him.

"So," he says. "You're the famous Robert Hardy."

"That's right," I tell him, meeting and holding his gaze.

"I've heard an awful lot about you, Mr. Hardy. I've actually had reason to come up against you in court on several occasions, but for one reason or the other, we've never actually met. But I'm fairly familiar with your work."

He reaches for a file on his desk and flips it open almost lazily.

"The People vs. Cital Manufacturing. We spent months building a case against one of the biggest polluters in the city, and you got them off on a technicality."

So he has done his research.

"That was one of my earlier cases," I say, and I realize too late that he has already put me on the defensive.

"Jacob Smith. Charged for illegally obtaining and selling the data of the users on his dating app. You got him off too. Belinda McCain. Endangering her employees. Found not guilty. On and on it goes."

"Is there a point to this, Mr. Simms?" I ask, feeling myself getting irritated.

"Oh, I'm just trying to show you why I'm such a fan of your work. You have defended some of the worst people to ever come through this city, Mr. Hardy. Frankly, it's laughable to hear you talk about fixing the judicial system when you've done more than most to exploit it for personal gain."

"All this tells me, Mr. Simms, is that you were rattled enough to look me up."

"Is that what you think, that I'm rattled?"

"I'm here, aren't I? I can't imagine you summoned me here to give me a pre-emptive tour of the premises."

"I'm glad you used the word 'summoned.' It tells me that even though you were stupid enough to actually run against me, on a deeper level, you understand how this works. You understand power. And you're right. I did summon you here. I wanted to look you in the eye when I tell you that you will never sit in this office."

"Rattled," I say, smiling slightly. "Well, thank you for the childish display of power, Mr. Simms. I'm quaking in my boots. Now, if you'll excuse me, I have a campaign to run."

I get up and straighten my coat. Simms stands up too, and when he takes a step toward me, his eyes are flashing dangerously. "Have you asked yourself, Mr. Hardy, why it is that I ran unopposed last time?"

"I imagine because no one had the balls to stand up to you?"

"It's because they know I would crush them. If I may offer you a piece of advice, you would be wise to reconsider your political ambitions. This is not your battlefield."

"Thank you for the advice, Mr. Simms. But I think I'll stick to the advice I get from my campaign team."

Simms smiles humorlessly. His eyes are still flashing, and I know that visual will stay with me long after I leave the room.

Gwen rushes up to me as soon as I step outside. "That was quick," she says, frowning slightly. "Oh, Mr. Simms?" She walks up to him, stopping well away and looking up at him. "There's a small press corps outside. I wonder if you would be okay with you and Robert giving a quick statement?"

Simms smile is similarly rigid, but he nods.

If I haven't yet accepted the reality of what I've just gotten myself into, those few minutes in front of the cameras bring it home with finality.

Simms grabs my hand as the cameras click. When he speaks, it is with the pleasant lightness he projects on television. The menace is gone. He looks, for all intents and purposes, like he just had a nice brunch with an old friend.

"I welcome the challenge by Mr. Hardy," he says to a rapt group of reporters. "It's an indicator of the beauty of our legal system and a credit to the ideology of democracy. I look forward to going up against him, and may the best man win."

I echo his words in my own speech, even though I'm sure I can't begin to match his false smiles and forced camaraderie. On that front, he has me well beaten.

"Okay, so that was definitely weird," Gwen says once we're back in the safety of my car. "I know Simms is a seasoned politician, but I wasn't fooled for a second. He looked like he was ready to punch you in the face. What did you say to him?"

I recount the encounter to her as best as I can remember it. I try to paint a picture of Simms towering over me, of his glowering, his veiled threats, but I can't help feeling like I haven't quite captured the spirit of the man.

"That sounds exactly like him," Gwen says. "From what I've heard anyway. But we knew this wasn't going to be easy, Robert."

"I know. I just wasn't expecting him to be so … raw. You

know?"

"There were no cameras around. He was being himself."

I pause. "Do you think he's the one behind the tape?"

Gwen shakes her head. "It doesn't seem like it. Did he imply anything of the sort during your meeting?"

"Not really, no. Just veiled threats."

"We can't rule out anything," she says. "Until we have more information, I suggest we keep our minds open."

"Speaking of which, do we have any more information on the tape? Any further communication?"

"That's what's so strange about it. Blackmailers generally make their demands known as early as possible, so it's weird that this one hasn't said anything else. We can't even be 100 percent sure that it *is* blackmail. But I have someone from IT waiting for us back at the office. I had him go over the tape, so let's see what he has dug up."

The 'someone from IT' is a gangly youth with huge glasses. He's buried behind a large laptop, and he nearly jumps out of the chair in fright when Gwen knocks the desk right in front of him repeatedly.

"Sorry," he says, putting a hand on his chest to calm himself. "I was plugged in."

"This is Charlie," Gwen says. "Charlie, what did you discover about the video?"

Charlie pushes his glasses further up his nose. It makes him look almost like a cartoon character with huge eyes. "Well, the person who made it definitely knows their way around video editing software. This isn't the original video or the full video. As far as I can tell, this clip has been heavily edited and enhanced, probably to highlight the subjects more clearly." He glances nervously at me.

"I did manage to find out where this is. The sheets from the bed have the crest of The Winstonia, a luxury hotel out in Chicago."

"Robert?" Gwen asks. "Do you remember when you were in Chicago?"

"I think I can work it out."

"Great. Anything else, Charles?"

"I'm afraid not," Charles says. "Whoever made this, they were very careful not to leave any digital footprints. Beyond what is in the video, I couldn't find any other clues."

"Okay. Well, thanks for trying. You can go back to your department. I'll seek you out if I need any other information."

Gwen sinks into the chair and stares off into the distance. I can almost hear the cogs in her brain working. "I need to ask you something, Robert," she finally says. "And I want you to be honest with me."

I nod, although I'm not sure I like where this is going.

"What happened to you eighteen months ago?"

"Short version? I went on a bit of a tear. Drugs, women, you know, a standard self-destructive episode. Except it lasted a bit longer than I would have liked."

"These women, they were random?"

"More or less. I mean, mostly, I picked them up wherever it was I was drinking. Why? It sounds like you're ramping up to something."

"I have a theory." She reaches for her bag and pulls out a small notebook. "I need you to remember the women, Robert. As many as you can, as much information as you can remember. Write them down for me."

"Is this your way of asking how many women I've been with?" I say, reaching for her waist and pulling her in. "I thought we already cleared that particular relationship hurdle?"

Gwen twists away, her eyes quickly going to the door.

"Not here, Robert," she says. "Someone might see us, and you already have enough on your plate."

"You're no fun," I tease her.

Not the best time for it, clearly. Her expression is hard, her face devoid of humor. "Right now, Robert, I'm trying to be your campaign manager. Not your girlfriend. And I don't think 'fun' is the quality you need in your campaign manager. Especially not in the middle of a crisis."

"I don't know if I would call it a crisis," I say, and instantly regret it.

"You should really take this more seriously, Robert," Gwen

says. "Whatever it is we're dealing with, it is clearly an attempt to derail your political career before it's even started. I mean, I knew you had a lot of messy baggage, but I didn't anticipate having to deal with it in this way."

It's a disquieting thought. She doesn't say it, but I know what she's thinking. Gwen was one of the few people I approached to be my campaign manager, and she only accepted after I promised to lay my entire history bare. She didn't want any skeletons in the closet, she said, ones that would come back to bite her in the ass later. And after I told her everything I thought was important, she came very close to pulling out. Apparently, it's not a good idea to run for public office with the kind of past I've had, but I was able to get her to see it as a challenge. Provided we kept everything in front of us, I was sure we would be able to handle anything that could put my candidacy at risk.

I'm sure she's not feeling too comfortable now. Only a week after announcing I am running, and she's already putting out fires.

"What's your theory?" I ask her.

"I keep trying to figure out how this kind of attack would benefit anyone, a rival, for example. And it occurred to me that this might be the work of a scorned lover. You don't even remember the woman in the video. Imagine how she feels, or how any of the women you used while you were on your 'bender' felt afterward. There is a possibility that we're dealing with one of the women from your past."

"Which is why you want the list."

"Have you ever had an STI, Robert?"

"What does that have to do with anything?"

"When you're diagnosed with any of the more contagious diseases, you are required to contact every single person you've had sexual contact with and inform them about the disease, in case you exposed them to it."

"I'm not sure where you're going with this."

"You need to go on an apology tour."

It takes a minute for the full meaning to sink in, and when it does, I almost burst out laughing. "You can't be serious."

"I'm dead serious."

"To be clear, you want me, a few days after I announced that I'm running for District Attorney, to start calling women I may have hurt in the past and apologize to them? Do you have any idea how crazy that sounds?"

"Actually, I want you to seek them out. Phone calls are a bit impersonal."

I keep waiting for the other shoe to drop, but it seems Gwen has definitely lost her mind. "Gwen. You must realize what this will do for my candidacy."

"What do you think it will do? Because if the person who is getting ready to blackmail you turns out to be one of these women, then apologizing may be the one thing that saves your campaign."

"If, Gwen. If. And it's a huge if. Because if it isn't, then I've just helped whoever they are heap dirt on myself."

"Well, you're not particularly innocent in all this. You did go on that bender. You did get filmed having sex with that woman, and God knows what else. These are *your* skeletons. I'm just suggesting it might be a good idea to own up to them instead of crossing your fingers and hoping they stay in the closet."

I fall silent, mostly because I literally have no idea what to say.

Gwen moves closer and puts her hand on my cheek. It's a simple gesture, and the fact that she seems to have abandoned her fear of us being seen gives it that much more weight.

"I know you've had a troubled past, Robert. I understand. You don't need to explain any of it to me. I get it. And I know who you are. I'll tell you what I told you when you first approached me to be your campaign manager. You're a deeply flawed person. But so am I. So are all of us. It shouldn't be the reason you don't get to make a difference."

I smile. I remember that meeting and the thing that struck me right away about Gwen. In the whole hour or so during which I narrated the darker aspects of my life to her, she never once flinched or recoiled in judgment. She is a beautiful woman, but her true beauty is in her knack for seeing the best in people. It's why I fell for her. And it's why I know she's right.

"Okay," I say. "I'll get started on the list."

"Excellent," Gwen says, and she bounces up on the balls of

her feet and plants a quick kiss on my lips.

"And I hope you realize what this means?"

"What?" I ask.

"You'll probably have to start with Amelia Brooks."

25
Amelia

Kieran has spent the entire lesson stealing glances at me. It's a step up from staring, which is how we got into this situation in the first place.

It's how I noticed him. He always sat in the middle of the lecture hall. He would later tell me it was the perfect place to sit if one wanted to blend in, be completely invisible. But I noticed him. It was hard not to. He was one of the few students who listened to everything I said with such rapt attention it was hard to miss. And once I did, my eyes kept returning to him. At first, it was out of simple curiosity. What was it about that quiet boy, sitting so low in his seat it was clear he was trying his hardest not to stand out ... what was it that struck me? He was staring, so that was something. And giving every indication that he was actually paying attention.

It took some time, but I eventually learned not to expect undivided attention while I was teaching. On a good day, my students stared at their laptops for the duration of the class. On other days, it was a struggle just getting them to look up. That's why I took notice of Kieran.

He is a beautiful young man. He has long dark hair that he always ties up in a bun. He is tall, and he looks very athletic. His eyes are steely blue, and he has the cutest smile.

Today, like the first time he introduced himself to me, he stays behind after the lecture. He waits for the room to clear out before stepping down and walking up to me. Unlike that day, his gait is confident, purposeful. He looks around once more, checking that we're truly alone, then he leans over and kisses me. It is chaste and sweet, a kiss hello.

"You know we can't do this here, Kieran," I tell him, stepping away and continuing to gather my things and shove them into my bag.

"You look stunning today," he says as if he hasn't heard me.

But then he always says that when he sees me. Even though I never vary my wardrobe by much. Blouse, pants. Shirt, pants. Heavy jacket, beanie, boots. He is so earnest, so irritatingly charming without realizing it.

"What do you need?" I ask him. I don't mean to sound rude, but I can't help it. It's been a long, exhausting day.

His smile falters, but it is back up almost immediately. "I need to see you tonight. Can I come over to your place?"

"I don't think that's a good idea."

"Why not? I miss you."

"I have work to do. Midterms are coming up, so I need to prepare for that."

"I can come keep you company while you work."

That's another of his unwittingly charming traits. Whether by design or not, he always sounds so eager to spend time with me.

"You would be a distraction." I risk a gentle pat on his cheek. "A gorgeous distraction, but a distraction, nonetheless. I'm sorry, Kieran."

I can tell he's not buying it. I'm not trying particularly hard to sell it, so I don't blame him.

I haven't told him yet, but I've decided I'm going to stop seeing him. I don't even know how any of this happened in the first place. I suppose it was gradual. A stolen glance here and there. A smile returned. A dangerous game of chicken. And then one afternoon, a huge mistake made in the heat of the moment. A mistake that happened again, and then again, and then again.

It was extremely reckless of me to allow anything at all to happen between us. I'm his lecturer; it's inappropriate to even look at him that way. Even though I'm actually not that much older than he is. But those are the counterarguments I draw up late at night when the guilt is eating away at me. Even if I can rationalize the relationship on the basis of age, there is the small matter of the university's code of conduct, the ethics handbook, and a slew of other legal documents that all say the same thing: teacher/student relationship = bad.

I'm risking both our lives and careers. If this comes out, I'll probably lose my job, and then I'll have to go back to working at some stupid firm, and I'm right back to square one. Kieran stands to get suspended. There is no version of this that has a happy ending.

Last night, I finally accepted that he is a guilty pleasure and that the best thing for me would be to give him up. I haven't figured out how to break it to him yet, though. It doesn't help that he's been hitting me with the puppy eyes for the whole lesson. And that he's now standing in front of me, drowning me in his scent.

He is incredibly perceptive, though. Even if I haven't mentioned it, he can feel me pulling away.

"I really need to see you, Miss Brooks," he says again. "Even if it's just for a little while."

"Why, Kieran? Why is it so important that you see me?"

"Can we go somewhere? Please?"

I let out an exasperated sigh. I pick up my bag and walk out of the room. I can hear Kieran rushing after me. I open the door to my office, wait for him to get in, and then swing the door shut. That's a mistake.

Kieran practically descends on me in a flurry of kisses. He grabs me, wraps his hands around me, and before I know it, I'm pushed up against the door, and his tongue is pushing past my lips. The intensity of it takes me completely by surprise, the wildness, the illicit nature making it hotter.

His hands fan out and brush the front of my blouse, then my shoulders. And now they're running down my back and pulling me into his chiseled body. I find myself kissing him back just as fiercely, pushing back, fumbling with his T-shirt, reaching down and squeezing the bulge in his pants.

He reaches down and grabs me by the ass. He lifts, and I wrap my legs around the backs of his thighs and interlock them with each other. His fingers move to my hair, running through my thick curls, tangling and untangling. They hold my head in place as he plunders me with his tongue. Excitement is shooting through me, making me weak, jumbling my thoughts.

A thought is dancing on the edge of my mind, but I can't form it, can't articulate it. It seemed important a few minutes ago … but that was before Kieran woke me up. And boy, am I awake. His fingers are now making inroads into my blouse, and after a few moments, I feel them against my skin, soft and warm. Why did I wear a bra today? Such a waste. I want to be closer to him. I want to feel his skin with my skin. I want to crush my body against his and fill myself with every inch of him.

I need to say something …

His fingers are sneaking into the edges of my bra. Working in, slowly, patiently. My breasts ache for the touch, tingle in anticipation.

And then I remember it.

It takes every ounce of mental strength I possess to break the kiss. I blink rapidly, trying to clear my eyes and my mind. Kieran is looking at me with confusion. God, he has such beautiful eyes.

We shouldn't be doing this. That's right. That was the objection.

But before I can voice it, a knock sounds on my door, impossibly loud because I'm leaning right against it.

Kieran steps away, and I slide to the floor a bit awkwardly. This is exactly why I was trying to end this. Too risky.

The person on the other side of the door knocks again, sharper, more urgent. I gesture wildly for Kieran to hide, and he opts to rush over to my desk and dive under it. Not perfect, but it will have to do. I make quick adjustments to my blouse and straighten my pants, then use my fingers to comb my hair back into place. I don't even want to think about how I look.

I swing the door open.

The woman standing in front of me looks familiar, but I can't begin to imagine where I've seen her before. She looks to be in her late thirties. She has short brown hair falling in curls to her shoulders. Her eyes are brown too, and she has a tiny little button nose that stands out in an otherwise pretty face. She smiles and extends a hand.

"Miss Brooks?"

"Yes?"

"Hi. My name is Gwen Michaels. I hope this isn't a bad time?" Her eyes travel over my shoulder and into my office.

"Not at all. We don't have an appointment, do we?"

"I don't believe so, no," she says. "But I'm hoping you'll see me anyway? I only need a few minutes of your time."

I hesitate. It would be a bad idea to invite her into the office. I don't know what Kieran is doing under that desk, but I doubt he will be able to keep it up much longer. Not with those long limbs of his.

"I was actually heading out. Is it okay if we talk on the way?"

"Yes, that's fine."

"Great. Let me just lock up real quick."

I dart back into the office and go over to the desk. "My place. Nine." I whisper so only Kieran can hear me. Then I grab my bag and leave, shutting the door behind me and falling into step behind the lady. Gwen, she had said her name was.

"Are you one of the lecturers at the university?" I ask her, still trying to figure out where I might have seen her.

"Here? Oh, no. I don't work here. I only came to speak with you."

"Well, how can I help you?" I ask stumped.

"I hope it's not too personal a question to ask, Miss Brooks, but how involved are you in local politics?"

I shrug. "No more than I need to be, I guess."

"Do you follow it? Watch or read about what's happening in the city and beyond?"

"I can't say that I do."

Gwen frowns. Now I'm definitely intrigued.

"Why?"

"I need your help with something, if I may cut straight to the chase. Or someone, to be more specific. I didn't introduce myself properly; I'm sorry. I'm a campaign manager with one of the top PR and Consulting firms in the country. I find myself in a slight pickle with one of my clients, and I was hoping you could help me out."

Still cryptic but getting warmer. I think I may have seen her on television or something.

"Like I said ... uh, Gwen, I'm not particularly knowledgeable in politics, so I don't think I can help you or your client."

We are now outside the main university annex. I stop and turn to face Gwen because my car is only a few feet away. "Sorry I wasn't of more use," I say, pulling out my car keys.

Gwen steps up to me, her whole demeanor suddenly different. "Look, Amy. I know it's a strange request, but I need you to come with me. It might be easier to show you what I'm talking about than to tell you."

It *is* a strange request. I don't know this woman, and I have no intention of going anywhere with her. I tell her as much, but she holds up a hand.

"We're just going over to my car over there." She points to a black SUV parked close to the library. It looks laughably out of place. "I'm not a serial killer, I promise. I just need you to meet someone, and then this will all make sense."

I don't know why I do it. I feel like I can trust her, even though I've only just met her. So I nod hesitantly, and Gwen sighs in obvious relief. She sets off at a brisk pace. I walk slowly behind her, reasoning that whatever she has planned, whoever she's hiding in the car, I'll at least have a better chance of reacting if I stay back a little.

When she gets to the car, she raps on the passenger side door, and it rolls down a fraction. I can't see inside from where I'm standing, so I edge slightly forward. I don't know why, but my heart has started to beat a little faster. Curiosity? Anxiety? Fear?

Then the car door opens, and a tall figure steps out. It feels like it happens in slow motion like my eyes are registering the man one frame at a time, starting from his highly polished leather shoes, to the immaculately tailored blue suit, all the way up to the man himself.

He looks a bit different, which is probably why I didn't recognize him right away. But I do recognize him. The fluttering in my chest stops, and my heart feels like a ten-pound rock.

"Hi, Amy," he says. He has the nerve to smile.

I shake my head and turn on my heel.

He must have sprinted to cover the distance between us because he is suddenly right beside me. "Amy, please, hear me out."

I quicken my steps, and when I realize he is still following me, I break into a trot.

"Amy!" He reaches over and tries to grab me, and that's what pushes me over the edge. I stop, whipping around as I swing. I catch him by surprise, which is how I'm able to get such a clean hit. The smacking sound echoes across the grounds, a sharp, ringing sound that fills me with savage pleasure.

Robert Hardy stands there, his hand over his cheek, a look of disbelief on his face. "Okay. I deserve that. Now, will you please hear me out?"

I lift my arm again, and he ducks. I turn and take off again, this time running at full pelt. I don't stop until I get to my car. My hands are shaking as I fumble with the keys. I open the car and get in. I put the car in gear and drive off. Through the rearview mirror, I catch a glimpse of Robert, still standing where I left him, his hand still over his cheek. He does not chase after me.

26
Robert

Gwen thinks this is a work meeting. I know because when she shows up at my place, she is still dressed in her work clothes, and she has the little crinkle in her forehead from frowning too much. She drags her feet into the living room as soon as I open the door, and she collapses face down into the couch. Her bag drops onto the floor with a dull thunk.

"Ah," she sighs into the cushion. "I've had the longest day."

I go over to her and squat on the couch just at her hip. I reach over and unbuckle the shoes from her feet, slide them off slowly. I run a hand over the lovely curve of her instep, then up along her leg. When I get to the calf, I start to massage gently.

She sighs deeply. "That feels so good." I can almost feel the tension leave her body, the way she lets go and allows herself to relax. It's easy to take for granted just how hard Gwen works; she never shows any signs of fatigue.

"No," she says suddenly, twisting away from my hands and turning around. She sits up and blinks to refocus. "If I get comfortable, I'll fall asleep. And then I won't be any use, and we won't get this meeting underway."

"What meeting?" I ask her, smiling slightly.

Gwen frowns, her lips pushed out in an uncertain pout. "You texted me to meet you here? You said it was urgent."

"Well, perhaps I shouldn't have used the word 'urgent.'"

"What's going on, Robert?" she asks. Her eyes take in my appearance for the first time, and the look of confusion does not leave her face.

"Is that an apron?" she asks as if she is seeing me for the first time. "Are you cooking?"

"Yes," I say cheerily. "I'm sorry if I alarmed you or gave you the wrong impression. I wanted to make you dinner, that's it."

It takes a second, but the relief slowly seeps into her face, and it breaks into a truly radiant smile. I think Gwen might have the most beautiful smile I have ever seen. She is a beautiful woman, but when she smiles, she's quite the vision.

"Oh my God, really?"

"Of course. I figured you need a bit of a breather. I know how hard you've been working for me, and I don't think I've gotten the chance to say thank you just yet."

She leans back into the chair, and her expression is suddenly tender. "You don't have to thank me, Robert. I'm just doing my job."

"I know," I say. "But you're doing much more than that. I believe it's called 'going above and beyond'?"

She saddles up closer to me on the couch, and I put an arm around her shoulder. Her head falls onto my chest. Her hair smells like coconut oil.

"Well, I guess I have a soft spot for this particular client," she says.

The oven timer dings, a sharp sound that cuts through the house, startling us both.

"That will be the chicken," I announce proudly.

I peck Gwen on the forehead, then get up and rush into the kitchen. I hear her soft footsteps behind me as I'm leaning into the oven to pull out the tray of sizzling, baked chicken.

"No," I tell her. "You're the guest. You should be sitting down with a glass of wine in your hand. Let me."

I lay the tray down and go over to her, grabbing her by the shoulders and steering her out of the kitchen. She protests weakly, but I give her a little shove, into one of the dining chairs.

"Relax, that's an order."

Another quick trip in and out of the kitchen, and I return with a bottle of wine and two glasses. I pour into both and extend one to Gwen.

"To you," I say, raising my glass. "I couldn't have done any of this without you."

Gwen raises her glass too. "To the future District Attorney of Glendale."

It takes a little longer to set the table up than I had anticipated. I was hoping to go all-in on the romantic theme; candles, rose petals strewn all around the table, soulful music to set the mood … but Gwen came over a bit early. I find myself scrambling to get the meal right. My chicken is perfectly roasted, but the mashed potatoes and gravy take a bit more time.

Gwen watches me with something approaching amusement as I shuttle back and forth, laying the table, setting the dishes down, lighting the few candles I could find. She takes the cue and goes over to my record player to pick the music. After a few moments rifling through my small vinyl connection, she chooses a simple classical piece. Not exactly panty-dropping, but it will do.

"You need to update your collection," she protests as she sits back down. "And don't feed me that bullshit about vinyl 'just being better.'"

"It is, though," I say. "You know I'm an old soul like that."

"Or maybe you're just old," Gwen teases.

"Well, the joke's on you, then. You're the one stuck with me."

She flashes me her sweet smile once again. "I'm not complaining."

Then, because she is still Gwen Michaels, she pulls out a tiny little notebook from the inside of her bra and scribbles down 'GET ROBERT NEW MUSIC.'

"Do you just walk around with a notebook inside your bra?"

"I walk around with all sorts of things inside my bra," Gwen says, her eyes flashing.

I want to tell her I can't wait to go foraging for these 'things,' but there will be plenty of time for that later. Right now, I just want to feed the woman.

I ladle a generous helping of mashed potatoes onto her plate, then dip the gravy boat over her plate. I cut the chicken into thin slices and stack several there too. She protests the entire time, muttering something about watching her weight, which is absurd because she has a perfect figure. Soft. Round. Full. With curves everywhere you look and touch. *Not now, Robert.*

She digs in, and it is immediately apparent just how hungry she was. I love watching Gwen eat. While most women would be worrying about being proper and ladylike, she has no such qualms. Gwen does everything with an almost childlike zeal and abandon. She is unapologetically herself, no matter what. It's one of the most striking things about her.

She doesn't speak until half her plate is cleared. Then she leans back in her chair and lets out a long sigh, hopefully, one of contentment.

"You outdid yourself today, Robert," she says. "This chicken is delicious."

"Thank you. I'm glad you like it."

"Ooh. I just got an idea. We should get you on one of those cooking shows. Or one of those lifestyle shows with cooking segments. It could help sell you to female voters, younger voters too ..."

I reach across the table and take her hand, just as she is reaching back into her blouse, no doubt for the notebook. "Can we not talk about work, just for tonight?" I ask her. "I have no doubt you'll represent me to the best of your ability, and I'd love to talk about our media strategy in greater detail. But tonight is not about the campaign. Tonight is about you and me."

Gwen is quiet for some time, but eventually, she nods. "You're right. Take the night off. I understand."

"Do you? Because I haven't seen my girlfriend in weeks."

She squeezes my hand as if to reassure me that she does. "You're right. Of course. I get carried away sometimes... And I still don't know how to draw the line between girlfriend and campaign manager. I'm sorry. This is a lovely dinner you've planned. The food is delicious. And I'm here with you. That's all I need, really."

"Good. Because I missed you."

"I missed you too."

"So you'll spend the night, then?"

Gwen laughs. "Are you trying to get into my pants, Robert Hardy?"

"I wouldn't dream of it, madam!" I say, and now we're both laughing.

Dinner proceeds much better after that. Gwen finally drops the work persona and allows the woman I fell for to bubble through to the surface. She wisecracks about my cooking, promising that she'll cook circles around me next time, all while wondering why I don't cook for her more often. She shares stories about her family;

her little nephew, who is all of ten years old, has apparently decided he doesn't like his given name and wants to be called 'Simba' instead.

It has been a while, but our organic banter flows as easily and effortlessly as ever. Once Gwen settles down, and the wine starts to kick in, she turns back into the charming, devastating knockout I met several months back. She is whip-smart and sarcastic, and she has a delightful sense of humor. Even after our plates are both cleared, and the candles have burned down to dim stubs, we sit there, chatting and laughing, like old friends.

It's the first time in almost a week that I haven't thought about Amy. Or her stinging rejection. Unconsciously, I reach up and rub my cheek, the exact spot where she slapped me. By the time I snap back to my senses and draw the hand away, Gwen has already noticed the motion, and her eyes, previously half-lidded from the wine, are suddenly wide open and alert. She rarely misses a thing, this woman. And on a good day, she can read my mind.

"Have you heard from her at all?" she asks. Direct. No point hiding it.

"No," I say. "And I don't expect to."

She opens her mouth to protest, but I head her off. "Come on, let's retire to the couch. It's definitely more comfortable."

She sees the feeble attempt to deflect. Luckily, she simply nods and stands up. She sways slightly as she tries to step away from the table, and I have to rush over and grab her before she topples over.

"Sorry," she says into my face. Her breath smells like wine. Her posture is loose, and a single sleeve of her blouse has slipped from her shoulder so that it lays exposed, impossibly soft and inviting. I can feel my pants growing taut.

I walk her slowly over to the couch. She mumbles something about her head swimming, and I smile. I lay her down slowly, then stretch out beside her, my arms around her. She closes her eyes and rests her head on my chest. She seems so peaceful, so carefree.

"Why don't you like to talk about Amy?" she asks suddenly, without opening her eyes.

I had forgotten; drunk Gwen has no filters.

"There's nothing to talk about," I say simply, my tone icier than I had intended.

"That's not true," Gwen says. "I know she's the reason you went off the rails. I know that whatever happened between you was bad enough she quit her job and applied for a teaching job at a community college. That doesn't seem like nothing."

I suppose I should have known she was going to ask at some point. Amy has always been there, hanging between us, an unspoken thing that Gwen always knew was a major issue. At first, I deflected her questions easily enough. And then when I couldn't dodge them anymore, I told her a version of the truth that I deemed sufficient: Amy and I had been together for a long time, but it didn't work out between us, and the resulting fallout affected us both, albeit in different ways. Gwen figured out some more details over time, subtly, through sneaky questions and her own deductions. But after some time she knew not to ask, and she accepted that I wasn't comfortable talking about it.

Of course, all it takes to tear down inhibition is a few glasses of wine. The incident with Amy last week certainly couldn't have made her any less curious.

"What do you really want to know, Gwen?" I ask her.

Her eyes flicker open. She straightens up and adjusts her frame so that she is looking right into my eyes.

"Are you still in love with her?" she asks. It's a rare moment of vulnerability. I doubt sober Gwen would have admitted to being jealous. Assuming that's what this is.

"Of course not," I say, taking care not to think about that one for too long. I draw a finger along her jawline, over her cheekbone, and let my hand disappear into her hair. I push her face even closer to mine. "I love *you*, Gwendoline Michaels."

It's nothing new. These are words I've said before. But for some reason, it feels like they should carry more weight now. Like I have to convince her of their truth more than I have before.

Her eyes search my face. They seem so vibrant, so alive. Finally, she starts to nod. "Okay."

She leans in and kisses me lightly on the lips. Feather-soft. Inquiring. But it's enough. The blood rushes back downwards, and the cumulative images of her legs as she lay on my couch, the hint of cleavage as I help her up off the table, and the feel of her weight on me spring all thought from my mind except that I want this woman.

I respond to the kiss with little restraint. My lips seize hers, and as the hand still buried in the tangle of her hair pushes her forward, the force of my response is enough to lift her slightly. She swivels her waist and hips, works herself into a sitting position, and throws her arms around me.

The wine makes her mouth even sweeter. I delve in with my tongue, past her teeth, meeting her own tongue, and pushing it back. I feel her moan and begin to grind on top of me. Her skirt is stretched tight across her thighs, straining, forbidding. I try to push it up, work it back and over her waist, but it's impossibly tight, and after a few seconds of both our fingers fumbling uselessly with the hem, I give up. Maybe if I lift her?

I lean forward with her still in my grasp. Her lips break from mine, and her head falls back. I lift her and lay her gently on her back. Her body has gone limp, though, and when I lean back in to resume the kiss, she is unresponsive.

I curse silently under my breath. She has apparently passed out, no doubt from all the alcohol and the exhaustion. Her breathing has slowed down to the point I know she'll be snoring in a few minutes.

Shaking my head, I get off the couch and scoop her into my arms. She mutters something as I'm carrying her into the bedroom, and I think I hear my name. But she drifts off again in a second, and when I lay her on the bed and pull the covers over her, she lets out a little snore.

Maybe next time, Robert.

Ignoring the pulsing boner stretching out the front of my pants, I switch off the lights and head back into the dining room. I clear the table, scraping the leftover food into a container and storing it in the refrigerator. I quickly do the dishes, clean up, and on a whim, decide to take the trash out.

As I'm stepping out of the door, my foot hits something hard, and I look down in alarm. It's a small brown box, which had apparently been placed right on my doorstep. A feeling of dread blossoms in the pit of my stomach and starts to radiate outwards. I know what it is even before I reach for it. Unmarked brown box. A slight rattling sound when I give it a shake.

This is clearly the second package from my blackmailer.

27
Amelia

It's only my second week of 'total freedom' and I hate it.

My house is eerily quiet. Having gotten used to the hustle and bustle of mid-town, and the general mayhem of living in an apartment complex, this place will take some adjusting to. The silence was a welcome relief at first. In the night, there was nothing to be heard for miles. No chatter over dinner floating through the open windows, no dull roar from a nearby party. Nothing. Just the sound of my own thoughts. And for me, a rare opportunity to work without being distracted.

I graded papers and planned my next lesson in record time. Without Ness' constant interruption, or whatever else was going on, I achieved peak productivity and when I was done with work, I treated myself to a long bath, then got in bed with a book and drifted off before my eyes hit the second paragraph. It was so peaceful, so tranquil, so perfect.

Soon, however, the silence took on a more menacing quality. Why was the neighborhood so quiet? I knew I had neighbors; I saw them during the day, and in the moments between leaving for work and coming back. But in the night, it seemed the whole street vanished. Was I really safe? Would anyone hear me if I was in need of help and I called out?

In the days immediately after my encounter with Robert, that silence turned against me. Robert, whose name I have been refusing to actively say or even think about. Without the background noise, I was alone with my thoughts in a way I had tried so hard to avoid. Even without trying, my mind wandered, and it seemed to particularly enjoy wandering to *him*.

Tonight has been worse than usual. Earlier, I saw an ad on television, a short clip effectively announcing Robert's candidacy. And suddenly, I understood what the woman had been talking about. Gwen, she had said her name was. Robert is running for political office.

It seems ludicrous to me that he would. Everything I know about Robert makes him the worst possible candidate for an elective post. Too many secrets, too dark a past. But I suppose I didn't know him as well as I thought I did. If I had, none of what went down between us would have happened. Clearly, Robert Hardy and the man I thought I was in love with are two different people.

Since the ad, my mind has been awash with memories of the bastard in spite of my best efforts. Eighteen months of successfully blocking him out, for the most part, and it is all undone by a single encounter. It feels like someone else's memory, which is perhaps why my mind keeps going back to that scene, replaying it, reconstructing it, and regretting it. I should have hit him harder. I should have hit him again. I shouldn't have fled; it made me look weak.

But nothing sticks to my caw quite like the question of what he wants from me.

To say Robert and I left things on bad terms would be a gross understatement. There was yelling. Things were thrown. A scene was caused, witnessed first by a rapt restaurant audience and then by a confused street. And then, much later, very briefly, by the internet. Ness forwarded me the YouTube link, but by the time I was composed enough to click on it, the video was nowhere to be found. He must have had it removed, which was maybe the only positive to come out of the whole mess.

So, what could he possibly want from me now? I made it clear I didn't want to see him ever again or hear from him. I came so close to leaving town, but Ness convinced me that it would be like letting him win. The best I could do was remove myself from his immediate surroundings, and slowly start to heal. And to Robert's credit, he did not try to look for me or contact me. Total radio silence from him. Until last week, that is.

My phone rings in the middle of my ruminations.

It sounds so loud, intrusive, the only sound I've heard all night. It breaks my train of thought and snaps me back to the present. I dimly register the name 'Kieran' on the caller ID. I glance at the clock and frown. It's almost midnight. Why would he be calling me at this hour?

"Miss Brooks?" His voice sounds slurred, heavy.

"Is everything okay, Kieran?"

"Yeah, yeah. Everything is fine." Silence. "Can I see you tonight?"

Of course. A booty call. From a child.

"It's late, Kieran. I have school tomorrow."

"I know. I'm in your class."

Funny. "Then you know seeing me is not possible."

"Why not?"

I open my mouth furiously, but then I realize I'm not actually sure why not. "As I said, I have to be up early tomorrow."

"I'll leave early, then," Kieran says without missing a beat. "Please? I miss you."

"Go to bed, Kieran," I say and hang up the phone. From the sounds of it, he is out with friends, somewhere noisy. Probably a little drunk. It's not a good sign if he's starting to drunk dial me. I really need to put a stop to this.

But then I realize that I don't have much of a night planned out anyway. That without any distraction, I'll be alone with my thoughts until I fall asleep, and judging by how much harder it has been getting to do that I could be in for a long one.

Maybe it's not such a bad idea for Kieran to come over. I could kick him out in the morning …

I grab the phone and compose a text, hit send before I can change my mind.

Be here in 20 minutes.

It takes him 15. I am wrapped in my bathrobe, preparing to get in the shower when I hear his car pull up in the driveway, and moments later, the doorbell. He must have been on his way when he made that phone call.

"You cannot call me like that," I say to him as the door swings open.

He is leaning on the door frame, his long limbs thrust into his pockets, a cheesy smile on his face. "I'm sorry," he says. "I was at a party, and someone handed me some weed."

Weed makes him horny. I hate that I'm starting to retain information about him. And apparently, when he gets horny, he thinks of me.

He steps into the house, and I close the door behind him. Somehow, I can't bring myself to admonish him anymore. It's getting harder to. He is so freaking adorable, and his attraction to me seems so earnest and endearing I almost can't stand it.

"I was just about to jump in the shower," I tell him. "There's mac and cheese in the freezer if you're hungry. I'll be a few minutes."

Kieran nods, and I leave him on the couch as I head into the bathroom.

The bathrooms may be my favorite thing about the new house. The one in my bedroom has a nice little tub tucked away in a corner, where I like to soak after a long day. But the one down the hallway is even better. No tub, but the shower system is complicated and beautiful. I can play around with the water pressure, the temperature, and even detach the showerhead for a therapeutic rub-down. I swear, I could stand under that deluge of searing hot water for hours. It's strangely calming.

I turn the heat all the way up, and the water gushes out over my body. I close my eyes and let out a deep sigh.

Somehow, I don't hear Kieran sneak into the bathroom. I'm completely unaware of his presence until his hands are on my body, and then my eyes fly open.

"Jeezus!" he exclaims as the water hits him too. "Isn't this too hot for you?"

"It's just right," I say.

I want to protest, but he steps in and puts his hands around me.

He is an interesting kid, Kieran. He has the body of a model; tall and lean, with a chiseled torso clearly maintained by rigorous exercise. But from what I understand, he doesn't play any sports. He is the dictionary definition of a nerd: he likes video games, comic books, and movies. He is shy and introverted, always preferring to be invisible rather than contribute to any social situation. But when we are alone together, Kieran turns into a different beast altogether. It's like I bring out the sexual deviant in him.

His hair is already wet, and he pushes it out of his face as he lowers his lips to mine. I think for a moment that he may be more beautiful than I am, and then I melt into him and lean into the kiss.

The water pours down between us, around us. It makes our bodies slick, and his hands roam with ease all over my backside. He grabs my ass and squeezes with intent. I gasp as the motion crushes me against his body, and his erect penis presses hard into my belly.

The kiss is growing in urgency. His lips are like soft, hot pillows, rubbing and dancing along and against mine. It may be the water, but I'm so turned on I can feel the muscles in my vagina start to clench and unclench.

He flips me around suddenly, almost roughly. I marvel for a second at the stark difference between Kieran, the man who is about to fuck me, and the shy boy who cannot hold my gaze in class and took weeks to gather up the courage to approach me. Then a firm hand is pressing onto my back, and I lean against the wall, pushing my ass out towards him.

Long, hot fingers pull my cheeks apart. I feel him reposition himself and stand directly behind me. It must be hard, with the water coming down like that. Slippery too. But the next moment, he is pushing into me, hot and long and heavenly, and his hands are now on my hips.

Everything feels hot. The walls I'm trying to cling on to, the floor underneath my feet, the man inside me ...

I can hear him grunting.

He starts off with a slow, deep thrusting motion, pulling all the way out and then sliding back in. I rock in time to his thrusts, pushing back, using the wall for support. His rhythm grows erratic gradually until suddenly, the fingers on my hips are digging into my flesh, his grunts are louder and harsher, and his hips are now slamming into me.

I can feel his whole body tense. Any time now, I think, squeezing my lips against his girth, egging him on.

Instead, he pulls out, just as suddenly as he swings me around, and steps towards me. Instinctively, I step back, but he follows me, looming over me, the hairs falling around his face, his jaw clenched. He circles my waist with his hands and lifts. I wrap my legs around him as he pins me against the wall.

He finds my aching pussy with ease and buries himself deep inside me. Now his lips are against my ear, and his hands are gripping my bottom. Most of my weight rests on the walls, but the firm pressure on my ass is a silent reassurance that he is in control.

He doesn't last much longer. His thrusts are manic, hard, and fast. My eyes flicker open, and I see him in the throes of bliss. It sends my own eyes rolling into the back of my head. His nails claw against my butt. His hips are like a piston, powering into me once, twice, thrice, and a final fourth time. Then it is all over. His lips are buried somewhere in my neck, and I think I feel teeth sink into the soft skin there.

After what seems like an eternity, he steps back, allowing his dick to slide out of me, and setting me gingerly on the floor. He stares at me tenderly, the shy boy peeking through the matted hair, the sexually charged man gone.

Without saying a word, he reaches over my head and grabs the shampoo. I stand there, almost in awe but not quite, as he starts to lather my hair. His fingers are gentle, almost reverent, as they work out the knots in my hair. He massages my scalp, letting the shampoo soak my head completely before washing it off. I feel strangely disarmed, standing there, letting this beautiful man wash me.

He does the same for the rest of me, but by this time, I'm caught up, and I return the favor.

The eerie silence of the house comes back to me, louder than ever except for the water running from our bodies, the soapy sludge pooling around our feet and then draining away, and the motions of our hands as we scrub each other.

Eventually, he deems me clean enough, and I have washed every inch of him twice over. I nod when he meets my eye, and he bends over, scoops me like a weightless toy, and carries me out of the shower.

I don't hate this. I think I could actually get used to it. I shouldn't. I probably won't. But I could.

His feet make soft squelching sounds as he pads over to my bedroom. I remember the first time he was in here he couldn't stop staring at the large, four-poster bed in the middle of the room. He makes his way over to that bed now and sits me on the edge. His eyes scan the room, landing on the towels folded neatly on the chest in the corner.

My eyes follow him as he crosses the room, and I think, not for the first time, that this is wrong. He is too good for me. Some girl somewhere is missing out on all this, and it's all my fault.

I notice that his erection is back as he towels me off. It's still impressive just how little time he needs to get going again. That, and he is high.

We climb into bed together. He is more deliberate now, slower, seemingly eager to savor instead of ravish. He starts a moist trail of kisses from my temple, running them all the way down to my belly button, and once his hands have pulled my knees apart, his head disappears between my legs.

He is no expert, certainly, but he is eager to please, and I concede he is doing a great job of that. His tongue lashes and teases, running first along my swollen lips before venturing in and locating my clitoris. Then he sets to work, still in no rush, licking and sucking and making all sorts of motions. He reads my body so well; well enough that he can tell when I'm about to come, and then his mouth is gone, and I hang for a moment, suspended on the precipice of ecstasy.

Don't stop I want to tell him. Keep going; I'm so close. But I know he wants us to come together, and I can't hold that against him.

Somehow, he feels bigger this time. Or it could be that I'm sore. It's a good ache, a sweet kind of agony. He fills me up and rocks slowly, letting me adjust to him, taking his time. I throw my legs up and trap him between them as he starts to grind and thrust.

We move like that for so long I feel my leg begin to cramp. His body, which was hot from the shower before, has started to get dotted by sweat. I close my eyes and will myself to remain present, but my mind has started to drift.

The thought slips into my mind unbidden. I would have climaxed already with Robert. Multiple times. I shake the unfair comparison from my mind. I blink quickly, and Kieran's face swims before me once more. He has quickened his pace and is starting to pound away inside me. He lifts himself off me, then grabs my legs and pushes them as far back as they can go, which in this case means my feet are now dangling somewhere close to my ears.

He pins me to the bed and uses the headrest to support himself as he drives deeper into me. I moan softly, lifting my hips slightly upward to meet his thrust. It undoes him completely. The first words he utters for hours now are all curse words. He loses control of his body as he climaxes. I can hear the soft creaking from the board where he is gripping. His legs jerk beneath him, and his torso convulses uncontrollably. I watch him quietly, trying not to acknowledge the disappointment surging through me. And the shame, at how easily my mind replaced him.

When he eventually slumps over to the side and looks at me and asks in the sweetest voice if I came, I plant a smile on my face and nod. Satisfied, he turns to the side, and in a few minutes, he is asleep.

I don't remember falling asleep. I remember struggling to, and then someone is shaking me, calling my name. It feels like I have sand behind my eyelids. I grumble in protest, but the voice is persistent, the shaking more urgent.

"You'll be late for work if you don't wake up."

Kieran is seated on the edge of the bed, fully dressed. It takes a lot of effort to sit up, but I do. It is still dark outside, but a quick glance at my clock tells me that it's 4 a.m.

"Thanks for waking me," I say in the middle of a yawn. I lean over to give Kieran a quick peck, but he pulls away.

"Is everything okay?" I ask, surprised. Kieran has never once recoiled from my touch.

He bites his lip, and his voice trembles slightly when he speaks. "Who is Robert?"

"What?"

"Robert. You said his name twice last night."

28
Robert

It was Gwen's idea that I go in alone. It's not exactly hard to figure out why. Somehow, it doesn't seem smart to show up at a woman's house to apologize for past wrongdoings in the company of another woman. I like to think that we have managed to keep our relationship fairly low-key, but it's not impossible to figure out we're together. As I can myself attest, women have a way of picking up on these things.

Bethany is one of the first names on my list, and the only woman I remember almost completely. It wasn't hard to find her; she lives just outside Glendale, according to the info Charles was able to draw up for us.

I step out of the car and walk up to the first house on a row of nearly identical houses on the street. Two burly gentlemen fall into step beside me, each frowning at nothing in particular. I'm still not comfortable with them around, but Gwen insists that I need a security team around me after the appearance of the second package. She was particularly livid when I told her the package had arrived just after she did at my apartment, and she has been uneasy ever since.

So I am now flanked, wherever I go, by the two statues. My Men in Black. Personally, I think it's a bit unnecessary. If the person had any intention of harming me, I feel like they have had ample opportunities to do so. I'm not exactly hard to find. If they know where I live, and all they've done is deliver a package, then I feel fairly confident that this isn't a security threat in the way Gwen thinks it is.

The one thing we agree on, however, is that I need to get a move on with the 'plan.' I need to start tracking down these women and owning my mistakes.

Amy was obviously a bust, but I have an idea how to get to her. Right now, the woman I'm going to see is one I hope will be as receptive to me now as she was when I first met her.

When the door opens and a woman steps out, I don't initially realize it's her. She has definitely filled out; her frame is wider, her face a little plumper, and the reason for it is immediately clear; she is bobbing a child up and down on her hip.

I know that a year is a long time, but the baby takes me completely by surprise. I may not remember much about the night we met, but I remember Bethany's wild, carefree party attitude. Somehow, it didn't seem like she had any interest in motherhood, let alone a domestic life.

"Robert?" Her surprise is brief, replaced moments later by a flash of what I assume is anger.

"Hi, Bethany," I say. For a brief moment, I am tempted to step backward; the last time I tried this, I was rewarded with a stinging slap for my troubles.

"What are you doing here?" she asks, and her expression has definitely turned cold. She has even stopped bouncing the baby up and down and is looking me over like I've just walked on to her porch with muddy shoes.

"Can I come in?" I ask, suddenly worried that someone could see me standing there, recognize me, and then that would be another thing I would have to deal with.

"I'm not sure I want you in my house," she says.

The baby stirs and then starts to fuss. Bethany tries to resume the rocking motion, but it's apparently too late. A piercing scream announces that the baby is now awake, and Bethany curses loudly.

"Come on, then," she says over her shoulder as she turns and walks into the house. "You have five minutes."

I give a quick nod to the Men in Black indicating that they wait for me outside. Then I step over the threshold and follow Bethany into the house, more nervous than I expected to be.

Everything about the house screams 'family.' Family photos lining the walls, toys scattered all over the house, the smell of burnt coffee lingering in the air. And the sound of a toddler screaming at the top of its lungs.

Bethany lays the baby down and starts to fuss with its diaper. I stand there awkwardly until she shoots a look at me, then I start to talk very fast.

"Right. Well, I'll just get to the point, Bethany. I don't know if you've heard, but I'm running for DA."

"I have," she says nonchalantly. "Bad idea."

"I beg your pardon?"

"I think that's a bad idea. But no matter. You were saying?"

"Uh ... yes. I'm running for DA. As you may know from our ... encounter, there are things about my past that are a little colorful, things that I would prefer to stay in the past."

"I don't see what that has got to do with me, Robert."

Her fingers are quick and practiced as she changes the diaper. She is finished before I've decided on what to even say. She turns to face me, her hand going to her hip, just in case I don't already know what she thinks of my sudden appearance.

"Look, Bethany." Honesty, then. "Someone is trying to blackmail me. They have gotten hold of some incriminating documents from my past ... photos, videos ... things which cast me in a certain light, which I think they intend to use to somehow derail my campaign ..."

"And you think that person is me?"

"I mean ... no, but is it?"

Bethany shakes her head in disbelief. "You know what, Robert? I'm happy this is happening to you. Frankly, I'm surprised it has taken this long for someone to hold up a mirror to you."

"I don't think ..."

"Do you even remember me, Robert? I mean, besides my name, which I'm shocked you *do* remember, and my face, which must be part of a revolving door of inconsequential women."

"I never said you were inconsequential, Bethany."

"But you don't remember me, do you?"

"Of course I do. I wouldn't be here if I didn't."

"Really? I thought you're here to cover your ass."

She is angry. And she has every right to be. I am suddenly overcome by a wave of exhaustion at my situation, and disgust at myself for getting here in the first place.

"We met at a bar," I say. "You were out with a group of your friends, celebrating a birthday or something, and I had drinks sent to you all night, which you kept returning, but I kept them coming until you relented and came over to talk to me."

"Huh," Bethany says. The baby is silent in her arms; it must have fallen asleep again. "Close enough, I suppose. But just like that night, you don't care about the details. It was a bachelorette party. It was the first bar we hit on an intended crawl through the city. I wasn't drinking, but that didn't stop you from sending the drinks. All night. I approached you to tell you to stop, that I wasn't drinking because I was pregnant. But you didn't care. I don't think you even heard me. No, you turned on the charm and proceeded to sell me on Robert Hardy, the big-time city lawyer."

"You were pregnant?" I ask, trying to recall our discussion on the night. My whole memory of it is foggy.

"Didn't stop you from sleeping with me. I'm not blaming you for that part, though. On some subconscious level, I suppose I wanted to. Against my better judgment, I was flattered by your attention and your relentless pursuit. You made me feel beautiful, wanted, something my husband had not been doing."

"Your husband?" And here I was thinking she was angry at me for failing to call her the next morning.

"Well. Ex-husband now. But you see my point, Robert? You don't care about anyone except yourself. If you did, if you listened to any of the women you blew through, I'm sure you wouldn't have any trouble figuring out which one would want to blackmail you. Assuming that's even what this is."

She steps away, and I watch in stunned silence as she lays the baby gently into a cot. She beckons that we should leave the room. I follow her into the kitchen, trying not to look at the towering mountain of unwashed dishes.

"To answer your question, no. I'm not the one who's blackmailing you. I have no reason to. I'm angry at you, yes, but really, I'm angrier with myself. It was my own fault, what happened, even if you played a big role in it. My bad decisions were just that; mine. I'm sure you were battling your own demons, so in a way, we used each other. But that was that. I've moved on with my life."

She catches me eyeing the sink, and a slight smile crosses her face. "I'm trying anyway," she adds, then laughs to herself.

"I'm sorry, Bethany," I tell her. "This wasn't just about me finding out who is behind the blackmail. I'm also trying to own up to my mistakes, be a better person. I'm sorry I was too self-obsessed to see you as anything more than a skirt. I'm sorry I didn't listen to you, and for the way I treated you."

She is silent for a long time. Her fingers twitch, and once or twice, she reaches almost absentmindedly for her pockets and then freezes halfway and lays her palms at her sides. I recognize the motion. She must be trying to give up smoking.

"I won't lie, I've thought about calling you, if only to talk. Once my marriage broke down, I even allowed myself to imagine ours wasn't just a one-night stand, that maybe there was something more. But like I said, I understand what happened that night. I get that we were both just trying to outrun our ghosts. Thank you for saying that, though. It means a lot." She smiles the first genuine smile I've gotten from her, and the relief that floods through me is almost like a shot of adrenaline.

"Did you mean it earlier?" I ask her, confident our truce means she will answer honestly. "You think I shouldn't be running?"

Bethany walks over to the coffeemaker and pours herself a cup. She lifts it in my direction, but I shake my head.

"How many women are left on this apology tour of yours?" she asks me.

"A few," I say, grinning in spite of myself.

"So you have to traverse the country seeking out this culprit, all while hoping none of this comes out in the media, and at the same time running your business and also a campaign?"

"Pretty much, yeah."

"Then no. You should definitely be running. I'm sure this is what all candidates have to deal with."

Gwen is waiting for me in the car. She reads from my expression that the 'meeting' went well, and she lets out a little whoop. "The first one is always the hardest," she comments, pulling out the notebook and crossing out Bethany's name.

Amy was the first, and I want to point it out, but I realize she means the first to strike off the list. "It wasn't actually that difficult," I say instead. "No one threw anything, which was a genuine surprise. Of course, it helps that there was a baby in the house, but still."

"See? I told you this would be good for you."

"You're right," I admit. "It felt really good, talking to her, apologizing. If I had known it was so cathartic, I would have done it a long time ago."

Gwen punches me playfully on the arm. "Let's hope the others will be as easy," she says. "Who do you want to do next? According to Charles' breakdown, I think … Sara is closest? She lives just a few blocks from here …"

I take a deep breath, "I kinda want to take another run at Amy."

Gwen's expression doesn't change to her credit. Her jaw clenches ever so slightly, but her smile doesn't falter. "Oh? I don't know if you remember, Robert, but the last time didn't go so well."

"I know. But I have an idea on how to get her on board."

29
Amelia

The summons comes just as I'm finishing up my afternoon class. It's the first time I've been called to the Dean's office. It feels just as scary as it did when I was a kid being called into the Principal's office. I didn't even know the Dean could do that.

My first thought is that someone has somehow found out about Kieran and me. When the blushing freshman whispers in my ear that Dean Patel would like to see me, my eyes automatically seek out Kieran. He gives me a subtle shake of the head, but that doesn't reassure me. Even if he knows nothing about it, the jig could still be up.

I should have put a stop to it when I had the chance. I shouldn't have let things go so far.

I try and fail to keep my voice steady as I dismiss the students. I sink into my chair and wait as the room clears slowly, gradually. I was hoping to catch Kieran before he leaves, maybe ask him if he knows anything about this, but he has been avoiding me. I was never able to satisfactorily explain why I would be mumbling another man's name while asleep, and he is punishing me the only way he knows how; by withholding his typically expressive attention. It's an effective strategy, I'll admit.

He chooses the furthest exit from the front of the lecture hall, and he blends into a group of other students so that it is virtually impossible for me to grab his attention. It seems like I'll be facing the music alone on this one.

I make my way to the Dean's office slowly, trying to think of ways to justify carrying on an affair with a student. It sounds so wrong when phrased like that.

Dean Patel is one of the friendliest people I've ever met. He has this delightfully zany energy that reminds me of some of my more eccentric high school teachers, and it has the effect of making you want to be his friend minutes after meeting the man. He is a big reason why I ended up accepting a teaching position at the community college; he made it seem like it was the best decision, the only decision, and he made me feel right at home when I did start teaching.

Which makes me feel even worse about having to see his disappointed face.

But neither of the faces that greet me first belong to Patel. In fact, I'm so surprised to see Robert and Gwen. I momentarily forget to scowl.

The Dean steps out from behind a bookshelf on the far side of the room. He beams at me, and that puts me even further off balance. This has nothing to do with Kieran and me, I realize.

"Ah. Amy!"

The Dean has always been flamboyant and expressive, particularly in his fashion. Today he is in a crisp blue shirt with a dotted black bowtie. He looks more like the host of an award ceremony than the Dean of a university.

"You wanted to see me?" I ask. I keep my attention on him. I know it's silly, but I'm telling myself that if I keep my attention focused on the Dean, if I completely ignore the other two people in the room, maybe I can will them away. I even allow myself to imagine that they are here for a different reason that has nothing to do with me.

"Yes, yes. Please. Sit."

I can feel Robert's stare burning a hole in the back of my head. I sit down and look over at Dean Patel expectantly.

"You must know who this is?" he points to Robert.

I shrug. "I have seen him on television, yes."

"There's that, yes. But Mr. Hardy informs me that you actually used to work for him?"

"I interned at his law firm when I got out of school," I say, resigned. What else has Robert been telling him?

"Wonderful! I had no idea! Well, Mr. Hardy has made a very interesting proposition for the university ... well, two propositions, actually. He is working on making our auditorium the venue for the first District Attorney debate! Isn't that incredible? That would be such good publicity for us, Amy, don't you think?"

I nod, unable to speak due to the swelling lump in my throat.

So this is how he thinks he is going to get my attention?

"Mr. Hardy is also willing to directly mentor some of our young legal minds, all through their time here and beyond, as they venture into the field! Much like he did with you, I suppose? Think about it, Amy. Your best and brightest students, getting regular one-on-one time with such a fine lawyer, and, as the lovely Miss Michaels here assures me, our next District Attorney!"

Patel is visibly excited, and I think I know why. The Lincoln Community College is a great institution, but it has never quite managed to shed the tag of 'small college' that so many of its peers place on it. For the Dean, a big part of the job was always increasing the stature of the university enough that it could be talked about in the same breath as some of the older, more established colleges.

Robert's proposals have no doubt appealed to this very sense; he feels it is a rare opportunity to put the university on the map, and on paper, it is. The only problem is that he is dealing with Robert Hardy.

"This all sounds great, sir," I tell him. "But I don't see where I come in."

Subtext: I know he isn't a politician just yet, but if he could hurry up and tell me what he wants from me, that would be swell.

"Well, for one, you teach some of our beginner law courses, so you would be the perfect person to work with Mr. Hardy on the mentorship program."

"Oh, but there are several other law professors at the university," I jump in. "I'm sure any one of them would be a better fit."

Why isn't the benevolent Mr. Hardy, DA-elect, saying anything? Why isn't he making this pitch himself?

"There's more, Amy. Mr. Hardy requires a small favor in return."

There it is. Maybe he is already a politician.

"It seems he has a small case he needs help with, as much of his attention must understandably turn to his campaign, and he cannot attend to it fully."

"So he needs a lawyer."

"He needs you, Amy."

Ha. As if.

I get up from the chair and finally turn to Robert and Gwen. "I appreciate the offer, Mr. Hardy, but I'm afraid I must respectfully decline it. I'm far too busy here, and I'm sure there are people more qualified than me you can seek out. I hope this doesn't mean you won't still want to work with my students?"

Dean Patel says something, but his voice comes as though from a mile away. Gwen has taken a step toward Robert, and now she stands on tiptoe and leans up to whisper something in his ear. Her hand goes to his waist as she does. It's such a small, seemingly insignificant gesture, but I notice it right away.

Robert turns to the Dean with a smile. I know that smile all too well.

"Mr. Patel, if I could have a quick word with Miss Brooks outside?"

The Dean nods eagerly.

And therein, I realize, is the genius of Robert's plan. This wasn't about getting me to help with a case. That wasn't his goal. This was about an audience with me, one where he was guaranteed I wouldn't run away or slap him across the face.

"Regardless of her response, by the way," Robert adds as he turns to leave the office. "My proposition stands. I will be happy to help the university in any way I can."

The Dean grins, his relief is evident. I try to think of ways to avoid this sidebar with Robert, but so far, I have nothing. I cannot run this time.

We walk a few feet away from the office, and I worry at first that he wants to lead us into an empty classroom, in which case I will have to put my foot down firmly. He may have tricked me into speaking with him, but I'm not going to be alone in a room with Robert Hardy, not if I can help it.

He seems to read my mind, though, and he stops at a seemingly random point in the hallway. Then he turns to face me, and it feels like déjà vu. How many times have we stood face to face like this, to talk, debate, fight?

"You're not going to hit me again, are you?" he asks, and I gather from the way his lips twitch that he is trying to make a joke.

Lighten the mood.

"What is this, Robert? Why are you stalking me?"

"I'm not stalking you."

"Then what do you call this? This is the second time in two weeks you're showing up at my place at work."

"I need your help, Amy."

"I told you I don't want anything to do with you, Robert. We agreed."

"I know. And I've left you alone this whole time, haven't I? But things have changed, and I really need your help."

"Like I told your girlfriend the last time, I don't know anything about politics."

It's a wild thing to say, an unfounded accusation based solely on how she touched him. But it's his reaction I'm looking for, and his face betrays him immediately. Surprise. Guilt? Defiance.

"Gwen isn't my girlfriend," he says, shrugging and then pocketing his hands. If he were hooked up to a lie detector test right now, the machine would be going haywire.

"You need to learn to lie better, Robert, if you're hoping to be a politician."

"Because there's no such thing as an honest politician?"

I laugh. "Remember when *I* was the naïve one? Anyway, I thought she was your campaign manager." I don't know why I'm pushing the subject. Part of me wants to hear him admit it if only to prove me right.

"She is," Robert says stiffly.

"But she's also your girlfriend."

Silence. Then: "So what if she is? That has nothing to do with anything."

It occurs to me that I'm in no position to judge him for that when a few minutes ago, I was shaking in fear of my inappropriate relationship with a student being found out. But he admitted it. Congratulations, Amy. You can still read him like a book. So he's dating. What now?

"What do you mean things have changed?"

Robert sighs, clearly relieved at the change of topic. He

reaches into his pocket and pulls out a stack of photos, which he hands to me.

It takes me a minute to figure out what I'm looking at, but it all falls into place fairly quickly. Photos of Robert, with various women. Photos of Robert at seedy bars, strip clubs, dimly lit streets. All with him clearly inebriated.

"You have a secret admirer."

"I'm afraid so. And normally, this would just be another Wednesday, but the timing couldn't be worse."

"When was this?" I ask, waving the stack of photos.

"These are from around nine months ago. After you broke my heart."

I shake my head. I'm not taking that bait. "So someone is trying to blackmail you, end your political career. Isn't this the sort of thing you thrive at?"

"Well, that's not what I need your help with. Gwen—"

"Who?"

"What do you mean, who? Gwen."

"Oh, your girlfriend?"

Don't banter with him, woman. Don't enjoy this. He is still an asshole.

An asshole with a girlfriend. Why does that bother me?

Robert goes on as if he hasn't heard me. "Gwen thinks this is the work of a scorned former lover. You know, one of the women I 'encountered' when I fell off the wagon last year."

"That's a long list."

"Which is why I'm recruiting the person who knows me best to help me figure it all out."

I hesitate. "I don't know if I'm that person anymore."

Robert shakes his head. His eyes are blazing into mine, burning with an intensity I remember so well.

"You'll always be that person, Amy."

I don't see the hand until it is resting on my shoulder. His touch takes me completely by surprise, shocking me so badly, I react instinctively. I lash out at the same time I'm stepping back. For the second time in as many meetings, my hand connects with his face.

"Shit, I'm sorry! That was unintentional!"

"I knew you wanted to hit me again," Robert says, smiling through the hand on his cheek. "Get it out of your system yet?"

"Maybe a few more. I'll let you know."

I realize suddenly that the invisible wall between us is coming down, that I am closer than I have been to having a normal interaction with him in such a long time. And I realize that I don't hate how that feels. It's like going back to a show you stopped watching or bumping into an old friend; it feels comfortable, familiar.

"Robert?"

We both snap around to see Gwen approaching, with a look of concern on her face.

"Is everything okay?" Her eyes dart between the two of us, and I feel a savage pleasure at the inkling of suspicion that settles over her beautiful features.

"Yeah, everything is great!" Robert says, a little too cheerfully. "Amy was just about to accept my offer. Amy?"

30
Amelia

Kieran isn't speaking to me. I noticed it after he spent the night at my place, and he wouldn't even meet my eye for the rest of the day. In class, he looked down for the entirety of the lesson, and afterward, he melted into a crowd of other students and was out of sight before I could get around my desk.

At first, I was too proud to reach out to him, reasoning that he would eventually swallow his pride and call me, or that he would go out with his friends again and drunk dial me. In all the scenarios I mapped out in my head, he was the one who came to me. I assumed he would because that's the kind of person he is. So when he didn't, I grew increasingly concerned, until I had to admit to myself that maybe I cared about him a little more than I had been willing to acknowledge.

Eventually, I caved and started to text him, but my messages went unanswered, and I felt myself descending into the dark place where I started to overthink the simplest things. I didn't want to flood his phone with messages because that's crazy girlfriend behavior, and I'm NOT his girlfriend. But when my calls also went unanswered, I figured I was definitely in trouble.

His distance unnerves me. I have become so used to him fawning over me, and the glow of his affection, so now he's stepped away I definitely feel it. The tricky thing is figuring out what to tell him. I have no recollection of saying Robert's name that night. I remember thinking about him at random points while we were making love. But I don't think I said his name out loud. So I could only have done it in my sleep. The memory is foggy, and it slips away from me every time I try to go back. Was I dreaming about him? Did he slip into my subconscious, replacing the man who was actually lying beside me?

All I remember is how hurt Kieran looked when he woke me up, and that wounded expression never left his face as he dressed hurriedly and left. No lingering last glance. No peck on the forehead. No covert squeeze of my bottom. He just slipped out quietly, without waiting for an answer to the question he had posed.

So what to tell him?

Perhaps I'll figure that out as soon as I can get him to stand still long enough to have a conversation with me. And that has proven especially difficult. He is much faster and definitely more athletic than I am. It's actually not that hard to avoid me, I have realized. I operate on a very small circuit; classroom, office, cafeteria, library, and then parking lot. Once in a while, I visit the teacher's lounge, but I haven't made the kind of friends that would make me go back regularly. My schedule is simple, primarily because I want it that way. If someone wants to avoid me, as Kieran clearly does, all they have to do is steer clear of these areas.

It's how I get the idea to track him down. All I have to do is find out where he goes, the places he frequents. It would be easier if I knew his friends, but there would be no way of getting any information out of them without seeming suspicious. Already, I feel like someone must have noticed how panicked I look and feel. I feel like someone is eventually going to stop me and ask me to explain my interest in a twenty-something-year-old student.

No, I will have to do this on my own.

The shame and judgment wash over me as I'm standing at the computer in the Records room, but only for a moment. I rationalize it as I always have. Yes, this has definitely gotten out of hand, but the time for backing out has come and gone. As of that night in my house, I have crossed the point of no return. I type in his name and click on the spreadsheet that pops up.

Kieran is twenty-three, which comes as a bit of a shock. It's easy to forget just how young he is. I resist the temptation to go over his admission details and head straight for his schedule. I look around the dusty room, my heart pounding, expecting someone to walk in at any time.

But no one does.

My eyes travel down the schedule, and I quickly surmise that Kieran is supposed to be in History. Relief floods through my body as I close the window and shut down the computer. This wasn't the hard part by any stretch of the imagination, but it still feels like a big win.

I can't remember the name of the kindly professor who teaches History, but I know where he holds his classes. I make my way there, heart pounding, trying to arrange my face into a convincingly nonchalant smile.

I stand at the door to the classroom and peer inside, realizing a second too late that I haven't thought about what I'm going to say. A hundred eyes turn to me, including those of the professor, who stops speaking and follows the gaze of his previously rapt audience. I search the room quickly, and I finally see Kieran, hunched over in the back of the room, inconspicuous as ever.

I snap my eyes back to the professor, grinning awkwardly, and signal for him to come over. This was definitely not well thought out. Thankfully, he shrugs and starts to walk over to me. "I'm so sorry to interrupt," I say, injecting as much sweetness into my voice as I can. "But I need to have a quick word with one of your students, Kieran."

The professor's thick brows knit together. "Is everything okay?"

"Oh, yes, yes. He's in my law class, you see, and there's a slight issue with his transcript I need to speak to him about."

"This could wait, surely?"

"I'm afraid not. I'm finishing up the class exams, and I need to get the transcripts in by end of the day. I wouldn't pull him out of class if it weren't important."

The professor nods, but I can see the suspicion still etched across his face. Whatever his doubts, he sticks his head back into the classroom and says something I can't hear. Moments later, Kieran's mop of hair emerges from around the door, and he looks at me with an expression I can't read.

"Hurry back if you can," the professor says, patting him on the back, then turning and walking back into the classroom.

That was weird, I think. I can already picture the rest of the students leaning across desks and whispering to each other: Did you see that? She pulled him out of class, what could that mean?

"Miss Brooks," Kieran says to me. He steps out of the doorframe and into the hallway, taking care to stand a little distance away from me.

"Look, I need to speak to you."

I'm reminded of the time he came up to me after class and

told me he wanted to see me, that he needed to see me. How the tables have turned.

"I was in the middle of a class," he says, shrugging.

"I can see that. You think it was easy for me, dragging you out here like that? God knows what your friends are thinking now."

For some reason, my words seem to harden his expression. He wasn't exactly grinning before, but now he's definitely upset. "I can't do this right now," he says, looking away.

"I know you're upset about what I said. But really, Kieran, it was a subconscious slip. I don't know what was going on ..." I start to reach out to him, but at that very moment, a group of giggling girls appears from around the corner, and I withdraw my hand quickly. I trail off, waiting for them to pass, noticing their curious glances and resenting the knowing smiles on their faces as they pass.

"Can we please go to my office?" I implore Kieran. "Five minutes, please."

He never looks into my eyes. I can tell he is trying not to. He ponders my proposal for a long time, or maybe my anxiety is making it seem like much longer than it really is. Then he nods curtly and takes off walking briskly in the direction of my office. I shuffle along behind him, torn between maintaining a respectable distance so as not to attract undue attention and staying with him in case he changes his mind and walks off in a different direction. Damn it, but he has a long stride.

He disappears around a corner, and I worry for a second that he has given me the slip again. But I find him waiting for me in my office, seated in the chair facing my desk, arms crossed in a very uncharacteristic manner.

"No, don't," he says when I reach back to close the door.

"What?" I ask, although I heard him perfectly.

"Leave the door open. Five minutes, right? No need to close the door."

I get it. He doesn't trust himself to be around me behind closed doors. It's a compliment, a reminder that in spite of his anger, he still acknowledges his attraction to me. Or I may be overthinking things. I'm seized by a sudden desire to mount him right there on the chair and shove my tongue down his throat.

"Right," I say instead. I step into the office and walk over to the other side of my desk. Might as well make it a proper meeting.

"Look," he says before I can figure out how to begin. "You don't owe me an explanation. You don't really owe me anything."

"I don't understand," I tell him.

"We've never talked about this." He makes a gesture, pointing from me to him. "We've never discussed what this is, so I have no right to demand anything from you."

"But you're still mad at me," I say tentatively.

A buzzing cuts into our little bubble, just as Kieran is opening his mouth to speak. My irritation is short-lived, however, as I realize the sound is coming from my own pocket, my phone ringing. I reach for it and silence it without even looking at it. "Sorry," I say to Kieran. "Continue."

"I'm not mad at you," he says. "I mean, not really. But I realize now that I haven't been upfront with you."

My phone buzzes again, and I silence it with an irritated flick of the wrist.

"What are you talking about, Kieran?"

"I like you, Miss Brooks. Okay? I always have. You're beautiful and smart and a little sad, which for some reason, I find oddly appealing. I never expected anything to happen between us. I assumed it was a little crush which would fade away with time. But it didn't. And then by some stroke of luck, something *did* happen, and it was a dream. Felt like a dream, anyway, one which I kept reliving, and I knew it was too good to be true, but there I was, and there you were, and my dream was a reality, if only for a while."

My mind is blank, except for the recurring thought that maybe Kieran should be majoring in poetry.

"I never asked about your past," he goes on, "because I didn't want to know. Not really. A gorgeous woman like you, of course, you have a past. I know it, but that doesn't stop me from getting jealous. And I am, Miss Brooks. Jealous. I can't stand the thought of you with someone else."

"Kieran," I say softly, trying to sound diplomatic. This conversation has not gone the way I expected at all. For one, I thought I would be doing all the talking. "You realize what we have been doing is wrong, right? You realize nothing can happen between us?"

"What am I to you?" he asks, out of the blue.

There is such heartbreaking sincerity in his voice, such adoration in his eyes. I don't know what to say to him. Even if I did, I wouldn't because I would hate to disappoint him.

"That's really why I'm upset," he says. "Because it occurred to me that I'm your dirty little secret. And I don't want to be anymore."

"What are you saying?" I'm almost afraid to ask. The words slip out, almost a whisper.

Kieran stands up. His jaw is set, his hands thrust into his pockets as if to keep them from doing something stupid. "I don't want to be a secret anymore. I should have done this the right way from the start. Hopefully, I still can. I want to take you out on a real date. No more sneaking around late at night. No more hiding. A real date. Food, drinks, kiss by the doorstep. That's all."

"That's all?" I ask, incredulous. "You must realize that is impossible, Kieran." I stand up as well if only so I don't strain my neck looking up at him.

Kieran shrugs, already turning away. This is an ultimatum, I realize. He is putting his foot down. Date or nothing at all. I'm not sure how to feel about it, but at that moment, I can't help smiling a little. Pride, maybe? I'm still trying to figure out what to say. He is walking to the door now, and I'm desperately trying to remember the arguments I had constructed as to why he and I are a bad idea. Why it would never work.

Before I can give voice to the chaotic thoughts, however, a shadow falls across my doorway, and I look up to see perhaps the person I would have liked to see the least.

Gwen is in her standard sharp business suit; crisp white blouse and short, fitted skirt stretched out by her thick thighs. Her smile is sweet and forced as she looks at Kieran, then around him and at me.

"Hi," she says to him.

Kieran mumbles something to her, then steps around her and walks away.

She dances into my office, irritatingly chipper. "You weren't answering your phone," she says, waving her own.

"As you can see, I was busy," I say without thinking. I see a flash of something in Gwen's eyes, but the next second it's gone, and her smile is back.

"Doesn't matter," she says. "We have that meeting with Robert today, remember? I sent you a reminder in the morning?"

I did see her reminder. And I ignored it. Just because I had agreed to work with Robert again didn't mean I was agreeing to being summoned on a whim, being at his beck and call. I am not his PA anymore. Worse, he is sending this woman to do his dirty work.

"As I said, I've been a bit busy."

"Well, I'm sure you will appreciate that Robert is just as busy, if not more, considering he has much more on his plate. I assume, having agreed to help him, you intend to actually do so?"

I'm not going to grace that with a response.

"Look, Amy. The first debate is coming up fast. I want to focus on prepping Robert for it, without having to worry about this other business. Robert was thrilled when you agreed to help him with that. It took a huge weight off his shoulders, especially considering the history between you two."

"You don't know anything about our history," I snap.

I expect Gwen to snap back or match the animosity I'm currently projecting in her direction. But she doesn't. She simply smiles, then takes a few more steps into the office, pausing when she's right in front of me.

"I know you're still in love with him," she says in a calm voice, barely above a whisper. "I saw the way you looked at him; I'm not stupid. Here's the thing, though. Robert is with me now, so if you agreed to help him as a front for weaseling your way back into his life, then I think you'll find that a bit difficult. Now, you don't need to come with me. This whole thing was Robert's idea. If it had been up to me, I would not have involved you at all, as I believe he can handle his problems himself. I won't lose sleep over you not coming. If anything, it will make my job ten times easier. So, what's it going to be?"

Her smile is smug now. Her eyes are gleaming, but the charm

I picked up when I first met her isn't there anymore. This woman is cold and calculating, and she has just thrown down the gauntlet. And I'll be damned if I don't put her in her place.

31
Robert

Amy and Gwen are both beaming when they walk into the office, but I am not fooled, not for a second. Animosity is streaming from them both like radiation. I can see it in the way they walk, extremely aware of each other, rigid, keeping the other always in sight but turned completely away from them. Gwen has a fixed smile on her face, one I've seen a hundred times; it's the one she uses for press and photos. Amy, on the other hand, isn't hiding her dislike very well. It has been a while, but I'm fairly certain I can still read her pretty well. And the look she throws Gwen when she walks up to me is one that could curdle milk.

"Hey," Gwen says, throwing her hands around me. It catches me off-guard because Gwen has always been very professional when we're not alone. The hug is a bit longer than necessary, and I definitely feel her press the length of her body against mine. All along, Amy's eyes are on her, unimpressed.

"Okay, okay," I say, shrugging her off.

"Sorry I took so long. Amy was a bit busy. Weren't you, Amy?" Her tone is mocking, even I can tell.

The smile Amy gives her is withering. She doesn't bother to respond but lowers herself into a chair and looks up at me. Something has definitely happened between them; I just know it.

"Right!" I say, trying to lighten the mood. The tension in the room is so thick I feel like cracking open a window. "Amy, thanks for coming. I hope we didn't pull you away from anything important. I spoke with your dean, and he implied your classes are usually in the mornings?"

"Usually, yes," she says. "And then I just sit idly by and wait for the next day's lesson."

Sarcasm. Always an endearing quality in a person.

"Okay," I say. "I'll try not to keep you too long."

I've never actually thought about how the two women would work together. Somehow, I always assumed they would get along just fine. Or that Amy would tell me to fuck off, and they wouldn't have to get along at all. It never once occurred to me that because of their individual connections to me, there would be some heat between them. Judging from the way Gwen rushed to embrace me, she wants Amy to know our relationship is more than just professional. Information Amy already had, but which seems to be eliciting a different reaction than when she first figured it out. Whatever happened between them must be serious.

I find myself thrust in the unfamiliar role of arbiter. Maybe it would have been a better idea to have this meeting with Amy alone, then bring Gwen in later?

"Well?" Amy says, snapping me back to the situation at hand.

"Oh. Sorry. Right. So, I had mentioned the case briefly to you, back at the university. I thought you might want to look at the documents." I grab the folder containing the documents and hand them over to Amy.

"I meant to ask," she says, emptying its contents onto her lap. "Why haven't you involved the police? If this is extortion, it might be better to report it and let them handle it."

"We don't know that it *is* extortion," Gwen says from the window on the far side of the room, where she is standing with her arms crossed.

Amy continues to stare at me, eyebrows raised, as if she hasn't heard Gwen speak.

"Uh, we wanted to be sure what we're dealing with before we go to the police," I say. "In both cases, there was no note or anything. No demands, no communication whatsoever. Just the photos and videos."

"That's weird," Amy says. She pulls out a stack of photos and flips through them one by one. "Why would anyone do that?"

"If we knew, we wouldn't need you," Gwen says. Amy shoots her a look, then goes back to the photos. She goes through them silently, taking a lot of time between photos as if she's scanning each one for clues. When she finishes, she turns to me. "You mentioned videos?"

I exchange a glance with Gwen, but she simply shrugs as if to say, 'Your problem.'

I was half-hoping I wouldn't have to show the video to Amy,

but I realize she needs all the information available. I pass her my laptop and retreat as she watches it, feeling embarrassed for perhaps the first time. I can't help staring at her, watching for her reaction. Her lip twitches once or twice, but she gets to the end of the video without comment.

"Have you figured anything about these women out? Do you have any new information?"

"One of our tech guys figured out the hotel where the video was shot, and I was able to come up with a loose timeline based on it, but I still have no information about the woman in the video."

"And the ones in the photos?"

"None on them either."

She continues to stare at the blank laptop screen, then shakes her head. "This still feels like a police matter, Robert. What do you want me to do, exactly?"

"See, part of the reason we haven't involved the police is the campaign. Gwen and I feel that this may be politically motivated, as the first package arrived almost immediately after I launched my campaign officially. In which event, it would be a bad idea to make this a public case. If any of this gets out without a proper containment strategy, it could be a problem for me, and we would be doing whoever is behind this a favor.

"However, Gwen has this theory that this is the work of a scorned lover, some woman trying to get back at me for something I did or did not do to her, and that it's not political at all. In both cases, we felt the best approach was one of discretion. So I drew up a list of all the women I … encountered over the last year or so, and I've been going around doing an apology tour."

"Assuming one of them is the one behind this?"

"Pretty much, yeah."

"And how has that worked out so far?"

"Not very well, to be honest. Which is where you come in. I know it's a lot to ask, but I was hoping you would step in, see if you can crack these women."

"What makes you think I'll have better luck than you? Also, if you're on an apology tour, then shouldn't the apologies come directly from you?"

"You wouldn't be doing apologies. Ideally, you'll be meeting with these women to see which of them is behind the photos and videos; that way, we narrow the list down as much as possible. I figure that way, I can focus on the campaign, and then once we've identified the culprit, we'll take it from there."

Amy smiles, but it isn't a happy smile. "So, basically, you want to use me as your blunt instrument, your bounty hunter?"

I know where she is going with this. It's an old fight of ours, that I use people for my own nefarious purposes and then dump them right after.

"I know it's a lot to ask," I tell her. "But no one knows me quite as well as you do, and I genuinely think you'd be much better at getting useful information out of these women than I am. The reception toward me has so far been frosty, to say the least."

"Can I see the list?"

I hand her a sheet of paper. "This is what I have so far. I'm still working on it, but I think this is everyone."

Her eyebrows go up slowly as she reads the list. There is the reaction I was looking for. "You went through all these women in a year?"

I glance nervously at Gwen, who is standing so still by the window she might as well be a statue. "More or less," I say. "I was going through a difficult time." I leave the rest unsaid, but I know she gets it. She was the one who pushed me over the edge, after all.

"I'll need a breakdown of what happened with all these women," she says after a while. "As best as you can remember. Each of them, when, where, in as much detail as possible. I assume you know where they are?"

"More or less," I say again.

Amy shakes her head. "I see you have this well under control."

"To be fair, I've been a bit busy trying to run a campaign here. So? Will you help?"

"Wait a minute," Amy says. "What if more stuff shows up? How sure are you that this is everything? What if there's more, worse than this?"

"I doubt there would be anything worse than a sex tape, to be honest. But assuming we approach this the right way, finding the person behind it solves the problem of more damning material. We'll be cutting the weeds off at the root."

Amy starts to nod. She licks her lips, and I know she's going to say yes. But at that moment, Gwen reactivates out of the corner of my eye. She punches the air jubilantly and lets out a little squeak. Amy and I both turn to her.

"Sorry," she says, visibly trying to compose herself. "Robert, I have some excellent news. Remember when I suggested you go on a cooking show? Well, a friend of a friend linked me up with Tiffany Cornish. You know Tiffany, right? From CBC's 'Breakfast with Tiffany'? It's a huge show. Ratings juggernaut. Anyway, I've been trying to get her to squeeze you in, and Tiffany just texted me. They're bumping tomorrow's guest, but you'd have to do the taping today!" She is literally bouncing up and down. Her excitement is palpable. It *is* good news, but somehow, I can't bring myself to match her enthusiasm.

"Wait. Today?" I ask.

At the same time, Amy is asking, "Did you just say you got him on a cooking show?"

Gwen looks from Amy to me, and the smile on her face falters a little. No prizes for guessing which question she chooses to respond to.

"Yes. Today, Robert. This is huge! Don't you get it?"

"No, no, I do. I just assumed morning shows are taped, you know, in the morning?"

"It's not actually live, Robert. It doesn't matter when it's taped. This is last minute too."

"But don't we have prep to do, for the debate?" I sound like a child trying to get out of doing chores. The truth is, I thought Gwen was joking when she first brought up the thing about the cooking show. Or drunk. Still, I can't help marveling at how quickly she has put the whole thing together. Very efficient.

"We'll prep after the taping. Oh. I actually have to prep you for the show now! I know Tiffany likes to be organic and off the cuff, but you still need to have your talking points handy, you know?" she drifts off, muttering to herself, no doubt creating lists and talking points in her head, no longer aware of her surroundings.

I turn to Amy, and her expression is one of genuine amusement. It catches me completely off-guard. "Amy?"

She starts to laugh then, slowly, gradually, suppressing the first few chuckles with limited success, before she loses the battle and breaks out in a fit of laughter. It is enough to snap Gwen back to the room and to draw an uncertain chuckle from me.

"I'm sorry," she says when she finally stops laughing. I'm just having a hard time picturing Robert at a cooking show." She continues to giggle, and I almost join her, but then I look over to Gwen, and the laughter dies at my lips.

"I'm sorry, but what is that supposed to mean?" she asks. She is using her deceptively calm voice.

Amy shrugs. "I just think that isn't Robert at all. A cooking show? I mean, what next, kissing babies? A quick game of tag with the local youth? Doesn't seem like something he would be doing, so it's probably going to come off as forced and transparent, which I realize is basically what politics is about, but still. I would play to your strengths, Robert. And a cooking show isn't the best showcase for who you are as a person, let alone what you hope to represent as a politician."

"I'm sorry," Gwen says again. She finally steps away from the window and walks up to Amy. Gwen isn't particularly tall, but at that moment, with Amy seated, she looks menacing, towering over her like that. "I was under the impression that I'm the campaign manager here. Your role, as far as I'm concerned, is rounding up Robert's past mistakes. You know, like yourself? Or did I get that wrong? Robert?"

"I don't … I …"

"If you could just stick to your job, Miss Brooks, I'll stick to mine, and we'll all be fine and dandy. In fact, I think that will be all for Miss Brooks. I believe she has all the information she needs for now?"

They both turn to me, and it is the single most terrifying moment of my life. Their expressions couldn't be more different. Amy's face is twisted in disbelief, defiance, and dislike. Gwen is looking at me with a smug assuredness. Yet they both say the same thing: Aren't you going to back me up here?

It's the worst possible position to be in. Right between a rock and a hard place, and I'm not sure which is which. I'm far too smart to pick a side, so I remain silent. Not that I would know which side to pick. The smart money would be on 'person you're currently sleeping with' but what if said person was being a bitch?

Amy saves me from having to respond, however. She gets up and straightens her dress.

"You're right, Gwen. I think my business here *is* done. I'll get started on these right away." She turns and walks out of the room without another word.

It takes a long time for Gwen to deflate. She stands there, her chest heaving, shaking her head from time to time as if trying to dislodge the memory of what just happened from her mind. Eventually, she turns to me and shakes her head. "Robert, I think your ex and I are going to have a problem."

32
Amelia

The restaurant Kieran picks is right in the middle of town. A few hours ago, I would have had a problem with that. I would have asked him to choose somewhere a little less conspicuous, where the chances of someone who knows me spotting us aren't so high. But that was a few hours ago. Before I was dragged to Robert's office and forced to deal with that woman.

The only emotions I could muster at that moment were anger and disbelief. And a certain desire to throw caution to the wind, a certain recklessness. Kieran answered my call on the second ring. Pick a restaurant, I told him. Let's have that date.

He's a coward, that Robert Hardy. I have half a mind to throw away his documents and tell him where to shove his case. But that's exactly what *she* wants. And that's who I should really direct my anger towards. The audacity of the woman. The sheer nerve. There's no way in hell I'm letting her win.

I'm still seething when I get to the restaurant, so I don't see Kieran standing at the reception, clearly waiting for me. He steps forward and wraps me in a hug. He steps back and plants a kiss on my cheek, then continues to hold me, staring right into my eyes.

"Is everything okay?" he asks, no doubt feeling the tension in my shoulders and seeing the lingering irritation in my expression.

"Yeah, why?" I ask him, trying to smile.

"You haven't pushed me away," he says.

It's true. I hadn't even realized it; this is the first time we're being openly 'intimate' in public. Usually, I stop him before he gets within three feet of me.

"Did you get a reservation?" I ask, changing the subject. Kieran swivels around and nods at a petite woman on the other side of the reception. She smiles and steps forward, informing us that our table is ready. We follow her into the fairly crowded restaurant, weaving our way through a clutter of tables and chairs crammed with chattering families, awkward couples, and gruff, unsmiling businessmen. She ushers us to our table with the promise that she will be right back with menus and fresh bread, then leaves with a quick aside that we make a lovely couple. Ugh.

It suddenly strikes me that this is really happening. I may be imagining it, but every other minute I swear someone glances over at us and frowns or shakes their head, and I'm sure they're putting two and two together, figuring us out, judging us. I feel like I have 'cougar' stamped across my forehead, and that Kieran may as well be wearing a diaper. *Which is absurd, Amy. You're not that old.*

"Are you sure you're okay?" Kieran asks again. He reaches across the table for my hand. Or he tries to. The motion surprises me, and I snatch my hand away, a bit too fast, knocking over the basket of bread. Kieran shows surprisingly quick reflexes; he stretches out a long arm and catches the basket before it falls. He manages to save some of it; the rest falls silently to the ground. Better the breadbasket than the pitcher of water. Our waiter is at the table in seconds, muttering apologies, fussing over us, and after repeated assurances from Kieran that 'it's all good,' sliding identical menus to each of us.

"Well?" Kieran prompts once we're alone again.

"Hmm?"

"You seem rattled. If this is too much …"

"Oh. No, Kieran. Not at all. I'm sorry."

It takes some time for me to compose myself, and some doing. I have to make a conscious effort not to think about Robert or Gwen because whenever I do, my fist clenches of its own accord. Gradually, though, I'm able to push the afternoon's shenanigans to the back of my mind and focus on the man in front of me.

He would never let anyone disrespect you like that. He would stand up for you. He would do anything for you. Stop it, Amy. Focus.

"I'm glad you called me," Kieran says after a while. "To be perfectly honest, I didn't think you would."

"I'm glad I called you as well," I say, spearing a piece of steak with my fork. "But I still think we need to talk, Kieran. Maybe not now, but still."

"Talk about what?" he asks.

"This. Us. I appreciate you being honest with me, and this is a lovely date, but this is much more complicated than that. I don't want to ruin a great meal, but ...""

Kieran puts his fork down and leans toward me over the table. His foot bumps me under the table, and I am uncomfortably aware that his knee is inches from my groin area.

"Is this about Robert?" he asks.

"What?"

He shakes his head as if in disgust. "I know I said I wouldn't ask, but I'm not blind, Amy. I recognized the woman I bumped into this morning in your office. Gwen Michaels. She is a campaign manager, and she is currently working for Robert Hardy. The same Robert Hardy you apparently worked for years ago."

As if this day couldn't get any more exhausting.

"Have you been looking me up, Kieran?" I ask.

"Is that him? Is that the Robert you were dreaming about?"

I can see he is beginning to get upset, so I reach out and take his hand. Just as I did earlier, he almost pulls it away, but I follow it and interlock my fingers with his.

"Listen to me," I tell him. "That man is a part of a long-forgotten chapter in my life. I don't want to lie to you or insult your intelligence. There is some history between us, yes. But that's just it. History. Nothing more, nothing less."

Kieran shakes his head. "You met up with him. That's why she was in your office this morning, isn't it? Doesn't seem like history."

"I'm helping with his campaign. That's it. He approached me some time back about doing some work for him, and I couldn't say no, as much as I wanted to. He is going to help put the university on the map, and he will help mentor some of my students, so I figure it's a small price to pay."

"So you're working with him?"

"Unfortunately, yes."

"And nothing else?"

"Not at all, no."

He lets out a long sigh, but his eyes continue to search mine, skeptical, analytical. Eventually, he nods uncertainly and lets his head drop. "What were you saying, though, about us? It's a great date but?"

I shake my head in resignation. It seems there's no getting out of this one. "It's not really a but. More like an asterisk. Because you're right, Kieran. You shouldn't be anyone's secret. You deserve so much more. You're a sweet guy, and you should be with someone who appreciates and deserves that. You deserve someone who can love you openly and loudly, because that's who you are, and it's beautiful."

"But I want you," he says simply.

"Don't you see? There is no version of this that ends well. I'll either ruin your life or my career, or both, and I can't do that to you. It's not worth it."

"I think it is," Kieran insists. "I think you're worth it and much more."

God. Where were you three years ago?

"Why are you here, then, if you don't think we have a shot? Why did you agree to the date?"

"Like I said, Kieran. You shouldn't be anyone's secret."

The rest of the date is marred by what I said to him, as expected. But I know I made the right decision. I can't throw him into the chaos that is my life right now. It sucks because it feels like he is the only good thing I have going on in my life right now, the last tether I have to a normal life because everything with Robert feels like a circus, a scene from a movie. With him, everything is complicated and way too intense and demanding. It's the exact opposite with Kieran. I finally understand his appeal; he represents everything Robert isn't. Openly sentimental, emotive, earnest, simple. I never have to guess what he is thinking or wonder how he feels about me. It's all right there, etched on the heart he proudly wears on his sleeve. It's no wonder I fell right into his arms after what Robert did to me.

But it has to end. I've known it for a while now, and I'm relieved I've been able to get it across to him. At least I think I have.

After our conversation, Kieran slips into an eerie silence which is not altogether strange for him but is unnerving, nonetheless. He finishes his meal in silence. He responds to my efforts at normal conversation with monosyllabic grunts. He declines to even look at the dessert menu, asking for the check and standing up to leave.

I feel guilty for having ruined the date, in spite of my best efforts, and for bringing him down, which I believe is a worse crime. I can't help feeling like he's just barely keeping it together, and he will unravel completely once he's alone. I'm sorely tempted to take him home with me, if only for one last night. But I know how charming he can be, and I'm sure that night will last forever. I'm completely at a loss on what to do.

But then I get distracted.

We're walking out of the restaurant's dining area when I see it. In the bar, there is a large flat-screen television, and as we pass, I see a vaguely familiar face on the screen, and the words 'HARDY HAS SKELETONS IN CLOSET: SIMMS' splashed across the bottom of the screen.

I stop and stare at the screen. I rush up to the bartender and point at the screen. "Could you turn that up, please?"

He fishes in his pocket for the remote control, and moments later, the sound fills the room.

It does not occur to me how odd I must look, standing in a room packed full of people, listening raptly to a politician on TV. Kieran stands at a distance, watching me; I am only peripherally aware of him.

I recognize the District Attorney more from his voice than his looks. It has been a while, and he has put on some weight since I last saw him, but his voice is the same gravelly baritone it has always been. He is speaking to a young, well-dressed reporter, who seems content to let him ramble on.

"… not as clean as people think. As anyone who knows me will attest, I am a firm believer in democracy, and in allowing the voice of the people to be heard. But democracy cannot come at the expense of morality. Of course, I have nothing personal against Mr. Hardy. As I've said in the past, I welcome the chance to prove that I'm still the best man for the job. But Mr. Hardy is not the perfect candidate he would like you to believe he is. I don't claim to be a saint, by any standards. But then again, I've always been on the right side of the law. Unlike Mr. Hardy, I haven't represented crooks and petty criminals, helping them escape the long arm of the law."

"Could you elaborate, Mr. Simms?" the reporter asks.

Simms raises both arms in a show of innocence. "I would rather not, actually. Because then it will seem like I'm going out of my way to unfairly bash an opponent, which I will not do. But the people of Glendale are intelligent. They would never willfully elect someone as dirty as Robert Hardy. So, all I ask is this: Do you really know the man who would be your new DA? Because, let me tell you, that man has more skeletons in his closet than a Halloween store."

The reporter chuckles, as do a handful of people around me. Words float by, curious, questioning.

"He has a point, you know."

"Does anyone really know this Robert Hardy guy?"

"I heard he once got a drug dealer out without even going to trial."

Not good. Not good at all. I glance at my watch. Somewhere, Robert is preparing to tape a silly cooking segment which will air in the morning, long after the damage from Simms' interview has been done.

I look around sharply when I feel something brush my arm, realizing a moment later that it is Kieran. I barely hear what he says. My mind is racing. I feel him tug at me, and then he is leading me away, out of the restaurant, and the fresh air hits me hard.

"You should go," Kieran says once we're outside. He attempts a reassuring smile that isn't lost on me. That's what spurs me into action. Of course, I should. Why am I still standing there, doing nothing?

I throw my arms around him and hug him briefly. "Thanks," I tell him. "I'll call you!"

And then I'm running fast, people zooming past me, the urgency making my heart race. I catch a glimpse of my reflection in the glass of a nearby building, and I think I look alive; my cheeks are flushed, my hair is coming loose and cascading behind me, my eyes are bright and glowing.

"Excuse me, sir," I grab the nearest person to me. "Which way to the CBC studios?"

33
Robert

"Are you ready?" Gwen asks.

Déjà vu.

Seems like only yesterday when she was asking me that when I was announcing my candidacy. Yesterday, and also a lifetime ago. It feels like so much has changed since then.

"Of course," I say, grinning at her. Just as she did on that day, she stands on her tippy toes and plants a kiss on my lips. Unlike the previous time, however, I grab her around the waist and kiss her back.

She tastes of coffee, and something fruity I think is her lipstick. Her body leans into mine, and for a moment, I forget where I am. My hand reaches down and traces the outline of her figure. Full. Thick. A reminder of just how much woman there is, behind the schedules and the cold efficiency. Beyond the machine lies a woman, dormant but very much alive.

My loins stir, a reminder that it *has* been a while. Too long. I pull her even closer, and she moans into my mouth as I tease her lips apart with my tongue.

"Stop it," she admonishes, but she does not pull away, and the pressure from her own lips contradicts the words she is saying. I know what she really wants, I think. She wants me to nibble gently at her lower lip, then pull away, grab the upper one with both of mine and suck softly. She wants me to finally draw my tongue into her mouth, to taste her, explore her. She wants …

"Really, Robert. Not here."

I don't know how she manages to speak. I can barely think myself. All the blood seems to have rushed out of my head.

I ignore her. My hands are itching to explore, so I let them. They travel with eagerness over the taut fabric of her skirt, feeling around the hem for weakness, sliding slowly upward until my fingers latch against what feels like a zipper. Jackpot.

Her protests have died off, and her body has gone completely limp. I unzip the skirt slowly, deliberately, ignoring the voice in my head screaming at me to hurry it up. Somewhere in the back of my mind is the niggling worry that someone is going to walk in on us, and it's both thrilling and scary at the same time.

I hear the soft rustle of fabric against skin, and then there is nothing between my hand and the soft skin of her thighs. Petal soft. Voluminous. How is she so thick? How is her body so perfect? My hands slide inside those thighs, and her gasp is loud and exciting. I probe further up, and my fingers brush against heat and damp tenderness. I'm filled with sudden lust, a powerful need to plunge myself into that heat and dampness, and the urge is almost overwhelming.

Screw it, I think, my eyes flying open.

I grab Gwen and push her against the dressing table. She doesn't need prompting, as she bends over and presents her posterior to me. Her thong is nestled somewhere between her cheeks. I wrap a finger around the string and pull it out slowly.

"Hurry up," I hear her say.

I reach down and start to fumble with my belt. My fingers won't cooperate. The clock in my head is ticking down, increasingly loud. They should be calling me in any minute now. Any second, a knock will sound on the door of the dressing room, a pale-faced intern will stick their head in the door and—

"Miss Michaels?"

The knock *does* come, and it is even more annoying than I thought it would be.

"Don't come in!" Gwen manages to yell, straightening up and whipping around. "Mr. Hardy is getting dressed!"

I grab her by the neck and kiss her once more.

"Oh my God, I want you so badly right now," she whispers to me. I grab her hand and place it on top of my pants so she can feel the erection threatening to rip straight through.

"We'll have to take a raincheck, unfortunately."

With great effort, she steps back and away from me, and I watch her with misty eyes. "Shame."

"You're telling me," she says. She leans down and picks up the skirt, shimmying into it with some difficulty.

"Take care of that." She points to my erection. "I'll go buy you some minutes."

She gives the boner a final pat, I imagine in apology, then she turns and walks out of the room. I hear her speaking quickly to the intern, their voices fading slowly as they walk down the hallway.

'Taking care' of the erection turns out to be incredibly difficult. It usually is, after such a long time without any action. I pace around the room, willing myself to think about bland, everyday things, but my mind keeps returning to Gwen, and the feel of her pressed up against me, and the sight of that red thong buried deep in her ass. And with each passing second, my dick throbs in agony.

When I hear the footsteps, I make up my mind. There is only one way that boner is going down, and that's the old-fashioned way. I don't know how much time Gwen has 'bought,' but it will have to do. I rush to the door as she is walking in. There's no time to waste, I think, and I grab her and pin her to the door she just walked in through.

It doesn't occur to me that she tastes different, feels different.

I have her pinned, so I don't register much until my tongue is foraging inside her, and my hand is burrowing in her hair. My other hand goes back down, intent on finishing what we started. That's when I hesitate. Where before there was a tight, short skirt, there seems to be a single flowing something. A dress?

I blink and open my eyes. And step away in horror.

"Amy?"

She looks even more shocked than I do. Her eyes are like bulbs, almost popping out of their sockets. Her cheeks are flushed, and there is a sheen of sweat running down her forehead.

"What the ..." she stammers. She licks her lips, clearly to encourage her dry mouth to function normally. She probably didn't intend to remind me that I was just kissing her, mere seconds ago.

Holy shit. I just kissed Amelia Brooks.

I'm trying to think of something to say. I'm struggling to make sense of her presence here. I'm wondering why the shock of it all hasn't killed my boner. But I don't get a chance to process it all. Naturally, impossibly, the door pushes open, and Gwen's face peers around the door, and she walks into the room.

Her smile vanishes as soon as she sees Amy. I feel like I'm

watching it unfold in slow motion. Her eyes go, ever so slowly, from my face, who knows what it looks like, to the resilient erection still tenting my pants (but starting to deflate, thankfully), all the way over to Amy, still standing by the door, thoroughly bewildered. I watch her put two and two together, and I jump back from Amy, a whole minute too late.

"What is this?" Gwen demands, her eyes blazing.

"I ... I don't ... she ... she just showed up ..."

Amy looks over at me, puzzled, but her eyes do the same dance Gwen's did, and she gets it. Her mouth forms a perfect little o.

"We don't have time for this now," Gwen says, putting up her hand as if to forestall any explanations until later. "Robert, you go on in five minutes. Tiffany is already impatient."

"Wait," Amy says suddenly. "That's why I'm here. You need to see this."

Gwen's surprise at the absurdity of the whole situation is matched only by her shock that Amy is addressing her directly. Amy pulls a phone from her bag, taps quickly on the screen and displays it so we both can see.

I realize what it is right away. Gwen does too. We exchange identical expressions of abhorrence as we listen. By the end, Gwen is shaking her head in disgust.

"The fucking douchebag," she says. "I suppose it's too much to expect politicians to run a clean campaign."

"What do we do?" I ask, relieved beyond belief that the focus has moved away from whose lips were on who. "Obviously, I need to respond to this, quickly."

"Right," Gwen says, starting to pace. "But this is the absolute worst platform."

"Told you," Amy mumbles under her breath. Gwen is in the zone and doesn't hear her.

"Still, if you could somehow let it be known, even in passing, that you're aware of Simms' interview and intend to respond to it ..."

"That won't be enough," Amy cuts in. "Simms made some pretty bold accusations. Robert needs at the very least to respond to them directly, or it looks like he has something to hide."

"I mean, I do," I say.

Another rap on the door. Gwen looks around wildly, then seems to make up her mind all at once. She rushes over to me and starts to fuss with my shirt and tie. I help her straighten everything out, so it doesn't look like I was just rolling around with two women who hate each other.

"You go on out, Robert," she says. "Start the segment as planned. Introductions ... Tiffany will bring out the recipe, ingredients and all that, and you can banter about it. They'll be a break after about fifteen minutes. We'll have figured out how to proceed by then."

"We?" I ask before I can stop myself.

"Yeah. Amy and I will talk it out, come up with a plan. Go ahead."

I can't help picturing coming back to find the dressing room turned over, the walls smeared with blood, the two women sprawled out on the floor, dead from each other's blows. But there is no time to protest.

Moments later, I'm walking down the hallway, following the pale-faced intern as he ushers me into a large studio set, a mini kitchen perfectly lit, with a myriad of cameras at almost every angle. I see what Gwen was talking about; it would be nearly impossible to tell that it isn't in fact six in the morning.

In the middle of the set, standing with her back to me, deep in conversation with one of the camera operators, is Tiffany Cornish.

She turns around as I approach, a smile sliding onto her face with an ease that suggests a lifetime in showbiz. "Robert!" she coos, extending a hand, which I take.

"Tiffany. It's such a pleasure to meet you."

"Oh, you're too kind."

She is a handsome woman, Tiffany. Definitely older, although the layers of make-up she is wearing do a good job of hiding it. Her hair is perfectly coiffed, and there are flecks of gold in the soft auburn curls. Her eyes are perhaps the most outstanding feature on her face. They're large and brown, but very sharp and alert.

"I'm so sorry to keep you waiting," I tell her. "My team had some last-minute ... information it needed to pass to me."

"Oh, yes," Tiffany says. "Must be this whole Simms

nonsense, no doubt?"

I'm only slightly surprised. The woman works in TV. Of course, she's heard. All the better. Now I can be upfront about hijacking her show.

"It is, in fact, yes."

"Total nonsense, if you ask me. I've known Jeremiah a long time, and let me tell you, it's preposterous for him, of all people, to talk about skeletons. And the idea that he is preaching morality is quite laughable."

"Sounds like there's a story there," I say.

"Oh, there are stories there, definitely. I wouldn't know where to begin. So? What did your team recommend? Shall we go on as planned? Or would you like a few minutes at the end to hit back? I think I can surrender the floor to you as we wait on our pie to bake."

"That's great, Tiffany. Let's do the introduction and take it from there?"

"Excellent."

In the excitement of the last half hour, I have forgotten all the prep Gwen took me through, so the first take is a complete disaster. I forget my lines a couple of times, and Tiffany eventually has to stop shooting to give me some notes on my posture and delivery. Apparently, I'm a bit too stiff, and I need to relax, imagine I'm in my own home, making dinner for my family.

It feels like hours before she finally calls for the first break, and I almost race away from the set, down the hall, and back to the dressing room.

I open the door tentatively, already worried at the absence of raised voices. I find Amy and Gwen seated across from each other, speaking in low voices. They turn around when I walk in. There is a surprising lack of hostility between them.

"Everything okay?" I prompt, approaching slowly.

Gwen laughs. "You may approach, Robert. We're not concealing any weapons."

"Bullshit. Let's see those hands."

She puts her hands up, smiling, and Amy does too.

I pull up a chair and sit down across from them both. "So, what's the plan?"

Amy takes a deep breath. "We have decided that the best course of action is for you to come clean. On live television."

I wait, certain there is more, looking to Gwen for the contradiction, but all she does is nod.

"About what," I ask. "The women?"

"Well, yes," Gwen says. "Simms threw down the gauntlet. He's a seasoned politician, so he knows what he's doing. It's a win-win situation for him. Either you give the people skeletons, or you deny it and let the accusation do his work for him. The truth is, this was probably not going to stay buried, not with the scrutiny that goes on in a political campaign. My initial plan was always to get out ahead of it, and I think this may actually be the best way to do so."

"You can't be serious," I say, shaking my head. "And you're in agreement on this?"

"On this, yes," Gwen says. "He has forced our hand, yes. But we can still turn this to our advantage. You trust us, don't you, Robert?"

I look from one to the other, thinking that this may have been the craziest day I've had in a while.

Rock. Hard place.

34
Robert

I remember Edward Peele, but only vaguely.

Anthony and Phil filled me in on his case just this morning, and they did their best to paint a vivid picture of the man who was giving them such a headache, but I can barely remember him. I thought it would come together once I met him, but the man who opens the door to me might as well be a stranger.

It's a lovely mansion. Too lovely, perhaps, for someone who was recently fired and was suing his former employers. Either the man comes from money, or he landed right on his feet after leaving Galweather & Meyer. I step into an exquisite foyer, and I quickly decide it must be the former. The house is old, the kind that I imagine has been passed down for generations. The paintings on the walls have that artistic touch, and the rug beneath my shoes feels thick and fluffy.

The man himself seems relatively unmoved by my appearance, almost as if he was expecting me. He is a skinny man, Edward. Not too tall, with thin, willowy arms pushing out of a fleece shirt. He has thick oval glasses which magnify his eyes almost comically. His lips are almost as thin as the rest of him as he looks me over. Yeah, I definitely do not remember this man who I have supposedly worked in the same building with for more than five years. But judging from the tension all over his body, he definitely remembers me, and I doubt it's for anything good.

He doesn't show his distaste too openly, though. He is perfectly civil, even warm, as he ushers me into his living room, but only after nodding pointedly at my shoes. I slip them off and follow him. His eyes never leave me; they follow me with a blank intensity as I move across the large room, as I look this way and that, momentarily distracted by a completely nude painting of a couple perched above the fireplace behind a plush-looking sofa. He sits down and indicates with a bored wave of his hand that I should do the same. I choose the seat closest to him on his left. His gaze stays on me long after I sit down.

I promptly realize he is playing the waiting game with me.

I remember the first time I went into Anthony and Phil's office, back when I was just starting out at the firm, and they just stood there for almost ten minutes, letting me take everything in, allowing me to feast my eyes on the spectacle of their office. As Phil liked to say, the only real reason to own anything was so you could watch people's reactions when they looked at it.

It feels like that is what Edward is doing; letting his affluence wash over me, showing me he is better than me, that I am in his lair, and I won't intimidate him.

Either that or this is a standard stare-down; two men sizing each other up before battle.

"So," Edward says after some time, breaking the ice. "They sent *you*."

He says the 'you' almost like an accusation, and his tone matches the vitriol of his voice.

"Yes," I say simply. "Me."

I can't tell if he is surprised or disappointed. I'm hoping it's surprise, but not the good kind. Like me showing up makes him realize how big a deal this really is.

"Shall I get right to it, then?" I ask.

Edward waves a hand and sits back in his chair.

"As you have probably already deduced, I'm here on behalf of Anthony Galweather and Phillip Meyer."

"I'm surprised you have time for the trivial business of representing scumbags," Edward says, a nasty smile on his face. "I would have thought you're far too busy with your ill-advised foray into politics. I read somewhere that you're 50 points off Simms in the latest projections."

"I'm not here in that capacity," I say, refusing to take the bait. "I'm here as Galweather and Meyer's legal counsel, in the frivolous lawsuit you brought on them."

"Frivolous? I hardly think so."

"I can't help noticing that you have no legal counsel present," I plow ahead. "If you wish to postpone this meeting until …"

"Oh, I don't think I need a lawyer for this," he says. He looks so smug it's infuriating.

"Well, then. The case. My clients would like to invite you to reconsider the facts of the case, and strongly advise you to drop your suit."

"Really?" The self-assured grin is back. "And why exactly would I do that?"

"Well, between you and me, Peele, we both know you have no case. This is frivolous at best. Your allegations are flimsy and based entirely on hearsay. Now, you could proceed with the suit, drag it through court for months on end, and at the end of it, you will lose, and you'll be hundreds of thousands of dollars poorer for it. And you'll be forgotten, along with every other disgruntled employee who has tried to fleece their former employer. You're a lawyer, you know how this works.

"Alternatively, you could do the smart thing and drop the case. Admit that it was driven by a personal grudge and save yourself the trouble of fighting a battle you're not going to win."

Edward stays silent for a long time. He almost looks like he's actually considering it. But I know his type, and the only thing he's considering is the best way to tell me to go fuck myself.

"Do you even know what the suit is about?" he eventually asks me.

"I was briefed, yes. You seem to think you were wrongfully terminated. Even though the letter of dismissal clearly states you violated the company's morality clause, which is grounds for firing."

"Hmm. That's one version of events, I suppose. Another one is that Anthony and Phil fired me because they knew my review was coming up, and as per my contract with them, I was in line for a promotion.

"I know you don't know me. We've worked in the same building for years, but you don't know who I am. I know you, of course. Teacher's pet; the intern terrorist. But if you bothered to actually interact with any of the other lawyers you work around, you would know I'm the longest-serving employee at Galweather & Meyer. I was the first brought in, and I've slaved for those assholes from day one. I wasn't the best lawyer, perhaps, but I was the hardest working. And when I finally got the partners to rework my contract, the only stipulation I provided was that I be promoted to name partner in five years, assuming I keep up my current level of work. I held up my end of the bargain. But when it came time to fulfill theirs,

Anthony and Phil got crafty. Suddenly, 'Galweather, Meyer & Peele' didn't seem so appealing after all. I doubt they ever truly meant to keep their promise, but rather than just face me like men and turn me down, they chose the coward's way.

"Now, I know the company policy and morality clauses almost back to front. What the dismissal letter you're using as your smoking gun alleges is that I carried on an inappropriate relationship with an employee for over three years, without following the proper channels laid out by the company. Stay with me, Hardy, this is where it gets interesting.

"If there was any actual intent by the company to enforce this rule or even any interest, then that would be another story. But Galweather & Meyer don't give a shit about who is sleeping with who, and that is a fact. It's why I find it so interesting that the partners sent you."

"What is that supposed to mean?" I ask although I'm pretty sure I know where he's going.

"You? Robert Hardy? The man whose name is synonymous with harassment? The man who routinely bullies interns and is celebrated for it? That's who they choose to send?"

"I'm not sure what you're implying, Peele, but I would consider my next words very carefully if I were you."

Edward puts up his hands in mock apology. "You're right. Let me see if I can stick to just the facts. The firm's morality clause also included guidelines on employee conduct, guidelines which protect employees from any form of harassment, be it physical, emotional or mental. Now, a whopping 80% of the women who worked for you in the capacity of 'Personal Assistant' resigned or were fired citing various reasons like 'gross incompetence' or 'unprofessionalism.' A good number of these women implied in their exit interviews that your treatment of them bordered on harassment. In other words, legitimate grounds for your termination.

"But never mind that. Let's bring this closer home, shall we? I was fired for carrying on 'inappropriate relations' with another employee. Now, I know for a fact that you were romantically involved with your last assistant, Amelia Brooks."

"You should get your facts right, Peele. I didn't get involved with Miss Brooks until after she quit her job working for me and joined another firm."

"Right. So you just started dating her out of the blue? No courtship, no build-up?"

"Frankly, I don't see what any of this has to do with your lawsuit."

"Don't you? Then I may have overestimated you. Here, I'll spell it out for you: Anthony and Phil had no just cause to fire me. And once I prove that in court, then I can pursue the other matter of their breach of contract. I appreciate your 'advice,' but I think I'm good."

Now it's my time to smile smugly. I always like going up against the stubborn, arrogant types. Much more fun to bring down.

"Well, I'm glad that's your position, Peele. I really am. Because Anthony and Phil insisted that I at least offer you an amicable settlement. I mean, I didn't want to, but you know how they can be. So, let's see. You're right about one thing. The dismissal letter is just smoke and mirrors. Of course, no one cares about who you're sleeping with at the firm. No, everyone is sleeping with everyone else. But do you want to know when people start to care? When there's sexual harassment involved."

The trip was worth it alone just for the look on his face right now. His mouth opens and closes silently like a fish out of water, and in that brief moment, his mask slips, and suddenly he doesn't look so unbothered.

"Now, here's the real tragedy, Peele. You think Anthony and Phil assigned this case to me because I've flouted the rules so often I know them inside and out? If only. You want to know why I don't know who you are? You were an average lawyer, at best. It's also why you would never have been promoted to name partner. I never noticed you because you're unremarkable. And you know why? You lack the killer instinct. You lack that ruthless streak that marks out the great ones from the other ones. I got this case because Anthony and Phil know there are no lines I won't cross. They know, for example, that I would have no problem proving that the relationship you carried on for three years was, in fact, abusive and that it started with a little incident we conveniently have on the company's security footage, of you getting a little violent with a co-worker ..."

"I wasn't being violent," Edward says, and now his

composure is all but gone. His face is deathly pale, and he has uncrossed his legs and leaned forward.

"Oh?" I say. "You were just being a little kinky, right? She likes it a little rough, being slapped around like that? Well, that may be the case. But imagine what that tape would look like to an all-female jury. Now, sure, you're probably thinking, I can get the woman to vouch for me, right? She is my girlfriend, after all. And you may be right. Maybe you can. But tell me one thing, Peele."

I lean forward in my own seat and stare right into his eyes. "Knowing the kind of person I am, knowing the kind of lawyer I am, who I've represented in the past, do you have any doubt I can make this case? Three months, a year, it doesn't matter. Do you really think it would be hard for me to convince a jury that you sexually harassed an employee, then intimidated her enough that she ended up in a relationship with you?"

It's a rhetorical question. He knows it too, because he purses his lips in frustration, his eyes darting this way and that. His brain is whirring; I can almost hear it. And I know I've got him.

It feels good to be back. All the political stuff had almost made me forget the thrill of the job, the rush you get when you beat your opponent before the case is even brought before a judge. It feels like putting on an old sweater and finding that it still fits.

I get up and straighten my pants. Peele's eyes are unfocused, his mind no doubt miles away. This should be fairly straightforward from here. He will realize, eventually, that his case, which he thought was solid, is maybe not so waterproof. He will weigh the risk of having to deal with rape charges with the satisfaction of getting back at his employer, and there is only one smart decision there.

"I look forward to hearing from you, Mr. Peele."

He stands up almost mechanically, and he follows me to the door silently. Still being a host. Almost on autopilot.

"Tell me one thing, Peele," I say, stopping at the door. "This clearly isn't about money for you. With your resume, I'm sure you can get a job at any other firm. What is this really about?"

I don't expect him to answer, and for a second, I don't think he will. Then he shrugs, defeated, and speaks in a tone so different I almost don't believe he is the same man who met me at this very foyer earlier.

"You wouldn't understand it, Hardy. Someone like me, I'm like a fly to Anthony and Phil. No matter how much I did for them, no matter how long I busted my ass for them, I am, as you pointed out, insignificant. But even if this case doesn't pan out, I know one thing. I know they know who I am now. I know that they see me now. Sucks, that the only way to get seen is to threaten to sue them, but here we are."

His words stay with me for a long time, even after I'm back in my car and I'm driving to my office. I don't know why, but something about his speech jarred a little memory loose in my mind. I didn't expect to feel sympathy for the man, but there it is, the temptation to empathize. Maybe I've benefited from the difference in perspective. Maybe it was harder for him, and for many other lawyers at G&M to make a name for themselves, to even rise to the top. It must be hell, feeling unappreciated, invisible.

And then it hits me so suddenly I slam the brakes and come to a complete stop. The car behind me hoots angrily, and the driver flips me off as he goes around me. But I don't care. Excitement is coursing through me. I pull the car over to the side, my hands shaking with excitement. I pull out my wallet and empty its contents onto the passenger seat. I should really have checked it when I was trying to remember the women.

My heart gives a little flutter when I find it; slightly tattered, the writing a little faded, but it is there; the name and number still visible.

I'm so stunned I stare at it for a full minute. Then I start to think, and to plan, and to smile.

I pull out my phone and dial Amy's number without thinking. It rings for a while, and I'm almost hanging up when I hear her voice.

"Amy? I have huge news. I just figured out the woman behind the tapes and photos. I know who she is."

35
Amelia

"Are you even listening to me?" Ness asks, her voice coming at me as if from very far away.

The truth is, I'm not. Not actively. She was saying something about her boyfriend, Jeremy, and without much encouragement, she lapsed into a long tirade about his faults. It's not really my fault that I drifted off. Somehow, I'm not surprised that the honeymoon period didn't last forever.

"Of course I am, Ness," I say, smiling sweetly.

"Really? What was I saying?"

"That Jeremy is a dick."

Ness narrows her eyes and frowns. "How is he a dick?"

"He ... doesn't ... listen to you? Okay, fine, you got me, I drifted off for a bit. But I got the highlights."

"Amy!"

"I'm sorry! I have a lot on my mind!"

"So do I! And we will get to your thing, but it's my turn to rant now, and you're not listening. Could you be any worse of a friend?"

I get up and walk over to the couch, where Ness is sprawled out. I sink into the comfy cushions beside her and wrap my arms around her. "I'm sorry. From the top. I'll listen better this time."

Ness pushes her lips out in an adorable pout. "What do you even have on your mind? Schoolwork? You're not secretly seeing someone, are you?"

Crap. The woman can read me like a book.

"No, no," I protest, giving her shoulders a little shake. "Let's do your thing first. What has Jeremy done? He isn't going down on you anymore?"

"I wish," Ness moans. "No, his sex game is still annoyingly on point. Too on point, if you ask me."

"Annoyingly? Is that a thing?"

"Obviously, Amy. The sex is supposed to gradually get worse

and worse until we stop having it at all and become this old married couple that yells at each other and communicates through grunts and scoffs."

"Let me get this straight. You're complaining that the sex *isn't* bad?"

Ness turns her head and looks at me like a toddler who just asked her what one plus one is. "I always forget that you're a virgin," she says, shaking her head sadly. "And therefore unfamiliar with the ways of the world."

"Uh, I am the farthest thing from a virgin, thank you very much." I want so desperately to tell her that I very recently had sex in the shower and that I'm cavorting with one of my students if only to see the expression on her face. Was cavorting. Shit.

Ness is still shaking her head. "It's been more than a year, sweetie. Your hymen regrew."

"Will you just explain what Jeremy did? God!"

"Okay, okay. Like I was saying before I noticed your eyes glazed over, he isn't trying anymore. He used to surprise me with the tiniest gestures, these random little things to let me know he was thinking of me. Like sending me flowers at work. Or making me breakfast in bed. Or taking me on a random trip. Lately, all we do is sit at home and watch old documentaries. I mean, the sex is still great, but it feels like it's only a matter of time before that goes too, you know?"

I nod, but I really don't. Not that I'd admit it and prove her wrong, but I really have no experience with this kind of thing. Robert and I dated for only a few months, and it was hot and torrid all the way through. There was no slump like the one Ness is referring to. We burned bright, and then we went out just like that.

"It makes sense," I say. "I mean, he got you. No need chasing you anymore."

Ness snorts. "Nobody's got me! And that doesn't sound like him. He wasn't chasing me out of some antiquated male notion of courtship. No, he was doing it to show me he thought I was gorgeous, to highlight the things he liked about me. So what happened? Does he not think I'm gorgeous anymore? Doesn't he like me?"

It sounds so strange, coming from her. Ness is the most

confident person I know. I've been dismissive of her issue, but if Jeremy is denting her self-esteem, then maybe there's more to this.

"You don't really think that, do you?" I ask her. "You know you're beautiful. I know Jeremy thinks so too. I mean, he can never keep his hands off you, so I guess this is a blip."

I feel like I don't really know what to say to her. Like I'm not equipped to deal with relationship matters. I can barely figure out my own issues, and Ness is supposed to be way savvier than me.

She gives me a little pat on the back as if to reassure me. And I realize she simply wanted to vent; the process of sharing was the therapy. She extricates herself from my arms, gets up, and walks away in the direction of the bathroom.

I try to imagine myself in her situation, and I keep coming up short. I can't even picture it, Robert and I, seated on a couch somewhere, silent. Him, with a book, and I lost in my phone. In that bubble of domesticated bliss.

Almost as if the act of thinking about the man summons him, my phone vibrates, and when I reach for it, I see that it's Robert calling. For one irrational second, I get a rush of anxiety, worrying that I won't be able to talk to him without him somehow reading my mind, figuring out the unwelcome thoughts I've just been entertaining.

I end up staring at the screen for far too long, and then I start to wonder what he'll read into it if I don't answer if I let it go to voicemail. But I remember that I'm supposed to be working with him, and maybe there is something important he needs to tell me, and I mentally slap my face, because this line of thought has been ridiculous.

"Hello?"

"Amy? I have huge news. I just figured out the woman behind the tapes and photos. I know who she is."

It takes me a minute to get on the same page. He sounds excited, and I don't immediately reconcile why. "Wait, what? The one who's been blackmailing you?"

"That's just it. It's not blackmail. At least I don't think it is. I think I figured out her angle."

"Okay …"

"It's a plea for attention. Sort of. I'll explain on the way."

"Uh, on the way ... where?"

"We're going to see her. I'm on my way to your place right now."

Panic.

"Wait. Here. Now? Huh?"

"Yeah. I just got off the highway. I should be there in ten minutes."

"You're coming here?"

"Yeah. You're coming with me, obviously."

"I don't think that's ... I can't, on short notice. I have work to do ..."

"I know you don't. It's the weekend. And your next class is on Monday."

"How do you know this?"

"I have your schedule, remember? To plan for meetings and stuff. Shit. Let me talk to you in a bit, Amy."

The line goes dead. I don't get a chance to voice the many reasons I'm not okay with random plans being sprung on me with no prior notice. I can't seem to think of them just yet, but I have some very strong objections to it.

It's great that he has figured it out, though. For one, it takes one massive problem off his plate, which even Gwen would admit was starting to get a little crowded. My new friend Gwen. More importantly, it means we don't have to worry about the big reveal with Simms. Following Robert's Breakfast show taping, during which he openly challenged the DA to a media sit-down in which they would both air their dirty laundry, Simms responded almost immediately. He agreed to the terms, and to an interview the coming Tuesday. Gwen is currently pulling out her hair figuring out how to sanitize Robert's past enough that he can talk about it on TV.

But if Robert has figured out the person behind this, then we might need to rethink the interview.

Ness re-enters the room, snapping me out of the reverie. It is a nasty reminder that I haven't yet told her about Robert coming back into my life. And he's probably just turning around the corner from my house.

I jump to my feet and rush to her, and only then notice the single sock she's brandishing in one of her hands.

"What's this, you slut?" she asks.

I literally have no idea, and I'm trying to figure out how to get her out of the house before Robert gets here. I look at the sock, puzzled at why she would pick it out. I have no recollection of it at all, and it's certainly not one of mine.

"I have no clue," I say, throwing a worried look out the window, listening for the telltale sound of a car pulling into the driveway. "So, listen, Ness. I just got called in to the university, and I have to rush. I don't mean to kick you out, but ..."

"This is a male sock, woman," she says, waving it in my face like an exhibit in a murder case.

"Is it?"

The memory clicks into place slowly. Kieran, slightly high, definitely horny, sneaking into my bathroom and slipping his hands over my body. He must have left the sock somewhere. I don't think I have been in there since, and even if I have, I doubt I would have seen it. Of course, Ness would, though. No doubt she's been over every inch of the bathroom looking for something to latch on to.

I sigh inwardly, already dreading the interrogation I know is on the way. The woman is like a dog with a bone, and the timing couldn't be worse. I look over to the window once again. How long has it been? Five minutes? I'm going to have to be more drastic.

"Can we do this later?" I ask her. "I really need to go."

"You better not think I'm letting you get away with this," she says. Thankfully, she yields to the not-so-gentle pressure I'm applying on her hand, and she allows me to push her a little toward the door.

"Of course, of course," I reassure her. "We'll talk about everything when I get back."

"Ooh," she goes. "So there *is* a new man in your life."

"I can neither confirm nor deny that," I say. I grab Ness's handbag as I pass the couch and thrust it into her hands.

"And here I was, thinking you could never surprise me."

We are outside the house now. Ness seems to have accepted that she's being kicked out, and she walks freely to her car.

"Weird, that they're calling you on a Friday," she comments.

"I thought you have a very specific schedule?"

"I do, but sometimes we get called in to sub, or to help administer exams. I don't really know why …"

The black Jeep is so silent I almost don't hear it. But I see it, and I forget what I was saying. I curse inwardly. Too slow, Amy.

Ness is watching me, so when I stop speaking and my eyes dart over to the car pulling into the driveway, she follows my gaze. I watch as her expression goes from mild curiosity to recognition, and then straight to disgust. I watch her put two and two together, and I just know I'm not ready for her reaction.

Robert is on the phone when he steps out of the car. I wonder for a moment how he knew where I live, imagine him keeping tabs on me. By the time he's fully out, closing the door behind him, Ness is already walking toward him.

I didn't even see her get out of the car. In the fraction of a second between me looking to see if Gwen is with Robert because that would make this so much easier, and then back to Ness, she is already out of her own car and past me.

I curse again and take off after her. It's a small miracle that she isn't running. That means she's mad but still processing it. And that only means there will be an eruption sooner or later.

"Ness! Listen to me, he's here for work." Her stride is longer than mine, and she gets to Robert before my words get to her.

Robert's initial reaction is that of someone meeting someone they should know but don't. He mumbles something into the phone, then puts it away and looks from Ness to me.

"What are you doing here?" Ness shoots at him, hands on hips.

"I'm sorry?" I can tell Robert is truly lost; in our brief time together, I never introduced him to my best friend. He heard a lot about her from me, but I never introduced them. Probably out of fear that they would instantly dislike each other, and their mutual hatred would level entire blocks.

"You have some nerve, weaseling your way back into her life after what you did to her." She points at him, then realizes she is still holding the sock from my bathroom.

"I'm sorry," Robert is saying, again. "Who are you?"

But Ness has already turned away from him. She levels the fullness of her accusatory gaze on me now.

"No, dude," I tell her. "Of course not. Like I told you, I'm sort of working with him now … on his campaign. I'm sorry I didn't tell you, okay? But I was afraid you'd react like this."

Her expression doesn't soften.

I grab her arm and pull her slightly away from Robert. Not exactly out of earshot, but she won't budge any further. "I swear, okay?" I say. "I'm helping with his campaign, and that's it. There's nothing else going on there."

"This is the work thing? This is why you were kicking me out of your house?"

"I was avoiding this very conversation."

She nods slowly. Then she leans in and whispers right into my ear. "Don't let him back in, Amy. I know you think it wasn't a big deal, but I saw what he did to you, and I won't let it happen again."

"I know, Ness." I don't know what else to say to her.

"I trust you," she says. "But I don't trust him."

"I can handle him," I say. "I wouldn't be helping him if I didn't think I could."

I can feel her relent, her body sort of deflates. She nods again, then she walks back up to Robert and says something to him that I don't quite catch. I have no doubt it's a threat of some sort, not least because Robert's jaw clenches, and he nods curtly.

Ness pats me once on the back as she leaves. She gets in her car without another word and pulls out of the driveway. Right before she leaves, she waves the sock at me one last time as if to say, 'We still have to talk about this.'

"I like her," Robert says, oddly cheerful. "That must be your friend, Vanessa?"

"No one calls her that. Ness. But yeah."

"Excellent. Now come on. We have a mystery to solve."

"Oh, you were serious."

"You thought I was joking? Get your jacket, Amy. We're going on a little road trip."

36
Amelia

It is incredibly difficult to say no to Robert Hardy. He has this natural charm, which translates into an ability to talk you into just about anything. It's what makes him such a good lawyer. It's how I fell for him in the first place. And it's how I end up in his car with him speeding down the highway on what is supposed to be my day off.

"Where are we going?" I ask.

"A little town called Haven," he responds.

"You mean out of town Haven?"

"I thought that was implied."

"No, it wasn't implied. You didn't tell me we're going out of town! How far is this place?"

Robert looks at his watch. "A little under four hours."

I shake my head, torn between disbelief and frustration. Here is the problem with Robert and his forked tongue: He gets you to say yes to things without even knowing what you're saying yes to. I don't know why I assumed we were going someplace close by. I realize he called it a road trip, but I just thought he was being comical and hyperbolic. Four hours? That means we will be on the road late into the night if we are to make it back in good time. Assuming he even plans on coming back today.

There is the very real possibility that the trip may be even longer, and that is something I'm definitely not prepared for.

"You're not mad, are you?" he asks.

I'm not. I'm just exasperated.

"I hate that about you," I tell him before I can stop myself. And why should I stop myself?

His smile falters, and I can see his knuckles whiten as he grips the steering wheel tighter. "What?" he asks, with the air of someone who would rather not know.

"The surprises. The manipulation. The presumption. You

could have told me about this before we left, given me all the information. You were purposely vague to get me to tag along. And that's partly on me; I should have asked. But still. It's the old Robert all over again. His time is more important than yours. Do as he says, ask questions later."

"That was not my intention at all," Robert says. "I wasn't trying to mislead you or anything. Believe it or not, I was motivated mainly by the time factor. I wanted to be on the road as soon as possible. If we make it to Haven before evening, then we can conclude our business and be back today, latest early morning tomorrow. I figured it would be easier to fill you in once we got going.

I appreciate that I may not have been very considerate to you, and for that, I apologize. I didn't mean to make you feel like that."

Ugh. I hate it when he shows feelings like an actual human being. Makes it slightly harder to be mad at him, but I'm sure I can pull it off. I'm not ready to accept his apology just yet. When I am, we will have to go back way further than today.

"So, fill me in, then," I say.

"I figured it out while speaking with a former employee of G&M. Long story short, he is suing the firm, and the partners wanted me to bring the hammer down on him. And I do. I go to see the guy, and I basically point out that his case is hopeless, and the best option is to settle out of court, right? But something about it doesn't make sense to me. He is a wealthy guy. He doesn't need the money. I ask him why he is suing his former bosses, and he says something about feeling invisible and wanting to make them see him and finally appreciate how much he did for them. And I guess the only way he could do that, the biggest splash he could make, was suing them.

And I just sort of made the connection. A lot of what happened to me after our … you know, our breakup. A lot of it is foggy, and I can barely remember what I did or who I did it with. I had completely forgotten about one of my first wild nights. But that conversation brought it back. Maybe it was because we had just gone over the names on the list with you a few days back, but it occurred to me that there was someone I completely forgot, someone who should be at the top of that list."

"You mean someone you slept with and then forgot about?"

I ask him. "Doesn't that apply to all the women you've slept with?"

"Well ..." The corner of his lip goes up a fraction. He keeps his eyes on the road, but I can feel the smile in his voice. "There are certain exceptions."

Jeez, Robert. Way to make a girl feel special.

"Essentially, Gwen was right," he continues. "This is a woman who I met and spent the night with, and even though I don't remember her or anything that went down, I know that I took her information down, so I know I must have made certain promises to her that I didn't fulfill."

"But why this one?" I ask. "What sets her apart?"

"That's what I hope to find out. Like I said, my memory is mostly foggy. Hopefully, she can help me fill in the blanks. I know this, though, she was the first one. I went on that bender *after* I left Haven, so whatever happened must have gone down there."

It still feels like we're going off a hunch at best, but I don't say it. Maybe there's something he isn't telling me. We'll see when we get there.

"What's her name?"

He dives into his breast pocket and pulls out a scrap of paper which he passes over to me. The writing is barely legible, the piece of paper has clearly been rotting away somewhere. But I can just about make out the name 'Celeste,' and the better part of what appears to be a phone number.

I'm not sure when I fall asleep. As we got outside the city the radio turned to static, and neither of us bothered to change it. It must have lulled me to sleep. I'm jolted awake by the feeling that we are no longer moving.

I rub my eyes and squint out the window. The sun is just beginning to set. We have stopped at what appears to be a roadside diner. Robert is watching me. I have no idea how long he has been sitting there, eyeballing me.

"Hey," he says. "We're almost there. I figured we might as well stop and get some food. I don't know about you, but I haven't eaten all day."

I shrug. "I could eat."

"Okay. I'll go see what they have. What would you like?"

He returns a few minutes later with bulging bags, which he deposits in the back seat before climbing in next to me. I feel self-conscious about my breath, so I reach back and grab a soda, take a swig before turning back to him.

"I'm surprised no one recognized you in there," I say.

He hands me a box with a burger and fries.

"I'm not," he says. "We're a long way from home. I don't expect many people outside Glendale follow local politics."

"But what would have happened if someone did?"

"Naturally, I would have had to grab the food and make a run for it. Obviously, when you see me running, you'd quickly put two and two together. You'd start the engine, throw the door open for me, and we would make our getaway before the first guy can even pull his camera out."

"You've clearly given this some thought."

He shrugs. "You asked. I'm actually supposed to be traveling with armed escorts, did you know?"

"Oh, yeah. I think I saw them once. Big, angry-looking guys in suits?"

"Yeah. They're not actually angry, believe it or not. Solid guys. It would be their job to get me out of a bad situation."

"Why didn't they tag along, then?" What I really want to ask him, what I've been dying to ask him since the thought first occurred to me a few hours ago, is why he didn't bring Gwen. She's his campaign manager. She would probably be more useful to him than I am.

It still surprises me how fast her feelings toward me changed. In the blink of an eye, all the suspicion and negativity just disappeared. Right around the time Robert was devouring me with his tongue, his boner digging into my thigh. *Don't think about the kiss. Do not, under any circumstances ...*

"What was that?" Robert asks, and I have to blink several times to refocus on his face. He looks almost comical, his cheeks puffed up as he chews.

"What was what?" I ask, reaching for my burger and taking a huge bite.

"Your cheeks just went red. What did you just think about?"

I swallow way too fast, and the food goes down the wrong hole. I'm almost grateful that I start choking because I'm pretty sure I would be blushing again. Robert reaches over and claps me on the back as I cough. He hands me a bottle of water, and I take a long sip. Tears stream down my face, clouding my vision. I'm sure I'm quite a sight.

But Robert only smiles.

"I was thinking about it too," he says after I've stopped coughing and crying and certainly blushing.

Of course, as soon as he says that, I feel my cheeks begin to heat up. "What?"

What sorcery is this? Am I transmitting my thoughts, somehow?

"I can't help it. I know it's not ... proper, but I have thought about it. A few times."

"And?" I ask. When did I start holding my breath?

"And I'm sorry I did it." My heart sinks a little, a reaction I did not expect. "I never got around to saying it, what with all the chaos of the taping, and planning the interview with Simms, but I've been meaning to speak to you about it. I just didn't know how to bring it up."

"It's a good thing we've wandered onto the topic then," I say. "Quite organically, too." I hope I don't actually sound as disappointed as I think I do.

Robert grins. "Indeed. So, it was an accident. I mistook you for Gwen ..."

And suddenly I don't want to hear it. I don't need to hear it. "You don't have to explain it to me, Robert. I figured out it was a mistake pretty easily."

"Oh. Right."

And now things are awkward. We both fall silent. I eventually remember that I'm still holding a burger, and I take another bite to distract myself. *Chew slower this time, you animal.*

Neither of us says another word until we're done eating. The only sounds in the car are those of us chewing, the low buzz of static on the radio, and the deafening sound of my mind clunking and banging as I try to figure out how to go back to small talk.

I land on: "How far are we?"

Robert consults his watch. We should be there in around twenty minutes. Maybe we should discuss strategy? We can't just walk up to her like that."

"I think we can. If your theory is correct, then she has no violent motives or any reason to run. If all she wanted was for you to reckon with what you did, then this turned out perfectly for her. She got you to go back to where it all started."

"Okay, then. I guess we'll go with 'walk up to her.'"

The atmosphere in the car is definitely different as we get back on the road. I can tell Robert is desperate to break the awkward silence too because after a short time he starts to fiddle with the radio. He finds a station playing some pop ballad, and that's what we listen to for the rest of the way.

He said twenty minutes, but it feels like a full hour before we pull up at an old building with a blinding array of neon lights, and a simple sign that says 'FLESH.'

37
Robert

FLESH the strip club is a simple establishment which does an excellent job of offering exactly what is advertised. It looks exactly as you would expect it to; a seedy, cheap joint with a handful of people swaying dizzily on low chairs.

All around the room, women are milling around completely naked. As per the sign. The entire staff is female, no doubt by design, except for two grim gentlemen at the door scowling at potential troublemakers.

It's a bit disconcerting, walking into such a blatant display of nudity. It is definitely unnerving walking in sober and in the company of a beautiful woman. In the company of a woman, I should say.

Amy and I are met as we walk in by a cute little blonde with a pixie cut and a large set of double Ds I would bet are not natural. I have no chance to inspect them, though, because I think I can feel Amy's eyes burning a hole through the side of my head.

"Welcome to FLESH!" pixie cut says, stepping up close to me. Far too close. I clear my throat and take a single step back, sliding a hand around Amy's waist. She stiffens, but she does not push my hand away. Or slap me across the face. Pixie cut notices the gesture and smiles apologetically.

"Hi. I'm looking for someone who works here. Her name is Celeste."

Pixie cut pauses, thinks for a moment, then shakes her head. "I'm not sure I know a Celeste. Come on in, take a seat, and I'll ask around."

I know what that means. Buy a drink, and maybe my memory will be refreshed. Fair enough, I suppose. I glance over at Amy, and her whole body betrays how little she wants to be here. I know what she's thinking. I know she's picturing me here, wondering how I could ever come to such a place. Because she doesn't understand rock bottom.

"I know," I tell her. "It's not exactly high end. But we're here for information, nothing else."

We're treated to a veritable buffet of body parts on our way to our table. I don't know if I've ever seen more breasts in such a short period of time before. And the women are so confident it feels almost dirty to look, even though they clearly want you to. One of the women stops right in front of me and asks me in a sultry voice if I would like a lap dance. I sidestep her while mumbling polite refusals, and she rounds up on Amy instead.

"What about you, gorgeous? He can watch."

Amy shakes her head, mortified. She seems almost to shrink as we finally sit down, and Pixie disappears, probably to 'ask' about Celeste.

We have been seated only a few feet away from the stage. I realize this a second too late, right as an announcer's voice cuts through the low hum of music, inviting someone called 'Vicky Stone' to the stage. And then, with an almost blinding light display, the stage erupts in glitter and blaring music, and a tall woman with a spectacular bush drops onto the stage from a previously unseen pole suspended in midair.

"I'm sorry," I say to Amy as she sinks into her chair in horror. "Might be better if you wait in the car? I'll get Celeste and ask her for a private word outside, then bring her over to the car."

She hesitates, her eyes glued to the stage. Vicky Stone drops all the way down to the floor, landing in perfect splits and treating everyone in the front row to an eyeful of bush. Amy nods slowly and stands up. I hand her the keys, and she turns and starts to make her way through the tables.

"So?" Pixie is back. "What can I get you?"

"Any information on Celeste?" I ask her. "It's the only name I have, sorry. I was here almost a year ago, so I don't know if she still works here."

Pixie continues to look pointedly at me, a slight smile on her face.

"Right, right. A beer, please." I slide a twenty over to her and her smile widens.

"There was a Celeste who used to work here, yes. But she quit around six months ago. Sorry."

"And you couldn't have volunteered this information a few

minutes ago?"

Pixie leans over, and her tits lean over right along with her. I can't help sneak a glance at them. Maybe they're real after all.

"You should stay for a bit. Have a couple of beers, get a dance or two. We have plenty of girls way hotter than your Celeste."

"That won't be necessary," I tell her. "Do you know how I can find her? Celeste? An address, maybe? The phone number she gave me doesn't work."

But Pixie is no longer paying attention. Her eyes have wandered away, over my shoulder. I turn around, a feeling of dread seizing me that I don't immediately understand. I follow her eyes and look to the far end, close to where the door is. Amy is pinned to a table, leaning away from a towering man with long unruly hair and a nasty expression. As I notice him, he raises a grimy finger towards Amy.

I bolt out of my seat and bound across the club. I move so fast I'm there before the man's hand is all the way up. My arm lashes out, slapping his advancing paw, and I step between him and Amy.

"Is there a problem here?" I bark at him.

He sways slightly on the spot. His eyes have that unfocused look of someone who is seconds away from passing out. He raises the hand I just slapped away, as if just now realizing what happened.

"This is none of your business," he slurs. "I was just asking the pretty little lady for a dance."

"Well, the lady is with me," I tell him, struggling to stay calm. My blood is boiling. "And as you can see, she does not work here."

"Hey, if the lady wants to give me a dance ..."

"I assure you, she does not."

The man sways some more, eventually managing to take the two steps to close the distance between us. I am hit by the overpowering smell of alcohol and stale sweat. I almost gag. Behind me, I feel Amy shudder, and I squeeze her hand gently.

"You're not from around here, are you?" the man asks. "Because if you were, you'd know that in Haven a man takes what he wants. And I want this pretty little flower to dance for me. Maybe I'll take her back to the private rooms, see if the carpet matches the drapes."

There is a single moment when all the sound seems to have been sucked from the room. Everything is on pause; the music, the chattering, the people. I see the man's lips moving, I can sense someone closing in from the right, almost in slow motion. And then I snap.

Sight and sound are restored in a whoosh. I snap my hand back, ball it into a fist on the swing, and crack it onto the drunk's face. I feel the satisfying crunch of bone breaking. He roars in pain and doubles over. I yank Amy's hand and give her a little push toward the door. The car, I mouth to her. When I turn back to the drunk, he is already swinging.

I duck the first punch, but I'm not so lucky with the second. There is a savage fury behind the blows; a man swinging in self-defense, not calculated or aimed, just sheer power as he throws his weight behind them. He catches me on the temple, and my head explodes into a million brilliant stars.

All hell breaks loose. I can barely follow what's happening. The scuffle has grown; predictably, the few patrons who had been enjoying the entertainment elect to join in, and it quickly descends into a melee. I swing without seeing who I'm hitting. I feel bodies and react with the nearest body part. I kick and punch and push and throw. There is no sense of direction, no idea where what is or which side is down. It's just complete chaos, with the sounds of shouting men and painful yells drowned out by the music.

At some point, impossibly strong hands close around my chest, and I feel myself lifted off my feet. Shit, I think. This is how it ends. I strain against the grip, but those fingers may as well be made from cast iron. Then I am being carried. The room is swimming around me, behind me, up then down. I catch a glimpse of the doorway, right before I'm sent flying through it.

I land with a grunt and a loud thud on the ground. The bouncer yells something in my direction about staying out. I'm just grateful to be free of his grip. I take in lungfuls of air, savoring the feeling of being alive.

Hands touch my face, soft hands, Amy's hands. They run over my right eye, which I now realize is swollen, and I wince sharply.

"I'm sorry!" she squeals. Her hands are shaking. Her breath is sharp and raspy.

I force myself to open my eyes and stare valiantly at the spot where her head is until at last, she swims into focus. "Are you okay?" I manage to ask her. "Are you hurt?"

"No, I'm fine," she says. Her hands are still on my face. Her eyes are wide. "But you ... we need to get you to a hospital."

"Oh, no. I'll be fine. Just a little brawl. Been a while since I was in one. I may have lost my killer instinct a bit, but overall I think that went pretty well."

She shakes her head. It makes mine swim. "Do you have a first aid kit in your car?" she asks me, and I nod.

She grabs me under the arms and helps me to my feet. I'm unsteady, and the world starts to spin again, but I grit my teeth and stand still until the wave of nausea passes. Amy helps me limp to the car. She opens the back door, and I collapse onto the back seat, which still has some of the bags and bottles from the diner.

I hear her rummage around the car. Moments later, something cold is slapped on my forehead. It feels wonderful.

She sets about cleaning my face. From the way she dabs and wipes, it seems the only serious damage done is the blow to my right eye.

"What do you think," I ask Amy, opening the functional eye to look at her. "Am I still beautiful?"

She laughs once, a short humorless sound. "This is a disaster. You have a TV interview on Tuesday."

"Eh, I'm sure it's nothing a little make-up can't conceal."

"I'm sure Gwen will be furious," she says.

I know she will. I haven't called her since before I left Glendale. In fact, she has no idea where I am right now. Or with who.

"We'll deal with Gwen later," I say. My head has stopped spinning, and I'm thrilled to find that I can sit up without wanting to vomit. "So? What's the prognosis? Give it to me straight, doc."

"How can you be joking at a time like this?" Amy asks. She sounds like her old self again, which is a massive relief. I don't think I've ever seen her as scared as she was back there.

"How can you not?" I respond.

I don't know what it is about almost dying that brings out the recklessness in me. I snake a hand around her waist and try to pull her to me. It's mostly impossible, given how awkwardly she's crouched while leaning around from the front seat.

"I'm sorry I put you through this whole thing," I say to her. "It was a bad idea. And it was pointless. We missed Celeste by a few months, apparently."

Amy can't seem to hold my gaze for long. Her eyes keep drifting down, and her cheeks are starting to darken, too. "Thanks for defending my honor," she says with a half-smile.

Someone raps sharply on the rear window. Amy jumps then shakes her head and turns around. As she leans over to lower the window, I get a great view of her ass, and it is the best one I've seen all night.

The window slides all the way down, and Pixie's head pokes through. She looks at my swollen eye and shakes her head.

"That's going to be one hell of a black eye," she says. She passes me something through the window; a bag of ice which I immediately press onto the eye. "Keep that on your eye for as long as you can."

"Thanks," Amy and I say simultaneously.

"That was very stupid of you," Pixie goes on. She glances over at Amy and smiles. "But also very gallant. Romantic, even."

Amy and I exchange glances. I'm sure we're both thinking the same thing; no point in correcting her.

"I seem to remember FLESH being a bit more friendly," I say.

"It is," Pixie says earnestly. "Most of the time anyway. But I did get you this." She hands me a slip of paper through the open window. I squint at it, not sure what I'm looking at.

"It's her address. Celeste. She lives a few miles East of here. You should be able to find the place easily enough."

"Look at that, the day wasn't a complete waste after all. Thank you, really."

"No problem," she says. Then, to Amy, "Hang on to him, sweetheart. He's a keeper." And she walks away.

"Do you hear that?" I reach out with my free hand and grab

Amy again. It's a bit easier to squeeze her through the space between the front seats this time, and I deposit her squarely on my lap. "Keeper, the lady said."

"I'm surprised you heard anything she said at all, with those giant fake breasts hanging right in front of you."

I knew they were fake.

"Oh, I don't know about that," I tell her. I like how she is splayed out on my thighs, the pressure of her ass, the feel of her body. "I seem to have been distracted."

Reckless. Inappropriate. Cheesy. But I don't care. All I can think is that she is right there, her lips slightly parted. Would it be so crazy if I just … leaned in a bit?

"So?" she asks. "What happens now?"

I shake my head to clear the lascivious thoughts. It was a moment of insanity, that is all.

"It seems our road trip will be extended a little longer."

That drunk idiot must have hit me pretty hard because, for a split second, I think I see Amy smile.

38
Robert

I'm in a stuffy room. It's cloudy, with the heavy scent of tobacco hanging in the air. Low jazz music is playing in the background, softly enough to seem part of the overall aesthetic and sound of the club. The hum of conversation is just distinguishable. I'm seated across a large, fat man with greasy hair and a red, pudgy face. He is twirling an unlit cigar between short, stumpy fingers. He watches a waiter saunter away, balancing a heavy tray in her hands, then his eyes snap to me, watery and eager. I can see his lips move, but his words don't immediately get to me. He is saying something about 'my girl,' something mildly offensive and decidedly presumptuous. He met her just this morning. And from the way he is talking, he was very impressed.

He is important. That much I know. I need him for my campaign, as far off as it is. He has been called the Kingmaker, the man with the golden touch. And so I have to smile and nod as he talks about my girlfriend, and how much he would love to take a run at her. It's all in good fun, I think. No harm done. Just men being men.

Except his smile is growing bolder, more lewd. The twinkle in his eye isn't fading; it's looking more and more dangerous if anything.

I smile and nod again, but this time he frowns. I'm serious, he says. What would it take to spend one night with her? Just the one night. A gentleman's agreement and that would be that. We could proceed with business afterward.

You do not insult the Kingmaker. Everyone knows that. Unless you want your career to go down the drain before you can even blink.

I try and swivel, ask him about his last candidate, how they managed to cut into what was at first an insurmountable lead by his opponent. But the Kingmaker isn't interested in talking politics. Not anymore. Or not yet. The woman, he says again, finally reaching for a dark Zippo lighter and lighting his cigar. Thick, putrid fumes billow up and around his face, and he looks at that moment like a classic 80s mob boss. What about the woman?

I'm not sure I can stall anymore. Neither can I get away with a non-response. The man is staring, awaiting his response.

I go for a soft maybe. I'm a lawyer, after all, so I'm certain I can make the words work for me. It's not a no, not at all. I'm personally on board with the whole idea, even though that couldn't be farther from the truth. But would he let me speak to her first, get her on board? She's a little hard-headed, you see. Just give me a couple of days to sell her on the idea; I'm sure she wouldn't mind spending a little time with someone of such stature.

His grin is wide. He looks positively giddy. Excellent, he declares, lifting his glass toward me. I clink his glass with mine, smiling awkwardly. Uncomfortably. He laughs, blowing a puff of smoke at me, and I shut my eyes.

When I open them, I'm looking into Amy's hurt eyes. She is speechless, wounded, stunned. I can explain, I tell her, pleading. I'm struggling to forestall the explosion I can see brewing behind her eyes. I know her well enough to know she's going to be yelling soon.

But I cannot explain. It was stupid of me to even mention it at all. I don't know what I was thinking. Sure, I was a little desperate. Maybe I expected her to react a little differently. But here we are, and there she is. There's no excuse in the world for what I did: Offering her to another man, so that he helps me to pursue my career.

She doesn't say anything for a long time, she just stares at me as I fumble with words. Then, she nods to herself, resolved, and she gets up to leave. I know I've lost her then. I can feel it, even as I get up and hurry after her. I'm almost unaware of the crowd around us at the restaurant, and then outside as she taps furiously at her phone to request a ride. I know it would be better to shut up, let her go, and maybe I can try and speak to her when she's calm. But I'm terrified she won't ever calm down, that even when she does, she won't want to speak to me.

I love you, I tell her. Please, I beg. But I've only made things worse. The words are like tiny little razor blades into her heart; she hears them, and she flinches, then recoils. The last I see of her she's disappearing into the back of a cab. A camera clicks somewhere close by, and only then do I realize how public our confrontation has been.

"Robert?"

I groan, half in pain but mostly in protest as Amy shakes me awake. My neck is as stiff as a board. I twist in the seat and struggle to turn around and face her. The dream was so vivid I can still feel my heart beating. It's almost like I'm still there in the street outside that restaurant, and not in the slightly stuffy back seat of my Jeep.

"We're here," Amy says.

I don't immediately register where 'here' is. I blink rapidly to clear my head and eyes of the dream. The events of the night come back to me very slowly. Strip club. Fight. Throbbing temple and right eye. Amy squeezed on my lap. A slip of paper with an address on it.

"Oh," I mumble, sitting up straight. "Here here?"

I look outside the window to my right, but it's too dark to make anything out. With a deep sigh, I drag myself up off the back seat and scramble into the front. I roll down the window and look outside. We're in front of a small, isolated house in the middle of nowhere. A single light illuminates the surrounding area. It appears to be a small compound, with the house the only building for many miles in every direction.

"Are you sure this is it?" I ask Amy.

She shrugs. "It is. I used Google Maps, and I'm fairly certain this is the only house in the area."

"What's the time?" I ask her, rubbing my eyes.

"A little after midnight."

"Hmm. I don't know if this is such a good idea after all. Maybe we should come back in the morning."

"The trip alone would take half the day, Robert," Amy says. "You said it yourself. We need to get this over with."

"I know. I know. But it just occurred to me how weird it would be to walk up to the woman's house at this hour."

"Well, what do you suggest, then?" Amy asks, a little exasperated.

I think about that for a minute. We really don't have much of an option. We could sleep in the car and wait until morning, but that would be a practical nightmare. We could also go find a hotel and spend the night, assuming we can figure out where we are. Neither of us brought a change of clothes or basic amenities. And we will still have to show up here in the morning, not exactly fresher, but with the added possibility that we'll miss Celeste entirely.

"I guess we'll have to risk it," I say finally. My stomach gives a low rumble, and I realize I haven't eaten in hours. "It's obviously not ideal, but we don't have much of a choice."

Amy nods then shifts in her seat and reaches out. Her fingers are tentative as she runs her hand over my face. She prods the area around my eye gently, watching me closely for a reaction.

"Well, the swelling has gone down, so that's a good thing," she says. "You'll have the bruise to deal with for a while, but that's about it."

"Happy days. It's not like I'm a public figure or anything."

"Oh, you're a public figure now, are you?"

"I would go so far as to claim I'm a celebrity," I say, grinning smugly.

"Huh." Amy's expression is amused. "Wonder why no one has recognized you this whole trip."

"Oh, shut up."

We get out of the car and walk slowly toward the compound, literally toward the light. The night is eerily quiet, no nocturnal insects making their presence known, no faraway sounds of the city rushing by. I suppose it's one advantage of living somewhere like this; complete and utter serenity. If you like that sort of thing.

After a slight hesitation, I give the small picket gate a little shove, and the door swings open. We trot up to the house, making loud crunching sounds on the gravel pathway. I figure anything to wake Celeste up if she's sleeping.

At the front door, I raise my fist and give it three sharp raps.

"Celeste?" I call out. I knock once more, then, when nothing happens, I walk around the porch and to the nearest window, where I cup my hands and try to peer into the house. I can make out vague shapes and shadows, but no movement.

It takes several attempts, each increasingly loud and desperate before we finally hear someone stirring in the house.

Moments later, a light flicks on inside the house, and we hear soft footsteps coming closer and closer, the sound of several locks clicking, and finally, the door opens a fraction.

A pale, oval face peers out through the gap in the door. Sleepy. Confused. Slightly familiar. Her eyes go from Amy to me, and I think for the first time about how we must look, a guy with a bruised face and a woman in a T-shirt and jeans, shivering due to the cold. I would be suspicious too. But she recognizes me. Her eyes pop, and I have no doubt she's fully awake now.

The door swings all the way open. She is standing there in cute little sleeping shorts and a baggy tee, almost unrecognizable from the girl I first met months ago.

"Robert fucking Hardy," she says, crossing her arms. I can't tell whether she's disappointed or simply stunned.

I guess it's a good sign that she hasn't thrown anything yet.

"Celeste," I say, nodding in greeting.

"Of course, you show up in the middle of the night."

"Sorry about that. I thought I'd find you at the club."

"Flesh? I left there months ago."

"Yeah, well, I didn't know that."

Her eyes flick over to Amy, who still hasn't said a word. "How rude of you, Robert. Aren't you going to introduce your friend?"

"Aren't you going to invite us in?" I ask her. I may be imagining it, but I can feel Amy shivering beside me.

Celeste steps aside to let us through. I walk in first, through a narrow hallway and into a crowded living room area. Crowded, as in messy and thoroughly lived in. We have to wade through assorted piles of clothes, books, and even dishes. Apparently, Celeste isn't a neat person. Or we caught her on cleaning day.

I ram my toe into something solid, and I let out a pained grunt. Furniture. A couch, I find out when I reach out and feel around. Celeste actually laughs; she is standing in the hallway, watching Amy and I try to make sense of her living room.

"I live alone," she says in defense. "I won't even lie that I had any intention of cleaning up. Find something to perch on. I think I have a couch in there somewhere."

Amy and I push aside enough things to make room on the couch and sit down.

Celeste comes up to us, then, her eyes twinkling. "This is her, isn't it?" she says, addressing me.

"What?"

She turns to Amy. "You're the woman who broke his heart, aren't you?"

Amy and I exchange identical expressions of shock. "I don't …" Amy stutters. "How do you …?"

Celeste only grins. "Of course. It makes sense, I suppose. But

... no, wait. You're not the woman he's been running around with, though. His campaign manager."

"We get it, Celeste," I say if only to spare Amy the indignity of having to answer. "You've been looking us up. Been doing a lot, haven't you?"

"Oh, you finally figured it out." She seems unperturbed. "Took you long enough. I'm surprised you did at all, to be honest."

"What is this about, Celeste? Why have you been torturing me?"

She shakes her head and skips away. "Not so fast, Mr. DA. Can I get you guys anything? Water? A beer?"

Amy and I say no at the same time. But Celeste is already gone, rummaging away in the next room, and moments later, she returns with two glasses of water. She looks around for a few moments, stumped, and then she shrugs and sets them down on the only clear patch of the floor.

"Maybe I do need to clean up a bit," she admits to herself. "I could have sworn I had a coffee table."

She attacks the nearest pile of paraphernalia, throws a few things around, and pulls out a thick, fluffy cushion. She pats it a few times to dislodge dust, then throws it down right in front of us and sinks into it.

"Do you even live here?" I ask, surveying the full extent of her mess.

"Actually, no," she says. "I spend most of my time in my room. And the kitchen maybe. I'm never in this particular room. As you can imagine, I don't get a lot of visitors."

"So, this is your attic?"

"Pretty much, yeah. We can move to my bedroom if you'd be more comfortable there ...?"

She says it with such brazen confidence I instantly remember the night we met. Shy, but once the ice has been broken, this woman is a force. It's starting to come back to me, tiny details, pieces of a larger puzzle.

"How did you know who I am?" Amy asks. Clearly, she is bothered by how much Celeste seems to know.

"Oh, has Robert not told you about me?"

"Only that you've been trying to blackmail him." There's a little hostility in the way she says it. I look over to her. Her posture is closed, her arms and legs crossed.

"I can understand why you'd think that, but no. I have no interest in blackmailing Robert. Not least because it would be too easy. A child could find dirt on him. There's so much there I don't know why no one has thought of it, to be honest. Especially now that you're running."

"Well, maybe no one else is inspired by jealous, personal motives," I say to her.

"Jealousy? What are you talking about?"

"It's obvious, isn't it? I spent the night with you, probably gave you some ideas. And then I left the next morning and didn't say a word, didn't call or reach out. I forgot about you, and now you're doing this to spite me."

It's infuriating how calm she's remained all along. Like she has an ace up her sleeve and is waiting for the perfect time to throw it out.

"And what exactly am I doing, then?" she asks.

"You know what."

"I do. But you clearly don't. So, let's hear it. What is it I've been doing to spite you?"

"The photos? The videos? Random, anonymous packages. You've obviously been trying to send me a message."

Celeste shakes her head. "The wrong one, clearly." To Amy, she says, "I didn't get your name."

"Amelia."

"To answer your question, Amelia, and his, too, because while he has figured out that I'm the person behind the documents he's been getting, he clearly doesn't remember what happened between us ... I'll just go back to the night in question, okay?"

"Let's see ... how far back do I need to go ... right. I was a new employee over at FLESH, then Haven's newest, shiniest establishment. I was coming off a failed venture into the legal field, having worked briefly as a paralegal before losing my job along with half the staff of the firm I was at. Anyway, I needed a way to make ends meet, so I took the only job I could get; one of the girls at

FLESH. Now, here's all you need to know about that job; those girls are basically all-purpose slaves. We were supposed to do whatever the clients asked of us. Waiting tables, serving them, entertaining them. We were the staff and the talent. The younger, sexier girls went right to the stage, others worked their way there. They make the most money, the stage girls, so it's naturally the most coveted job. But it also had its cons. The stage girls attract the most attention from clients and the most requests for 'private sessions.' I don't need to tell you what went on back there, but it wasn't a whole lot of fun.

Being new, I was pushed to the stage the first few nights. I wasn't particularly good at it, to be honest. I'm not the best dancer, and I certainly didn't know too much about looking and acting sexy. A lot of the other girls started to get jealous because the owner kept pushing me up there, and they felt they deserved it more. So, all this means I'm not particularly well-liked, I hate it there, and I'm desperate for a way out. Enter this charming guy from out of town, clearly looking to blow off some steam. I don't know why he notices me, but he does. I serve him drinks, and finally, he asks if he can get a private dance. At first, I panic, thinking it's going to be just as bad as I expect because nothing good happens in those back rooms.

But he is nice to me. He isn't touchy; he doesn't immediately try to get me on my back. He wants to hear my story. He actually listens when I tell it to him. Slowly, he starts to open up too. He is a big shot lawyer from the big city. He is punishing himself because he just messed up his relationship irrevocably, and he doesn't think he'll ever get back what he had with this woman."

I shift uncomfortably in my seat. I don't need to look at Amy to know she's staring daggers at me. I can feel the heat of her gaze burning a hole in my temple. I don't remember this story, as well as Celeste clearly does, so I can't object to any of it. Maybe I should have come alone.

"I tell him I need to get back, my shift is almost up, but he won't let me go. He wants to take me home, he says. He likes talking to me. He's the first person who hasn't treated me like a piece of meat, so I'm flattered. I go with him to a hotel. He tells me he is sorry about my situation, that he would be happy to help. Would I be okay with coming back to the city with him, and he could help me find a job and get myself set up? It sounds ridiculous. This man is a stranger. He has been nice to me, but serial killers can be nice too.

There's no reason why he would help me, right? But he is charming, the bastard, and he convinces me he has no bad intentions, that he really does want to help and that's it.

We make love as if to seal the deal. I know he isn't making love to me so much as the ghost of the woman he claims broke his heart, but I don't care. He has given me hope. I write my name and contacts on a piece of paper and give it to him. I can't go with him right away, obviously. I need to quit my job at FLESH, sell my house, get my things in order. We agree that he'll give me a call when he gets back to the city, and he can come to get me once he has a lead on a job. He falls asleep in my arms, and that's that. When I wake up the next morning, he is gone."

I almost don't want to hear the rest, because I can guess what happens. I can't remember it, but I can guess. I would have forgotten all about Celeste that morning. The alcohol would have worn off, and I would have had no memory of our shared experience. I probably woke up to a woman and assumed it had been a casual one-night stand I picked up at a bar, and I left because that's what I do; I leave before it gets awkward.

There is a long silence after Celeste finishes her story. None of us knows what to say, how to react. I'm swimming in a deadly concoction of shame and guilt.

"That's how I know who you are," Celeste concludes. "Because he wouldn't stop talking about you, and how much you meant to him."

"What was your plan, then?" Amy asks. I chance a glance at her. Her expression has not changed. "You said you weren't blackmailing him. What were you doing?"

"Oh, I just wanted him to remember me. I wanted to show him who he really is; that he isn't the guy he pretended to be when he met me. He isn't nice or charming or thoughtful. He's just a guy who uses people, and once he's done, he walks away and forgets about them. I wanted him to see his true self in those photos and videos."

39
Amelia

The drive back to Glendale is initially uncomfortable and much quieter.

I know Robert is trying to wrap his head around what we just heard because the same story is running through my mind. In the end, it seems Gwen was always right about the woman behind the 'blackmail.' We gave it such prominence, we worried about it so much, yet in the end, it was as personal a motivation as I've ever seen.

I know, too, why Celeste bothered me so much. She is me. Under slightly different circumstances, I would probably make the same choices she did. I was that girl, meeting Robert and becoming instantly smitten. I can't judge her because I've been in her shoes. I know what it feels like to be seen by him, to feel like he cares about you. I can almost imagine what it's like to then have that taken away. I don't know if I would have gone as far as she did to remind him what he did to her, but I understand it. I understand her.

I disagree with her assessment of Robert, though. Or at least I don't agree with it entirely. He may have been that guy once upon a time, but not anymore. The change is subtle, but it's there. If nothing else, the fact that he went on the trip at all means he's willing to make amends.

But the thing that bothers me the most is what Celeste said about me. Well, what she said about Robert in relation to me.

I have done my best to block it out, but I still think about what happened between us. Subconsciously. Reluctantly. Always, I assume I was the one who was hurt the most. I still believe I was. He pawned me off to a disgusting man for personal gain, without a second thought. He basically gave me away like property and had the nerve to try and justify his indecent proposal. There is no excusing that, as he learned from his myriad attempts to apologize to me.

Still, I've never stopped to think about what it did to him. I mean, I knew he went on a self-destructive trip through half the strip clubs and gambling dens in the city. But I always assumed it was his way of showing he was unfazed by the break-up. That he could bounce back that fast. It never occurred to me right up until Celeste implied it, that he was on a downward spiral of guilt and regret. And that, I have no idea how to feel about.

"Hungry?" Robert asks suddenly, cutting into my train of thought.

I clear my throat, and my voice sounds scratchy from the long silence. I nod. It's easy to ignore the baser urges when you're busy picking up the pieces of your blown mind.

It's harder to find somewhere to eat this time around. It's late, and Haven isn't exactly a bustling metropolis. Robert pulls up at a gas station off the Interstate, and we pick up coffee and donuts. It's all there is, but it will do.

"I'm sorry the road trip went off the rails a little bit," Robert says, finally breaking the silence. "If I'd known how wild it would get, I wouldn't have involved you at all."

I shake my head. "No. I'm glad you did. This has been eye-opening."

Robert looks over at me, and his frown is suspicious. "In what way?"

"For one, we've finally put this blackmail business behind us. Now you can focus on the campaign."

"True. And yet not what you meant."

"I guess I didn't understand why you hit rock bottom like that."

"And you do now?"

"I think I do."

"I hope you're not buying into Celeste's absurd theory that I was doing it out of heartbreak and rejection."

"Don't do that, Robert."

"Do what?" He tries to make his voice light and conversational, but I notice he can't quite meet my eyes.

"Don't hide behind humor and try to laugh this away. For once, just speak honestly. Just be open with me."

"Okay," he says in a low voice. "Maybe it's not such an absurd theory."

Even that feels like a gift, like he has admitted way too much and is about to immediately retract it. But he doesn't. He lets the words sit, their implication hanging heavy between us.

"I know what I did was shitty," he goes on. "I shouldn't have even considered it, I know, much less brought it up to you. There isn't a day I haven't thought back and wished I'd done things differently. I know I messed up, Amy. I've known it for a year, and it has haunted me to no end. But I feel like you never gave me a chance to make amends. You didn't even want to hear me out. You already had one foot out the door, and I gave you the perfect excuse to put the other one out."

It's the fight we never had, the conversation I so desperately tried to avoid. Because talking about it means reliving it, and that means fresh heartbreak.

"I don't think you realize how you make people feel, Robert," I say. "It took meeting Celeste for me to confirm it, but I've always known it. At least that's how you made me feel, anyway. You elevate someone, and you make them feel so important, so beautiful, and so loved. Yet you remain distant, always, never giving yourself fully, always just out of reach. So, we try harder and harder. But you never cave. And then we start to worry. Maybe I don't really mean that much to him. Maybe I'm alone in this. And then something like that happens, you essentially give me away to another man, and my worst fears are confirmed. You couldn't possibly do that if you cared about me."

"Except I did care about you, Amy. More than I've ever cared about anyone else. Hell, I loved you, and that's not an emotion that comes easily for me. I made a mistake, sure. But that's the kind of thing we were supposed to work through."

He's not wrong. I've been so hung up on what he did, clinging on to my hurt because if I took any focus away from it, our relationship would swing into sharper focus.

"I was scared," I admit. "Things were going so great, and I had not expected that at all. And then that whole thing happened, and part of me was relieved because it meant you were still you, and I could pump the breaks on us. Maybe I was too quick to jump ship."

"I was scared too," Robert says.

"Really?"

"Yeah. I mean, I had never been in anything that serious

279

before. Maybe part of me consciously sabotaged it because it was getting to a point I wasn't sure I was ready for."

It is such a relief to hear him say it. It feels like the most earnest he has ever been with me, and I don't want the spell to be broken. I realize suddenly that I'm not mad at him anymore. If I'm being honest, I don't think I've been for a long time.

"It was still a dick move, though," I say.

Robert laughs, and the tension between us snaps like a taut string.

"I can't argue with that."

He reaches out and takes my hand. His fingers interlock with mine. At that moment, the road trip doesn't seem like such a bad idea.

"You don't need to …" I protest as Robert parks the car in my driveway and starts to get out.

"Nonsense," he says. "I promised your scary friend I'd get you home safely. That involves walking you to your door."

And so, he does. There's something of a giddy teenager in him as he jogs to the other side of the car and opens the door for me, then takes my hand and helps me out the car. He extends a hooked elbow and I slip my hand inside it. For the whole three feet to my doorstep.

This is it, then, I think. The end of the line. It has been a strange trip. I could never have guessed that the biggest knot we would untangle was the one between us.

There is a sense of finality to it all as we stand awkwardly in front of my door. We both know that as soon as I step into my house, as soon as he turns and walks away, what we shared will be gone. The real world will rematerialize, with all its problems and finely drawn lines. It was so much simpler when it was just the two of us in a car, alone in the universe.

I don't want to go in, and from the way he is standing, Robert doesn't want to leave either. So, we stand there for several precious moments, each of us terrified of being the one to say 'boo.' Robert is still holding my hand, and his fingers start to slide and move against mine, probably absentmindedly. But it is enough to distract me.

We speak at the same time. I mumble something about the time, and he starts to apologize again for stealing me. Then we both grin and shake our heads at each other. This would be cute if it weren't also very childish.

Get a grip, Amy.

"Well, then," I declare with as much conviction as I can muster. "Goodnight, I guess?"

"Right," Robert says. His fingers haven't stopped tracing patterns all over my hand. Dizzying patterns. Suggestive patterns. "Goodnight, Amelia."

He lets go all at once, and he steps back with a wry smile. "We should do this more often."

"What, stand awkwardly by my doorstep?"

"Yeah. Obviously. But maybe go on random road trips first?"

"Hmm. We'll see." I fumble around in my bag and pull out my keys. It's good to have somewhere else to look, something else on which to focus. I unlock the door and step in quickly. As the door swings shut behind me, I lean against it and let out a deep sigh.

That was close. Too close.

A soft timid knock sounds from the other side of the door. I can feel the last vestiges of my logic desert me as I open it. It's his smile that sends me over the edge. I don't know what it is he was going to say. I don't care. I throw my arms around him. He grabs me by the waist and lifts me into the air, and when he brings me down, his lips meet mine in a deep kiss.

I feel myself being carried backward. I hear the door slamming shut, and I'm still being carried. I drag my lips from his and point in the general direction of my bedroom. I keep my eyes shut because I don't want to see the reflection of my need in his eyes. I don't want to allow myself to question this, to overthink it.

I had forgotten how strong he is. I'm a feather pillow in his arms as he crosses the living room, turns into the hallway, and proceeds down to the farthest bedroom on the right. All in relative darkness. I hope he doesn't stub his toe again.

And then we're in my bedroom, and he sets me on my feet. I look up at him; he is taking my room in, scanning, assessing.

A sudden, unwelcome thought slips into my mind; I'm filthy.

281

I haven't showered since before we've left. I'm not exactly presentable. Do I have time to slip away and freshen up? I turn and try to walk away, but Robert's arm goes around my waist, and he pulls me back in.

"Where do you think you're going?" he asks. Has his voice always been that sexy?

"I need to …"

But he is kissing me once more. His lips are gentle yet firm. He uses his tongue to break down my feeble resistance, and I moan and spill completely into his arms. He kisses me like he has not seen me in months. I kiss him back like I've been longing to for months because I have. We move together in sync and in rhythm, and I am only aware of the lushness of his lips, the slick congress of his tongue, and the impossible hardness of his body.

I don't remember moving, but suddenly I'm at the edge of the bed. The wooden surface presses against the back of my thigh, and on the other side, Robert crushes his body.

"I need to shower," I whisper. "I've just been on a long trip, you see."

Robert shakes his head. "You're perfect."

Charming bastard.

His hands travel down my body, pausing to cup the curve of my butt and then moving slowly back up to rest on the exposed skin just below where my T-shirt ends. Long fingers snake their way past the fabric and crawl over my lower back. They raise goosebumps as they go. Up, then around, pulling the T-shirt with them. I lift my hands and help him pull it off. He reaches around to the back of my bra and unclasps it with a deft, practiced snap.

He takes a step back, like a painter admiring his masterpiece.

I blush at the expression on his face. His lips are pushed out as he whistles and shakes his head.

"God, I've missed you," he says. His eyes never leave my breasts, so I assume he's addressing them. His gaze alone causes my nipples to stiffen. I feel more naked than I have in a long time, so I reach out and pull him back to me, start to unbutton his shirt.

My hands are shaking. My fingers are clumsy, anxious, uncertain. I take way too long to get his shirt off. He gets antsy and resumes attending to my upper body with his hands. He cups, circles, and teases my breasts, making me impatient. When his shirt finally drops to the floor, he is already tugging down my pants and pulling my legs out of them. Pants and panties both.

Robert lifts me once more, throws me onto the bed, and climbs up with me. I reach for him, my lips already parting, but he only kisses my hand and pushes it away. He moves his torso down along my body, lower and lower until his head is at the tuft of hair I suddenly regret not trimming. Somehow, it sends a shockwave through me when he buries his head there and inhales deep.

He kisses the folds of my lips, runs his tongue along them. Already, my legs are trembling. I can feel the muscles of my vagina clench, and I know this is going to be a brief session. My hands tangle and untangle imaginary knots in his hair. He kisses around my clitoris, meaning only to tease, but I have a lot of pent up frustration, and the waves of pleasure set my torso rocking. I arch my back upwards. I'm thrashing this way and that, even before he really gets to work. I won't last. I'm not sure I want to.

He senses the change in my body. He always has. He knows exactly what he is doing to me. Right as I'm going over the edge, right as I'm starting to moan uncontrollably, I feel him shift and mount me.

He buries himself inside me with a deep, slow stroke. I watch with half-lidded eyes as his hips rock in time with the motion of his thrust, and it is beautiful. I have missed this so much. He fills me to the core. Somehow, he feels just right.

His face swims somewhere above me. He grabs me by the neck and kisses me once. It's a fierce, passionate kiss, but his hands are gentle, as is his expression. He doesn't say a word; he simply stares deep into my eyes as he starts to push into me. It's unnerving and more intimate than anything anyone has ever done to me. More powerful than the orgasm that tears through me moments later, strange and wonderful, and more than I can bear.

40
Robert

Gwen isn't exactly saying it, but I can tell she's mad. It's been two days since the road trip. Two days since I left without telling her and went on an 'adventure' with my ex-girlfriend. And since I returned from Amy's house, deliriously happy, to find her perched on my couch, bouncing her leg.

I've always admired Gwen's ability to prioritize, and at that moment, I watched as she went from cold fury to concern over my darkening eye, then slowly settling into a silent resentment. I knew that one. It was a staple of hers. And what it said was that there was a fight to be had, as soon as she finished with the matter at hand.

But that moment never came. After fussing over my eye for an unhealthy amount of time, she conceded that I needed to rest; she could tell from how exhausted I looked that it had been a long, draining trip. So, she crumpled up the arguments I knew she had carefully laid out and thrust them in her back pocket. To be continued, her expression said. She did not get into bed with me. She did not join me in the shower. I fell asleep almost immediately, and when I woke up, I found her curled up on the couch.

The next day presented new challenges. While the bruise was mostly healed, it had left a nasty orange discoloration that stubbornly rejected any attempts to conceal it with make-up. Gwen tried everything to hide it, emptying out the contents of her make-up kit and going to work on my face for almost an hour. In the end, she had to admit defeat. "We'll just have to hope it's gone by Tuesday," she sighed.

She spent the rest of the time grilling me as I would be grilled in my meeting with Simms. She had prepared an extensive list of the questions I was going to be responding to, including detailed branches accounting for any possible deviations. It was all very thorough.

Gwen had received the news of Celeste with such apathy I wondered if she knew all along. She didn't seem to think it was a big deal at all; after giving me her best 'I told you so' eye roll, she went right back into her questionnaire, and that was that. Not that I was fooled. I knew it was going to come up again, and I knew I wouldn't be ready for it; Gwen was shrewd like that.

I was right on both counts. Her prayer has been answered; it is impossible to make out the bruise, thanks to crafty make-up application. And then, right as I am going into the interview, seconds before I step out of my dressing room, she grabs my hand, and I turn to her, confused.

"Did you sleep with her on your trip?" she asks.

I have been thinking about what happened with Amy a lot, while simultaneously trying not to think about it. Gwen's question isn't exactly unexpected, but I'm still caught flat-footed when she hits me with it.

"Of course not," I say automatically. It feels like a technicality, but I'm not exactly lying. Nothing actually happened *during* the trip. Somehow, I doubt Gwen would appreciate the nuance of the lie. I try to go in for a peck, but Gwen leans away.

"Go on, then. You don't want to keep Tiffany waiting."

It's not exactly 'Breakfast with Tiffany.' Tiffany is her usual cheery self, and she welcomes me on set like a long-lost friend, but the atmosphere is definitely different. For one, there is the sallow, cold face of Jeremiah Simms watching my every move, his grey eyes battering me all the way up the makeshift dais. The handshake he gives me is no different from his last; firm, painful, clearly meant to intimidate. I try my best to stare him down, but the man is a small mountain, and I soon get a crick in my neck.

Tiffany has done the smart thing and set us up apart from each other; we are seated on either side of her, surrounded by at least five cameras in every direction.

Simms is the picture of composure; this is clearly something he has done many times. He is in his element in front of cameras. I, on the other hand, am slightly shaken, no thanks to Gwen and her tactics. Tiffany leans in once we're both seated and quickly goes over the rules. Keep it clean, gentlemen. No foul language. No talking over each other. As much as possible, let *her* moderate the discussion.

Before I'm completely ready, we are live. Tiffany introduces each of us in turn; Simms as the most recognizable politician in town AND the incumbent DA, and me as the scruffy challenger ready to take on the establishment. The tone of the interview is supposed to be light but serious, and already I can see her trying to straddle it.

"So, gentlemen. I'll get right to it. It's early days, of course, but we've already seen several polls predicting a significant edge for you, Mr. Simms. What are your thoughts on this? Do you have this thing in the bag, as the polls would have us believe?"

Simms sits back and puts on an excellent impression of thinking about the question. As if we haven't both been prepped within an inch of our lives.

"I wouldn't say I have it in the bag, no. As it is, I think the polls reflect the feelings of the people, and at the moment, they will naturally gravitate toward that which they know. Mr. Hardy has done an excellent job of introducing himself to the public, and it's a long way to the election, so I would take those numbers with a pinch of salt."

"But you're confident you can win?"

"Yes, of course. I believe I have done a good job for as long as I have been in office, and I have much more to do. I'm confident the people will give me the chance to do so."

She turns to me. "What about you, Mr. Hardy? Any takeaways from the early polls?"

"I'm not giving them too much thought right about now, no. It's still early, and I'm still in the process of rolling out the fundamentals of my campaign. I trust that once I've done this fully, I can then start to make inroads and actually challenge Mr. Simms."

Back and forth we go. I'm surprised at how well Gwen has coached me, because I can hear myself, see myself on the monitors, and I look and sound the part. More impressively, I can not only match Simms' subtle hostility, but I get one up over him on a few of the more innocuous questions, which makes his mood darken slowly as the interview progresses. I know, because it is getting harder and harder for him to respond genially with the false charm he has mastered. Thirty minutes in, it's clear he's irritated and impatient.

And with unerring timing, Tiffany dives into the heart of the interview.

"Mr. Simms. Some would say you fired the first shots a few days ago when you called out your opponent in a televised interview. You said, and I quote, 'Democracy cannot come at the expense of morality. Of course, I have nothing against Mr. Hardy. But Mr.

Hardy is not the perfect candidate he would like you to believe he is. I don't claim to be a saint, by any standards. But then again, I've always been on the right side of the law.' What did you mean by this?"

Simms shifts in his seat. "If you watched the interview or read the transcript a little further down, you would have seen that I was simply referring to Mr. Hardy's history of representing unscrupulous individuals, including criminals and corrupt individuals. All of it is part of public record."

"It's interesting that you mention corruption, Mr. Simms," I cut in. Tiffany flashes me a warning look. "Isn't it true that your office has refused, on several occasions, to respond to requests for external audits, preferring to keep it in-house?"

"That's inaccurate. There is a system in place to ensure ..."

"And these individuals you claim to be corrupt criminals. Isn't it your job to prosecute them? So, what does it say about your office if criminals are constantly walking scot-free? Is it that you're incompetent? Or is it possible they are not, in fact, guilty, as you believe, and as the court rules them not to be?"

"This isn't a courtroom, Mr. Hardy. I'm afraid there is much more to running a campaign than slinging wild accusations."

"Remind me, then. Which of us went on live television to 'sling wild accusations'?"

"Gentlemen, please!" Tiffany holds her hands up, and we both fall silent. If this were a boxing match, I would just have gotten away with throwing in a couple of jabs after the bell rang. Simms looks furious.

"Let's address this, then, shall we?" Tiffany says. "As I understand, you have both agreed to lay all your cards on the table here today, regarding any skeletons you may have which could be used against the other. Is that accurate?"

Simms grunts, and I nod.

"Good. So, I will ask each of you, in turn, to speak directly into the camera and own up to your skeletons. I'll start with you, Mr. Hardy."

If it had been up to me, we would have called this interview off. Amy and I already figured out the person behind the photos and videos. There is no blackmail, so there is no need to confess anything. I pointed this out to Gwen, but she wouldn't budge. This was no longer just about the blackmail. It was now about me showing that I'm human, I make mistakes, and that I'm ready to own up to them. She is convinced it will go a long way in fixing my 'problematic perception issue,' particularly among female voters.

"If the people of Glendale do elect me as their District Attorney, I will insist on complete transparency for my office and myself. So, I would like to start now, by inviting you all into my private life. I have nothing to hide. And here's how I'm going to prove it. My team has uploaded every shred of data and documentation that can be used against me to a website that will go live as soon as this interview is over. Every parking ticket, every case I've tried in court, every personal disagreement. I invite you all to visit the website, robhardy.com, and see for yourself. All my skeletons laid bare."

I can tell from Simms' expression that he didn't expect me to say that. He probably thought I would somehow bluff my way out of actually giving away any real information. No doubt, he still doesn't believe I have. I can picture him rushing out of the interview as soon as it's over and yelling at his closest aide to hand him a phone or tablet so he can see for himself. Well, it's all there, Simms. Enjoy.

It turns out he has nothing to confess himself. He makes a meal out of 'applauding my honesty,' but when Tiffany stops him speaking in circles, he says that his skeletons comprise largely of his failures in office, most of which are part of the public record.

Tiffany is disappointed, as I'm sure her viewers are too. There were no explosive reveals, no scandals rearing their heads on national TV. But she nods and concludes the interview.

"Well, folks, that is all from us here on GBC Exclusive with me, Tiffany Cornish, and our special guests Jeremiah Simms and Robert Hardy. We may not have gotten the juicy scandals, but we did get something better; the promise of a clean campaign."

From the look on Simms' face, a clean campaign is the farthest thing from his mind.

41
Amelia

It feels good to be back at work.

It's like returning to earth after a space mission, that comfortable feeling of going back to familiarity and routine.

I arrive earlier than usual, just so I can sit at my desk in front of the class and bask in the beauty of the day. And to watch the students as they file in. I'm half-hoping I will catch Kieran before he disappears into the back of the room, from where he will vanish after the class. I haven't checked in on him since the lunch 'date' at the restaurant; I have no idea how he's doing.

But Kieran doesn't show up. He isn't late, as I assume he's going to be. Thirty minutes in, an hour later, I have to force myself to stop throwing looks at the door, expecting him to stride in on his long legs, wearing his trademark awkward smile. My heart sinks at the realization that I'll have to hunt him down again. And then at the thought that maybe he isn't okay at all.

Everything with Robert has happened so fast it feels like the rest of my life is scrambling to keep up. It has only been a few days since he first approached me about helping him with his campaign problem, and yet it feels like weeks. I have barely had time to process what I said to Kieran and how he must have taken it. I need to find a way to check in on him; it would be very easy for a lovesick kid to run his mouth out of spite. I finally did the right thing in ending the inappropriate affair; now, I just need to cover my tracks.

A shadow falls over my desk as the class is clearing out, and I look up to see a familiar face. I don't remember his name, but I know him; he is one of my students. One of the cool kids, he always sits in the front with a gang of his friends. Never says much, but he is always whispering asides to his gang and snickering when I look away.

"Hey, Miss Brooks," he drawls with a cocky swagger drawn from every high school movie ever.

"How can I help you?" I ask him. I throw all my stuff into my bag and sling it over my shoulder to hurry him up. His name is floating around in my head, but I can't quite reach it.

"Maybe *I* can help *you*," he says, grinning stupidly and pointing from him to me.

"What are you talking about?"

"I just thought, you know, maybe I could be your next boy toy?" And he bursts out laughing.

The shock of his words hits me like a slap across the face. And the realization that he knows something, that someone knows about Kieran and me is very unpleasant. I struggle to keep my face straight as I look into the kid's smiling face.

"I don't know what you think you're talking about," I say.

Now would be a good time to walk away. Don't give him anything else. Don't fuel the fire of gossip and rumor. But I'm desperate to know more. How does he know? Who else knows? Has Kieran been talking?

"I'm just saying, Miss B., you're fine as hell, we always thought so. If we knew you were into young guys, that would have been a game-changer, you know what I mean?"

It's at this point I decide to drop all pretense. "Who told you that?" I ask him, taking a step toward him, fighting the urge to grab him by his flowery shirt and shake all the information out of him.

"Nah," he drawls. "No one told me shit. We all have eyes, you know. People see things, talk, you know."

I do know. I try to think back, to pinpoint a single incident which would have set tongues wagging. That time I dragged Kieran from another class? Definitely suspicious? Or maybe I didn't wipe my digital footprint from the computer I used to find his schedule? Neither seems enough to arouse suspicion, but I guess I'll never know.

"I guess that's a no, then? On the boy toy thing? You don't need to worry about me. I can keep a secret."

"You're being absurd," I tell him.

And then I'm out of the classroom. Every part of my body is screaming for me to run. I'm so paranoid I feel like everyone knows, everyone is staring at me as I walk past them, that as soon as I do, they point and whisper behind my back. I don't even know where I'm going; I just know I need to find Kieran, quick.

As I turn the corner into my office, I pull out my phone and text Kieran.

MY OFFICE! NOW! EMERGENCY!

I shut myself in the office and allow the panic to set in. And the day started so well.

I'm pacing, my mind racing, trying to think of a course of action. It all depends on Kieran. If he has indeed been telling people about us, then it might be difficult to deny it. Even if I could, he has evidence of our interactions; phone-calls, messages, maybe even photos. I was sloppy. I got complacent. I should have been more discreet, more careful. I should have …

Or maybe he hasn't actually told anyone, and the idiot in my classroom was speculating. But that's more a blind hope than anything else. Either way, the first thing I need to do is get Kieran to delete all evidence of our interactions.

Right on cue, a knock sounds on my door, and he pops his head around and into the office. "Amy?" He looks worried, and I don't immediately register why.

"Are you okay?"

"Yeah, why?"

"Your text said emergency."

"Oh. No, no. I'm fine. I need to speak to you. Get in here, quick. And close the door behind you."

As he does, I walk around the office, peering out the windows and shutting blinds like a crazy person. When I'm satisfied we're alone, I round up on Kieran.

"Have you told anyone about us?" I ask him in a whisper.

"What? No. Of course not. I wouldn't do that."

"Are you sure?"

"Yeah, I'm sure. I know you broke up with me, but I wouldn't."

He seems way too calm and composed for someone who was just broken up with. Or maybe I just overestimated the level of his affection towards me. It wouldn't be the first time I've done that.

"Why weren't you in class today?" I ask him, remembering.

"Oh, I dropped it."

"What?"

"I dropped it."

"You dropped my class?"

He nods.

"Why?"

"I think you know why."

"Because of what I said at the restaurant? Come on, Kieran. You can't be serious. Because of what happened between us? I thought we agreed that was a mistake ..."

"We didn't agree," Kieran says. "There was no agreement. You decided that."

"Look, Kieran." I start to reach out, to touch him maybe, but I realize too late that it would send the wrong message, and I let my hand fall awkwardly to the side. "What happened between us was a personal matter. In spite of how things ended, you shouldn't risk your academic future. It's not smart."

"Well, I'm not dropping it entirely. Just for this semester. I can take it next year, or maybe I can find another ..."

"Another course instructor? So, this *is* about me."

"I won't lie and say it isn't, Amy. You know how I feel about you. It will be torture for me to sit in your class day in day out after all that has happened between us. I couldn't bear it. I couldn't sit there and pretend I'm not distracted, that I'm not fantasizing about you or remembering something we did together. I respect your decision to end things. I won't bother you anymore. I just need some time to heal, and I don't think six hours a week in your class is the best way to do that."

That one silences me. I get where he's coming from. And he's right. I never thought about any of this before when I was texting him, encouraging his infatuation. I never stopped to think about what would happen if it all went to shit. I understand, and yet I can't bear the thought that I've made him lose interest in law. It's literally my one job not to do that.

"There's a program coming up," I say, grasping at straws. "A mentorship program where you get to be guided by ..." I realize too late where that train of thought ends. Kieran's eyes narrow. He knows too.

"Guided by your boyfriend, Robert Hardy."

I don't know what to say anymore. I feel like I'm making things worse, no matter how hard I try. I need him to listen to me. I need this conversation to go back to the simple discussion of who said what to who. Anything but this mess.

"Well, that's even more reason for me to drop the class, then," Kieran says. His entire body language has changed. His tone is gruff, clipped. "I definitely won't be taking career tips from your boyfriend."

And with that, he turns to walk out of the room.

"Kieran, wait, please."

He stops at the door and looks back at me.

"You're sure you didn't tell anyone about us?"

"Unbelievable," Kieran says with a shake of his head. "That's all you care about, isn't it? That no one finds out about us. Not how I feel. No, fuck that. The most important thing is that I keep your secret. It's why you called me in here, right? To make sure I don't talk. Well, you don't need to worry about me. I haven't told anyone, and I won't. We never happened."

Yesterday, I was on the moon. Giddy. Happy. Excited. Right now, I feel like my heart has been yanked out of my body and stomped on. I don't even try and stop Kieran as he leaves. I wouldn't know what to say. I slump in my chair and let my head fall onto the table. How did I get here?

The phone rings, extremely loud as it is inches from my head. I have no doubt that this is more bad news. Indeed, when Dean Patel's voice asks me to meet him in his office right away, I'm not even surprised.

This is it, Amy. This is how it all ends.

42
Amelia

The last time I did a walk of shame was in high school. I had been out with a couple of my friends, and somehow, I thought it was a good idea to spend the night at one of their houses. I remember the morning after in all its awkward detail. The futile shower. The nagging feeling that everyone I walked past could tell I was in yesterday's clothes. The knowing smiles as I snuck back home. And, at the end of it, the absolute panic at arriving home and finding both my parents waiting, arms-crossed, in my room.

This feels like that, but much worse.

Maybe if Dean Patel had been clearer and given me more information, I wouldn't feel so panicked. Because it's the uncertainty that is killing me. He sounded serious, somber even, on the phone. But all he said was that he would like to see me in his office. Nothing more, so I'm left in the uncomfortable position of trying to guess what else this could be about, even though I know I'm simply lying to myself. False hope is still hope, though. What are the chances this *isn't* about the inappropriate relationship with a student?

As expected, the walk to Patel's office is long and stressful. I attract stares every step of the way, and none of them are casual or fleeting. They know. If I know one thing about rumors, it's that they spread alarmingly fast. And with these young students and their social media obsession, I shudder to think just how far the story has gotten.

So, it is with thoroughly frayed nerves and trembling fingers that I finally find myself at the door to the Dean's office. I take a deep breath and filter it out through gritted teeth. It doesn't calm me down. I knock on the door, wait for the invitation, and push in.

I haven't known Dean Patel a long time, but I feel like I do. I have gotten used to his easy smiles, his comically inappropriate banter, and his overall warmth. It is, therefore, the first sign of the gravity of the situation that he greets me with an expression I have never seen on his face before: disappointment. This is not the man who welcomed me to the university with open arms; this is a different animal. This man is quiet and intense and primly professional. It's the first time I've understood why he is the Dean after all.

"Miss Brooks, please sit."

It's so weird; I've never noticed just how much I appreciate the little touches he incorporates into face to face interactions, those things he does to lighten the mood, make you feel comfortable. I see it now. I would give anything for a gentle pat on the shoulder, or one of his corny dad jokes. Anything to let me know he is still my friend.

"So." He walks around to his side of the desk and sits down. "I have heard some disturbing rumors involving you, and I would like to clear things up with you before we can take any further action."

"Okay …"

"Now, I usually don't like to get involved in the petty gossip peddled by student magazines. I encourage it, certainly, for the purposes of journalistic integrity. I believe our journalism department has a role to play in our little campus community, and part of that is sharing the stories about other students, and to a lesser degree, some of the teachers.

"Now, I'll admit that I don't always read the student publications. But recently, a particular article was brought to my attention, one I found disturbing. Are you familiar with the article?"

I shake my head. "I'm not … I don't read the publication."

Patel slides open a drawer on his desk and pulls out a folded newspaper. It looks old and worn. I can tell it has been passed around quite a bit. He hands it to me across the desk. I'm about to ask which article I'm supposed to be looking at, but I don't need to. The article at the bottom of the page has been circled out in bold marker.

Illicit Affair Gone Sour?

A campus student has been left licking his wounds following the abrupt end of his brief but fiery romance with a professor at the university. The relationship was kept hush-hush for the better part of two months, but we can reliably report the two lovebirds were recently spotted hand in hand at a local restaurant.

Fresh details later emerged that the relationship is, in fact, a love triangle, with one of the parties also being involved with a local politician. It is unclear what caused the split, but it is likely the discovery that he was being played led our young Romeo to question his status, and the ensuing fallout resulted in heartbreak.

Student-teacher relationships are of course strictly forbidden by the university, but who doesn't love a rebel? For more on this developing story, be sure to check out next week's publication, and to tune in to tonight's podcast, featuring a special guest who will be discussing the dynamics of an illicit affair.

The paper is dated two days ago, which means it has had enough time to make the rounds on campus. Whatever was discussed on the podcast certainly couldn't have helped. I'm grateful that the paper didn't mention any names; I don't understand why seeing as they seem to know exactly who is involved. I can only assume there is some rule against publishing such information; otherwise, I would be on the front page. It's a small mercy, but I'll take it.

"Well?" Patel asks. He is watching me carefully as I read the article. Looking for a reaction, a tell. It can't be hard to find; my face grows increasingly hot as I read the article, and by the end, I feel like puking.

"This has no names," I say.

"No," Patel agrees. "I think that may be a stylistic choice, you know, keep the reader guessing, build suspense for the next issue … it's worked too. This edition was sold out. It went viral, too. It was all over the internet."

I can imagine Patel sitting down at his computer, trying to send an email and being met with countless spam emails urging him to 'check something out' and then summoning his secretary to help him make sense of it.

"Still," he goes on. "I think there's plenty of information we can infer from what little the article *does* say. I find it odd, for example, that the article mentions a local politician, mere weeks after we had that sit-down with Mr. Hardy.

"And I spoke with some faculty members, and some of them implied that there was reason to believe this student mentioned is one of yours. So, it follows that the professor is you, Miss Brooks."

Of course, it is. I made no attempts to keep my affair with Kieran secret. I got complacent, and therefore careless. It was right there for anyone who cared enough to look. And clearly, someone did. This is my own fault. Whatever happens now, I have to take responsibility for my recklessness.

"Is any of this true, then?" Patel asks me, his thick eyebrows going up a fraction. I can almost see the plea in his eyes for me to say no, to deny it so he can keep the idea he has of me intact.

I nod once. Something is caught in my throat, and I find that it is suddenly very difficult to get any words out or look directly at him. Guilt and shame wash over me. I feel like I'm back in that bedroom as a teen, facing my parents, knowing there's no getting out of this. If this is anything like that, Patel will tell me he isn't mad, just disappointed, and the quiet displeasure will make me feel ten times worse.

His eyes pop at my silent admission. He leans back in his chair and buries his head in his hands. He is silent for a long moment, during which I wonder what is going to happen to me. And then I remember the bit about a local politician, and nausea rises once more. I can't jeopardize Robert's campaign any further.

"I'm not involved with him," I say. Patel looks up at me, confused. "The local politician. Robert Hardy. I'm not involved with him, as the article claims."

"Oh." Patel frowns. "But the rest is true? You were involved with a student?"

"Not anymore," I say, a little desperately. "I tried to break things off earlier, I really did..."

"You realize this is in direct contravention of the school rules?"

"I do, and I'm sorry. I know I shouldn't have ..."

"Then why did you, Amy? I don't understand. I thought I knew you. I would never have expected this from you."

There it is. The disappointment.

Why did I indeed? It's an excellent question. I don't think I know how to answer it. I felt lonely? I liked the attention of a sweet, beautiful boy? It was simple, uncomplicated? I was reaching out in fear of having to confront my feelings of inadequacy and confusion? All kernels of truth. None adequate for this situation.

"I don't know, to be honest. It's complicated."

Patel nods slowly, almost as if he understands what I'm not

saying.

"You're young," he says, mostly to himself. "Younger than most of our instructors. You see these young students, and they're not that much younger than you are. You only just finished school yourself, so it's easy to relate to them. Maybe you resent that you have to be the adult, you have to be the one putting your foot down and making them listen to you. Maybe this one student doesn't make you feel like you're the teacher, maybe he reminds you of your own youth. One thing leads to another …" He trails off. It's almost like he is trying to make sense of it in his head like he's cooking up a scenario in which my actions would be justifiable. I'm not sure what to make of that.

"What happens now?" I ask him.

He shakes his head. He looks genuinely pained. "It's out of my hands now, I'm afraid. There will be an investigation, and you will have to appear in front of a disciplinary hearing. I can't imagine it will be pleasant. Best case scenario, you get suspended for some time. The university will be eager to make an example of you, so it could be much worse."

"What does that mean? Worse, how?"

"You could lose your job."

No surprises there, I suppose.

"And the student?" For some reason, I still don't want to say Kieran's name. Irrationally, I still believe I can protect him from all this.

"He'll have to go in front of the disciplinary committee as well. The cases will be handled separately. Generally, though, the university tends to be a little harder on the instructor in such a case."

"Surely it shouldn't matter this much?" I ask. "I mean, we're consenting adults. No one is hurting anyone."

"I agree with you, Amy. This particular rule is from a different era. But it is still a rule, and the university will have to act on it."

"I understand."

"The bigger problem, of course, is the school magazine."

"How so?"

"We need to shut this story down. Already it has done so

much damage. It will be practically impossible to stifle it, but we have to try. Campus gossip is one thing, but we can't have a licensed publication verifying or even commenting on such a story. It gives it wings, and we don't need that."

Another small mercy; he has softened a little. He is back to using my first name, and in saying 'we,' he is implying that this is now *our* problem. Together. And that he will help me figure it out.

"For what it's worth, I'm sorry," I say as I'm leaving the office. "It was reckless of me and unprofessional. I take full responsibility for it."

Dean Patel nods grimly. "I understand. Of course, I understand. I was young once. I remember what it was like."

He comes over and pats me on the shoulder. His smile is a little stiff, but it's all the reassuring I need. Maybe things are not so bad, after all.

I'm so ready for this day to just be over. It has been mentally and emotionally draining, to say the least. I need to lie down and forget about everything, just get out of my own head for a little bit. I want to be alone. Which is why I curse out loud when I get back to my office and find Gwen standing there, poring over a book on my shelf.

She is probably the last person I want to see at this moment.

So much has been going on, it's easy to forget what an eventful weekend I just had. With her boyfriend. I haven't even had time to obsess about it. But I know for a fact I'm not ready to deal with her just yet.

She beams and walks over to me, which is far more intimate than I expect from her. Gwen and I have never really been friendly; if anything, our relationship was very frosty up until Robert's TV interview, and then we sort of agreed to a silent truce. But neither of us likes the other, and we both know it. So, when she steps in for a hug, I'm too stunned to receive or return it. I simply stand there, rigid, as she squeezes me and singsongs 'hello' in my ear.

If my reaction surprises her, she doesn't show it. She smiles and takes my hand, leading me to sit on the chair closest to the desk. She remains standing, but she leans on the desk and faces me.

"Is everything okay?" I ask her.

"Oh, everything is great. The campaign is going really well. Robert is going to launch this website revealing his skeletons, and I think it's going to create a lot of publicity for him. Some of it won't be good, obviously, but that's how publicity works."

"That's great, Gwen."

Would it be impolite to ask her what the hell she wants? I don't think I have the patience for subtlety today. Thankfully, she correctly interprets my pointed silence as a prompt to get to the point.

"I wanted to talk to you about Robert," Gwen says. She has dropped her voice to a conspiratory whisper.

"What about him?" I ask without missing a beat.

"I know you two went on that trip over the weekend." It's a statement. No vocal inflection. But there is also an accusation hidden in there somewhere.

"Yeah," I tell her. "I'm sure Robert told you all about it."

"Here's the thing, Amy. I'm going to be straight with you. I don't know what happened with you and Robert over the weekend. I mean, it's strange enough that he showed up with a black eye. I haven't asked him about that yet. I was hoping to hear it from you first."

I'm familiar with this strategy. This whole thing, her being nice to me, it's an act. This is really an ambush, a subtle interrogation. She's playing good cop, hoping she can get me to admit to something and possibly contradict whatever Robert will tell her. I'm not falling for that one.

"As I said, I'm sure Robert has told you all about the trip. Now, if you'll excuse me, I really need to get going."

There is a flash of annoyance on her face, but only for a second. I don't know what she expected from this interaction. I can see her pondering what to say next, how to counter my non-response. I'm not going to give her a chance to. I gather up my things and sling my bag over the shoulder.

Gwen follows me out and all the way to my car. "We still need to talk about the upcoming debate," she says. "The campus was approved as the venue, so I'll need your help getting everything set up."

"That might be a bit problematic," I tell her through the window. "I'm going on leave for a few weeks."

I stop short of telling her that it's administrative leave, that I may be suspended. And that there is a very real possibility I won't be coming back.

43
Robert

I once thought that running a campaign was the hardest part of running for office. How wrong I was. I have found out today that setting up an office is far more challenging.

I'm used to Gwen handling this sort of thing. She is so much better at it, and she makes it seem effortless. But Gwen isn't here yet, so I'm left to handle orders and requests, to direct traffic this way and that, and to sign for things I didn't even know I needed.

This has been in the books for some time now. As Gwen kept saying, I need an actual campaign office, because it doesn't make sense for me to keep working out of my house or from Galweather & Meyer. A campaign office communicates intent and professionality.

The building we move into is a bit smaller than I expected, but its location is prime; it's only a few blocks away from G&M, and it is smack in the middle of town. In its initial state, it didn't look like much. But over the last few weeks, Gwen has transformed it into a tiny little haven. It has an open-floor aesthetic, with the only offices being those of the campaign manager and my own. The rest of the staff is scattered around the office, in tiny little cubicles that are private but not isolated. The portions of the wall that are done are covered in large banners with my face and my slogan.

As of today, we have a skeleton crew present. There is still some work being done, so the foot traffic is significant. In one corner of the office, a group of IT guys are frowning over laptops. Next to them, two sprightly-looking interns are responding to phone calls, which seem to be coming in every second. I tried to say hi to them when I walked in this morning, but they could only smile and nod; it seems we are already swamped.

The reason for the chaos, of course, is that someone thought it was a good idea to set up a website and dump their personal information on it. We expected some traffic, but even our wildest estimates were off by miles. In less than twelve hours of being live, the website has attracted a myriad of visits. Shortly after it launched, the phone calls started coming in, then the emails, then the notifications.

The IT specialists also double up as my social media team, and if they are to be believed, I have made quite the splash online. There are pages cropping up discussing some of my old cases. I am being praised and reviled in equal measure. Strangely enough, the things I expected to cause a stir have barely made a blip. There is no discussion on Celeste's photos, for example. Nothing about the encounters with the women. People seem more preoccupied with my career, and the mystery of my 'perfect record', which stood for over three years.

All of which means I'm lost in a sea of people, with no idea how to handle the situation. I try calling Gwen a few times, but she left early, insisting she had to work on something real quick and that she would be back 'before the nerds burned the building down.'

I walk around the office, looking for problems to fix, things to do. The part of the job I'm good at is of no use here. I'm a motivator; I can get people to work, even if my methods are a bit extreme. Here, there is no need for that. Everyone knows their role and is driven to work by the sheer load of work that needs to be done. So, after my fifth trip around the office, I retire to my office and put my feet up. I pull over the folder with my talking points for the debate and flip it open.

I read the first few talking points over and over again, the words seeping through my brain without actually registering. I'm distracted, and I think I know why.

I haven't seen or spoken to Amy in almost a week. Part of that is by default; I have been busy with the new office and dealing with the fallout from the interview with Simms. The website hasn't made it any easier, either. Beyond that, I've been dealing with Gwen's silent assault. In typical fashion, she didn't bring up the road trip again after the interview. No further questions, no clarifications, nothing. For anyone else, this would be okay. But I know the woman too well to accept that this is over.

She has thawed, somewhat. She isn't outwardly hostile toward me. But she's not the same Gwen either. Something is different about her. She has always been laser-focused on getting the job right, but since the road trip, she's thrown herself into her work with renewed zeal, almost like she's using it as an outlet for pent-up frustration. Naturally, the relationship has suffered a little. She hasn't touched me in days; I don't think she wants to. But the truth of the matter is that I can't stop thinking about Amy. My immediate concern regarding the situation with Gwen is almost always overshadowed by my new and confusing feelings surrounding Amy.

The road trip was a spontaneous thing, but it revealed so much to me that I didn't know. By some miracle, Amy and I were able to resolve the core issues that drove us apart, which I would never have imagined possible. As a result, it felt like I got my Amy back. And once the dam broke, all those pesky feelings I had long buried swam back to the surface. Feelings. Questions. Memories.

So, it's no surprise that the minute I have nothing else to do, my brain immediately switches back to the road trip, and Haven, and those tense but earnest moments in my car. And then I find myself replaying the night at her place.

When my phone rings, I grab it eagerly. It's irrational to expect Amy to call me, and yet I do. Her silence is strange. Unexpected. I know we didn't exactly set boundaries after that night, but I would have expected her to at least call, even just to check-in.

But it's not Amy calling. It's Gwen, the person I *should* be thinking about.

"Have the nerds driven you crazy yet?" she asks, ignoring the unenthusiastic hello with which I answer the phone.

"They have. I'm hiding away in my office."

"I thought that might happen. Want to get away for a few hours?"

I hesitate because that sounds nothing like her. "Get away with you?"

"With me, yeah."

"In the middle of the day? When we're supposed to be working?"

"Precisely."

"Who is this, and what have you done with Gwen?"

"Hardy ha, Robert. But I'm serious. Let's take the day off, go somewhere."

"Did you have any place in mind?"

"I do, actually. Meet me at your place in fifteen minutes?"

"My place?"

"Yeah. Your apartment."

"Is that why you ditched me this morning? To go plan something?"

"Your place, Robert. Fourteen minutes."

It's a strange request, not least because Gwen doesn't make recreational plans while she's supposed to be working. She definitely doesn't take days off, and she certainly wouldn't take her foot off the pedal this close to the debate. Something is up. Her demeanor is different too. She didn't sound frosty over the phone, as she has this past week. She sounded like her old self.

If her intention is to lure me in with mystery, then she has succeeded. I leave one of the senior technicians in charge and call it a day. I pass by the IT corner where I'm reliably informed that my website is still straining to handle the traffic and that the interest generated by the online conversation has resulted in a spike in my poll numbers. Then I get into the car and drive off, pleasantly surprised by Gwen's sudden transformation and curious as to what she has in store.

I knock a few times, then push the door to my apartment and walk in. My eyes dart around the living room, and I don't see anything different at first. Eventually, though, they fall on something red on the floor, and when I get down to look at it, I notice several others lining up the path out of the living room, all the way to the bedroom door. Rose petals. Laid out like breadcrumbs to lead the way.

"Robert? Is that you?"

"Gwen?"

"Come on into the bedroom."

"I thought you said we're going out?"

Silence.

I take off my coat and walk over to the bedroom door. The rose petals end right at the door. I swing it open and look inside. My jaw falls to the floor.

Gwen is standing in front of my bed, dressed in an outfit I don't immediately understand. She is essentially naked, except for a sheer, see-through full-body mesh piece that barely conceals her body. It's like a net, stretched taut over her body, with dark strips of tape covering her nipples. From her thighs, all the way down is a pair of latex boots, held up by a garter that circles and accentuates her panties. If I'm not mistaken, Gwen is dressed as a dominatrix.

"Holy shit …" I stop mid-sentence because Gwen pulls out a leather crop from somewhere and swings it wildly through the air, making a low whistling sound. It's terrifying and exciting in equal measure. The words die on my lips. My mind clears, and I stand there mutely, waiting for her next move.

The bedroom has been similarly transformed. Soft rose petals all over the floor and on the bed. A handful of candles wafting scented air around the room. Most distinctly, though, a single hard chair propped against one wall, prominently standing out against the rest of the furniture in the room.

"You will address me as 'Mistress'," Gwen says. Her voice is completely different. Deeper, more authoritative. "And you will not speak unless spoken to. Do you understand?"

"Yes," I say.

The leather crop whistles through the air once more.

"Yes, Mistress," I say.

"Good. Now, you will do exactly as I say, when I say it, without hesitation or objection. If you do not, I will punish you as I see fit. Do you understand?"

"Yes, Mistress."

This is such a strange experience; I can't wrap my head around it. I have no idea where she got this idea from, the whole kinky BDSM thing. All I know is that I have to follow the woman's every instruction. Or else.

"Take your clothes off."

I do so quickly. Awkwardly. My legs get stuck in the pants, and I have to struggle out of them for a few embarrassing seconds before finally getting them off. I stop once they're off, stand there in my boxers, but Gwen nods at them, and I step out of those, too.

It's the first time I have been naked in front of her in a while. Her eyes travel over my body from head to toe. She swings the crop idly in her hand, occasionally bringing it up and slapping it gently against her palm. Then she walks up to me in five-inch heels, her hips swinging seductively. She pauses when she gets to me, then starts to circle me. Inspecting me. Taking every inch in. For a brief moment, I feel vulnerable. And then scared. What if she has figured out what happened between Amy and me? What if this is her weird way of dragging the truth out of me? Or worse, punishing me for it?

"Get down on your knees," she says suddenly from behind me.

"What?" I ask, confused.

I see a flash of movement out of the corner of my eye. I hear it before I feel it; the leather crop, sings as it cuts through the air, and then pain blossoms around my lower back. The surprise dulls the pain for a moment. She is actually doing this.

"On your knees. Don't make me ask again."

I obey without another word. She didn't hit me hard, but the place where the crop landed feels raw and itchy. I get down on my knees, feeling incredibly exposed with my back turned to her like this.

"Crawl over to that chair and sit down facing me."

I crawl, on all fours, towards the chair. I can feel Gwen behind me, can hear the soft clicking sounds of her heels on the floor, and I know she is following me. I get the chair and pull myself up, turn around and sit down. The wood feels cold on my bare ass. I look up at Gwen, and she is smiling.

She drops the crop and gets down on her knees as well. Her hands are firm as she grips my legs and pushes them apart. Not so gently. Her eyes never leave mine as she lowers her head onto my lap. I watch as her tongue lashes out and tastes the slit of my dick. And as she wraps her ruby-red lips around my head and sucks once, her tongue still darting back and forth, teasing the slit.

She starts to bob her head up and down slowly and then pick up the pace gradually. Her mouth is like a vice around my shaft. She feels wet and tight and warm all at once. I throw my head back. I'm not used to this, not from her. I can't think straight. I had a thought that was floating on the edge of my mind, but all I can think of now is that I'm about to come, too soon, and I need to focus away from the spectacle in front of me.

Gwen's eyes are still on me. I feel self-conscious in the way she is staring at me, even as her head moves up and down, even as she swings a hand around and starts to fondle my balls.

Without warning, she parts her lips as far as they can go, and she takes me in as deep as I can go. I can hear the soft sounds of suction, can feel the wonderful warmth of her throat. I buck and jerk on the chair. I don't know what to do with my hands. I bury them in my hair, then I tear them away and grip the chair beneath me, then I give up entirely and leave them to clench and flail. I'm coming. Damn it; I'm coming.

Gwen stops suddenly. It's like she senses my orgasm approaching. She slurps as she pulls away, a single line of my juices running down her chin.

"You will not come without my permission," she whispers, less firm but still ringing with authority.

I bite my lip and nod, though I'm not certain I can do what she's asking. I'm too far gone already.

Gwen straightens up and swivels around, giving me a gorgeous view of her pert little bottom. Sexy. Inviting. Unable to stop myself, I reach over and give her a loud smack right across the cheek.

I half-expect her to retaliate somehow, but she doesn't. She simply takes my hand and pulls me up, then leads me to the bed and pushes me onto it. She climbs in, heels still on, and mounts me. She reaches around me to the closet by the side of the bed and pulls out a pair of handcuffs. Silently, she secures my wrists to the bedpost, then repositions herself on top of me.

She rocks back and forth, brushing against my still-erect dick and drawing an involuntary groan from me. I want so badly to grab her and flip her over, push into her, and pound away. But she knows I'm frustrated. She senses it, so she takes her time, teasing me. She rocks against me again. The fabric of her lace panties is very soft, and the motion of her grinding against me is actually really pleasant.

Eventually, she reaches down and slowly parts the hem of her panties. I hear the mesh bodysuit rip. She guides herself down and onto me, enveloping me in heat and damp ecstasy.

Her riding is slow and measured. Erratic, too. She isn't relying on any definite rhythm. One second she's sliding along gently, almost dancing, the next she's bouncing up and down hard enough that the slapping sounds of our thighs fill the room around us.

I close my eyes and let my head sink into the pillow. Somehow, it heightens the experience; hearing Gwen starting to moan, feeling her body start to tremble. I'm beyond gone myself. It's like I've been tightly wound, like I've bottled up the tension in my body, right to the breaking point.

The next thing I know, I'm straining against the handcuffs, and there are sounds coming from my mouth. My hips jerk upwards as I climax, and I grind my hips to meet Gwen's motion. My eyesight is reduced to a couple of single bright spots in the backs of my eyelids. My whole world erupts, a collision of sound and feeling until I am only dimly aware of the woman on top of me, and the vague scent of candles burning in the distance.

Hours later, when my hands have gone numb, and I've slipped in and out of consciousness more times than I can remember, I feel Gwen's hands on my face, and I force my eyes open.

"I'm fighting for us, okay?" she says. "I know I let the job get between us sometimes, and I'm not always the woman you need me to be. But I want you to know that I'm working on that, and I'm committed to making this work."

It's only then I understand what this was about. She was claiming me. The whole dominatrix thing was her way of letting me know she wasn't going to relinquish her hold of me that easily. Almost as if she suspected she would have to.

44
Robert

The first thing that throws me is the number of people in attendance. Lincoln Community College's auditorium is large enough for the typical function. On this occasion, it seems small. People are crammed into every space imaginable. I didn't expect a turnout of this magnitude, and it immediately increases the pressure I was pretending not to feel.

The second is my cheat sheet. Gwen had written up a series of questions I'm expecting to have to respond to, along with detailed responses and breakdowns of my policy and plans. The knowledge that I could always refer to the cheat sheet was what kept me from internalizing it. In the week leading up to the debate, I didn't go over it as thoroughly as I should have. I didn't think I needed to, to be honest. And then, right before we left for the university, the folder containing my cheat sheet vanished. Or someone misplaced it. We turned the office inside out, but in the end, we had to leave without it because we were running late.

So, I'm essentially flying blind. Gwen has scribbled quick footnotes onto a different piece of paper, but it's not nearly as detailed, and it lacks the scope of the previous one. I'm doing my best not to panic, but I keep thinking I'm going to be unable to answer one question or another, and it will look very bad if a candidate running for DA is not familiar with his own reform policy. There's no time for regret, as Gwen has reminded me countless times. The priority now is to focus on getting my ideas across. Easy enough in theory. Gwen has always had way more faith in me than I do myself.

But the thing that has unnerved me the most, and I hate to admit it, is the absence of one Amelia Brooks.

It's been three weeks now since I saw or spoke to her. A few days is acceptable, I guess. Give or take. A week, even. I understand that people get busy. Life happens. She was probably busy at school. In those initial days, I actively resisted the idea that she was deliberately not speaking to me. It didn't seem likely. Not after the weekend we spent together.

Two weeks later, I had to finally accept that maybe there was more to it. It coincided, in the most unfortunate manner, with Gwen's renewed efforts to 'fix' our relationship, so even thinking about Amy felt like a risk. But it finally started to bother me. So, I called her. And texted her. None of my calls went through. My messages were not returned. On the other hand, Gwen was trying harder than ever before. On both fronts. Excellent campaign manager. Attentive and loving girlfriend.

And so, we rolled into debate week on the back of a personal mystery. I was desperate for information on Amy. I had started to worry that maybe something had happened to her. I managed to stop myself going to her house only by convincing myself it would be safer to see her at the debate. She would be there, surely? I mean, she worked at the university. And even though she is no longer an active member of my campaign team, she is still invested enough to come watch me, right?

Well, so far, I have seen no sign of her. I half-hoped she would come backstage to look for me, but she didn't.

When the moderator pokes his head through the thick curtain backstage and announces that we should head out onto the stage, the combined stress and pressure are almost too much for me. I'm not ready. Nothing is in place. This is going to be a disaster; I can feel it.

Gwen is right there by my side, as always, reassuring me, motivating me. I see her lips move, but her words don't reach me at all. Something about being myself, I think.

I have gotten sick of the sight of Jonathan Simms by now. This is one too many times I think as I walk out onto the podium. There are no lecterns. Apparently, the organizers felt there was no need to have the candidates stand for the entire debate. They ditched the lecterns in favor of simple chairs with tiny little desks on the side. Keep the candidates comfortable.

I catch a glimpse of Dean Patel in the front row just behind the moderators' panel. He waves surreptitiously, and I throw him a questioning look: Where is Amy? I'm sure he gets it, but I can't decode the rueful shrug he gives me in return.

Then the lights are dimmed behind the panel, and a voice announces to everyone assembled that the debate will begin shortly, and would everyone please take their seats and maintain silence?

I'm distracted from the get-go. My mind keeps drifting away from the auditorium. I don't hear the moderators when they first introduce themselves, so when it's my turn to introduce myself and give my opening statement, I don't know how to address them.

"Thank you to … uh … the moderators," I say. "My name is Robert Hardy. I'm a lawyer, having worked for the better part of my career at Galweather and Meyer. I have been involved for a very long time with the judicial system. I'm running for District Attorney because I understand the system, and I want to help make it better. I have seen the issues, the inadequacies, the inefficiencies. I would like to be part of the process of reform."

Simms' opening statement is frustratingly concise; he knows what the job demands, and he believes he is still the best man for the job.

He gets more confident and more articulate as the debate goes on. He delivers his points in the unrushed cadence of a man who knows what he's doing. He never seems rattled. Nothing catches him off guard. He is charming and intelligent and everything I'm not at that moment.

For me, the night gets steadily worse. As I suspected, I need the cheat sheet. Several times I mess up my talking points, mixing one with the other or making moot points. I know it's going badly because the audience, made up primarily of students, gradually loses interest, and half of them pull out their phones. And I know it because Simms has never looked calmer, so this is definitely playing to his advantage.

"You're on the record saying your first priority will be to weed out corruption in the DA office and beyond," one of the moderators asks me about half an hour into the debate. It almost seems like he is genuinely throwing me a softball.

I glance down at the substitute cheat sheet. Under the heading corruption, there is a simple instruction scrawled down in Gwen's handwriting: GO ON THE OFFENSIVE.

"In my experience," I say, "and by this, I mean the years I've spent defending against those who are falsely accused by the state of crimes they did not commit. In my time as a defense attorney, I have found that the office of the DA, in its current state, routinely brings charges against marginalized individuals and communities, while ignoring the larger, more blatant offenders who are in positions of power or influence. It's almost as if there is a method to it like there is a system in place which determines which cases are worth pursuing and which ones are not. If elected as the DA, I will redefine the prosecution threshold, and ensure there is a transparent process of trying cases."

Simms is practically bouncing in his seat.

"Mr. Simms? You have a rebuttal?"

"With respect to Mr. Hardy, his 'years in the judicial system' have clearly been wasted. He seems to display a lack of understanding of the fundamental workings of the very office he seeks to occupy. I welcome you, Robert, to *my* office, where I will instruct one of our interns to break down the way we make decisions on which cases to prosecute. I assure you it is quite transparent."

Someone in the audience laughs. Another person starts to clap, and to my dismay, he is soon joined by someone else, and then the whole auditorium is applauding. It is the single most embarrassing thing that has ever happened to me.

I want this to be over. I admit it; I was not ready for this debate. All the goodwill I've accumulated from my website reveal has slowly dissipated. All they are going to remember of me is this moment, being humiliated by Simms.

Yet it isn't over.

To round up the interview, the moderators invite questions from the audience. One of the first hands to shoot up is that of a small, mousy girl seated at the front.

"Hi. My name is Betty Flack, and I have a question for Mr. Hardy. Mr. Hardy, what are your thoughts on teacher/student relationships within the context of an institution such as this?"

It's an odd question to ask, especially in this forum. Even more baffling, it is received with murmurs and muttering by members of the audience.

"I would say it depends on the institution's policy on the same. For most, such relationships are frowned upon or considered inappropriate."

"So, if the campus policy on this reflects that view, then is it your position that any offenders should be dealt with to the full extent of the law?"

She is leading me somewhere, but I cannot tell where.

"I believe any legally binding agreement should be followed to the letter," I say. "And that includes the contract between a student and the institution they enroll at, as well as that between a teacher and that same institution. If the contract is violated, then yes. The punishment should be followed as recommended by the code of conduct or rulebook."

"With no exceptions?"

But the moderator cuts in, citing time, and he moves on to another student. It may well be the strangest exchange I've ever been a part of, but I don't dwell on it. I'm torn between relief that this debate is finally coming to an end and frustration at how poorly I did. I had gained some ground on Simms in the most recent polls; tonight, all that ground has been taken back and then some.

As soon as the closing speeches are concluded, I speed-walk off the stage and head backstage.

Gwen's expression says it all. She pats me reassuringly on the back. "It wasn't that bad," she says, but even *she* doesn't believe it.

"Let's just go," I say, pushing past her and sinking into a chair. I rub my temples, feeling the early signs of a migraine coming on. I need a drink. Gwen nods and leaves, no doubt to bring the car around. I close my eyes and sigh. Is a do-over too much to wish for at this point? Do I even want one? If only Amy had been here, maybe things wouldn't have gone so wrong. Amy.

I bolt upright and scan the space around me. I need to ask … someone. Noticing one of the students who were part of the organizing committee on the far end of the stage, I jump to my feet and hurry toward her. She cowers as I approach, gripping her clipboard tight to her chest and taking a terrified step backward.

"Hi. No need to be afraid, I just want to speak with you."

She swallows and nods.

"Do you know Miss Amelia Brooks? She is a lecturer here, teaches law?"

The girl nods again.

"Great! Was she in today? Do you know where I can find her?"

"Miss Brooks hasn't been on campus in almost a month, sir."

"What? Why?"

"No one knows for sure. The administration says she is on leave, but there is a rumor going around that she was suspended."

I mouth wordlessly at her, and she understands my plea for more details.

"Well, the rumor was started by the school magazine, that there was a lecturer having a relationship with a student. It was all over the campus. But a few days later, the story just died. The magazine was supposed to run a follow-up story, but they never did. The thing that got people talking, though, was the fact that Miss Brooks went on leave just after that story came out, so everyone assumed she was the lecturer mentioned in the article."

I shake my head in disbelief. None of this makes any sense. I know Amy, and she would never get involved with a student. I realize suddenly what the girl, Betty, was actually referring to in her question. What did I think of teacher/student relationships? I knew there was something else there.

I need to get to the bottom of this. I turn around and scan the place, and I see Gwen walking toward me. She tells me the car is ready; I shake my head and grab her by the arm, pulling her to the side and away from others.

"Why isn't Amy here?" I ask her.

"At the debate?"

"No, Gwen, at the university. What is going on with her?"

It's a mark of my desperation that the only person I can ask right now is Gwen. Desperate times.

"Haven't you heard? Amy was suspended. She was sleeping with a student."

45
Amelia

"Come on, Amy. Walk around, mingle."

Ness prods me playfully in the arm, then pushes me in the direction of a small group of people. She is much stronger than me, so I am powerless to resist. I stop myself just as I'm about to bump into one of the people in the circle, but the motion has carried me close enough to them that they notice me, and a few of them turn around.

"Hi," I mumble, smiling awkwardly.

The guy closest to me steps back to make room for me to join the circle. He smiles back politely when I remain rooted to the spot.

"You must be Amelia," he says, offering me his hand.

I shake it and nod. "Amy, yes."

"We've heard a lot about you, Amy," a short lady with blonde curls says. There are a couple of murmurs and grunts from the rest.

"All good things, I hope?" I say. Ugh. Small talk. The bane of my existence. And one of the biggest reasons I can't stand parties.

"Not at all," the lady says, laughing slightly. "Ness is a wild one, and you being her best friend …"

She couldn't be more wrong. Ness and I are like polar opposites. Sometimes even *I* wonder why we're such good friends when we don't have much in common.

"What have you heard about me, for instance?" I ask. I'm curious to hear how Ness has presented me to her other friends.

"Oh, you know, just tales of your exploits, the two of you. Parties, boys, you know how it is."

I stare at her, and I'm overcome by such sudden revulsion I almost throw up. The woman knows nothing about me, but she assumes she does just because she heard a few stories from Ness? How pathetic. I'm somehow able to stifle my stronger emotions and walk away from the circle of idiots. If only I could just keep going, all the way to my own house and my bed.

"Can we have your attention, please?"

I look around, along with everyone else in the room. Ness is standing with Jeremy next to the fireplace. She is beaming, wider and brighter than she usually does. Once she is satisfied that every eye in the room is on them, she gives Jeremy a glowing look and then turns back to us.

"I hope everyone is having fun, yeah?"

The response is a singular roar of agreement.

"Great!" Ness goes on. "Jeremy and I are thrilled you could join us for our first party. Here's to many more, am I right?"

Cheers. Raised glasses. I roll my eyes and pine once more for my bed.

"Before everyone gets wasted, though, Jeremy and I have some news we would like to share with you. Now, anyone who knows me well enough knows that I'm a bit skeptical about love, and the idea of 'the one.' Just as anyone who knows Jeremy knows that he is the exact opposite. So, it's a minor miracle that we met, and an even bigger one that we fell in love. I never thought I'd ever say these words. I never dreamed I would one day stand in front of my friends with someone like Jeremy by my side. And I definitely didn't think I would ever get married."

Gasps. A squeal of delight from the other end of the room.

"That's right, people. Jeremy and I are engaged!"

She sticks out her hand and brandishes an enormous ring she had definitely not been wearing before. The room erupts. Everyone around me is clapping and whooping. The diamond from the ring twinkles in the moonlight, and the ladies in the room swarm Ness like a horde of angry bees.

I wish I was surprised by the news, but I'm not. It's huge news. As she said, Ness is the last person I would have expected to pack it up and settle down. She is too much of a free spirit. She never stands still long enough. She resents the idea of marriage and monogamy. An engagement should be totally out of character for her. But I've seen enough of her and Jeremy to know this was inevitable. My 'time off' from the university meant I got to spend a lot more time with them, and they are just as insufferable as they were when they first started seeing each other. Even when she complained about him, Ness was never able to shake the bug. She resisted, but it was no use denying it; she was in love with him. And once she admitted it, my best friend turned into a sixteen-year-old girl.

"Raise your hand if you're surprised by that," a voice cuts in from nowhere.

I look up to see a familiar face standing next to me. It takes a second to place him; he has shaved his head completely, but the shy smile is still a dead giveaway.

"Ethan!" I am genuinely happy to see him. A familiar face in a sea of strangers.

"Oh, you remember me?"

"How could I not? We had that excellent first date."

"And then you never called me after."

I shrug. "You never gave me your number."

Ethan laughs. He seems to have grown in confidence since our 'date.' "It's good to see you, Amy. I'm surprised we haven't bumped into each other before today."

"Ah, you know how it is. Work. Life. But it's good to see you too."

He points at Ness and Jeremy, who are still surrounded by half the party people. "Like I was saying, no surprises there."

"I don't know. I saw it coming, but I didn't think she'd go through with it. Not marriage, anyway. She says she was a love skeptic? That's a gross understatement."

"Jeremy literally swore he would never get married. No way he was boxing all that up and tying it to one woman, he used to say. I guess they just hadn't met each other."

"Well, I'm happy for them," I say.

Someone rushes past me, and I catch a whiff of their perfume, doused over the distinct smell of body sweat. The food in my belly churns and swims. I turn my head for a hit of fresh air.

"Are you sure about that?" Ethan asks. His smile falters ever so slightly. "You look pale. Are you okay?"

"I think I might be coming down with something, actually," I say. "I've been filling a bit under the weather lately."

"Oh, I'm sorry about that. You should go see a doctor."

"Thanks. It's probably nothing. It's actually a great excuse for me to sneak off. Would you tell Ness I had to run? Let me go sleep it off at home."

Ethan extends his hand and lays it over my forehead. He frowns as he does so. "This doesn't seem like nothing, Amy. Feels like a fever. You should definitely get checked out."

"Really, Ethan. I'm sure I'll be fine."

"I can drive you. Mercy West isn't too far from here."

He is already grabbing my hand and trying to steer me in the direction of the door. I'm too weak to resist, so I let him.

"When did these symptoms start?" Ethan asks me. We are out the front door. The fresh air feels incredible as it hits my face. I didn't realize how stuffy Ness's house was.

"It comes and goes," I tell him. "Started about a week …"

I stop right there, my foot suspended in midair. No fucking way.

"Amy? Is everything okay?"

His voice sounds distorted like it's being filtered through a wall. My mind is racing, trying to work out the possibility, the impossibility.

"I don't need to go to a hospital, Ethan," I tell him, snapping out of my trance. "Thanks for your concern."

And I take off running. I can hear Ethan yelling behind me. I think he tries to run after me, but he gives up soon. I remember as I'm running that I drove to Ness' place and that it would have been a better idea to take my car. But it's too late. Urgency is spurring my feet on. I don't think I've run in a long time; my lungs are burning, and my breaths are coming in short gasps. But the discomfort is completely overshadowed by the feeling of dread crawling all over my skin like a poison.

It can't be.

I burst through the doors of the local drug store, miraculously still open, and almost collapse to the ground. I bend over, hands on knees, struggling to catch my breath. The attendant watches me with some amusement. I must be quite a sight if I've managed to drag his attention from the boxing match he was just watching.

Once I'm able to breathe normally again, I head straight for the third aisle and grab the first box I see. I slap a crisp note onto the counter and leave.

I can't run all the way home, I realize. Urgency or not. It's getting late, and it's not safe. I can't go back to the party either, because that would be weird. The only option is to call a cab, so I pull my phone out and do so.

My heart sinks even lower when the cab pulls up at my house. There is a Jeep parked in my driveway, and standing by the passenger door is Robert Hardy. I stuff the box into my bag and pay the driver. I take a deep breath before stepping out of the car.

Robert watches me approach silently. I don't realize it until I'm close enough, but he is visibly angry. His posture is rigid and agitated. He has stuffed his fists in his pockets, which I know is his way of trying to stop himself from doing something rash with his hands. Then there's the pulsing vein right in the middle of his forehead.

"What the fuck, Amy?" he explodes at me.

I take a step back. "What?"

"You were suspended? You were fucking a student?"

Not the best time to deal with this, to be honest. I have a more pressing matter. I don't know how he learned about my relationship with Kieran. I don't imagine it was particularly difficult, especially if he spoke to anyone at the university.

"I need to go to the bathroom," I say, and I sidestep his stunned face. "I'll be right back. Sorry!"

It takes several tries to get the door open. My fingers are shaking, and my nerves are shot to pieces. Robert is saying something behind me, but I tune him out. Not now.

I push the door open and make a beeline for the bathroom. I grab the box and rip into it, glancing once at the illustrated instructions before pulling the little stick out. Pee. Panic. Flush. Panic some more.

Robert is seated on the couch when I walk back to the living room. He looks up at me, ready to explode again. But then he catches the look on my face, and his eyes travel down to my hand. I don't know what I expected, but it wasn't for him to open his arms and gather me in a hug. Silent. Emotional. I don't realize I'm crying until he wipes the tears from my face with tender, gentle thumbs.

"Does that mean …" he asks as the little stick slips from my hand and falls to the floor.

"Yeah," I tell him. "I'm pregnant."

46
Robert

There is no good way to have 'the talk.' Not when the person you hope to have it with has already figured out your intentions and is doing the best to counteract it. That's what it feels like, at any rate.

Over the last few days, Gwen has buried herself in work, even more than she did during the run-up to the debate. It's understandable, of course; there *is* more to do now than there was before the epic disaster that was the debate. And I may be slightly off pace because the interview, and the campaign in general, have ceased to hold any significance to me. I keep going over the thought that maybe I just don't care about being DA anymore. Not with the other, more pressing news that I'm going to be a father. Everything else has faded into static. Background noise.

The talk. It has been coming, if I'm being honest, ever since Amy reappeared in my life. I always knew, from the moment she ran from me, that all paths led here, inevitably. I've simply been putting it off, because how do you have that conversation with the woman who is also running your campaign? Sorry, I slept with my ex, but please don't abandon my campaign team? Also, I'm not sure I want to be with you anymore? You don't, that's how. Unless your weekend of frolicking with said ex turns into something more complicated, and then that conversation becomes a necessity.

Or maybe she hasn't become unavailable at all, and I'm simply projecting my fear of the inevitable confrontation onto her. Maybe it doesn't mean anything that she hasn't said anything to me that doesn't involve work for over a week. Or that her daily routine has narrowed down to showing up at the office for an hour or two in the morning, and then disappearing for the rest of the day. "Working," she says simply when I ask where she goes. It definitely doesn't set off any alarm bells that a few days after showing me a side of her I didn't think existed in the bedroom, she hasn't so much as brought up that encounter again.

I don't know if I would ever have worked up the courage to approach her myself. I suppose I'll never know. I'm just grateful when she finally pops into my office one morning and asks if she can have a quick word with me. Something about her energy is off. She seems nervous, prickly, as she walks in and takes a seat across from me. Or, as my brain registers it, as far from me as she can.

My first thought is that this is not the best place for it. I don't know what she has in mind, but I'm fully intending to seize the opportunity and tell her what's been on my mind these past few days. Then I realize that there is never a good enough place for this kind of discussion. The best I can hope for is some degree of privacy.

She stares silently at me, and I wonder why. She has nothing to be nervous about, does she?

"You've been busy," I say, trying and failing to pass it off as an offhand comment. Even I can hear the accusation in my voice. 'Where have you been?'

Gwen shrugs. "Yeah. I've had some fires to put out on the back of the debate, as you know."

I notice she doesn't look me in the eye.

"So," I say. Suddenly, I don't want to be the one to go first. "What did you want to talk to me about?"

"I ... uh ... well. It's about the campaign."

"Oh. Okay."

She frowns. "Did you ... is there something else *you* wanted to talk about?"

"Not ... I ... We're okay, right? I mean, I know I took a hit during the debate, but it wasn't that bad, was it?"

"I'll be honest with you, Robert. It's not looking good. I mean, it's not terrible, but it's not ideal either. As it is, your numbers are lower than our most optimistic projections. I've been doing some crisis management as best as I can, but even with aggressive publicity, we still have a huge mess on our hands. I promised when I took you on that I would always be honest, so that's what I'm going to do. Realistically, I don't think you can win this race."

It's not exactly shocking news, but it's no fun hearing it either.

"Okay, so what are you recommending?"

"Recommending?"

"Yeah. I assume you're presenting a problem and recommendations on fixing it?"

"Oh. No. That's not what I came in here to talk to you about."

"No?"

Gwen takes a deep breath. "I was approached yesterday by a representative of the Glendale Reform Party."

"Right …"

"They're thinking about making a late play, sponsoring someone to run for DA. It's late, for sure, but not too late for someone to make a ripple in the pool. If anything, a new candidate has the advantage of freshness and instant memorability."

"And they want me? I thought the whole point of my campaign was that I'm representing the common man and not some big political machine …" I trail off because Gwen is suddenly looking pained. It's the closest I've ever seen her come to blushing, and I suspect it isn't out of personal embarrassment.

"What?" I ask her.

"It's not you they want, Robert," she says quietly, then goes back to staring at the floor.

"You? They want you?"

"Well, I don't know why, but yeah."

My initial confusion soon gives way to disbelief, and then, in spite of myself, I'm impressed. A third candidate would definitely shake things up, particularly for potential voters tired of the silent war between me and Simms. Gwen as that third candidate? That is actually genius.

"Wow," I say.

It's all I can think to say. The more I consider it, the more I realize the serious and immediate potential of Gwen as a candidate. She is smart, politically savvy, beautiful. She understands the game, so she would not be out of place. And she knows how to scrap. I have no doubt she would have done much better than me at the debate. And at the interview. Not to mention the fact that she has zero scandals to worry about. Glendale's first female DA? The media would eat it up.

But my fantasizing is quickly cut short by the implications of that reality.

"Wait," I say, holding up a hand. "That would mean you're

running against me."

Gwen's expression is unreadable as she flicks her eyes back to mine. "If I accepted, then yes. It would."

"If you accepted? As in you haven't?"

"As I said, I was approached. That was it. The man only said the Reform Party was very impressed with the work I've been doing, but that they think I would make a far better candidate. He was very convincing, to be honest, and he seemed to have done his research. But yeah. He told me they have been following my work and would be interested in sitting down to have a discussion about it. Left me with a phone number."

"They said I'm screwed, didn't they?"

"Not exactly."

"What, then?"

"He implied indirectly that I backed the wrong horse."

"Wow."

I'm not even sure how I feel about it. Oddly enough, I'm not nearly as mad as I should be. Someone just tried to poach my campaign manager and have her run against me. I should be livid. But once more, I'm discovering just how insignificant it all feels.

"So?" I ask her. "Are you going to call them?"

"I don't really know. I'd never thought about it up till that point."

"And now that you have?"

Silence. Once more, she averts her eyes, focuses instead on the same spot on the floor. I don't know if she's actually hesitant or just afraid to hurt my feelings. I have no doubt her head has been turned.

"Are you handing in your resignation, Gwen? Is that what this is?"

She shakes her head. "Not at all, no. When I signed up for this, I promised I'd see it through to the end. I knew it would be difficult. I knew there would be stumbling blocks. But I'm no quitter. I'll stick it out to the end …"

I get the feeling she may not be talking about the campaign anymore. Nothing about these past weeks has given me any impression she wants to stay. And now that she's been given an easy out, I would understand if she was entertaining second thoughts.

"So why tell me about the Reform Party at all?"

"I have no secrets from you, Robert. Well, not as far as our professional relationship is concerned."

Now I'm positive we're not talking about the campaign. I start to mentally retrace my steps in the conversation, trying to work out when we took that turn.

"I wanted to be open with you," Gwen goes on. "In case you come to find out about it later, and you think I betrayed you."

I can't help feeling impressed at how swiftly she has turned the tables on me. Almost effortlessly, too. I was skirting the issue, trying to figure out the best approach. And here I am, in the line of fire without saying a word. It's ingenious, really. The woman *does* have the political animal in her.

"What are you really asking, Gwen? What is this *really* about?"

Gwen gets up from the seat she was in and walks over to me. All the way up to me until she is standing right in front of me. At the perfect distance, that is, to hit me.

"You slept with her," she says simply. It doesn't sound like a question. She isn't inviting me to challenge or correct her; she is stating a fact and informing me that she knows the answer. Lie at your own peril, her eyes say. Except I'm not going to lie. I decided a while back to tell her the truth. I was uncertain about when and where, but the confrontation was always on the books.

I nod. Once. A tiny upward motion of the head, then an even tinier one downward. Blink, and you'll miss it. But Gwen doesn't blink. Her eyes are like live coals; she watches me with a discomfiting intensity, her face barely registering the silent confession.

I brace for the hit, but it never comes.

"In Haven, during your road trip." Another declaration.

"No."

"Before?"

"After."

"Where?"

"At her place."

"How many times?"

"What?"

"How many times, Robert?"

"I haven't done it again if that's what you're asking. I hope that's what you're asking."

"Were you going to tell me?"

"Of course, I was."

"So, you lied to me."

"I did?"

"You told me you no longer had feelings for her. I asked you when you sought her out months ago. I asked you, and you said you were over her."

"Honestly, Gwen, I thought I was. I really did. I know it doesn't seem like it, but I didn't go out of my way to hurt you. It just happened."

"It just happened? You mean it was an accident? So, you aren't just about to dump me for her?"

"No, I mean it wasn't planned."

"It seems like it was. You called her when you found out you'd be going on that trip. Even if it was only subliminal, you called her and not me. You must have known something would happen. Maybe you hoped it would?"

"Look, Amy and I had a lot of unfinished business. A lot of things went unsaid; a lot of feelings were unresolved. I didn't want us to keep going on like we were, like there was still unspoken enmity between us. I missed my friend. I didn't expect us to reconnect like that, but we did."

"You're avoiding my question, Robert."

"I'm not ... what question?"

"You're leaving me for her, aren't you?"

I hesitate for only a fraction of a second, but it's enough. Gwen nods, her worst fear confirmed, and she finally takes a step back from me. She keeps going until her back hits a hard surface, and she sits down on the desk behind her.

"I wish I could say I'm surprised," she says, almost to herself. "And to think I actually encouraged you to seek her out."

I expected her to react differently; I'll admit it. But deep down, I know this is all I'm going to get. Gwen was never the most expressive person or the most emotionally vulnerable. She never lets her guard down, never lets her feelings show. It's what makes her great at her job.

She sits quietly on that desk for a long time, and I stand here, guilt washing over me. I thought it would be a relief to finally get this conversation out of the way, but I feel like crap. In spite of everything, I really did love Gwen.

"I really tried, you know," she says, turning to me with glistening eyes. "I was never the relationship type, but I tried with you. I even dressed up for you, did the whole kink thing, even though I'm not big on it. But if we're being honest, I was always better as your campaign manager. And maybe not even that; look how the campaign turned out."

"Don't be silly. You did a great job."

Gwen smiles, a little sadly. "Couldn't help noticing the past tense there. I guess that saves me from having to ask where we stand. No sticking it out this time, eh?"

"You said it yourself, Gwen. My chances of winning are pretty slim. No point wasting even more resources. And you've been my biggest resource. No, I won't hold you back any longer. Your talents are wasted on me."

"What are you saying?"

"I'm saying that maybe you should give the Reform Party a call. The man was right; you'd make an excellent candidate."

"I don't know if I want that."

I step forward, close in on her, and give her a friendly little nudge on the chin. "Bullshit, Gwen. You know you'd be great at it. If you could make me look half-decent, imagine how much easier it would be to represent yourself. I can't beat Simms, but I know you can."

"I think you could beat him too. If the debate hadn't been so … tricky. And if you weren't so distracted with Amy and the pregnancy …"

My eyes go wide, and I take an involuntary step backward.

"How do you know about that?"

"About Amy's pregnancy?"

"Yeah."

"Oh. I mean, I'm not so proud of it, but I've been keeping tabs on her."

I shake my head in disbelief. That must be how she found out about Amy's relationship with her student.

"Do you know whose it is?" Gwen asks.

"What?"

"The baby. Do you know for sure that it's yours?"

For a long time, I'm too stunned to speak. And then the anger settles in at the pit of my stomach. Anger at the possibility of that baby being anyone else's. And at the fact that it has never occurred to me to think about that.

47
Amelia

My favorite thing about Dr. Whitlock is his hands. I have been to many doctors before, and none of them had better hands than his. They are kind and gentle, soft, and clean. And they are warm. Which, as I've come to learn, is a rarity.

The hands are part of an overall package that I'm actually quite fond of. Dr. Whitlock is himself easygoing and friendly. He made me feel right at home the first time I came to see him, and we have become odd friends since. He always reserves his warmest hugs for me, and he swears that he looks forward to our appointments the most out of all his patients.

"I really do, look," he said when I told him I didn't believe him. And he showed me his calendar, which had the date of my appointment circled in red marker and a tiny little heart.

This visit is a little different. When he was setting the date, Dr. Whitlock mentioned that the visit was the first 'big one.' "Where we figure out what's really going on in there." There was a little more gravity to his voice than usual, and he only slipped back to his jocular self once he had completed my examination.

I am relatively nervous as I walk into the clinic. Up to this point, the pregnancy has seemed like a distant dream, something happening to someone else. I've been putting off even thinking about it, but something tells me I won't be able to after today. Today, things get real.

The staff greets me with their usual warmth and bubbliness. A couple of nurses try and distract me by making jokes, like one who asks if I'm sure I didn't just have a big dinner. It's helpful, going into the OBGYN's office, even if that OB is someone I'm very comfortable with.

As expected, Whitlock's face positively lights up when he sees me. "Sorry, gorgeous," he jokes. "The model auditions are in the next building."

He bounces to his feet and drags me into a hug, squeezing me like he hopes something will fall out. One of the first things Whitlock told me when we met was that he is gay. It felt like a little too much information for a first-time meeting, but I understood what he was going for. He wanted to put me at ease, to make me feel safe. And I do. With anyone else, this hug would have felt weird.

In the time during which he examines me, he slips in and out of his joker persona. He theatrically looks away when I undress. He pretends to frown as he helps me onto the exam table; when he puts my feet up in stirrups, he says he is terrified of 'lady bits' and to help him out with directions. But he is also serious and professional without being too somber. In the end, I do a lot of tests, which would typically be scary, but it never seems that way thanks to Whitlock.

He is all smiles as he goes over my test results.

"These are all excellent," he assures me. "You're in perfect health, so there's nothing to be alarmed about. Your bloodwork, urine tests, and STD tests all came back clear, which is good."

It's minor miracle is what it is. As Ness was only too keen to point out, I've been a 'lowkey ho' the past few months.

"Nothing on the genetic screening tests, either. Have you had any major health issues, any serious conditions?"

"I don't think so, no."

"Any mental illnesses? Depression, anxiety?"

"No."

"Drug allergies?"

"Not that I know of."

"Okay. Now we just need to do an ultrasound to give us a better picture of how the baby is sitting, and from that, we can determine conception date and expected date of delivery."

I can feel the color drain from my face. Dr. Whitlock notices it right away; his eyes travel over my face, and I feel like I'm growing paler by the second.

"Is everything okay, Amy?"

I clear my throat and attempt to keep my voice calm. "Yes, yes. I'm sorry. Just a brief wave of nausea."

"Oh. You've been getting nausea, then?" He glances at his watch. "Morning sickness. Always a fun experience."

"Not regularly, but yeah. I do get random bouts of nausea."

He starts talking about other symptoms I can expect in the first trimester, but my mind drifts off almost immediately.

The thought first occurred to me when I was breaking the news of my pregnancy to Ness. It was a few days after her engagement party, and I had finally forced myself to go over to her place and talk to her about it. Her reaction was exactly as I expected it to be; she was delighted at the news that I had been having sex, then horrified that I wasn't being safe while doing so, and then she shot straight to horror when I told her about Robert. But as I did, I realized that there was more than a slim possibility that the baby might be Kieran's.

And that disturbing thought has embedded itself into my subconscious ever since.

Realistically, it could be either of theirs. There was a worrying overlap between my last encounter with Kieran and my tryst with Robert. Not too big a window; certainly, big enough for me to not feel like a complete whore, which is what Ness has taken to calling me. She says it in jest, but it cuts deep all the same.

So, I did the only thing that made sense to me at the time. The pregnancy alone was such a big shock for me that I didn't think I could take any more big news. Worrying about the father of my child? There was no way I was mentally ready to deal with that mess. I blocked out all thoughts pertaining to it from that moment, and I've been actively avoiding them ever since. I can't worry about that now. I don't know if there will be a time when I'll feel like I can.

Enter Dr. Whitlock, and the cheery prospect of an ultrasound is suddenly more menacing. It's still early; I'm only around seven weeks pregnant, but if an ultrasound can determine the date of conception, then that might shed a little more light on the brewing dilemma. The only problem is that I'm not sure I want to know.

"Dr. Whitlock?"

"Yes, darling?"

"How accurate is this ultrasound? Can you tell me the exact date my baby was conceived?"

"Oh, yeah. Totally. There's a bit of math involved, but it's fairly straightforward. We just have to know the date of your last period, and then—"

"Can we skip that part?"

"The ultrasound?"

"Yeah."

His brows knit together. I can almost see the gears turning in his head. "Amy, dear. This is your first antenatal visit. It's generally a good idea to get a sense of how the baby is doing, and an ultrasound will provide us the best possible picture—"

"Okay, but can you do it without telling me the date of conception?"

"Uh … usually, it's the gender most people would rather not know aboutm…"

"Please, Dr. Whitlock. We can do it on the next ultrasound. Please."

He shrugs and agrees, but I can see he is still confused. He glances at my file as if to gather his thoughts, and then the easy smile is back on his face.

"Well, then. Ultrasound. If you don't mind me saying, Amy. I didn't expect to see you alone today. The ultrasound is often a bonding opportunity for the parents. I didn't see a Mr …?"

"There's no Mr. Anything, Doctor," is what I want to say. It's probably what I would have said, in an appropriately curt tone of voice, if the door didn't suddenly fly open, and a gangly youth with wild eyes spill into the room.

"Excuse me, sir." Dr. Whitlock is all serious again. Gravel in his voice. Authority. Indignation. "This is a private consultation."

Kieran looks around the room, and his eyes fall on me. He starts to move in my direction, but moments later, a large man with thick arms and a barrel chest squeezes into the room right behind him, dashes forward and puts a hand on his chest. Kieran is stopped in his tracks. I can tell the man is strong; Kieran is visibly struggling against the single hand on his chest, but he might as well be bound in chains.

"Sorry, Doc," the man booms in the direction of Whitlock. "He sprinted past me. Slippery fellow."

To Kieran, he grunts and grabs him more firmly by the hand. "Come on, you."

"No, wait," I call out from the exam table. I remember, too late, that I'm only dressed in a flimsy hospital gown. One that is billowing freely around my thighs. "He's with me."

"I'm sorry, Amy," Whitlock says. "Private consultation. Only immediate family members can be in here with you. Or, in this case, the father."

For the second time in mere minutes, the color drains so fast from my face I can almost feel myself go transparent. I look helplessly over at Kieran, then back at Dr. Whitlock. There are too many men in the room. Why are there so many men in the room?

"I'm the father," Kieran declares, making a final, desperate bid for freedom from his captor's vice grip. The shock of the statement is enough to slacken the hold somehow, because his arm comes free, and before anyone else can react, he swims away and steps further into the room, moving toward me.

The muscle man starts to follow him, but Whitlock puts up a hand and shakes his head. "It's fine. I've got this." The man throws Kieran one final disgusted look, then he turns and walks out of the room.

I'm too embarrassed to meet Whitlock's gaze, so I turn to Kieran instead, and I channel all my frustration toward him. "What the fuck are you doing here?" I spit at him.

"I'm here for your check-up," he says simply, and he seems so calm it infuriates me even more.

"It's my check-up. It has nothing to do with you."

"I don't understand."

"How did you even find out about this?"

Kieran smiles, pulls out a phone from his pocket, and waves it in my face. "I added your calendar to my phone so I could work with your schedule. Forgot to take it out. I was going to this morning, but then I saw that you had an appointment at a clinic. With an OBGYN."

He turns around, looking for Dr. Whitlock as if he just remembered he is also in the room. All evidence of mirth is gone from Whitlock's face. He is looking from Kieran to me and back again, and the rigidity of his posture is telling.

"This has nothing to do with you, Kieran," I say, and his eyes snap back to me. "And you really shouldn't be here."

"What are you talking about, Amy? You're pregnant. I'm

obviously the father!"

"This really isn't the best place, or time, for this, Kieran."

"You're right! It's not the best place to find out you're going to be a father! How long have you known this? Huh? When were you planning on telling me?"

I feel trapped. I am stuck in a small, crowded room with the full extent of my indiscretions about to blow up in my face.

"There's nothing to tell you, Kieran," I hear myself say, my voice small. "It's not your baby."

The small, crowded room seems to get much smaller. It's like the air is being sucked from it, and the walls are closing in on me, slowly, surely, pulling in to crush me to death. It would be a relief, really. I could close my eyes and open my arms to receive death. At least then I wouldn't have to deal with this.

"What?" Kieran asks. He looks over at Dr. Whitlock, who has finally figured out what is going on and is making a concerted attempt to back out of the room.

This is my purgatory.

"What?" Kieran asks again. "What do you ... whose is it, then?"

I've never believed in cosmic intervention, but when the door opens once more and Robert steps into the exam room as if in answer to the question, it's hard not to imagine a group of gods sitting somewhere laughing their asses off.

Kieran is confused and shocked. Whitlock is intrigued and shocked. Their expressions are like mirrors of each other, both reflecting the emotions coursing through my own head at the moment.

I don't know how I'm even able to register such a thought, but Robert looks dashing, like the proverbial prince rushing in to save me, the damsel in distress. His hair is slightly longer, and his beard is unruly, bordering on unkempt. He looks rugged and wild, and his eyes are burning with what I realize seconds later is anger.

He looks first at Dr. Whitlock, barely registers him, then at me for the briefest second, and then they fall on Kieran, and that's when his features fully settle into the anger.

"Is this him?" he asks, and I realize he is talking to me.

I open my mouth to answer, but my voice is apparently gone. Robert takes the silence as agreement; without another word, he charges toward Kieran. It's like I'm watching it in slow motion; his mouth opens ever so slowly, the sounds coming from it distorted and unfamiliar. As he gets to Kieran, he twists his body sideways and pulls his arm back. No one reacts fast enough. I blink, and the next second, a sickening crunch echoes through the room, a guttural yell rips through the air, and a stream of blood flashes through the space between Robert and Kieran.

Someone curses. Robert shakes his hand in pain. Kieran stumbles backward, loses his balance, and falls into a low chair adjacent to a table full of medical equipment. They all go tumbling to the ground in a deafening cacophony of sound.

The door opens again, the large muscle man from earlier charging in and scanning the room for the danger. It's not hard to spot it. Robert is massaging his hand, and the flailing limbs from Kieran on the ground are a dead giveaway.

The man takes a step toward Robert, but to my surprise, Robert holds up a hand, and the man remains frozen in his tracks.

"Amy?" he calls, even though I'm only a few feet from him.

I must look terrified because his expression softens as he looks at me.

"Why didn't you tell me about him?"

Yup. Purgatory.

I don't know what to say to him. He looks hurt, disillusioned. I want to run from the scene and never look back. This has gone south so fast I can't believe how peaceful everything was only a few minutes ago.

"It's complicated, Robert," I start to say, even before I know what it is I *want* to tell him. I just know he's furious, and it's all my fault. And that I need to make him understand it's not that simple. I didn't mean for any of this to happen …

Everyone in the room is frozen, even the muscle man. It's strange how quickly he took action with Kieran compared to how neutralized he seems right now.

"Him?" Robert spits, casting a throwaway look at Kieran. "He is a child, Amy! You let him cost you your job, and now this?"

"I'm sorry. Can we not do this here, please ..."

"Is it mine?" he asks suddenly, cutting me off. His eyes flick down to my belly then back up to my face.

I can tell from his face he doesn't really want to know. The tough exterior he displays is falling apart; here is a man on the verge of vulnerability, desperate for one answer, but knowing it may well be the other. I can't bear to break his heart. Never again.

"Of course, it's yours," I tell him.

There is a flicker of hope in his eyes. But only for a second. The doubt flares deep within those very eyes, and his posture doesn't change.

"You're not sure, are you? You're just telling me what I want to hear, but you don't know for sure."

I cannot lie to him. He will see right through it. But I cannot assure him either. He isn't wrong; I'm not sure. But even that admission would break his heart. So, I remain silent, hoping he can read in my eyes that I love him, that none of this matters.

Whatever he reads in my eyes, it's not that. He turns without another word and storms out of the room. No one says anything. Kieran gets gingerly to his feet, his face covered in blood. Whitlock walks slowly over to me and slides his hand onto my back. Patting me. Comforting me. He has the best hands of any doctor I know. But for once, his touch does not bring me any comfort.

48
Robert

I remember everything about Leonard Perkins.

I remember the shiny leather jacket he wore when he first came to our house. I was around ten or eleven. I'm the one who got the door because my mom and dad were in the kitchen yelling at each other. Neither of them heard the doorbell. They didn't notice they had a visitor until I stood on the kitchen counter and waved my hands in between them.

I remember thinking he looked cool in that leather jacket. And, as I opened the door to let him in, he stepped aside, and I caught a glimpse of a sleek, matte black motorbike perched at the entrance to our house. And I thought Leonard Perkins was the coolest man I had ever seen.

I remember his smile, his deep baritone voice as he asked if Mr. and Mrs. Hardy were in. I remember the distinct smell of a cologne I would spend the better part of my teenage years searching for. I remember the highly polished shoes, the perfectly fitted pants. The black suitcase. The dark sunglasses. The aura of the man was undeniable and intoxicating.

I was sent from the room with strict instructions never to come out, but I didn't go to my room. I circled back to the kitchen and pressed my ear against the door, and that was how I came to learn that my parents were getting a divorce.

It wasn't a long meeting, but it was the first of many.

Leonard Perkins showed up at our house so many times after that; mother started setting a place for him at the dinner table. Always, he came in that stylish leather jacket. Always impeccably dressed. Always smelling amazing. And the way he spoke! It was all too much for an impressionable boy. I admired everything about him, so much so that I started to dress like him, try and speak like him. It didn't work out all too often, but I could pretend I was him for a day or two, and that was all I needed.

When my parents eventually finalized their divorce, Leonard Perkins came over to me and told me he saw a lot of himself in me.

He could have meant it literally, as I was hidden away in one of my dad's oversized suits and a leather jacket I'd stolen from one of my friends. But I knew he meant he could see me following in his footsteps.

And that is exactly what I did. I decided there and then that I was going to be a lawyer like Leonard Perkins, and I started to work toward it.

My memory of him is still intact, down to the tiniest details. It's how I'm able to trace him all these years later. It's how I know I've got the right house when, days after announcing the end of my candidacy, I'm knocking on his door.

Leonard has aged gracefully. He has lost his youth, obviously, but the aura is still there, that undefinable quality that appealed so much to me as a child.

His style is still impeccable. Even at 70, he is still in a dress shirt and well-fitted pants. He has ditched the leather coat for a simple, thick wooly sweater, but it suits him. He would not be out of place walking into a random courtroom.

Remarkably, he recognizes me. He stares for a long time after he opens the door, and I start to fumble with my words, but he shakes his head to stop my ramblings. He remembers, he says. And he calls me out by name. It's like I'm 11 again, and the validation I so desperately sought is finally within reach.

When I was looking for his address, I did some research on Leonard. I don't know why, but I never have before. I found out that he has led a pretty good life. For a long time in his career, he was considered one of the best attorneys in the country. Then he switched exclusively to divorce law, and some of that shine gradually wore off. He retired quietly a few years ago and now lives alone in a small town outside Glendale.

It's hard to gauge his success from his house. While the man himself is flashy and attention-grabbing, his house is anything but. It's a small, intimate little condo, perfect for a bachelor, as he appears to be. That doesn't really surprise me. For someone who has spent so much time intervening between broken marriages, it's no surprise he didn't go that way himself.

He invites me to sit with him in the back, and he drags two chairs out and places them in a lovely mini garden with excellent shade. He is apparently a part-time farmer; the garden has a couple of fully-grown lemon trees, the fruit just starting to come out.

It's actually very tranquil. Away from the noise of the city, perfect for sitting down and just enjoying the day.

"This is lovely," I tell him as we sit down. I indicate the garden, but I also mean his life. I don't need to stretch my imagination to picture myself in such a setting in my later years.

"It's my little slice of heaven," he says.

He excuses himself and disappears back into the house. The spring in his step is no longer there, understandably, his walk is more of a shuffle. Time has done the one thing I didn't think possible as a child; it has slowed Leonard down.

He returns a couple of minutes later with two cold beers and hands me one.

"I would have brought you a lemonade, but I always wanted to have a beer with you," he says, sinking into his chair.

"You did?"

"Yeah. You were a good kid. Smart. Observant. I think you probably saw what was happening with your parents better than even they did. I always wanted to pull you aside, take you away from it all."

"That would have made my childhood," I say. "You made quite the impression on me."

"Did I?"

"Yeah. How did you even recognize me? It's been over thirty years."

Leonard grins. "I have a thing with faces. Your eyes. I remember your eyes. I remember every little kid I had to look in the eye and explain to why I was breaking their parents up. They always blamed me for it. Part of the job, I suppose. But not you. Even at your age, you were exceptionally smart. You knew what was actually going on. Of course, I remember you."

"I'm sorry I never came to visit you before," I tell him. "Looks like you're doing well enough, though. I might get into divorce law if it will buy me a nice little place like this."

Leonard laughs. The corners of his eyes crinkle up when he does. "It's a nasty business. I wouldn't recommend it."

"Can't be any worse than criminal law, I'm sure."

"Let me tell you something, son. If you want to see what crazy looks like, sit in during divorce talks. Criminals have nothing on married couples, I tell you."

I don't doubt it.

"How did you do it?" I ask him. "You must have seen the worst cases, practicing for all those years. How did you stay sane?"

"It's pretty easy if you see it as a corrective measure. Most people rush into marriage without thinking about the future or knowing what they really want. And they change. The one thing that always happens is change. Two, three years in, neither of them are the versions of each other they married. Life has happened; they have different goals, and they want different things. So, the resentment kicks in, then the cheating, inevitably, because they want to be with someone who suits the person they are years later, and their partner isn't that someone anymore. Not everyone goes for divorce. But I think it's noble to admit that your marriage failed and to leave while you can. That's the mentality I had; I was helping people do what was best for themselves."

"That's fascinating," I say. "I don't think I've ever thought of it like that."

"Is that why you're here? Looking to drag me out of retirement?"

"Huh? Oh, you mean for …? No, no. I'm not married."

"No? Don't get me wrong. I'm happy to see you. I always wondered how you turned out. I heard you became a lawyer, and I liked to think I had a little something to do with that."

"You did. More than a little something."

"And then I heard you got into politics?"

"Briefly. It was ill-advised, though. I stepped away from it."

"Did you really?"

"Quite recently, in fact. I realized I never really wanted to get into politics. I only did so out of some idea I formed when I started out, that there was this path I had to follow in my life. So, I mapped out these goals, and I set out to knock them off my list, and politics just happened to be one of them. I think I realized a bit late that it wasn't for me."

Leonard nods slowly, impressed. "Introspection. Not

everyone has that. It's admirable when you can look into your own heart and decide what you want."

"True. I just wish I'd done it earlier."

"Well, then, I'm stumped. That means this visit is purely social?"

I take a deep breath and turn around in my chair so I'm facing Leonard. "I need to ask you something. I've always wondered, but I was never able to confirm it. What happened with my parents? What's the real reason they got divorced?"

"Ah." Leonard nods. "Right. Well, the short version is that they fell out of love. I saw it a lot, couples finding out after several years together that they didn't even like each other anymore. With your parents, though, from what I remember, things had gotten very toxic, very fast. I know you must have assumed it had something to do with you, but it didn't. If anything, you're the reason they stuck it out so long."

"I know. And I hated my dad for it."

"How do you mean?"

"He wanted to leave. He threatened to leave on so many occasions, but he never did. I saw how miserable they both were, and I never understood why he didn't just leave. They weren't doing anyone a favor by staying. If anything, I'm sure it fucked me up more to be around parents who didn't want anything to do with each other."

"It's not that simple, you know. I'm sure they both wanted what was best for you, and at the time, that meant staying. There are exceptions, obviously, but it's generally considered better for a child to grow up around both his parents."

"Is that why you don't have kids?" I ask him. "If you don't mind me asking."

"In some ways, yes. I believe you should be there for your child, no matter what. And I never want to put my child in a situation where something I do makes them resent me. I've seen enough to know that we are all messed up in one way or another by our parents. In spite of their best efforts, and sometimes because of them. I don't believe anyone should be a parent unless they've figured themselves out, and they are sure the only things left to pass on to their kids are positive traits."

I hear him. I hear what he is saying and what he isn't. If it were up to me, I don't think I would willingly father a child. I'm too messed up. There's too much damage there, some of it from my own relationship with my parents. But it's no longer up to me. The decision, if it can be considered a decision, is no longer purely mine. In running away from Amy yet again, I have proved that I'm no better than my dad. In staying with Gwen for so long, even when I knew I wasn't as invested as she was, I'm no different from him, staying in a dysfunctional relationship. We really do become our parents.

"So, Robert," Leonard says, and his expression is shrewd. "Are you going to tell me about this woman, or are we going to keep speaking in metaphors?"

I grin. Still sharp, Leonard.

"I've been a coward, Leonard," I tell him. "I've been rash, and stupid, and a coward."

"I think I know what you seem to be having trouble figuring out how to ask."

"Yeah?"

"You want to know if it's possible for you to have a life outside the job. You want to know if it's possible for you to have the kind of relationship your parents never did."

"Well, is it?"

"I think you know the answer to that question, Robert. I think you know, and that's why you came looking for me. You want me to tell you that it isn't possible … that love is a myth, that marriage is a ticking time bomb. And you want to use that as the excuse not to try. I won't do that. But I will tell you this: you're not your father."

Epilogue
Amelia

My hearing is a small, private affair in one of the university boardrooms far from the public flogging I had been imagining it was going to be. For some reason, whenever I thought about it, I pictured a Victorian-style court, complete with stuffy, overdressed barristers frowning down on me. I imagined the university board of governors looking at me through lowered glasses and shaking their heads in disgust. I assumed there was going to be a mean old man with a gavel and one bad eye, his hand twitching as he read me the verdict and condemned me to some inhumane punishment.

None of that is even close to reality.

I'm ushered into a large, tastefully furnished room I didn't even know existed in the university. There is a single large mahogany table in the middle of the room, and around it, six people sit patiently. I don't recognize any of them, except for Dean Patel, looking shrunken at the far end of the table. I assume the others are members of the university board of governors or representatives of the school appointed to sit at my disciplinary hearing.

None of them look as menacing as I thought they were going to look. I even get a few smiles as I waddle up to the table, though that might have something to do with my appearance; I have started to get heavy, and my belly is poking out a little bit. Because I'm always out of breath now, it saps all the energy out of me just to get to the chair and sit down. They all watch me silently. One of the ladies starts to get up, presumably to help me settle into the chair. I give her a smile and shake my head.

A few minutes pass, during which I look around the table nervously. I try to catch Dean Patel's eye, but he's lost in muted conversation with the woman next to him.

Finally, the man in the middle raps the desk softly with his knuckles, calling attention to him. He is clearly in charge; he has that authoritative posture, the easy confidence of someone used to giving commands, and having them followed.

"Good morning, everybody," he says, then nods at the murmured responses. "I'll start by introducing myself, for those who don't know me. My name is Arthur Beck, and I'm the head of the university board of governors. I'll ask that everyone introduce themselves when they speak, to keep things moving. Now, Ms. Brooks. Do you have any questions before we begin?"

"No."

"Good. Now, we decided to hold separate hearings for you and Mr. Parker, to maintain the integrity of the proceedings. Is everyone set?" He looks around at his fellow committee members, and they all nod or mumble their agreement.

"Well, then. Dean Patel? Your statement, please."

Dean Patel looks out of place in the midst of the suits and fine dresses around him. He is by far the most approachable of the lot, but that may just be because I know him personally. He gives me a quick smile to reassure me, and it actually calms me down.

This is it, then. After months of agonizing, here we are, finally.

Dean Patel introduces himself, then goes into a detailed account of what happened. He refers to a piece of paper as he recounts the affair, starting with his discovery of the article in the school paper and the small investigation he undertook to determine its validity. He doesn't go into detail on the relationship itself, saying all he knows is that it was brief and that it was over by the time the article was came out. I know it's his job, that he has to give the committee as much information as possible, but it feels like he's still rooting for me, and I'm grateful for it.

The Dean actually called me a few days ago, to check on me and see if I was ready for the hearing. During the call, he advised me to bring a legal representative, but I told him I didn't think I'd need one. I've already made up my mind about this hearing; I'm not going to fight it.

Beck calls on me. "Am I to understand that you're representing yourself?" he asks me, and I struggle to my feet.

"Yes, I am."

"Very well, then." He notices me straining to stand up and waves a hand. "You don't need to get up, Miss Brooks. Please."

I sink back into the chair gratefully. Dr. Whitlock told me a certain degree of fatigue is to be expected, but it seems like I'm exhausted all the time. I can't even walk to the kitchen and back to my room without getting completely winded.

"First of all," I begin, "I wish to thank the University board and Dean Patel for giving me the opportunity to teach here. It's a privilege I did not take lightly. I admit, therefore, that I contravened the university policy on student/teacher relationships. I take full responsibility for my actions, and I would like to urge the committee to focus the full brunt of its disciplinary process on me. The student in question, Mr. Parker, is guilty only of going along with his instructor. He shouldn't have to suffer for my mistake.

"As for the relationship itself, I initiated it. I'm not proud of it, but I was in an emotionally vulnerable state, and I took advantage of a young man's innocence. I carried on a sexual relationship with Mr. Parker for exactly four weeks, starting in March of this year. I ended the relationship thereafter, later than I would have liked, but I acknowledged the inappropriate nature of our interaction.

"I am ready to accept whatever punishment the committee deems appropriate. In light of this, however, I wish to also tender my resignation from my teaching post, effective immediately. I am grateful for the opportunity to have worked here. I accept that I cannot continue to do so in the aftermath of my transgression."

There is a long silence after I finish speaking. A few of the committee members exchange uncertain glances.

Beck shuffles his papers, seemingly rattled. "You are aware, Miss Brooks, that the committee is still tasked with determining whether your actions merit punishment? And that regardless of this decision on your part, we are still required to deliberate and decide on the case?"

"Of course, Mr. Beck."

"Very well. Following your admission, I don't believe we need to hear any further testimony ...?"

He looks around the table once more, collecting nods.

"Then I'll ask you to kindly step outside, Miss Brooks, and give us a few minutes to deliberate. The clerk will summon you when we're done."

Well, that was quick.

I nod and start the arduous process of standing up. I get

gingerly to my feet, which are already swollen, and I push the chair back.

I know something is wrong as soon as I try to take a step. Nausea hits me suddenly and hard. One minute I'm trying to put one foot in front of the other, the next moment I can't tell which side of the room is up and which is down. My head starts to swim, and I lose all sense of balance and direction. I can hear voices behind me. Someone is shouting something. I try to turn around, and I catch a glimpse of one of the women pointing—at me, I realize.

And of someone else—Dean Patel, rushing toward me. "Amy!" I hear him gasp. "We need to get you to the hospital. You're bleeding."

My hand weighs a ton as I reach around to the back of my dress and swipe at the seat. My fingers come away slick, and when I bring them up to my eyes, they swim in and out of focus. But they are stained bright red. The effort to keep standing is suddenly too much. My knees give way, and I'm swallowed up by a void, feeling like I'm falling.

The last thing I'm aware of is shouting and firm hands holding me as I sink to the ground. Then it all goes dark.

The first face I see when I wake up is that of Dr. Whitlock. There are stress lines all across his forehead, and his smile seems forced.

"Hey," he says as I blink to refocus my eyes. "Welcome back."

I shake my head to clear it. It takes all my strength to sit up, and Dr. Whitlock puts a hand on me to try and push me down, but I do it nonetheless.

"What happened?" I ask him. It all comes rushing back to me now, the boardroom, the screams, my blood-stained fingers. I reach down and grab the bed covers, yank them away. I don't know what I was expecting to see, but the presence of my belly is such a massive relief.

"Doctor? What happened? I was bleeding. I … Did I lose …?"

I can't bring myself to say it. I just stare at Whitlock, my eyes begging, desperate.

"You're fine, Amy, relax," he says. "Your baby is fine, too. You had a threatened miscarriage. It's not uncommon this early in a pregnancy, but we're monitoring the baby now, and it isn't in any danger."

"I passed out …"

"You've been under a lot of stress, from what I hear. The man who brought you in told me you were in the middle of some sort of meeting, that it has to do with your job. You must have been under a lot of pressure, and your body just gave out."

"I've had some abdominal pain as well …"

"That would be the threatened miscarriage. Usually, it is accompanied by some spotting. But as I said, you're out of the woods now. We just have to keep you supine for a few hours, and then we can examine you again and decide whether it would be safer to monitor you overnight."

I let out a breath, slowly, expelling air through gritted teeth.

"No more running around for you, though," Whitlock says. "I'm prescribing bed rest for you for the next few hours. Starting now, okay?" He pushes the hair out of my face, then reaches over and draws the covers back over me. "Breathe, Amy. Everything is okay."

I nod and thank him. That was a scary experience.

"Oh, by the way, there are some people here to see you. I asked them to wait outside, but you don't have to see them if you don't want to."

"No, no. It's fine. What people?"

Ness is the first to burst into the room, in typical fashion. She's dragging Jeremy by the hand, and from the looks of it, that grip is vice-like. She descends on me in a fit of tears and hugs me tight. She is sorry she wasn't there, she blubbers. She was so worried. So worried! And from the second I get discharged, she isn't going to leave my side.

Jeremy smiles awkwardly. He winks at me as they walk out of the room and wishes me a quick recovery.

I didn't expect Dean Patel to still be at the hospital, but

apparently, he waited after bringing me in to make sure I'm okay. It's a small gesture, but it means a lot.

"You gave us quite the scare," he says after fussing over my pillows for a full minute. "But on the plus side, that little incident may have helped them make a decision on your case."

"What? Really? What did they decide?"

"After a very brief consideration, Beck agreed that your resignation changes things and that there's no reason to punish you any further."

"Oh my God, really?"

"Yeah! And, thanks to yours truly, they agreed to take a look at the school policy, maybe make a few changes."

"That's the second-best news I've heard today. Thank you! Wait, what about Kieran?"

"Academic probation for a few weeks. Nothing that will affect his record. It all worked out, Amy."

It almost doesn't seem real, just how well everything has worked out.

"By the way, I was a little surprised by your decision to resign. What's the plan? What are you going to do?"

"Honestly, I'm not sure. But I don't think I have to worry about it just yet. You may have noticed the distended belly? I'll probably have my hands full for a little while."

The visit I'm looking forward to the most doesn't happen till much later in the day. I'm lying in bed, trying to swallow my disappointment at Robert's absence, when a feeble knock sounds on the door, and I look up to see Dr. Whitlock.

"Let me know if I need to call security, okay?"

And he steps aside.

Robert looks like he did when I first met him. He is clean-shaven, which highlights the Hollywood-like cut of his jaw. He looks beautiful in a fitted suit, wearing that smile he reserves just for me. His hands are behind his back as he walks toward me. I'm so happy to see him that I just stare at him sheepishly, like a lovesick teen.

"Hey, gorgeous," he says. He leans in and plants a kiss on my forehead. His scent washes over me, and I'm tempted to pull him in.

It's been a while, and my body seems to know it.

"I didn't think you'd show," I tell him.

"Why, because of that little tussle a few weeks ago? Water under the bridge. Kieran and I are actually friends now."

"Bullshit."

"I'm serious. I've decided to mentor him. He is a good young lawyer, and I'm sure he's going places."

"You're joking."

"I'm not. I've had some time to think about it, and I decided the way I acted was unacceptable. I owe you an apology as well."

I look down, and my eyes are suddenly moist. "I thought you left me again."

Robert steps in and gives me a one-handed hug. His left hand is still hidden away behind his back. "Never again, Amy. I'll never leave your side again for the rest of my life."

He says it with such earnest intensity it doesn't even register as cheesy.

"I found out about the baby," I tell him. He shakes his head and puts a finger on my lips to shush me. "It's our baby," he says. "Yours and mine. That's the end of that."

That brings the tears out. I try to blink them back, but I only succeed in pushing them down my cheeks faster. "I missed you so much," I say, and now I'm fully crying. My shoulders are shaking, and the waterworks are on full display. I probably look a mess, but Robert just smiles and hugs me again.

"I missed you too," he says.

"What's that behind your back?" I ask, the curiosity finally getting the better of me.

Robert smiles and shakes his head. "I need to ask you something first before we get to that."

"Okay …?"

"How would you feel about working with me again? Not for me, not as my employee, but as my partner? We could start our own firm. I've already started working on the paperwork."

"Do you mean that?"

"Of course."

"I would love to. Yes! Now give me my ring already!"

"Oh, you think this is a ring? You think I'm proposing?"

"I know you are. You love me, and you've already said you'll never leave me again. Come on, Hardy, let's hear the poetry."

He leans in and kisses me full on the lips. I'm still teary. Whatever make-up I have is gone. But I've never felt more beautiful in my life. Robert kisses me, and I know it's all I ever wanted. I am happy at that moment. And I know that as long as he's beside me, I always will be.

THE END

Dear reader,

thank you so much for reading my book, it really means the world to me! If you liked it and want to do me a little favor, please leave a short review on Amazon – that would be too wonderful!

XOXO
Sarah

Made in the USA
Middletown, DE
15 November 2023

42802375R00199